M.J. Arlidge has worked in television for the last twenty years, specialising in high-end drama production, including prime-time crime serials *Silent Witness*, *Torn* and *Innocent*. In 2015, his audiobook exclusive *Six Degrees of Assassination* was a number one bestseller. His debut thriller, *Eeny Meeny*, was the UK's bestselling crime debut of 2014 and has been followed by ten more DI Helen Grace thrillers – all *Sunday Times* bestsellers.

Lisa Hall is the bestselling author of six psychological thrillers and the Hotel Hollywood time-slip murder mystery series. Her debut novel, *Between You and Me*, was a Kindle UK number one bestseller, sitting in the top spot for over four weeks. Lisa has a first-class honours degree in English Literature and Creative Writing. She lives in Kent with her husband and their three children. Readers can follow Lisa on Twitter @LisaHallAuthor.

T0385334

# THE
# MISTAKE

## M.J. ARLIDGE

## LISA HALL

ORION

An Orion Paperback
First published in Great Britain in 2025 by Orion Fiction,
an imprint of The Orion Publishing Group Ltd,
Carmelite House, 50 Victoria Embankment
London EC4Y 0DZ

An Hachette UK Company

The authorised representative in the EEA is Hachette Ireland,
8 Castlecourt Centre, Dublin 15, D15 XTP3,
Ireland (email: info@hbgi.ie)

1 3 5 7 9 10 8 6 4 2

A CIP catalogue record for this book is
available from the British Library.

ISBN (Mass Market Paperback) 9781 3987 1666 7
ISBN (Ebook) 9781 3987 1665 0
ISBN (Audio) 9781 3987 1664 3

Typeset at The Spartan Press Ltd,
Lymington, Hants

Printed and bound in Great Britain by Clays Ltd,
Elcograf S.p.A.

MIX
Paper | Supporting
responsible forestry
FSC® C104740

www.orionbooks.co.uk

# THE
# MISTAKE

# *Prologue*

There have been rumours for years that these woods are haunted. That screams and cries echo through the trees once the sun has gone down, legends of a maid murdered by a lover, of a servant man found hanging from the old oak that grows beside the stream, its roots stretching out far below the waterline. The cry that splits the air now is sharp enough to make your blood run cold. The shrill, insistent cry of a baby.

The wails, high-pitched and frantic, rise up towards the thick summer leaves of the old oak before being swallowed by the rush of water. The stream is swollen by the rain of the past few days, August storms that split the skies with thunder and lightning, fat raindrops bouncing off pavements. The stink of the river fills the air, thick with sulphide. The baby cries again, her face red, her fists pumping as rain drips from the canopy above her, splattering the mulchy leaves, her face, the blanket that covers her. No one comes.

An owl takes flight, swooping across the night sky, its white wings an elegant blur. A rat, whiskery and pointy, sniffs the ground a few feet away before stepping towards the bag the baby lies in. Sleek and fat, the rat tugs at the plastic with its razor-sharp teeth, nipping and tearing. The baby cries again, a cry of distress and panic that would cut a mother to the bone, and the rat whisks away, sloping into the hollow of the oak tree. The clear night air is chilly and damp, despite it being the tail end of summer, and the baby hitches in a breath, her chest heaving. Her chubby hands fall to her sides, rustling against the bag covering her tiny body, damp from the rotting leaves seeping through a hole in the plastic, soaking the edges of her sleepsuit. Cries turn to whimpers, faint and whispery, drifting away towards the stream before they can rise into the night sky. Whimpers turn to gasps, the gasps to silence.

And still nobody comes.

# The Pregnancy

# Natalie

Natalie splashes her face with cold water, pausing for a moment when she thinks she hears the sound of the doorbell, the faint chime breaking into her thoughts. Reaching for a towel, she presses it to her cheeks, swiping away the water and avoiding her pale reflection in the bathroom mirror. She still feels nauseous, and there is no mistaking the dark circles under her eyes. The ring of the doorbell comes again, followed by a frantic rapping at the door, and Natalie hangs the towel back up and hurries to the top of the stairs.

The knocking repeats, sharp and fast, and Natalie can feel the crash of her own pulse in her ears, her heart thundering in her chest. There is something urgent about it, and she wonders if it's Pete, if he forgot his keys. She's sure Pete is out on a site visit today, looking over the contract details of the new housing development going up on the other side of the woods, on the newer side of West Marsham village. He never usually comes home in the day when he's out on site. Running down the stairs, trying to ignore the churning in her stomach, Natalie reaches the front door and yanks it open, breathless.

'Eve!'

'Hi, love.' Eve leans over to kiss her on the cheek as she squeezes past, heading towards the kitchen. Natalie's eyes go to the clock on the wall. It's only 12.30 p.m. She wasn't expecting her best friend until one o'clock. 'I did ring the door but there was no answer, so I thought I'd better knock. I thought you must not have heard the bell.'

'Sorry, I was in the bathroom.' Natalie eyes the Camembert Eve is pulling out of a plastic bag and placing on the kitchen worktop, inhaling its faint musty scent. She's not sure if she can eat that.

'I know, I'm early.' Eve grins. 'My eleven o'clock client cancelled on me. We haven't had a proper catch-up for ages.'

'You're not worried they cancelled?' Natalie doesn't know how Eve does it. She couldn't be a bereavement counsellor, listening to other people's heartbreak all day long.

'People cancel all the time.' Eve pulls out a baguette, some fancy charcuterie meats, grapes and a bottle of red wine. Natalie thinks about the quiche in the fridge that she'd been planning on serving up with a salad for their lunch. Maybe Pete can take it to work tomorrow. 'You OK? You look a bit peaky.'

'Just tired. Hectic week.'

'You sit down, let me sort lunch.' Eve bustles around the kitchen as if it is her own, sliding the cheese into the oven with the bread, and arranging the meat on a wooden board Pete bought on a whim in a fancy kitchen shop at Bluewater, as Natalie sinks onto a stool at the island.

'I got us a bottle of that nice Chianti,' Eve says, placing two wine glasses beside the place settings. 'The one we drank two bottles of last time.'

Natalie pauses, her hands fluttering below the table. 'Not for me.'

'Emily's picking Zadie up from school for you, though, isn't she? We can just have one bottle, I promise it won't turn into a late one.' The women meet regularly for lunches that go on until dark, if Pete, Natalie's husband, is around to watch the kids. Natalie doesn't go out much – much less than some of the other mums from school – so lunch with Eve is her only chance to get some time to herself. Sometimes they meet in Maidstone, in one of the little cafés; other times they take it in turns to host at home, on the days when Natalie only works half a day at the HR department for a national charity. On rare occasions they head up to Stratford for lunch at Westfield, giggling on the train home with the taste of too much wine on their tongues. Usually she wouldn't be bothered about whether it turned into a late one.

Usually Natalie would have opened the wine while she waited for Eve to arrive.

'No, honestly. Just sparkling water for me.' Natalie slides from the stool and heads for the huge American-style fridge, pulling out a cold bottle of water.

'Are you OK?' Eve frowns, as she moves to the oven to check on the food.

'I'm fine. I don't fancy it today, that's all.'

Eve waits until they are both sat at the island, the Camembert steaming in front of them, before she speaks.

'What is it?' Eve leans across the worktop, reaching for Natalie's hand. 'What's going on? Is it Pete?'

'No, it's not Pete. Pete's great. He's won the contract for that big housing development on the other side of the village. You won't believe who owns the development company.'

'Who?'

'Vanessa Taylor.'

Eve's eyes widen. Like Natalie, she's never met Vanessa but she knows exactly who she is. '*That* Vanessa Taylor? As in Pete's ex-girlfriend, Vanessa Taylor?'

'The one and the same.' Natalie had had the same reaction when Pete told her, shaking his head in disbelief.

'What a small world,' he'd said. 'I couldn't believe it when her name popped up in my inbox, but I suppose it was always going to happen. I'm surprised we haven't run into her before. After all, I don't think she ever left West Marsham.'

Natalie had nodded and murmured her surprise, but Pete had picked up on her anxiety.

'You're not worried, are you? God, that was years ago, we were kids when we went out.' He'd pulled her into a hug, resting his chin on her hair. 'She's probably all fat and wrinkly now, and anyway I only have eyes for you.'

Natalie had laughed, knowing she was being silly. This was Pete, after all. Faithful as a Labrador, was Pete.

7

'Well, if it's not Pete, then what is it?' Eve asks. 'You seem out of sorts, and it's not just tiredness. And sparkling water? You always have a glass of red, no matter what kind of day you're having.'

Natalie says nothing for a moment, tugging her hand away from Eve's and sipping at her water. It has a flat, mineral taste despite the bubbles, and her stomach rolls again.

'Natalie? Come on. I've known you for sixteen years, I know when something's up. I've lived through baby vaccination worries and mortgage trouble with you.' Eve pauses, a smile tugging at her lips. 'I was even there when that woman in the threading place over-plucked your eyebrows so badly we thought it was 1997 again.'

At this, Natalie would usually have roared with laughter (despite the fact that the eyebrow thing was a *very* painful memory) but when she raises her eyes to Eve's, Natalie has to struggle not to blink, afraid that if she does, a fat tear will slide its way down her cheek. 'I'm pregnant.'

'Pregnant?' Eve presses her hands to her mouth, her eyes wide. 'Oh, Nat, this is wonderful news. How far along are you?'

'Nine weeks.' The memory of cold porcelain against her cheek this morning as she threw up her morning cup of tea rises in Natalie's mind and she has to swallow hard.

'Will you be OK to eat the cheese? I think it's all right if it's piping hot.' Eve frowns. 'What did Pete say when you told him? Did you do the whole Instagram-worthy baby sleepsuit layout thing? Or did you dress Zadie in an "I'm the big sister" T-shirt? Do people actually do that?' Eve takes a mouthful of wine as Natalie doesn't reply. 'Wait. What *did* Pete say? This is good news, isn't it?'

Natalie lifts her shoulders in a tiny shrug, reaching for the napkin Eve has set out. She wishes it was paper, so she could shred it and make use of the nervous energy that ricochets around her body, but it's cloth, so she settles for folding and refolding it. 'I haven't told him yet.'

'What? Why not?' Eve gently removes the napkin and takes hold of Natalie's hands again. 'You guys are rock-solid – sickeningly so, in my opinion. And you already have two beautiful kids … a third one would be the icing on the cake.'

'It's not that simple,' Natalie says. 'Zadie is eight years old – she's going to secondary school in a couple of years. Emily is about to leave for university. I don't know if this is the right time.'

'The right time? I remember you saying that when you got pregnant with Zadie. And I'm pretty sure you probably said it about Emily as well.'

Natalie winces a little. She vividly remembers the day she locked herself in the bathroom of the tiny flat she shared with two others, her heart thumping as two pink lines showed themselves in startling clarity, signalling the arrival of Emily. She'd been in her final year at university, as had Pete, both of them just a few months out from final exams. Pete had been thrilled, Natalie's parents not so. In fact, they were so not thrilled that Natalie has barely spoken to them since, and Emily has only met them once. Zadie, not at all. Not that Natalie is devastated by this. Growing up with an overbearing father and a mother who could only get through life by self-medicating, lurching from one imagined crisis to another, means that Natalie had almost felt relieved when they cut her off. Relieved that she wouldn't have to protect Emily from the same shit she experienced growing up.

It had been slightly easier with Zadie. Natalie and Eve had been good friends – *best* friends – for almost eight years by then. Eve's parents had died when she was in her twenties, so she understood that untethered feeling Natalie had whenever she thought about her mother, and neither of them had any siblings. When Natalie had told Eve she was pregnant with Zadie, Eve had filled the gap left by Natalie's mother, offering moral support, the connection between them moving from friendship to sisterly, if not quite maternal.

'Eve, I'm forty next month. The girls are growing up. It's been eight years since I've had to go through antenatal appointments, dirty nappies and sleepless nights. I'm not sure I'd be able to cope.'

'That part doesn't last forever, though, does it?' Eve gives Natalie a gentle smile, as she dunks a piece of bread into the cheese. 'Look at Zadie now – proper little comic, isn't she? She has us in stitches. And Emily. You must be so proud of her, going off to the next stage in her life. The world is her oyster.'

'Exactly. How are they going to react to having a new baby in the house? Having to share my and Pete's attention? What if Emily thinks I'm replacing her?' Natalie sighs, pushing her plate away. There is something too big in her gut that crushes her appetite, and it's nothing to do with the tiny bundle of cells in her belly. 'I'm just not sure, Eve. I don't know if I can go through it all again.'

Eve tops up her wine glass, even though Natalie had barely noticed her empty it the first time. 'You can't be thinking of…'

Natalie blinks, her eyes stinging. 'I don't know, Eve. I don't know what to do. Part of me loves the idea of a little baby. But the other part of me… I *like* where I am now. I like our life. To go back to the beginning would be… I don't know. Part of me thinks it would be…' Natalie swallows, the words sharp and angular in her throat. 'It would be easier to just… terminate.'

'Natalie, there's nothing *easy* about a termination.'

'I'm not saying that literally,' Natalie replies quickly. 'I'm just saying… having a baby is a massive adjustment. I have to make sure it's the right decision. And millions of women have terminations every day—'

'That doesn't mean it's the easy way out.' Eve's tone is sharp. Her eyes glitter, and Natalie realises she looks as though she might cry. 'There's a huge knock-on effect emotionally for women who have had a termination. It's not as simple as getting rid of it and never thinking about it again.'

'Eve? I didn't mean it like that.' The atmosphere has changed between them in a way Natalie can't put her finger on. 'And I never meant to upset you, I'm just … I don't know, I'm all over the place.' Eve sniffs, as a tear slides down one cheek. 'Oh, Eve, please don't cry.'

'I'm sorry. I know this is a difficult time for you, and I …' Eve hiccups as a sob escapes her throat.

'What is it?' Natalie asks gently, pulling Eve's hands into her. 'You can tell me.'

'OK.' Eve draws in a shaky breath, and nods. 'OK. Sorry, this is so difficult.' She pauses, almost visibly pulling herself together. 'You know I can't have children.' She says it bluntly but Natalie knows the words cut her. 'I never told you why.' There is a pause where Natalie feels her breath stick in her throat, and then Eve continues, her voice hoarse, as if she has to force the words out. 'Oh God, I haven't spoken about this for years. I had an abortion.'

'Oh, Eve.'

'It was ages ago, back in the nineties. I was seventeen. I wasn't with the father – he was just a drunken fling, and even if I was, it wasn't the right time for me. I was at college, working part-time in Zara, out partying every night. I would have made a crap mother. But it didn't go to plan, and I got an infection and it left me sterile.' Eve gulps a huge mouthful of wine, blinking. 'It wasn't a decision I made lightly, but at the same time I always thought there'd be another baby.'

'You were in a different situation,' Natalie says. 'You didn't really have any other option.'

'Well, I did,' Eve says bitterly. 'I could have had the baby. I probably would have been married by now, had more babies. But once you tell a man you can't give him children it kind of knocks you off the marriage pedestal. It was the worst mistake I've ever made, and now it's too late – I don't think I'll ever get married. I'm forty-five, for God's sake.'

Natalie never knew any of this. She has known Eve since she went back to work when Emily was almost two. She was assigned the desk beside Eve's – before Eve realised that HR for a charity wasn't her dream job, and she retrained as a counsellor. Although Eve has had boyfriends who have come and gone over the years, Natalie always thought it was her choice. That Eve was the one who made the decision to let them go. She always thought Eve loved her boozy, travel-filled, single lifestyle.

'I'm sorry.' Eve swipes at her eyes with her napkin. 'I'm not saying I've had a terrible life or anything, because I haven't. But what I am saying...' She leans in, holding Natalie's gaze. 'What I am saying is that I have regretted what I did every day. Every day I think about that baby and wonder what it would have been like. What would they be doing? What relationship would we have? I look at you and Emily and I always wonder.'

'I'm so sorry, Eve. I had no idea.' Natalie feels as if a weight has been placed on her shoulders. Not a burden as such, but the weight of guilt for all the times she asked Eve to have the kids, not knowing Eve was pining for her own lost child all this time.

Eve sniffs, pats her cheeks briskly and smiles, albeit shakily. 'Enough. Enough about that. I am thrilled for you, and I just want you to make sure you are absolutely sure about any decision you do make. You know I'll support you whatever you decide.'

'I know.' Natalie reaches out and squeezes Eve's hand. 'Sorry to lay this on you at lunch.'

'Don't be daft, it's what friends are for. Listen, have you seen a doctor yet?'

Natalie nods. 'Two weeks ago, after I did the test.' The doctor – in his late sixties and at the surgery since the dawn of time, it seemed – had congratulated her in a hurried way, without offering any other options.

'Wow. You've known for two weeks?'

The smell of the bread hits Natalie's senses and she wants to groan aloud. Her nausea has died down, and now she's starving. She piles salted butter onto a chunk of warm bread and takes a huge bite, chewing frantically before she speaks.

'I wanted to get my head round it all before I told Pete. I'm going to have to tell him soon, I have a dating scan in two weeks.'

'You don't have to tell Pete yet, not if you're not ready.'

'Eve—'

'I'll go with you.' Eve raises her eyebrows. 'If you don't want to tell Pete yet, I'll go to the dating scan with you. Then you've got a bit more time to decide what you think you want to do, and the best way to break the news to him.'

'You would do that?'

'Of course.' Eve raises her glass in a toast, waiting for Natalie to clink her water glass against it. 'What are friends for?'

Later, Zadie is in bed after a bath and a story, and Emily is out with Jake, her boyfriend. Pete texts Natalie to say he'll be home late, and she resists the urge to collapse on the sofa. Eve's reaction to the news of her pregnancy has shocked Natalie, and she can't shake the look on Eve's face as she told her how much she regretted getting rid of her baby. Despite the exhaustion tugging at her bones, Natalie heads upstairs to the landing and stands beneath the loft hatch. Listening to make sure Zadie is asleep, once she is satisfied all is silent, Natalie slowly unhooks the latch, climbing the steps into the wide, draughty space. Turning on the light, she shuffles her way over the dusty boards to the boxes pressed against the wall. Pulling one towards her, she flicks the lid open, running a finger over the contents inside. *An old scan photo, dated 2005.* Emily's scan. The first time she and Pete saw this miracle baby they'd accidentally created. With a smile, Natalie tucks it back into the box before dipping in and pulling out something else. *Tiny, pink knitted bootees.* Pete's mum had sent them over from Australia when she heard Emily was going to be a girl. Natalie had wept over the parcel, after her own mother had stopped taking her calls. *A hospital band.* So tiny it only just loops around Natalie's thumb. *Zadie Esther Maxwell. DOB 3/10/2014.* Zadie's hospital bracelet. She had been tiny, barely six pounds. They'd named her Esther for Pete's mum. Natalie presses a hand to her stomach, breathing in the musty attic air. She's not sure how she feels about anything any more. Tucking the tiny baby bootees into the pocket of her jogging bottoms, she descends back to the landing. *Tomorrow*, she thinks. *I'll tell Pete tomorrow.*

# *Pete*

Pete is running late even though he left site early, and even though he promised Natalie he would be on time to meet her for dinner. He had wanted to go to that fancy new Italian restaurant on the other side of town, but she wanted to go to their usual place, despite the fact they've eaten everything on the menu and she and Eve lunch there all the time. Natalie gets her way tonight, which is no surprise to Pete, even though the old place is further away from work for him.

Nevertheless, Pete is feeling chipper. Natalie called and asked him to dinner, saying she's got something to tell him, and he's got a feeling in his bones that it might be about that promotion she was talking about. If she gets it, it means they'll have enough money to cover Emily's rent at uni for the first year without dipping into their savings. He's got something to tell her, too, and as he gets out of the car, he taps his jacket pocket, checking the envelope is still there.

'Sorry I'm late.' Natalie twists away slightly, offering up a cheek as Pete arrives at the table, reaching down to kiss her. 'I got held up.'

'Of course you did.' Natalie rolls her eyes, but her tone is good-natured, which Pete takes as a sign that she's probably got good news for him. She smiles as he sits down opposite her, but her face is pale and tired, and Pete feels a tiny flicker of concern. He knows he's been working long hours on the new contract, but finally it's starting to pay off. Natalie has been working and taking care of the kids on her own, and he knows she's already struggling with the idea of Emily going away to university after her A levels, because he came home late one evening about a month ago and

15

she was asleep, clutching a tiny pair of Emily's baby bootees. 'I ordered for you,' she says. 'I'm starving.'

'Well, I'm here now, and I've got something for you.' Pete pulls out the slim envelope. He can't wait to see her face when she opens it. 'This is the reason I was late.'

Natalie takes it with a curious smile, pulling the slim cardboard wallet from the envelope. 'Pete …' Her eyes widen and her hand goes to her mouth, and Pete feels a thrill run through him. He knew she'd be pleased.

'Four tickets to Oz,' he grins. He's waited years for this, ever since his parents decided to emigrate when he left for university, back to New South Wales where his mum grew up. Pete had grown up in West Marsham hearing stories of barbecues on the beach, surfing the best waves and blisteringly hot summer days, but when his parents had made the announcement, he'd just got into his dream university. He'd made the difficult decision to stay while his parents and younger brother packed up and moved their lives halfway across the world. 'I went to the travel agent and booked it straight from work. I know I could have booked it online, but there's something a bit more special about going into the shop and booking with a real person, isn't there?'

'When are these for?' Natalie raises her eyes to his, before she looks back down at the tickets.

'Christmas. Well, the seventeenth of December, actually. I thought we could do three weeks. We can stay with Mum and Dad, spend some time with the rest of the family. The girls can finally meet their cousins. They'll have to miss the first week back at school, but Emily will only have revision at sixth form, and I can get away for that long – the site will be closed until the beginning of January at the earliest. The girls are going to love it. It's just a small town, but Mum and Dad are only a ten-minute walk from the beach, there's a nature reserve nearby, and if we want to go to the city, Newcastle is only 20 kilometres away. And there's this, too …' On a roll now, Pete pulls out another envelope from his jacket pocket. This is the one he's really excited about.

'What is this?'

'It's a plot of land.' Pete unfolds the page he's printed from the internet, and smooths it out so Natalie can read it. 'It's about ten minutes from my parents – further inland, but still close to the sea.' Pete's parents live in the same town his mother grew up in, two streets back from the ocean in Fern Bay, New South Wales. Pete has always felt that a part of him belongs in Australia, despite only visiting once when he was a child. He had spent most of that holiday in the ocean with his cousins, or poking around looking for insects that may or may not be deadly, the heat scorching his scalp as his mother shouted at him to wear a hat. He's never felt heat like it since – a dusty, dry warmth that filtered deep down into his lungs. 'There's an old house on there at the moment, but Dad looked into it and there's permission to knock it down and rebuild.' Pete can hardly contain his excitement. 'Just think, Nat, we could finally do it. We could finally live the dream. I could build the house, and we could move out there once the girls are grown up. If we're sensible we could keep our house, and build this one and split our time between here and Australia, like we always talked about.'

'Like *you* always talked about,' Natalie says quietly, the smile long gone from her face. The waiter places their food in front of them – spaghetti aglio e olio for Natalie, a spicy pepperoni pizza for Pete – but Pete has lost his appetite.

'I thought that's what you wanted, too?' Pete feels a flicker of something bigger than annoyance, but not quite anger. 'Let's go out there and see Mum and Dad for Christmas – you know Mum hasn't been right since she had that fall in February. We can look at the plot and you can see how you feel. We don't have to make a decision right now.' Although Pete knows his dad will look at it for them and put in an offer on their behalf if he asks him to.

'I can't go to Australia, Pete.' Natalie shoves the paperwork back at him.

'What? Don't be daft. I'll speak to your boss if you want, explain the situation. You can take unpaid leave if you don't have enough holiday. We can afford it.'

'*No*, Pete. I'm telling you I can't go to Australia. Not in December.' Natalie takes a deep breath, her face turning crimson as she tries not to cry. 'I'm … I'm pregnant. Fourteen weeks.'

Pete feels as though Natalie has punched him in the gut. 'What? Are you joking?'

Natalie shakes her head. 'No, I'm not joking. Why would I joke about something like that?'

'Well…' Pete blusters, not sure what to say or how to say it. 'This is … unexpected. But it's not the end of the world, right?' Natalie looks up at him and opens her mouth, but Pete carries on before she can speak. 'I mean, we're not going to keep it, are we? We can't.'

'What do you mean *we can't?*' Natalie hisses across the table at him.

'It's not…' Pete doesn't know how to articulate what he wants to say. He wants to say, *this isn't what we want*. 'I mean, we're just getting ourselves on our feet. You're going for that promotion at work.' Natalie snorts. 'The business is doing well, and I've just won this huge contract which means we can finally afford to go and visit my parents. We can finally afford to look at doing what we always dreamt of. The girls are getting bigger. We're so close to …' He trails off. *We're so close to getting our lives back*, is what he wants to say.

'Bloody hell, Pete, I can't believe you're saying this.' Natalie chokes the words out, her voice full of muted fury.

'What am I supposed to say? You're pregnant – *fourteen weeks*.' Pete feels his own blood start to rise. 'When did you find out?'

'A couple of weeks ago.' Natalie won't look at him as she stirs her fork through her rapidly cooling spaghetti.

'A couple of *weeks*? Sorry if I'm shocked, Nat, but you've had a couple of weeks to get used to it. *Wait*. So you only did a test at twelve weeks? Didn't you... I don't know, feel different or anything before?' Now he thinks about it, she has been going to bed early, and she has looked a bit peaky in the mornings.

'I thought it was just a bug.' Natalie shifts in her chair. 'I thought that's why I was so tired. Listen, Pete, I've been thinking about it.'

'Clearly.'

Natalie glares at him, and Pete gets the impression that if looks could kill, he would have been vaporised. 'I can't...' She leans in, lowering her voice as the waiter hovers nearby. 'I can't do it, Pete. I can't get an abortion.'

'Don't you think we should talk about it? Think it through?'

'Don't you think I have been? All I've done is think about it!' Natalie's voice breaks on the last word and her eyes fill. Pete reaches for her hand – an automatic response, despite the way he feels right now – and she lets him link his fingers through hers. 'It's all I've thought about since I did the test. Worrying about the girls and how it's going to affect them. Worrying about you, and what it's going to do to us. But I just don't think I could live with myself if I... you know. Got rid of it.' Her hand goes to her belly in an unconscious movement.

'How much time do we have before we need to make a final decision?'

Natalie slides her hand away, her features hardening. 'I don't think you understand, Pete. I've made the final decision. It's my body, and I'm telling you I can't do it. I can't get rid of this baby. In fact, I can't believe you could just throw away a life we've made together so easily.'

'Hey, come on. That's not fair.' Pete shakes his head. She always does this. Finds a way to make him feel like absolute shit every time his opinion is different from hers. 'It's not that – it's going to be a massive upheaval in our lives. Of course I'd rather this hadn't happened, but if you've decided you want to keep it, then I don't really have much choice, do I?'

'No, you don't.' Natalie scrapes her chair back and Pete scoops the tickets and paperwork for the plot of land off the table, throwing a few banknotes down to cover the uneaten meal.

They walk back to Pete's car (God, if he'd known, he would have swung by the house and picked her up instead of telling her to get a cab) and ride home in silence. Pete is relieved to see the downstairs lights are off when they arrive back at the house, meaning Zadie is in bed and Emily will be holed up in her room, noise-cancelling headphones drowning out the sound of their arrival. He doesn't want to see the girls tonight, knowing their world is about to be turned upside down.

In the kitchen Natalie makes herself a cup of tea, and as she moves past him towards the stairs he reaches out and grasps her by the arm, pulling her towards him. She resists for a moment, but softens as he puts his arms around her, resting his chin on her hair.

'I love you, you know that?' he says, feeling her nod against his chest. 'It's just a surprise, that's all. You knocked me off my feet, again.'

Natalie lets out a little burst of laughter. They'd met crossing the square at university; Natalie had been carrying a stack of books higher than she could see over, and she had literally knocked him flying. Pete has spent twenty years telling people she swept him off his feet.

'It's going to be tough, but we'll make it work. We did it before, didn't we?'

Natalie lifts her face and Pete kisses her mouth, tasting chamomile on her breath. 'I love you, Pete.'

'It'll all be OK. Go on, get up to bed. Get some rest.' He swats her on the bum as she turns to leave, waiting until he hears the bedroom door close and the soft creak of the bed as she climbs in before he pulls the envelope from his pocket. *Gutted.* That's how he feels. As though Natalie has reached inside him and scooped out all the hopes and dreams he's held close for years, leaving a gaping hole. It's not just about the house, though – it's his parents, too. They came over when Zadie was born, and he's not seen them in person since. They FaceTime every week, and his mum is always sending him silly emails and text messages, but it's not the same. Even though they live on separate continents, Pete is still close to his parents, and the thought of them being ten minutes down the road instead of eleven time zones away made him feel lighter somehow. He knows Natalie will never understand that, given her relationship – or lack of – with her own parents.

Sliding the paper with the plot details from the envelope, Pete makes a mental note to go into the travel agents' tomorrow and see if he can get a refund on the tickets, before he tears the plot information slowly and deliberately into confetti-sized pieces. He stares out of the kitchen window, out into the thick darkness of the woods beyond the back gate. *Tonight was meant to be a* celebration, he thinks, watching the trees sway in the wind. He was meant to be having a glass of champagne with Natalie, celebrating their freedom, making plans for their future, for a new life in Australia, and instead … Instead, they're going back to the beginning. Outside, an owl hoots, sending a shiver down Pete's spine. *I'm going to be a father again.* And as much as he hates to admit it, the thought makes him nauseous.

# *Natalie*

'I can't believe you! You're being *so* unreasonable.' Emily's face is a thunderous storm cloud as she glares at her mother.

Natalie is in the kitchen, scrubbing burnt-on baked beans from the bottom of a pan Emily used for lunch. This isn't the first row she's had with Emily since she and Pete sat the girls down to tell them she was pregnant, and she's sure it won't be the last. 'Emily, please. I hardly think being forty-one weeks pregnant is unreasonable,' she says mildly. She's actually nearly two weeks overdue, and feeling every single second of it. She'd spent Christmas like a puffed-up balloon, instead of serenely nursing a newborn and watching Pete cook the turkey dinner.

'You don't understand how important it is – you didn't come to the last one either. This is the open day for *literally* the only uni I want to get into. Jake said he'll take me, seeing as you can't, and I don't see why you're making such a big deal out of it.' Emily slouches against the kitchen worktop.

*Because he's only had his licence for three months*, Natalie wants to say, among other reasons, as she forces herself to take a deep breath. 'There's another open day there next month. I thought that's the one you were going to, anyway, not this one.' The baby should have been six weeks old by that point, but now Natalie's starting to believe she'll still be pregnant when the next open day rolls around.

'For f— God's sake, Mum,' Emily huffs. 'Jake is happy to take me, and he's even found a B and B so we don't have to drive to Durham and back in one day.'

'Oh hell, no.' Natalie throws the scouring pad into the sink and turns to face Emily, her belly twinging. 'You actually think I'm going to let you stay out overnight with Jake?'

'We've been going out for almost a *year*.'

'And you're still only seventeen. Jake is twenty. I know exactly why a twenty-year-old man would want you to stay out overnight. Sorry, Emily, it's not happening.'

'I *knew it*,' Emily hisses. 'I knew you hated him because he's older. That's why you never want him to come over. That's why you keep saying no when I ask if I can go out.'

'No, Emily, that's not it at all,' Natalie says through gritted teeth, as if she doesn't know that even when Emily doesn't go out, she sneaks Jake in through her bedroom window. Her belly tightens again and she presses her hand to her forehead, feeling weirdly hot. 'I don't want you out all hours because you're supposed to be revising for your mocks. There'll be no point in going to any open days at all, if you're not studying for your exams.'

Emily gives her a spiteful glare, full of teenage vitriol as Natalie turns to place the saucepan on the draining board. As she twists, there is an odd popping sensation in her belly, and then water trickles down her legs.

'Oh.' Natalie looks down, and then at the remaining pile of lunch dishes waiting to go in the dishwasher. Relief is the first emotion she feels, even knowing the pain ahead of her. Relief that this long nine months of heartburn, insomnia, sickness and exhaustion is finally over. 'Oh. *Oh*.' A familiar cramp grips her belly and she groans, pressing her hands to her huge stomach.

'Mum?' Emily drops her furious expression and steps towards her, her eyes wide. 'Mum? Are you OK? Is it happening?'

Natalie closes her eyes and nods, trying to smile. 'I think my waters have just broken. Can you pass me my phone?' Pete has been called out to site, to sort out some problem with the drainage even though it's two days after Christmas and the site is meant to be shut. She dials Pete's number, listening as it rings four times and then cuts to voicemail.

'For fuck's sake.' Another cramp comes in a wave and Natalie winces, her breath coming out long and slow.

'Mummy? Mum?' Zadie appears beside Emily in the kitchen doorway, and Natalie feels a bead of sweat form at her temple as she smiles through gritted teeth.

'It's OK, darling. Mummy's fine. The baby's going to be born, that's all.' She pulls in a breath. 'Emily, try your dad again, would you?'

Emily dials Pete again, casting frantic glances in Natalie's direction as her mother grips the kitchen worktop until her knuckles turn white. 'Voicemail again. What shall I do?'

'Leave. A. Message.' Natalie huffs, before snatching the phone from Emily's hand. 'Pete? Get home *now*. My waters just broke, I need to go to the hospital.'

Zadie's eyes fill with tears and Natalie bends awkwardly, scooping her in for a hug. 'Why don't you go and— *Ooof.*' Her belly tightens. 'Go and watch some telly with Em? It's meant to snow tonight, so maybe you two can go out in the garden later and Em might make you hot chocolate?' Zadie nods, and Natalie gives Emily a grateful smile as she leads her sister into the sitting room, their argument forgotten for now.

Twenty minutes later, Natalie is pacing the hallway, her overnight bag at her feet, as the contractions come five minutes apart. She can't help the groans that emerge every time the pain takes a stranglehold on her stomach, and every groan makes Zadie cry just a little bit louder, the sound whittling under Natalie's skin and scraping her nerve endings. Finally, Pete flies through the front door, bringing icy December air with him.

'Where the hell have you been?' Natalie growls at him as he fumbles with her bag, dropping the car keys as he tries to take her arm.

'I got cut off as I tried to answer your call,' he pants. 'The signal over there is terrible, but I jumped in the car as soon as I got your voicemail. Shush, Zadie darling, it's OK.' Pete reaches out and pats Zadie on the head, before guiding Natalie to the car. 'And then the traffic was horrendous – every man, woman and child is out at the sales…I know we have to go through town to get to the hospital, but I just thought *to hell with it*, we'll use the bus lanes, we've got a good excuse—'

'Pete?'

'Yeah?'

'Shut the fuck up.'


Natalie lies back against the hospital pillow, sweaty and exhausted. She's lost track of how long she's been here – whether it's day or night, even. Pete sits in the plastic chair beside the bed, his phone in his hands. He kept stroking her hair off her forehead and squeezing her hand, until she told him to stop. She knows he wants to help, but every time he did it she wanted to punch him in the face. It wasn't like this last time, she's sure of it. Both the girls were quick, natural births – with Zadie she hadn't even had any gas and air – and she had joked with Pete that finally she had found a sport she was good at. Worry flits across her mind. *Are the girls OK? How long have they been on their own for?* She had called Eve and asked her to come and sit with the girls once they made it to the hospital. Now she wonders if she should check with Pete, make sure Eve is still there, but before she can speak another contraction squeezes her belly. She's too exhausted to do anything more than whimper.

Pete's phone blares to life, his ringtone cutting through the pain, and she sees his face illuminated by the screen as he holds it up apologetically.

'Sorry, babe, I really need to take this. That bloody drainage.' Pete drops a kiss on her forehead. 'I'll be back in a tick, OK?'

Natalie doesn't even have the energy to be furious. Another contraction comes, and she sucks deeply on the gas and air, even though it makes her dizzy and her throat feel thick, barely realising when the midwife comes in and gently lifts the blanket covering her lower half.

'I need to push,' Natalie says, the feeling coming almost as a relief. She squeezes her eyes closed, pushing hard, as the midwife encourages her to *breathe, keep breathing, Natalie, come on.*

Exhausted, Natalie bears down as hard as she can, only slumping back against the pillow as the contraction fades. *I want Pete*, she thinks. She tugs at the sleeve of the midwife's uniform. 'Pete isn't here. I need to wait for Pete, he's going to miss it all.' But then there is another contraction and she has to push again, screwing up her face and trying her hardest even though she's tired, *so, so tired.*

'Nat, I'm here.' Pete's face appears in the corner of her vision, flustered and breathless. 'I'm here. Oh, God, this is actually happening.' But Natalie is too worn out to do anything other than close her eyes as the midwife braces for another contraction. When it comes, Natalie just doesn't have the energy for it.

Moments later, the room feels crowded and Natalie feels the first inklings of panic through a haze of exhaustion. There are three midwives and a consultant all gathered around the monitor, murmuring to one another before the consultant – a man with grey hair swished stiffly back from his forehead – smiles down at Natalie.

'Natalie, I'm Mr Goodfellow. I've had a look at Baby, and things aren't progressing as quickly as I'd like. Baby seems to be getting a little bit distressed in there, and I think we need to get him out as soon as possible.'

*Her. It's a girl*, Natalie wants to say, even though she never asked at the scan. She knows, though; she knows this baby is another girl.

'With the next contraction, I'm going to need you to push as hard as you can for me. I'm going to make a small incision, and then we'll get this baby out in a jiffy.' Mr Goodfellow pats her hand. 'Nurse, get the forceps ready, please.'

The nurses begin bustling around Natalie, doing things she doesn't fully understand, and then there is the next wave of pain and Natalie grits her teeth and pushes as hard as she can.

'Oh my God, Nat,' Pete breathes, 'she's here. You did it. God, you're amazing.' He leans down and kisses her sweaty forehead.

*I did it*, Natalie thinks. *We did it. We have another baby. Erin*, if she really is a girl, *Arlo*, if he's a boy. It has taken Natalie and Pete ages to decide on names, and when Eve suggested Erin, which had been her grandmother's name, Natalie had loved it immediately. So had Pete, luckily, although Natalie has never told him the name was Eve's suggestion. Natalie feels hot tears slide out and into her hair, waiting for the wail that will split the air and announce the baby's arrival. But there is nothing. No cry, no shriek. Natalie looks up at Pete, who is pressing his hand to his mouth as the nurses hurry the baby away, towards the resus station.

'Pete? What is it? Why isn't she crying?' Panic is back, licking at Natalie's still-swollen belly.

'Mrs Maxwell, congratulations, you have a beautiful baby girl.' One of the nurses appears by the bed and Natalie drags her gaze to meet her eyes.

'Why isn't she crying? What's going on?'

'Baby just needs a little bit of help, that's all. The doctor is with her now, and as soon as we can we'll get her over to you.'

Time seems to stretch out like toffee, seconds turning into minutes, minutes turning into hours. Pete is still clutching Natalie's hand, and she is vaguely aware that he is squeezing it too hard, crushing the tiny bones of her fingers. Finally, *finally*, a cry rents the air, high-pitched and utterly furious. At first Natalie isn't sure if she's imagined it, and then it comes again, just as angry, and then the nurse is there, placing the baby – fists clenched and eyes screwed shut – onto Natalie's chest. She's saying something about skin to skin, but Natalie isn't listening; all she can hear is that beautiful, ear-splitting wail.

'She's OK,' Pete breathes in her ear, reaching out a finger as the baby quiets, wrapping her tiny fingers around his. 'You scared us there for a moment, little one.'

'Erin,' Natalie says, suddenly feeling light-headed. 'Welcome to the world, Erin.'

'Nat?' Pete's face is alarmingly close to hers, but Natalie can't speak as black spots dapple her vision and she feels awfully sick and faint. 'Natalie? Are you OK?'

'Mrs Maxwell?' Mr Goodfellow, the consultant, is back and she doesn't know why he's here; the baby is born. Shouldn't he be looking after another mother now? 'Natalie, you're bleeding very heavily, and we can't stop it. *Natalie.* Natalie, you're haemorrhaging. We need to get you down to theatre now. We need to perform a hysterectomy in order to stop the bleeding.'

Natalie nods, vaguely aware that the baby is no longer lying on her chest but too woozy to do anything about it. She doesn't care what happens, what they do to her. She just wants to see her baby. As they rush her bed along the corridor, bright lights flashing overhead, Pete runs alongside, his face twisted with worry. He reaches out and squeezes her hand, and this time she lets him.

The room is dark and Natalie is tucked away in her hospital bed, the curtains blocking out the rest of the exhausted mums on the ward. Pete left a couple of hours ago, heading back to the house to break the news to the girls about their new baby sister. He'd fussed over Natalie as they wheeled her from the recovery room to the ward, explaining that she'd lost so much blood, he'd thought she would die. Telling her how she'd gone so pale it was as though she'd failed to exist, a ghost of a woman. That they'd taken everything away inside her, it was the only way to save her, but she'd barely registered what he was saying. Now, it's 3 a.m., the witching hour, and Erin begins to stir in her cot beside the bed, a murmur that quickly becomes a full-on wail. Natalie pushes back the blankets, before pressing the buzzer for the nurse. The anaesthetic has worn off and her belly is a raging inferno of pain. Erin cries louder, her tiny face red and furious.

'I'm coming. It's OK,' Natalie puffs, just as a nurse whips her head through the gap in the curtains.

'Baby's hungry, mum!' The nurse says. 'I'll pass her to you, you're not going to be able to lift her yourself.'

Natalie pushes her way up the pillows into a sitting position. *Oh, God, the pain.* She isn't expecting it – after the girls she'd ached, of course, and she'd been ridiculously out of breath, but this is like no pain she's ever felt before.

'Here you go.' The nurse places the baby in Natalie's arms, and Natalie sinks back onto the bed, allowing the nurse to get her into a comfortable position. 'Let me know if you need a bit of pain relief.'

Erin feeds for what feels like hours, and when she's finished Natalie buzzes for the nurse to put Erin back in her cot, feeling oddly disconnected as she watches the nurse do a quick nappy change before laying Erin down. The pain relief the nurse bought hasn't done much, but as Natalie lies down she feels a wave of exhaustion. Both Emily and Zadie had slept well their first night in the hospital, and Natalie craves sleep like a drug, even if it is just for a couple of hours. Her eyes droop closed, and just as she is on the edge of dozing off – a blissfully dark oblivion laid out before her – there is a muted cry. Natalie squeezes her eyes closed, but it comes again, before ramping up into another angry wail.

'OK. It's OK,' Natalie says again, once more pushing herself back up the pillows and pressing the buzzer for the nurse. She wants to weep at the pain as Erin screams, aware that all the other babies in the ward are sleeping soundly. *Why is she crying?* She fed less than an hour ago; she's clean and dry. The sound seems to ricochet off the curtains as Natalie feels more and more out of her depth, a swimmer grasping for the bottom of the pond with her feet. This wasn't how it was before, with Emily and Zadie. Neither of them cried like this. *What's wrong with my baby?* Natalie looks down into the cot at Erin's angry little face, at the red cheeks and gaping mouth, the dark curls plastered into sweaty little horns at her temples. She is utterly furious, this new child of Natalie's. Furious with the world. Furious with *her*.

# *Pete*

Shit. *Shit.* Pete squints at his phone, hoping he's read the screen wrong. *7.41am. Shit.* He scrambles out of bed, his pulse frantic in his ears as he turns on the shower and jumps in before the water even has a chance to heat up. Five days after Erin made her traumatic way into the world, Natalie is still in hospital and Pete is desperately trying to juggle visiting her with keeping the girls fed and watered.

'Em! Zadie!' he calls out as he hurries towards the stairs, wrapped in a towel, his neck and shoulders still splattered with water. 'Get up! Back to school today!'

*How does Nat do it?* he thinks as he heads for the kitchen, unable to even contemplate packed lunches, school bags or even *getting dressed* until he has a shot of strong caffeine running through his veins. He pushes away the thought that actually, he should be returning to work today after the Christmas holidays with a killer tan and a strong temptation to drop his rs the way his mum does in her broad Aussie accent. Instead, he has to get the girls to school, check in with Dave, his foreman, then go into town to pick up a travel system so he's ready to bring Natalie and Erin home when they are discharged, before heading to the hospital to see them both.

A waft of coffee on the air hits him as he pushes open the kitchen door, and he frowns for just a second before clutching his towel tighter around his waist.

'Fucking hell!' he yelps. 'What are you doing here?'

Eve smiles as she pours him a mug of coffee and hands it to him. 'I knew the girls were going back to school today and I thought you might need a hand. Good job I did pop in, Zadie needs to be at school in half an hour.'

Pete glances at the worktop, where two neatly made packed lunches sit – sandwiches, bottles of water, fruit and something that looks suspiciously like a home-made brownie. 'And you didn't think to knock the door?'

'You must have been in the shower.' Eve turns back to the work surface and begins to wipe it down with a damp cloth.

Pete feels exposed, as if he's been caught doing something he shouldn't. Maybe it's down to the fact that while Pete only has a towel to cover his modesty, Eve is fully dressed, in her usual multilayered hippie outfit of a maxi-dress and cardigan despite the frigid temperatures outside, her long hair in a French plait hanging over one shoulder. Pete always says to Natalie that Eve would start a commune with her if she could only get Pete out of the way. Or at least, she would if she had any other friends to join them. 'Well, I'm up now. See.' He gestures to the towel. 'So, thanks, but you can go. I need to get the girls ready. You can see we're running a bit behind.' He's going to have to have a word with Natalie about Eve once she's home. There's something so ... *unnerving* about the way she just let herself into the house. If there was no reply when she knocked, why didn't she just call him?

'Sure.' Eve tosses the cloth into the sink and wipes her hands on a tea towel. 'The girls' school bags are on the table, and I made sure to sign Zadie's homework book. You and Nat forgot.'

'Right.' Pete shifts, eager now for Eve to get the hell out of his house. She steps round him, almost too close for comfort, and grabs her bag.

'Just one thing before I go,' she says, with a slight frown. 'You did iron Zadie's school uniform, right?'

Even with Eve's help (Pete couldn't throw her out after she ended up ironing Zadie's uniform for him – he's not a complete dick) it's still a struggle to get everyone out of the house on time.

'Emily!' Pete yells up the stairs for what feels like the thirtieth time. 'We are *leaving*. Right *now*.'

'OK, OK, I'm coming.' Emily comes barrelling down the stairs, but not so fast that Pete doesn't clock the heavy eyeliner she's wearing.

'Is that really school appropriate?'

'What?'

'The eyeliner.'

'Oh, for God's sake, Dad. Mum doesn't have a problem with it.' Emily hefts her bag onto her shoulder. 'Oh, yum, I love your home-made brownies. Thanks, Eve.'

Eve's cheeks pinken as Emily leans in and gives her a kiss goodbye. 'Have a good day, love.'

'For Christ's sake, can everyone just *get out of the house*,' Pete roars, shooing Zadie towards the front door. He pulls the door closed, checking as he does that he did actually pick up his keys, and turns to the car, stopping dead as he sees what is on the driveway.

'What the hell is this?' Pete steps forward as Eve presses her hands to her cheeks, unable to hold in her smile.

'Surprise!'

'What the . . . ?' It's a travel system, brand spanking new, with a pink ribbon tied around the handle. It's the really, *really* expensive one that Natalie has spent three months salivating over, the one that Pete said they couldn't get because it was just too expensive. Pete is all for good quality gear, but this was off the scale. The other two girls had coped with regular-priced travel systems, and his and Natalie's inability to agree on what they were actually able to afford is part of the reason that he has to go and buy one today. Or, maybe not.

'I know you guys need a travel system to bring Erin home, and I know that Natalie has had her eye on this one for months. She mentioned it often enough.' Eve gives a little laugh and nudges Pete. 'Go on, have a look. I got everything – it even comes with a sun parasol and a cup holder!'

Pete feels a bit sick as he takes in the fancy system. Zadie steps forward and grabs the handle, wheeling it back and forth in place. 'Zade, leave it. Get in the car.' He pauses, waiting until Zadie is in the car before he turns back to Eve. 'Eve, this is too much. We can't accept it.'

'Nonsense.' Eve flaps a hand.

'It's fifteen hundred quid!' Realising he's raised his voice, Pete leans in. 'It's *fifteen hundred quid*, Eve,' he hisses. 'That's not a little gift for a new baby. That's ... That's—'

'Pete. Please. It's not like I have anything else to spend my money on.' Eve looks away with a little sniff, but this is Pete she's talking to. Pete is immune to what he calls Eve's emotional warfare. She might be able to manipulate Natalie, but not him.

'There are plenty of things you could spend your money on. Bloody hell, Eve.' Pete runs a hand through his hair. He doesn't have time for this. Not this morning.

'Pete, come on. It's a gift. You need a travel system, this is the one Natalie wants.' Eve looks up at him slyly. 'You know if you don't accept it, you'll have to go out and buy one today anyway, so ...'

Pete glances at the car, where Emily mimes tapping a watch at him. Eve has a point, even though it pains him to admit it.

'Fine. Thank you. But we'll pay you back.' He doesn't know when, but they will. 'Sorry, Eve, I really have to dash.'

Hoping he hasn't made a mistake in accepting the gift, Pete jumps into the car, throwing it into gear and pulling off the drive. As Zadie chatters in his ear, he glances in the rear-view mirror. Eve stands on the drive, one hand raised in farewell. A shiver ripples through him, something about the scene seeming oddly domestic and yet off-kilter, as if viewed through warped glass.

'Dad?' Emily turns to him with a frown.

Pete lowers his gaze to the road, patting Emily's hand. 'Sorry, kiddo. Someone just walked over my grave, that's all.'

# *Natalie*

Natalie has been in hospital for a week, thanks to an infection after her emergency operation, and she's sick of it. She's sick of staring at the same curtain surrounding her bed on the ward. Sick of the same beeps of machinery and rumble of trolleys, the same saccharin-sweet tones of the nurses, the same faintly antiseptic smell on the air. Sick of the pain in her abdomen every time she holds Erin, or tries to walk, or does anything, quite frankly.

It has become quite clear in the few days since Erin's birth that Erin is a poor sleeper. Natalie is exhausted, and as she peers into the cot now, she feels an undeniable frisson of terror as Erin stirs.

'No, no, shhhh.' Natalie cautiously backs away, wincing as she manoeuvres herself back onto the bed. Several women and their babies have come and gone on the ward since the night of Erin's birth. One woman – according to the story she told a weary Natalie, anyway – fired her baby out of her womb in minutes without a single drug. Another, a woman in the bed next to Natalie, had had twins and when she arrived, Natalie thought she recognised a kindred spirit in the woman's exhausted face. She imagined them whisper-chatting together over their feeding babies' heads in the gloom of the early hours, comparing birth stories and sleep tips. But, it turned out, the twins slept wonderfully, waking only to feed. Natalie felt even more exhausted as she frantically tried to hush Erin before she could wake the sleeping twin boys, before, to her relief, the woman was discharged after only two nights.

Now, the doors to the ward creak open and she looks up, glad she's pulled back her privacy curtain. Visiting hours start at eleven o'clock, and while she knows the girls won't be there today, she's been expecting Pete. Her eyes go to the clock on the wall. It's almost three o'clock now. She feels starved of conversation, the nurses too busy to chat and the other new mums only wanting advice once they find out Erin is her third baby. This interest in her wanes when Erin begins to cry and it becomes painfully obvious to the other mothers that Natalie clearly doesn't have any idea what to do with her screaming child. It isn't Pete who enters the ward. Instead, it's the family of the woman in the bed opposite her: kids, her husband and what look like her parents, bearing flowers and balloons. They are noisy and overbearing, and Natalie casts another anxious glance towards the plastic cot as Erin screws her face up.

Natalie heaves herself off the bed on shaky legs, wishing it wasn't another two hours until her next shot of pain relief as she awkwardly lifts Erin, who begins to wail – a deafening, piercing cry.

'OK, shh, shh,' Natalie soothes, feeling utterly useless as she latches Erin on for the third time in less than two hours, her cracked nipple on fire as Erin begins to feed. Her scalp prickles as she hears the woman in the opposite bed tell her family, 'That baby has cried *all night*,' in a muted tone that isn't quite quiet enough.

Natalie feels her cheeks burn as Erin twists her head away, fed but still furious. Natalie puts her on her shoulder, patting her back, and squeezes her eyes closed, hoping against all hope that Erin will let out an almighty burp and then please, *please* stop crying.

'Hey, you. Someone's a cross little monkey.'

Natalie's eyes ping open and there is a rush of relief through her veins as Eve leans in and gives Natalie a kiss, before holding out her arms. 'Do you want me to take her?'

'Yes please.' Natalie feels inordinately grateful as Eve takes Erin and begins to wind her. 'She cried all night and that woman across the way there is pissed off about it, by all accounts.'

'What a *miserable cow.*' Eve raises her voice and Natalie stifles a giggle, before pressing a hand to her belly. It feels good to laugh, but by God, it's painful. 'How are you feeling?'

'Oh, you know.' Despite her breezy tone, Natalie can't stop the tears that spring to her eyes, and Eve knows her well enough to not let them go unnoticed.

'Oh, sweetie.' Eve shifts closer to her, propping Erin on one arm in a deft manoeuvre. 'Is it baby blues? You've been stuck in here for ages.'

Natalie sniffs, swiping her hand over her damp cheek. 'Everything just feels a bit ... *big,*' she says, quietly. 'Overwhelming, you know. I thought I was going to come in, pop out a baby and be home for New Year, and instead ...' Natalie has to swallow, the words getting stuck behind the lump in her throat. 'Instead I had a *hysterectomy.* They took everything, Eve. I couldn't have another baby now even if I wanted one.' *This wasn't what I signed up for,* Natalie thinks, as Eve wraps her free arm around her shoulder. She wanted a baby, not for half her insides – and the ability to have any more children – to be taken from her.

'I get it,' Eve soothes, pressing a kiss to Natalie's sweaty hairline. 'You know I understand. But I'm here for you, OK? If you want to talk about anything at all, even if it's just to rage. Your hormones are going to be all over the place for a bit, I should imagine.'

'Thank you.'

'I mean it.' Eve holds Natalie's gaze intently. 'I didn't have anyone to talk to when I ... Well, when I was in a similar situation, and I don't want you to ever feel as lonely as I did then.' She nudges Natalie, breaking the tension in the air, as Erin stirs in her arms. 'Now, how long before you can bust this joint?'

'Hopefully any day now. They think they caught the infection in time, and I do feel much better, even if I am still sore. I can't wait to get home.' Natalie pauses for a moment as she tries to figure out what day it is. 'Oh shit, it's Wednesday! I need to text Pete and make sure the girls got off to school all right this morning. He is coming in to see us today, but he's got a few things he needs to sort out first.' Natalie reaches for her phone, as Erin lets out an almighty burp.

'There we go!' Eve laughs, as Erin sighs against her shoulder. 'No need to text Pete, I can confirm everything is under control. I even ironed Zadie's uniform for the week... you *know* how I feel about ironing.'

Natalie feels oddly weepy, the bridge of her nose fizzing. 'Oh God, Eve, you are an angel. I don't know what I'd do without you.'

'Don't be silly.' Eve looks bashful as she adjusts Erin in her arms. Erin is actually *sleeping*, and Natalie feels her heart swell. Look at those eyelashes, resting on her cheeks. How could she have ever thought there was something wrong with her baby?

'I should probably let you get back to work,' Natalie says, with a twinge of regret. 'I know you've got clients coming out of your ears.' Natalie has always felt a little envious of Eve, since she retrained to be a counsellor. Natalie wishes she felt as passionately about the charity as Eve does about her clients, although now she thinks about it, she wonders if Eve's workaholic attitude is a way of filling the void left by her empty womb.

'I cancelled my clients this afternoon,' Eve says. 'I wanted to make sure I didn't have to rush back, just in case you needed the company.' She wears a look of satisfaction that Natalie doesn't quite understand. 'You haven't checked your WhatsApp today, have you?'

Natalie shakes her head. 'The hospital WiFi is terrible,' she says as she lifts her phone, scrolling to the app. Eve watches as Natalie opens the message she sent her first thing this morning.

'Eve? What is this?' Natalie raises her eyes from the photo of the travel system to Eve's face. 'Did you ...? You didn't?'

'I did. I wanted to. I'm surprised Pete didn't call and tell you,' Eve says.

'Pete knows?' Natalie's heart stutters in her chest. She knows how Pete feels about Eve: knows that he finds her interfering and intense; that he thinks Eve uses her emotions to manipulate Natalie.

'Of course. I took it over there this morning. He was surprised, but pleased, I think. I thought he would have been in to see you by now, seeing as he didn't have to go to town after all.'

'It's too much, Eve.' Natalie's mind races as she alternates between wondering what Pete's reaction really was, to imagining Erin lying peacefully in the pram, before briefly wondering where Pete is, if he didn't have to go into town. 'We can't accept it.'

'Oh God, not you, too,' Eve teases. 'I've already had this conversation with Pete.'

Natalie dreads to think what Pete's response was to Eve – what biting comment he made, dressed up as something milder. 'It's just… It's a big purchase, Eve. It's the kind of thing the baby's parents should be buying.'

There is the briefest flash of something that could be hurt across Eve's face as she gets to her feet, gently laying Erin in her cot. Erin purses her mouth for a moment, but thankfully stays silent. 'Why don't you two have a chat about it when you get home? You need something to bring Erin home in, so it'll do for now. If you change your minds, then I'll return it, no problem.' Eve keeps her eyes on the cot as she speaks, tucking the little blanket around Erin's body.

'You're sure?' Natalie feels weepy again, her throat constricting. 'It's not that I'm not grateful, I just—'

'Don't be daft. I know you're grateful. Listen, darling, I've just remembered I have a stack of paperwork to get done before the morning, but you'll be OK, I promise. Text me if they say you can come home tomorrow, and absolutely let me know if you need anything *at all*.' Eve swoops down and hugs her, leaving the heavy scent of her perfume on Natalie's skin, as she holds on a little too tightly, for a little too long, reluctant to let Eve go and find herself alone in this claustrophobic ward again. 'I mean it. Text me any time. You know I'd do absolutely anything for you.'

# *Pete*

Usually, Pete loves Easter weekend. Usually, Pete and Natalie would be away for the week with the kids, and Pete's best mate Stu and his family. They've tried to make a tradition of it since the kids were tiny – Stu is the closest thing Pete has had to a brother since his younger brother left for Australia with their parents, and they've made some brilliant memories together (not all of them PG rated). This year, though, when Pete met Stu for a beer to talk about where they were going to go – please God, not Butlins this time – Stu had sipped his pint and said he hoped Pete didn't mind, but he was taking Mari and the kids to Tenerife. 'I'm sure you guys will want to be at home this year, what with Erin being so little.'

Pete had nodded and said of course, it made more sense for the Maxwells to stay home. Natalie probably wouldn't feel up to it, even though her scar has healed well. But deep down Pete harbours suspicion that Stu and Mari didn't want to spend their Easter break listening to Erin cry. Because that's all Erin seems to have spent the first three months of her life doing – days and nights broken by a piercing cry that seems to burrow under your skin. If Pete is brutally honest, if he was Stu, he wouldn't want to listen to it either.

Pete has floated the idea to Natalie that maybe they could go away on their own, just the five of them. Somewhere further up north, like the Lake District. They could rent a lodge, hike the trails; he could take the girls out on a rowing boat on Windermere. Natalie had looked at him as though he was mad.

'Pete, do you even know when Easter is this year? *March*. You want to go hiking and boating with an eight-year-old and a

40

three-month-old in *March*? Of course I don't want to go away for Easter.'

And of course, she was right. The weather outside this Easter Saturday is atrocious – cold and drizzly; the trees at the end of the garden marking the beginning of the woods groan and sway in the blustery wind. When they had viewed the house, on a bright, sunny day in August, the woods being at the end of the garden had been one of the things that Pete fell in love with. He'd grown up in West Marsham, a Kent boy through and through, and a large part of his childhood had been spent sprinting across the village on his bike, to play in the woods until the sun went down. Even after dark, the woods had held a secret thrill for the kids of West Marsham, whispered ghost stories of jilted brides and hanged men a deterrent from staying out too late. The idea that his kids could grow up with the magical playground that was the woods on their doorstep was enough to make him look past the bathroom that needed replacing, and the missing tiles on the roof. Even Natalie, who had followed him to West Marsham after university, fell in love with the idea of living on the edge of their very own forest. But today, the woods look anything but inviting. Before Erin was born Natalie wouldn't have minded the weather – she's normally so keen on the girls getting out and away from their screens and into the fresh air that she's more than happy to put on wellies and take Zadie jumping in the puddles, but since Erin arrived Natalie hasn't seemed to want to do much more than lie in bed, or on the sofa.

He glances over at the sofa now, where Natalie sits staring mindlessly at the television. Erin is upstairs asleep – finally. She'd woken at five o'clock that morning, her screams slicing into a dream Pete was having about Chelsea winning the FA Cup. According to Natalie, Erin had woken every two hours through the night, but Pete was exhausted and hadn't heard a thing after midnight, when Zadie had come in to tell him she'd wet the bed. It's the third time this month, and Pete does wonder if they should start to be concerned by it, but when he raised it with Natalie she said it was probably Pete's fault for letting Zadie have juice with her dinner. Zadie sits on the floor in front of the telly, colouring in, her tongue sticking out of the corner of her mouth in that way she has when she's concentrating. Pete's heart squeezes when he takes in the scene. It's been a busy few months since Erin arrived, and if he's totally honest, he had forgotten how exhausting it is to have a new baby.

'Daddy, I'm bored.' Zadie throws her pencil down and comes to hang off his leg.

'We could go to the woods?' Pete leans down and ruffles her hair, casting a quick glance in Natalie's direction. Even as he says it, he regrets it. There is nothing appealing about rain dripping down the back of your collar, while the trees are shrouded in a disorientating, damp fog that echoes your words back at you whenever you speak.

'It's *raining*,' Zadie says with disgust. 'Where is Uncle Stu? Why aren't we on holiday with them? Lola says they're going somewhere really hot.'

Natalie stares at the television, leaving Pete to come up with an answer. 'We just didn't this year,' he says, 'but next year we'll definitely do something – and we'll make sure it's somewhere hot.'

'But that's aaaaaages way.' Zadie is perilously close to that stage of combined boredom and tiredness that means a tantrum she's too old for is on the horizon.

'Zadie.' Natalie's voice is a warning, but still she doesn't look away from the TV.

'Where's Emily?' Pete asks Zadie. 'Maybe she'll play Xbox with you. Or she might do your nail varnish.'

'She's *out*,' Zadie pouts, her voice rising. 'With Jake. With stinky, old, horrible Jake.' She shouts his name and then there comes a wail from the baby monitor.

'Zadie, *please*.' Natalie gets to her feet. 'I've only just got her down. Pete, calm her down, would you?' With a nod in Zadie's direction, Natalie hurries upstairs. Moments later, he hears her talking in hushed tones to Erin, then a blissful silence.

'Zade, come on, don't be a brat.' Pete scoops her up, tipping her upside down until she shrieks with laughter. He pops her head first onto the sofa and turns on the Disney Channel, as the front door opens.

'Em?' As Pete hears Emily's footsteps thud up the stairs, his phone pings with a text message. It's from Vanessa. It still feels odd to see her name pop up on his phone. Obviously mobiles hadn't really been a thing when they were together, and then Pete hadn't really thought about her much after he met and married Natalie. Not until her name appeared in his inbox with that lucrative house-building contract attached. Now, Pete sees her most days – she seems to find quite a few jobs that require coming in and out of his office.

Good sales day! Three sold off plan – some of us are going to the Kings Arms for a few drinks if you fancy? V

There is nothing Pete would like more than to be in the pub with a cold pint, football on in the background, maybe a kebab on the way home. It's been a long time since he and Natalie have done that. Leaving Zadie in front of the telly, he hurries upstairs and taps lightly on Emily's bedroom door. She is rummaging in a drawer as he enters, her face flustered as she turns to him with a frown.

'Good day?' Pete asks, perching on the end of her bed.

'Yeah. Wish we were in Tenerife with Uncle Stu, though.' Emily pulls a face.

'Me, too. Listen, would you mind looking after Zadie and Erin, if I take Mum to the pub for a couple of hours? Mum just fed Erin so hopefully she'll sleep.' Emily raises her eyebrows. 'She'll sleep on you, at least, if you sit in front of the telly with Zadie.

43

I'll get you a takeaway...' Pete waggles his own eyebrows, and Emily laughs.

'Nope, sorry.' Emily shakes her head, bending down to peer into the drawer again. 'I only came back to get a jacket and to find my ID. Jake and I are going out tonight.'

'You've been out all day, Em.'

'And?' She stands, sliding her ID into her wallet. 'I'm a teenager, and it's a bank holiday weekend. It's what I'm supposed to be doing.'

Pete can see her point, but even so. She's spending far too much time with Jake – she seems to be out all the time, so God only knows when she's actually getting any studying done. 'Sorry, Em, but no. You've been out all day and I'm taking your mum out for a bit of a break.' Emily opens her mouth to argue, but Pete carries on. 'Everything your mum does for you, the least you can do is look after your sisters for a couple of hours. Now, text Jake and tell him your plans have changed, or I'll do it for you.'

Pete kisses her forehead in an attempt to soften her mutinous expression, and heads for the bedroom he shares with Natalie. She is lying on the bed with the blinds shut, and she raises a finger to her lips with a frown as he steps inside.

'Let's go to the pub.' Pete scooches on to the bed next to Natalie and kisses her forehead, ignoring the faintly sour scent rising from her hair. 'A few people from work are there and they've invited us.'

'Why?'

'I thought it might be nice. A couple of drinks, maybe stop for a bite to eat on the way home.' They haven't been out for dinner since the night Natalie told him she was pregnant. She was too sick for the rest of the pregnancy, and since Erin came along they've both been too busy and too tired.

'Oh, Pete, I don't think so.'

'Come on, it'll be fun. Better than sitting in here all night.'

'I'm too tired... and what about the kids?'

'You'll feel better once you've had a shower and washed your hair.' Pete gives her hand a tug. 'Emily's going to watch the kids, let's go and have some fun. It's been ages since we've been out together.'

Natalie pushes him away, rolling over to face the cot where Erin now sleeps soundly. 'I can't believe you.'

'What? I just want to spend some time together out of the house.'

Natalie rolls back to face him, her mouth downturned. 'Pete, I'm fucking exhausted, can't you see that? I've been up God knows how many times in the night with Erin. The last thing I feel like doing while she is *actually* asleep is putting on make-up and going out for a drink.'

'I thought it might be fun, that's all. Just for an hour?'

'No, Pete. Look, you go if you want to. I need to get some rest, but if you want to go then just go. There's no point in you moping around the house when you'd rather be somewhere else. In fact, please do go – just give me a bit of peace.' And she turns her back on him again.

Any guilt that Pete feels at leaving Natalie home alone with the children disappears the moment he pushes open the door to the pub. A wave of warm, hop-scented air hits him, and the atmosphere hums with laughter and conversation, the rain outside pushing punters in from the High Street. He spots Vanessa's slim figure at the bar, her dark hair rippling down her back, and as he begins to weave his way between drinkers towards her, she turns and spots him.

'Pete!' A wide grin splits her face and Pete finds himself returning it. 'I'm so glad you made it!' She squeezes his arm and turns to wave at the bartender. 'What are you having? This one's on me.'

'Errr … a pint of Goose Island, please. Cheers.' Pete takes the pint and Vanessa clinks her glass of white wine against it. It's been a long time since a woman has bought Pete a drink – even longer since he and Vanessa were in a pub together, pooling their money for two halves of shandy and praying they didn't get ID'd – and it feels a little bit odd. 'Good sales day, then, eh?'

'Brilliant. They'll all be sold off plan before you've even started the next phase at this rate! Where's your wife? I thought you were bringing her?' Pete had texted back before he'd spoken to Natalie, and he pauses for a moment as Vanessa waits expectantly for an answer.

'Oh, she's … She's a bit knackered, you know? New baby. I'll just stay for one or two and then I'd better get back to her.'

Famous last words. Pete really does only mean to stay for one or two, but then Dave arrives, and he gets on well with Dave. He's the best foreman Pete's ever had, and it's only right that Pete buys him a few drinks. Then, as darkness falls outside a band comes on and they're playing old nineties Britpop tunes, the stuff Natalie and Pete were dancing to at university. It's almost closing time when the strains of 'Don't Look Back in Anger' fade away and Pete finds himself with one arm around Vanessa and one around Josh, the estate agent, as they sway to the music. There are long, loud drawn-out goodbyes as people leave, and Pete is more than a little tipsy, his throat hurting from singing, as he fumbles his key into the front door, sneaking his way upstairs and into the bedroom.

'Good night?' Natalie's voice is low as she sits up in bed, feeding Erin a bottle, the bedside lamp giving off a soft golden glow.

'Sorry I'm so late,' Pete stifles a hiccup, frowning as he notices the bottle. He didn't know Natalie was going to stop breastfeeding. 'There was a band playing Oasis …'

'Sounds like you had a good time.' Pete tries to listen really hard through his beer fog, and he doesn't think there's an undertone to her words, but he's not sure. 'Who was there?'

Pete sits on the edge of the bed, his back to Natalie as he pulls off his socks and tugs his T-shirt over his head. There was a time when he and Natalie might have laughed about the frequency of Vanessa's visits to his site office – for help with the printer and to ask whether he used the last of the milk – but for whatever reason, he hasn't mentioned them to her so far.

'Just Josh, Dave … a few of the other lads.'

'Nice. Well, at least you all have two days off to get over your hangovers,' Natalie says dryly as she places the baby in the crib and switches off the lamp, leaving Pete to lie cotton-mouthed and wide awake beside her. As Natalie rolls away from him, he reaches out and presses a hand against the small of her back. He's not entirely sure why he didn't mention Vanessa.

# Natalie

There's no milk. Or bread. Natalie closes the fridge door and rests her forehead against it. She's going to have to go out and get some, despite the dragging exhaustion nagging at her very bones. The temptation to ask Eve to drop some groceries over after her last client leaves is strong, but Natalie bats the thought away before it can fully form. She can't ask Eve to pitch in again. Just yesterday Eve had very kindly collected, and then dropped off, Zadie's refill for her inhaler, even though she must have been busy. Natalie yanks the fridge door open again and surveys the contents with a critical eye. There might be no milk, but there is, however, a ginger shot in the bottom of the fridge, promising revitalisation and an energy boost. Natalie twists off the cap and necks it in one, her face twisting at the fiery taste. Maybe that will give her the oomph she needs to get out to the supermarket. Erin squirms in her bouncy chair, gurgling as Natalie leans over her.

'Hello, you,' she says, holding out a finger that Erin reaches for and grips in an iron fist. The baby pulls, yanking Natalie's finger towards her mouth. 'Hey, missy! That's not your lunch.' Natalie blows a raspberry, her mood lifting, suddenly sure the ginger shot is working its magic. Erin startles at the noise before she erupts into a smile, her eyes never leaving Natalie's face.

'Oh.' Natalie presses her free hand to her mouth, her heart filling her chest. 'Thank you, beautiful girl.' She frees her finger and pulls off the blanket covering Erin's lap, spotting a damp patch at the top of her thigh where her nappy has leaked.

'Come on, baby,' she says, scooping up Erin before she can launch into that ear-splitting wail that makes Natalie's skin shrivel. 'We need to go shopping.' She carries Erin upstairs, laying her gently on the changing table before pulling the drawer open for a fresh outfit.

'What the...?' Natalie pauses, staring down into the drawer that holds Erin's tiny sleepsuits. Instead of the hastily folded outfits thrown into the space, every outfit is neatly folded, rolled and placed in colour co-ordinated rows. *Eve.* It has to have been Eve that did this. Pete would never do something this organised, and as for Emily... Natalie's lucky if Emily is even speaking to her these days.

She pulls out a clean sleepsuit and begins to stuff Erin's legs into it, but she can't stop thinking about the rows of neat outfits. Something about it makes her feel oddly displaced – off-kilter. There is something weirdly unsettling about the regimented way they are lined up in the drawer, so at odds with the rest of their chaotic household. It makes Natalie feel as if she is an intruder, living someone else's life. Once Erin is clean and dry, Natalie turns her attention to her own appearance. She washed her hair yesterday, but she looks pale and drawn, and she pulls out the make-up bag on top of the dresser.

'How about some lipstick?' she says to Erin. 'Maybe Mummy should try and look pretty for a visit to the shops.' She opens a MAC lipstick in a nude pink, but the end has been mashed into the lid, rendering it unusable. She throws it back into the make-up bag, swapping it for a Glossier lipstick called Fuzz, but when she slides the lid off, that, too, is squashed and ruined.

'*Zadie*,' she sighs, tears pricking her eyes. She just wanted to look nice, for the first time in months, but Zadie's obsession with make-up has scuppered that plan. 'It's only the supermarket anyway,' she says as she picks Erin up out of the cot, blinking rapidly. Erin offers up another of those rare gummy smiles and Natalie grins back, her tears drying up. When Erin smiles at her like that, things don't seem half as bad.

*

Natalie realises as she pulls into the car park of the supermarket and wrestles Erin into the baby seat of the shopping trolley that she has not timed this trip particularly well. Erin begins to grizzle as she enters the supermarket, the sound sparking a flicker of anxiety in Natalie's veins. She's due a feed, and Natalie could kick herself for not realising. By the time Natalie reaches the chilled section Erin is wailing at her highest volume, her legs scrunching into her belly as her face turns an alarming shade of purple. Natalie's thoughts feel scattered and fragmented as she scans the shelves looking for semi-skimmed milk, but all she can see is full-cream, and that makes Zadie sick. Erin's shrieks pierce her eardrums, and she feels as if someone is raking their fingernails over her exposed nerve endings.

'Excuse me?' An older lady taps Natalie on the arm as she finally spots the right milk and snatches up two cartons, throwing them into the trolley.

'Yes?' *Please don't ask me for help*, Natalie thinks desperately. *Please just let me get out of here.*

'Can't you shut that child up?'

Natalie feels as if someone has punched her in her solar plexus. *'What?'*

'Can't you stop that baby crying? You are her mother, aren't you? Surely you can stop her screaming like that. Some of us are trying to shop in peace.'

There is a moment in her head where Natalie sees herself shove the trolley into the woman's belly, sending her sprawling into the fridge, icy cold milk cartons bursting all over her perfect helmet of lacquered hair. *I'm going mad*, she thinks as Erin screams on, and she turns on her heel, hurrying towards the till before she does something she regrets. Fuck the bread. She's not hungry anyway.

At the till the young lad scans her shopping, as Natalie frantically tries to stop her racing pulse. Erin has cried herself to gasps and whimpers, and to Natalie's horror she feels herself join her as a sob erupts from her throat.

'Are you ... OK?' The checkout assistant asks. He looks terrified. To Natalie's horror she realises she recognises him; she thinks he used to be in Emily's class at school.

Natalie nods, averting her gaze as tears drip off her chin, her cheeks burning. 'The baby was crying,' she says. 'An old lady was quite rude to me.'

The boy just nods and hands over her change, clearly at a loss as to what to say. Natalie pushes the trolley hastily towards the exit before Erin can start wailing again. She makes no attempt to stop the tears pouring in a constant stream from her eyes, and as she passes the old woman at the self-checkout, their eyes meeting over the till screen, Natalie looks away first.

'Natalie?' Eve's voice rings through the shriek of Erin's cries, and Natalie lifts her head from where she sits at the kitchen table, hands over her eyes. She hadn't even heard the doorbell ring, so Eve must have let herself in.

'Nat, are you OK?' Eve moves through the kitchen, giving Natalie a concerned glance from where she stoops to lift Erin from her bouncy chair. 'Shush, good girl. Shhhhh.'

'I'm fine.' Natalie swipes at her eyes, aware that there is a stain on her T-shirt, and a ripe smell emitting from her armpits. *Did I shower today?* She can't remember.

'You don't look fine.' Eve bounces a still-wailing Erin in her arms. 'This one's hungry. Have you got a bottle?'

Natalie runs her eyes over the kitchen worktop: the dirty breakfast dishes, Zadie's Shreddies dried on and stiff; the empty bread wrapper; the greasy smear of butter glistening in the puddle of afternoon sunlight that hits the side. Six bottles sit on the draining board, every one of them lined with old milk.

'I need to wash some up. Hang on.'

'I'll do it.' Eve hands Erin to Natalie, the baby stiff and angry as she screams in Natalie's ear. Eve washes up a bottle and sterilises it with boiling water, before efficiently making up the milk and handing it to Natalie. In the silence that follows, Eve turns to the dishwasher, opening it to find clean dishes, and starts unloading it.

'I sent you a couple of texts,' Eve says as she puts clean glasses in the top cupboard, 'but you didn't reply so I thought I'd pop in and see how you're getting on. I'm glad I did now.'

Natalie vaguely remembers texts coming through, but she'd still been upset over the encounter at the supermarket, and she was going to reply later. She must have forgotten. 'Don't you have clients this afternoon, though?'

'It's OK. I've just ... rescheduled a few things. Cancelled a couple of appointments.'

'Eve, you shouldn't do that. Don't you only get paid if you actually see the client?'

'Honestly, Nat? It's one afternoon. I think you're more important right now, and it's not like Pete's here to look after you. So, what's happened to get you in this state?'

Something prickles along the nape of Natalie's neck at the idea of Eve cancelling work for her, but she brushes it away. 'I'm OK, really. I just need to ...' Natalie waves a hand in the direction of the bomb-site that is her kitchen. Zadie's left her PE kit on the floor, Emily's shoes are jumbled in a heap by the back door, and Natalie doesn't even know when anyone last opened the post. Plus, the bin needs emptying.

'Where's Zadie?'

'After school club. She'll be home at five. Stu's dropping her off on his way home from picking up Lola.' Natalie glances at the clock. It's 4.15 now.

Eve loads the dirty dishes and then turns to Natalie, wiping her hands on a tea towel. 'How are you really, Nat? Don't tell me *fine*, because I won't believe you.'

'It's been a bit of a shit day.' Natalie's eyes fill with tears. 'I'm just ... so tired,' she says, as Erin twists her head away from the now empty bottle. 'Erin doesn't sleep, at all. She keeps me up half the night; it feels like the moment I lie down she wakes up again.

Pete is up and out of the house at five o'clock every morning, and he's not been getting home until after Zadie's gone to bed.'

'Have you tried getting out of the house?' Eve asks gently. 'Getting some fresh air, maybe meeting up with some other new mums?'

Natalie lets out a harsh bark of laughter that jolts Erin, who lets out a cry. 'I tried going to the supermarket earlier and even that turned into a nightmare.' Natalie recounts the tale of the awful old lady at the milk fridge.

Eve holds out her arms and Natalie lays a crying Erin in them, taking the packet of tissues Eve has laid on the table and wiping her eyes.

'Every baby is different, Nat, you know that. And that old lady… She's probably forgotten what it was like to have a young baby.'

'But she hates me, Eve. My own baby hates me.' Natalie's throat thickens and she has to force the words out. 'She cries *all the time* from the moment I pick her up. She won't feed from me, she only wants a bottle.'

'She can probably feel you're tense,' Eve suggests, as Erin drops off in her arms. She lays her gently back in her bouncy chair and then moves to the fridge, pulling out cheese, garlic, tomatoes and pasta and starting to chop.

'I don't know how to feel any other way when she just screams twenty-four hours a day,' Natalie says. 'Zadie keeps wetting the bed, so I'm up half the night with her, if Erin does actually sleep. Pete keeps giving her juice with her dinner, and then he sleeps right through all the commotion – I think he's woken up once. Add into that, Zadie is refusing to eat anything I put in front of her. I'm just… sick of them all.' The words come out in a rush tinged with tears, and Natalie has no choice but to let out the sob that is threatening to strangle her. All she's done since she got home is cry.

'Oh, love.' Eve shakes pasta into a pot of boiling water and then pulls Natalie into a hug, letting her cry until there is nothing left. 'Have you thought about seeing the GP?'

'The GP? What for?' Natalie frowns. 'I'm not *depressed*, Eve. I'm just exhausted.'

'I'm not saying you're depressed, but if you speak to the GP he might be able to help. Give you some advice on getting Erin to sleep, or suggest some support groups or something.' The air fills with the delicious scent of garlic as Eve throws the chopped vegetables into the pan and comes to sit beside Natalie, taking her hands in hers.

'I don't need to see the GP.'

'Darl, it's not a sign of weakness. You're a new mum – take all the help you can get! No one's going to judge you—'

'Mum! I'm back!' Zadie's voice rings out from the hallway, and then she bustles into the kitchen, her backpack almost as big as she is. 'Aunty Eve! Yay!' Zadie throws herself into Eve's arms, as Natalie frantically shushes her so she doesn't wake the baby.

'I hope you're hungry, madam,' Eve says with a laugh as she spins Zadie around the now spotlessly clean kitchen.

'*Starving*,' Zadie says, grinning to reveal a missing front tooth as Eve deposits her on a kitchen chair.

'I hope you're going to be able to eat this big bowl of pasta with *no teeth*,' Eve teases as she drains the pasta and stirs it into the tomato sauce.

'The tooth fairy was meant to bring me a pound last night, but she was on holiday,' Zadie says, sticking her tongue on the gap. *Shit*. Natalie forgot all about it.

'She'll come tonight. Apparently it rained in Spain so she came home.' Eve winks. Zadie giggles and Natalie watches with a knot of hard, green envy in her stomach as Zadie pounces on the bowl of pasta Eve hands her and proceeds to eat every bite. When she's done, Eve clears the plates and Natalie walks her to the front door, already dreading the moment she leaves.

'Listen, I'm not trying to interfere, but just think about it, OK?' Eve says, as she steps out on to the front path. 'Even if you just make an appointment and talk, get things off your chest, it might help. And tell Pete to fucking step up. There shouldn't be anything more important to him than you.'

'OK. I'll think about it.'

'Nat, you've got a beautiful family in there – you are so, so lucky to have them all. I don't want to see things fall apart for you. Promise me, you'll make an appointment.'

'Sure.' Natalie wants Eve to go now. It's not fair of her, saying things like that and making Natalie feel guilty for having a family, and she seems to have taken against Pete more than usual lately. It's not Natalie's fault Eve can't have children, and she listened to her before, when Eve said she shouldn't have an abortion. Eve kisses her cheek and walks away. Natalie closes the door before she even reaches the end of the path.

After Eve has left, Natalie baths Erin and feeds her, and as she moves to the bedroom window to close the curtains, Erin begins to cry again. Desperately, Natalie grips the fabric of the curtains as she stares out on to the woods below. The trees shake and twist in the wind, as if being bent by the force of Erin's screams, and Natalie has a horrible sense of déjà vu. She thinks about the nightmare she's been having on repeat ever since Erin was born, where the doctor can't stop the bleeding in the delivery room, of the way it makes her feel as though she's fading away to nothing, leaving behind a soulless husk. *I don't know how much longer I can do this for*, she thinks. She doesn't know what she'll do if Erin doesn't stop crying.

# Pete

The printer whirs into life and Pete takes a moment to rub his eyes, scraping his hands down and over the stubble on his chin. Tapping his phone screen, he sees it's almost seven o'clock and his heart sinks. Another night that he's worked too late to get back in time to help Natalie bath Erin and help get Zadie to bed. He opens the next drawing on the list and sends that to the printer, too. He's still got to pop in on the show house before he leaves. They're having a little opening ceremony – just drinks for the site team – before they officially start showing potential buyers around tomorrow. He doesn't really fancy it, but he's going to get it in the neck from Natalie anyway, so he might as well go.

Twenty minutes later, Pete makes his way up the path to the show home. He doesn't want to blow his own trumpet or anything, but it really is spectacular, and pride straightens his spine as he pushes the front door open. Who would have thought that Pete Maxwell, that scrawny kid from the other side of the village (the side with the smaller houses and the mums who nattered over the front garden fences, cigs hanging from their mouths) would be the one to build West Marsham's most prestigious housing development?

'Vanessa.' Pete smiles as Vanessa appears in the doorway. She's wearing a fitted red dress that Pete knows the boys on site will have talked about today, and her dark hair tumbles down her back.

'You made it! Though you're a bit late, I'm afraid.' Vanessa gestures behind her towards the darkened kitchen. 'The lads all swooped in for a few beers, cheered themselves, and then went to the pub for Fatmir's leaving drinks.'

'Ah, bugger. I didn't realise they were leaving this early.'

'I could still show you round the house, though?' Vanessa raises her eyebrows. 'Come on, you should at least see the finished product. You did build it, after all.'

Pete grins. 'Yeah, go on, then. I suppose I should see what you've done with the old place.' He follows her into an immaculate sitting room, the walls a calming shade of taupe, with a huge flat-screen TV on the wall in front of two sofas that look far too expensive to sit on. There are no sticky handprints on the wall, no toys cluttering the plush rug, and the only sound is the hiss of a discreet air freshener that puffs the scent of jasmine and rose into the air. It's certainly a more calming space than the one Pete returns home to after a long day at work.

He follows Vanessa into the kitchen – gleaming appliances, white cupboard doors and a strategically placed bowl of exotic fruit on the worktop – through a laundry room and into a spacious garage, before heading upstairs. The master bathroom is just as opulent as the rest of the house, and when they reach the master bedroom Pete pauses on the threshold.

'You've done a cracking job,' he says to Vanessa. 'This is just … God, what I wouldn't have given to grow up somewhere like this when I was a kid.'

'It wasn't all me,' Vanessa says, blushing slightly. 'I had a few ideas, but it was down to the interior team to execute it. And what are you on about? I remember your house being brilliant fun. Your mum always had something nice in the oven, and your dad was so funny.'

'Yeah, it was a bit of a madhouse.' Pete looks at his phone. He had forgotten how much time Vanessa spent at his house when they were seeing each other. They were only teenagers, and Vanessa's mum always seemed more than happy to let Vanessa have dinner at theirs. It's weird to think about it, but Vanessa had probably spent more time with his mum than Natalie has in all the time they've been married. 'Thanks for showing me round, but I should probably get off home.'

Vanessa glances at the slim Cartier watch on her wrist. 'Oh gosh, me, too.' She pulls a face. 'I'm supposed to be going to a yoga class in twenty minutes but to be honest, I'd rather just have a glass of wine.'

Pete laughs, but secretly he feels the same. The thought of a nice, cold pint sounds like heaven, and he's late already.

'Tell you what.' Vanessa pauses as they walk down the front path together after locking the house up. 'Why don't we stop in the pub for a quick drink? If you don't mind giving me a lift, that is? The lads are only in town, and Fatmir did say he was hoping you'd pop in to say goodbye on your way home. I'd be more than happy to skip yoga for one night.'

Pete hesitates for a moment. He should go home, back to Natalie and the kids. But last week when he was late home, Natalie had shoved a screaming Erin in his arms before he'd even managed to get through the door properly, before marching upstairs and disappearing into the bedroom. He'd had toast for dinner at about ten o'clock that night, once Erin had gone off to sleep.

'Let me make a phone call.' Pete lifts his mobile and dials Natalie's number, exhaling with relief when it goes to voicemail. 'Nat? It's me. Something's come up at work, and I need to sort it before I can leave. I'm not sure what time I'll be back.' He pauses. 'Love you.'

The popular gastropub chosen for the leaving do is packed with people, and Pete's site team are more than a little rowdy when he and Vanessa walk in. Pete buys a round, clapping Fatmir on the back – he is genuinely going to miss him; they've worked together since Pete first started the business – and then joins Vanessa at the table she's managed to snag in the corner.

'Cheers.' Pete clinks his pint against her glass of white wine.

'They're a good team,' Vanessa says, her eyes going to the rest of the lads. 'They work really well together, and they're exactly what

I was hoping for when I sent you the tender. I've heard nothing but good things about you guys.'

'We try our best.' Pete has wondered more than once why Vanessa chose to send the contract to him to price, and even more why she gave the contract to him. He knows he isn't the cheapest around. Something eases in his chest now at the realisation that it's got nothing to do with their past. Of course it never did. It's his reputation.

'So . . .' Vanessa takes a sip of wine, her eyes closing briefly as the alcohol hits her tongue. 'God, that's good. How is Natalie? I can't believe I still haven't met her. All this time both of us have been living back in West Marsham, it's hard to see how we haven't run into each other somewhere.'

Pete thinks Vanessa probably frequents slightly different parts of West Marsham than he and Natalie do. He can't see elegant Vanessa in her classy suits and red lipstick queuing up for a kebab on a Wednesday evening. 'Nat's good,' he says. 'Tired, you know. New baby and all that.'

'I bet it's lovely, having a tiny baby about the place now the other girls . . . Emily and Zadie, isn't it? Now they're a bit older.'

'Well, swings and roundabouts, you know?' Pete has only drunk half of his pint, but he skipped lunch and it feels as if it's gone straight to his head. 'You forget how tough it is . . . the night feeds, feeling knackered all the time.'

'Ah. Things feeling a bit tough?'

'Something like that.' Pete sips at his pint again, and feels everything he wants to say – but can't – bubbling beneath the surface. 'It's been a mental few months, really.'

'Not helped by everything being crazy busy here. You must be doing something right, though. The houses are flying off plan before you can even get them up.'

'That's about all I'm getting right at the moment.' Pete smiles but it turns into a grimace. 'How's your mum, anyway?'

'You tell me.' Vanessa rolls her eyes.

Pete hasn't seen Vanessa's mum for years, but he remembers that they weren't particularly close. 'Oh?'

'She got remarried – *again* – a couple of years ago, so I haven't really seen her for ages. You know how she always used to be, head in the clouds whenever she had a new fella ... She's ten times worse now.' Vanessa sighs. 'What about your parents? How's Oz?'

'Oh, you know. Same as they ever were. They love it out there, though.' Pete remembers the day they'd sat him and his brother down to tell them about their plan to move to the other side of the world – remembers the way he'd broken down when he told Vanessa what was happening. Pete had been devastated, because even though he wanted to go with them, he'd had his own life plan, plus he hadn't wanted to leave Vanessa. They'd been together for three years at that point, and he thought he potentially could marry her. But then his parents had left, he'd gone to uni, met Natalie and left her anyway.

'Do you get to see them very much? I bet they were thrilled about the baby. I can imagine your mum flying over, telling everyone she met on the plane she was going to meet her new grandchild. I remember how she was that time your brother found that tiny puppy in the woods.' Vanessa laughs.

'She never did manage to persuade Dad to keep it.' Pete smiles as he shakes his head. 'It's hard, with the distance. We don't get to see them as often as we'd like. They haven't been over since Zadie was born, so they haven't even met Erin. And Natalie doesn't speak to her parents at all, so ...'

'Wow. So you guys have done it all on your own.' Vanessa sits back, signalling to a drinks waiter for another round for their table. 'It must have been tough ... I know how close you were to your parents.'

'Yeah.' Pete nods. 'Actually, yeah, it has been tough this time around.'

'A new baby is a big adjustment.'

'I don't think I realised how much of an adjustment. We have two kids together already, and I thought having a third would just... slot in, I guess. By now, anyway.'

'And it's not worked out that way?' Vanessa sips her wine, never taking her eyes off him, and for the first time in a long time Pete feels as though someone is actually *listening* to him.

'No. Erin is... She's a difficult baby. She cries a lot, and I know it's tough for Nat. It's been tough on all of us. I come home after hours on site and Nat just shoves the baby at me and shuts herself away in the bedroom. I can't remember the last time we ate a meal together. I can't remember the last time she even properly talked to me. It's almost as if she can't stand to be around me. Don't get me wrong, I love them all,' Pete says, hastily gulping at his beer, 'but it's been a bigger upheaval than we were all expecting, I think.'

'Have you tried talking to Natalie about how you feel?'

Pete shakes his head. 'There's no point – any time I try to raise anything like that, she just shuts me down and reminds me it's her that's home all day with the kids. Sorry. Ignore me. You didn't come out to listen to me moan.'

Vanessa smiles, shaking her head. 'Come on, Pete, don't be daft. We're old friends. If you can't talk to your old friends, who can you talk to? It sounds like Natalie is...' she trails off.

'What?'

'Honestly?' Vanessa meets his gaze, the candle on the table giving her face a golden glow. 'You can tell me if I'm out of order, but it sounds to me as though Natalie is being a little selfish.'

Pete sits back, stunned for a moment. This is the thought he's been privately harbouring ever since Natalie sat across the table from him and told him she was keeping the baby, regardless of what he wanted. 'I just don't want this to be it, you know?' he agrees. 'We were meant to go to Australia to look at a plot of land – we were meant to travel and do things together once the girls were older. I even bought tickets,' he gives a rueful huff of laughter, 'to go to Australia for Christmas last year, but of course everything is on hold now.' Pete feels as if his entire life is on hold, and he's treading water.

Fresh drinks arrive – a shandy for Pete, as he's driving, and another glass of Sauvignon for Vanessa. Pete uses the distraction to change the subject, feeling disloyal at speaking so frankly to someone – to *Vanessa*, of all people – other than Natalie. 'What about you?'

Vanessa frowns. 'What about me?'

'What have you been up to since…?' Pete trails off, not sure how to finish the sentence. *Since I swanned off to uni and left you behind with your useless mum? Since I chucked you for Natalie?*

'Since college?' Vanessa makes it easy for him. 'Oh, you know. Becoming a hotshot property developer. Riding roughshod over the little people who contest any inch of space being built on.' She lets out a familiar peal of laughter. 'I'm *kidding*. I guess you could say I'm the polar opposite to you.' Vanessa smiles as she reaches for her wine, and Pete feels an odd flutter in his stomach. 'No kids at all. And I don't think I really want them, to be honest.' She flushes. 'I know, it probably sounds weird. Everyone always expects women to want a family but… no, not for me.'

'What made you…?' Pete swallows. 'I mean, what made you feel that way?' He remembers her always liking kids; at least, she was good with his little brother.

'You know my dad left when I was really young?' Vanessa says. 'Skipped out on me and my mum for a woman two streets away, so that was great.' She takes a mouthful of wine, but Pete can see the hurt on her face. 'Watching him bring up two boys with his new wife, while he blanked me if he saw me in the corner shop… I just thought, *I never want that.* I wouldn't want to recreate that for my own kid.'

'Jesus, I'm sorry.'

'God, Pete, don't be. I'm all right. I've got a pretty brilliant life – posh flat in the centre of town, a nice car, a good job. I love to travel and kids would just hold me back.' The words are right, but the smile Vanessa offers up as she speaks lacks conviction.

'Really?' Pete leans forward, keen to know more. 'I wish I'd travelled after uni – I wanted to do Asia, but it didn't work out that way.' *Nappies and broken sleep.* That's how it worked out for Pete after uni.

'You've never been?' Vanessa's mouth drops open. 'You didn't ever stop off on your way to visit your mum and dad? I thought it was the law that if you travelled to Oz, you had to stop off in Thailand on the way.' She lets out a peal of laughter and Pete finds himself smiling. 'I spent last Christmas there.'

'In Thailand?'

'Yep.' Vanessa nods. 'Karon Beach. Sun, sea and some of the most incredible sights I've ever seen. I loved it even more than Vietnam and Singapore. I'm headed to Santorini for two weeks at the beginning of September, and I'll probably try and get away again for Christmas.' She eyes him with a smirk. 'Somewhere hot. I've always fancied seeing the Sydney Opera House, unless you can give me any recommendations?'

'All I can recommend is Dad's barbecue skills. And you need to get the iconic photo for your Instagram.' *Is she flirting with me? Am I flirting back?* Pete feels a pang of guilt as he realises he's actually enjoying himself. 'So, Santorini … That'll be a nice romantic getaway for you and the other half. I've always wanted to go.'

'Other half?' Vanessa pulls a face. 'No, Pete, no other half. Flying solo, that's me. Literally.'

'Oh.' Pete didn't think he already knew this, but still he doesn't feel shocked to learn Vanessa is single. 'Sorry, I just assumed—'

'I'm going with an old girlfriend from school – remember Sophie?' Vanessa says, the air suddenly thick between them. 'Then Christmas, I don't know. I'll probably decide nearer the time and do something alone.'

'It all sounds incredibly glamorous and exciting,' Pete says, draining his pint. He can't deny the little flicker of envy that sparks at the thought of just packing up and going on an exotic holiday at the drop of a hat. Going away was a military operation before Erin was born – he dreads to think what their next trip away is going to be like.

Mirroring him, Vanessa finishes her wine, screwing up her face when she realises her glass is empty. 'I love my life, I really do, but … it's lonely sometimes. There's only so many times you can go home to a cold, dark house and feel OK about it. It would be nice to have someone to share it all with.' She glances up at him. 'Someone who wants to travel and see the world, have adventures. I suppose I just haven't met the right person yet.'

Vanessa pushes her empty glass away and slides her phone into her bag. The pub has emptied out, the site team moving on to somewhere more lively, and the bar staff are cleaning in an attempt to get them to leave. Pete signals to the waiter for the bill, refusing to let Vanessa go Dutch, even though she offers, and it seems to be the natural thing when they step onto the pavement outside for Pete to offer to walk Vanessa back to her flat. They chat idly as they walk over the bridge across the fast-flowing river running through the town, the street lights casting an orange glow ahead of them. Pete wonders how many times he's walked Vanessa home in his life – too many to count – and it feels weirdly familiar as he glances down at her. As though he's stepped back in time.

'This is me,' she says as they reach Montpellier Square and the imposing old building where Vanessa has an apartment. 'Thanks for the wine.'

'No problem.' Pete shoves his hands in his pockets and glances towards town, to where he's left his car. 'Thanks for a nice evening.'

'Pete?'

'Yes?' He turns back to where Vanessa stands on the doorstep, the door open behind her.

'Do you want to come in for a coffee?'

Pete pauses, his pulse increasing. He should go home, he knows that. But it's almost eleven o'clock and the kids will be in bed. Natalie will be curled up with her back to him, her breathing deep and even in that way he can tell means she'll be pretending to be asleep, and Vanessa's words come back to him. *There's only so many times you can go home to a cold, dark house and feel OK about it.*

'Uh, sure, OK. Just a quick one.' And he steps inside, the door to Vanessa's flat closing tightly behind him.

# Natalie

Natalie understands why some women do a moonlight flit, she thinks, trying to ignore Erin as she screams from her cot. She wonders what would happen if she drove her car to Beachy Head and left her phone and wallet on the cliff edge before vanishing into the ether. Would that eventually make Erin stop crying? Would anyone in this house even notice? The mountain of laundry on the bed in front of her doesn't seem to be getting any smaller as she sorts and folds, Erin's cries scraping over her skin like nails on a chalkboard. After folding Zadie's T-shirts into Emily's pile for the third time, Natalie throws the laundry onto the bed and moves to the cot, gripping the rails until her knuckles turn white.

'Stop. Please, stop,' she hisses through gritted teeth as Erin cries on and on, kicking her legs furiously. 'What do you want? I've done *everything*.' Natalie has been awake since five o'clock, after getting up three times in the night to Erin. She's fed her, burped her, changed her nappy and even tried bathing her in an attempt to calm her down but still, every time Natalie thinks she might have dropped off, she starts to grizzle again. Natalie doesn't even want to have the windows open now, despite the warmth of the day, worrying about what the neighbours might think of the incessant crying. She leans down and picks Erin up again, laying her on the changing mat to check her nappy for the third time and rub some baby Bonjela on her gums.

Saturdays never used to be like this, Natalie thinks, as she picks Erin up and begins to pace the bedroom, jiggling her in her arms. Before, when they were still at uni, Natalie always looked forward to Saturday. She and Pete would wake late in the morning, both of them fuzzy-headed from the night before. They'd sleep in, have lazy hangover sex, stop at the café for a fry-up, and then head back into town in the early evening to meet friends for cheap cocktails and a kebab on the way home. Now, Zadie is at a friend's house for a sleepover (please, God, she doesn't wet the bed there), Pete is – surprise, surprise – at work, and Emily is out with Jake at the cinema, even though, once again, Natalie had found herself pressing the importance of Emily's looming exams on her. Emily has assured Natalie she is prepared for her exam on Monday, and to be honest, today Natalie just couldn't find the energy for yet another row over it all.

'So, it's not OK for me to go out on a date with my boyfriend, because I'm meant to be studying,' Emily had thrown the words at Natalie earlier this morning, 'but it's OK for me to spend hours walking Erin around town in her pram so you can have a bit of peace? Yeah, that's fair, isn't it?'

Natalie had felt sick at the words, knowing deep down that Emily had a point. Sometimes she did ask Emily to take Zadie out to play in the woods, or to walk Erin around town just so Natalie could have half an hour to get on top of things – to feel as though she wasn't about to lose her mind. So, instead of another argument, she had just sighed and nodded, flinching when the door slammed closed behind Emily.

Erin continues to cry – an angry shriek that Natalie swears could be used as a torture device – and she flips her over, dangling the baby along one arm on her stomach. Tiger in a tree, Natalie thinks it's called. The sure-fire pose to get a baby off to sleep, whether they're windy, colicky or just plain tired: that's what she's read. But still, Erin doesn't stop, and Natalie jiggles her harder. Where the fuck is Pete? She honestly can't believe that anything at work could be more important than spending time at home. He's never here lately, that bloody construction site taking up every minute of his day. Pete has always had a good work ethic – it's one of the things she loves about him – but just lately she never sees him. He used to come home late once or twice a week, maybe, but never later than seven o'clock, and even then he'd still sneak up and make sure he tucked Zadie in. Recently, though, he's been coming home long after she's gone to sleep (for that brief respite Erin allows her between ten and midnight), three or four times a week, and for the last two weeks, it's been Saturday mornings, too.

Natalie can't take it any more. Erin's wails grow louder, and she feels it. That sickening, overwhelming urge to shake her. Just once. Just enough to stop the incessant noise for one moment. Her throat closing over, her stomach rolling, Natalie lays Erin in the cot with rather more force than she should and hurries from the bedroom, closing the door tightly behind her. She fumbles in her pocket for her phone and dials, feeling breathless with fear and disgust at herself.

'Hello?'

'Eve?' Natalie can barely speak, the words snagging painfully in the back of her throat. 'Eve, please can you come? I need you.'

Natalie sits at the bottom of the stairs, her head in her hands as Eve steps through the front door moments later. She must have run from her own house two streets away, cutting through the woods to get to Natalie this quickly. Overhead, muted cries come from the bedroom, furious and insistent.

'Nat? Oh, God, Nat, what's happened? Are you OK?' Eve comes to crouch beside Natalie on the stairs as she raises her tear-stained face.

'She won't stop,' she says blankly. 'The baby. She just won't stop crying, Eve. I'm at my wits' end.'

'Where's Pete? At the pub? Or sleeping it off upstairs?' Eve looks up, as if Pete will magically appear in the hallway.

'Work. Where else?'

''Course he is.' Eve's tone is dry. 'Don't you wonder what he's up to, being gone for fourteen hours a day?'

68

'He's *working*,' Natalie says, her chest aching. 'That's all he ever does at the moment. Although I don't blame him for not wanting to come home to all this. Sorry, Eve, for pulling you away from your weekend. I forgot you were meant to be meeting Kate for a drink today.'

'I cancelled that. We had a bit of a tiff the last time we went out, and I'm done with her. I did tell you that the other night.' Eve stands and pulls Natalie to her feet. 'Right, you're going back to bed.'

'No, I—'

'*Natalie.* You're going back to bed. Where are Emily and Zadie?' She listens as Natalie tells her. 'I'm going to take care of Miss Erin, and you're going to get some sleep.' Eve's voice softens. 'You can't carry on like this, Nat, and I wouldn't be much of a friend if I let you.'

Natalie allows Eve to lead her upstairs, wincing as the bedroom door opens and Erin's wails hit her ears. Without fuss or bustle, Eve leans down into the cot and picks Erin up, pointing at the bed. 'Sleep, now. I mean it. I'll wake you up this afternoon.'

Natalie hears Eve murmuring to Erin as she makes her way downstairs, and then it's as though a light is switched off and she falls into oblivion. She wakes some time later, her pulse racing as she tries to piece together the remnants of a dream – something dark and unsettling that's left her with a dry mouth. Despite the dream, she feels refreshed and she reaches across the bed to where Pete lies, only her hand meets dead air. *Pete isn't here. Pete's at work. The baby. Eve came over to look after the baby.*

Sliding out of bed, Natalie swigs from the stale glass of water on the bedside table and then moves to the bedroom door. As she opens it and steps out on to the landing, something feels wrong. Off, somehow. She pauses at the top of the stairs, trying to put her finger on what feels different, her heart leaping into her mouth as she realises. The house is silent. There is no crying from Erin. There is no sound of the television chattering away to itself, no movement coming from the kitchen. No Eve. No Erin.

On wobbly legs, Natalie makes her way downstairs. Peering into the sitting room, she sees the throw blankets that Zadie likes to snuggle under, even on warm days, are neatly folded on the arm of the couch. Natalie's empty mug from this morning is no longer on the coffee table. In the kitchen the bin has been emptied, the post neatly stacked and the jumble of baby bottles that were lying in the sink, waiting to be washed, are gone. Not for the first time after one of Eve's visits, Natalie feels the disturbing sensation that she's woken up in someone else's house. Someone else's life. There is no sign of Eve or Erin, or indeed any sign they were ever here at all.

'Eve?' Maybe they're in the garden, but even as Natalie moves to the back door she knows they're not there. She pulls out her mobile and dials Eve's number. It goes straight to voicemail, a robotic voice telling her to leave a message.

Natalie moves back through the house, the feeling that something is wrong growing ever more insistent, the silence growing thicker and thicker until it threatens to suffocate her. In the hallway, she pauses, her hand going to her mouth. Erin's pram is gone, and so is the changing bag Natalie leaves beside it. Erin's raincoat is missing, too, even though it's blue skies and sunshine outside. A stirring of panic uncoils in Natalie's stomach and she remembers the broken fragment of her dream. *Someone had come in the house and taken the baby.* Feeling nauseous, Natalie dials Eve's number again, but once again it rings out and goes to voicemail. With shaking hands, Natalie calls Pete.

'Come on, come on,' she mutters under her breath as she paces the hallway, willing him to pick up. It rings out, Pete's chirpy voicemail greeting meeting her ear, and she jabs at the screen to hang up. *Where would Eve go?* It's not as though she knows where to take a six-month-old baby. What if something happens? Does Eve know the name of Erin's doctor? A tornado whips up inside

Natalie – a whirl of panic and fear and something else she can't describe – and she shoves her feet into a pair of Emily's trainers, ready to head out and look for her child. As she reaches the front door, it swings open and Eve stands there, Erin sleeping peacefully in the pram in front of her, looking every inch the doting mum that Natalie wishes she was.

'Where have you been? I've been going frantic.' Natalie stands to one side as Eve carefully bumps the pram over the threshold and wheels it into the hallway, all while Erin slumbers on.

'Shhhh, don't wake her. She's so tired, poor thing.' Eve fusses with the pram, rearranging the blankets and tucking the changing bag underneath. 'I took her for a walk to settle her – it took a while but she's fast asleep now.' Natalie steps aside as Eve pulls Erin's raincoat out and hangs it up. 'I didn't know if it would rain, but it's beautiful out. How are you feeling now?'

'Better. Thanks.' Natalie was feeling better when she woke up, but right now she doesn't know how to feel. Part of her is grateful to Eve for giving her a few hours' peace to catch up on her sleep. Another part of her is filled with a white-hot resentment at being shushed over her own baby. Yet another part of her feels inadequate and useless at Eve managing to take better care of Erin than she can herself. She swallows down all these feelings and takes the changing bag out from under the pram, hanging it in its usual place.

'See, I told you all you needed was a good rest,' Eve says, oblivious to the tangled emotions running through Natalie's body. 'But honestly, Nat, you can't carry on this way. Did you book that GP appointment?'

'Not yet.' She keeps meaning to, but everything is so overwhelming at the moment, it just feels like another job to do.

'You need to, Nat. You promised you would.' Eve gives her a long look as she steps over the threshold, out onto the front path. 'It's not fair on you to keep struggling on, and it's not fair on the rest of the family to have to watch you struggle.'

'I said I'll do it.' The resentment is rising, threatening to bubble up and over, and Natalie takes a step back, preparing to close the door.

'Good. Let me know what the doctor says.' Eve reaches out and squeezes her hand. 'And if Erin ever gets in that state again, you know where I am. She loved having a little walk. I took her out to the park and we fed the ducks. Have you not taken her before? She was so excited when they all came running over to her when they realised we had bread. And then she got fussed over by an old couple. They said they were missing their grandchildren. All the excitement must have worn her out. After that, she went right off to sleep.' Eve looks down into the pram at Erin, her face almost glowing. 'I'm always happy to do it.'

'Of course.' Natalie forces a smile, the last shreds of any rest and relaxation vanishing into thin air. Eve's outing with Erin sounds completely foreign to Natalie, and she feels it again – the sharp, rusty lick of envy. 'Thanks again.'

Closing the door, Natalie leans her forehead against the cool wood with a sigh before turning to the sleeping baby in the pram. She looks angelic, her dark hair curling gently against her forehead – *so thick! She gets it from Pete* – and her lips pouting into a tiny pink rosebud. Natalie fights back the tears that tighten her throat, too afraid to lean in and scoop the baby into her arms in case she wakes her. Instead, she leans over the pram, close enough for her breath to stir the curl on Erin's forehead.

'Why do you hate me?' she asks, in a broken whisper.

# *Pete*

If there's one place Pete never expected to be again, it's lying naked in Vanessa Taylor's bed late on a Tuesday evening, but here he is, and it's not the first time. In the three months that have passed since he took Vanessa to the leaving do, he's spent more time in this flat than he would ever care to admit. That first night, nothing had happened. He really had had coffee, and then when he left they might have kissed briefly, but it was enough to pour petrol on the tiny spark that still existed between them, and since then the fire has raged out of control. What started as a brief fumble in the darkened site office two nights after that fateful drink (Pete doesn't count the kiss at Vanessa's flat – he'd had a couple of beers, but the site office was stone cold sober), when Vanessa had gasped breathily against his neck as he pressed himself against the length of her body, has morphed into regular sex and the chance for Pete to express how he really feels about things at home.

When he's with Vanessa things seem… easier, somehow. As though Pete is a teenager again, stripped free of worry and responsibility. They take trips down memory lane, remembering the parties they went to, the people they went to school with, playing a version of Where Are They Now? Vanessa has kept tabs via social media on a few people they knew from when they were dating, but Pete has no idea.

'I did look for you a few times,' Vanessa says once. 'On Facebook. I always wondered what you were up to after… well, after we broke up. But I couldn't find you.' Pete doesn't do social media; he has no interest in it whatsoever. 'I couldn't believe it when people kept recommending this building company to me,

73

and it turned out you were the managing director. Pete Maxwell, back in my life after all this time.'

'Small world, eh?' Pete had kissed her then, feeling slightly uncomfortable. They talk about Pete's life at home, about the kids, about the way Natalie makes him feel when she repeatedly pushes him away. The only thing they don't ever really discuss is why they broke up. How Pete left Vanessa for Natalie.

He keeps telling himself this is just a temporary thing, and every time he leaves Vanessa's flat, he walks away hating himself, hoping Natalie is asleep when he gets in so he can shower away the smell of another woman before she notices. Each time it happens, he tells himself that this time is the last time, but when Vanessa appears in his office doorway long after the other lads have left for the night, smiling at him with those crimson lips, as though she's actually pleased to see him, he has to ask himself why he is really working so late. If Pete is honest, it's not just the lure of Vanessa's body and what she can do with her mouth that has him so drawn in. It's the way she lets him talk with no judgement – without jumping in with her own version of events, the way Natalie does. It's the way she's familiar, but different. Exciting. And the flat – it's a completely different vibe to Pete's own house. At home, chaos reigns. Natalie doesn't seem to do anything around the house while he's gone all day, and he regularly comes home to mountains of unwashed dishes while the dishwasher sits unemptied, the kids' shoes and bags dumped in the hallway and piles of washing that either need to be washed, folded or put away. Here, Vanessa's flat is tidy and clutter-free, with plants lining every windowsill. The only trinkets she has are items she's collected on her travels, like statues of Ganesha and Buddha, and there is always the faint clean scent of an expensive air freshener. Pete feels as though he can relax here, among the soft white covers of Vanessa's bed, with no hint of baby sick or that stale sour smell he catches from Natalie sometimes.

And then, if he's really digging deep into the honesty box, there's the thrill of it. There's a part of him that enjoys the heart-thumping, spine-tingling blast he gets from his illicit meetings with Vanessa, a sharp, dizzying contrast to the drudgery of his everyday life. The other night, Eve had mentioned the gastropub where he and Vanessa had had drinks at the leaving do in conversation with Natalie, catching his eye as she mentioned it, and for a moment he had thought his heart would stop in his chest. He'd waited for her to say something else, something damning, with his pulse a crashing tattoo in his ears, but she'd moved on to some fallout she'd had with a friend, and he'd had to resist the urge to say, 'another one bites the dust.' It seems only his wife can tolerate Eve for longer than a few months. But even that brief moment of fear had given him some sort of sickening charge, and it wasn't enough to stop him coming back to Vanessa for more.

'Pete? Red or white?' Vanessa calls from the kitchen, where she's fixing post-coital snacks and drinks.

'Either. Just one glass, though, I have to drive back soon.' Pete knows Vanessa will try and pour him an extra glass in an attempt to make him stay longer, something he finds flattering every time, even though he never stays for the whole night. Vanessa has made noises once or twice about how nice it would be for them to wake up together, but Pete has gently reminded her it simply can't happen.

Lying back against the thick pillows, Pete lets himself wonder about how things would be if Natalie hadn't got pregnant. He doesn't think he'd be lying here, that's for sure. They would have gone to Australia for Christmas, and his mum would have been able to see Zadie and Emily face to face, instead of just over a glitchy FaceTime call. He and Natalie would have ventured out to the other side of the bay where the plot of land sits; they would have walked around it, Pete gesturing to show where the house would sit, where the garden boundary would lie. He would have sketched out a pool area, a play area and a patio for Natalie to sit and read in the summer. As it is, Pete had an email from his brother this morning to say the plot has been sold, and as he read it he could almost feel his dream slipping through his fingers like sand. Pete feels a sickening lurch of resentment, and before he can bat it away, the thought rises in his mind. *If Natalie hadn't got pregnant, none of this would be happening.* If Erin wasn't here, they could be living their dream. Pete would be drawing up plans for the new house now. Natalie would be her usual bright, funny self, and he wouldn't be here, in his ex-girlfriend's bed, feeling sick and guilty. He reaches for the water glass beside the bed, trying to wash away the bitterness of his own thoughts.

'Here we are.' Vanessa appears in the doorway, wearing the kind of underwear that Natalie rejected years ago, carrying a tray with expensive Parma ham and cheeses, two glasses and a bottle of cold white wine. 'I hope you're hungry.' She places the tray on the bedside table and opens the wine, pouring him a generous glass.

Pete takes the wine and shuffles up the bed, making room for Vanessa as she slides in beside him.

'I was thinking,' she says, 'we could maybe take a trip to Whitstable now the weather is getting a little nicer. Maybe go out for some oysters, get a hotel … You could tell Natalie there's a conference.' She nuzzles against him, but Pete doesn't react. 'What do you think? Pete?'

'Hmmm?' Pete drags himself out of his own thoughts, aware that he's not heard a word she's said.

'You're in your own little world. What's wrong?'

'Just thinking.'

'Oh?'

'About Australia. I wish we could have gone out for Christmas but … You know. I just feel a bit low about it all. I was so excited to have bought the tickets, and then …' He trails off. Although he tells Vanessa how he feels about things, he's still reluctant to call Natalie by her name in front of his mistress.

'Do you ever wonder what it would have been like?' Vanessa traces a pattern over his bare thigh with one finger.

'What do you mean?' Pete shifts his leg, dislodging her hand.

Vanessa shrugs, pulling herself back into a sitting position. 'Just… do you ever think about how things might have been if we hadn't broken up?'

'Ness, we were kids.'

'I know,' she says. 'But I wonder about it, don't you? I still don't think I would have wanted children. I would have been happy enough for it to just be me and you. We could have travelled together, seen the world a bit. Maybe we both would have been happier.'

'Happier? Vanessa, I…'

Vanessa turns to face him, her brows drawn together in a frown, 'You're not happy, Pete, I know you're not. You come here and tell me several times a week you're not happy, but it doesn't have to be that way. Life's too short to wonder about all the what ifs. All I'm saying is, if things had been different, if it were me and you, we could pack a bag and go to Australia tomorrow.'

'But things aren't different. So—'

'They could be.' Vanessa's voice is barely above a whisper. 'It could be me and you.'

'Me and you?' Pete frowns. 'Sorry, Ness. What exactly are you saying?'

Vanessa turns to the bedside table and takes a mouthful of wine before she turns back on to her side to face him, her hair falling over one shoulder. 'What I'm saying, Pete, is that maybe it's time to be honest about what you really want.'

'Vanessa—' Pete feels a pang of alarm, his stomach sinking.

'Pete, please just let me talk. I need to tell you something.' She is hesitant, her fingers knotting in the duvet as she takes a deep breath. 'Oh God, I wasn't going to say it, but… The fact is, I'm in love with you. I think I always have been, ever since we were kids.' As she raises her eyes to his, a tear spills over one cheek. 'I know

77

it's wrong – everything about this is wrong. I know you're married, and I know this whole thing is going to end up being painful for everyone … but after everything you've told me, I can't help thinking you would be so much happier if you left Natalie. You would be so much happier with *me*. We want the same things. We laugh *all* the time, we have a shared history … and I know it'll be tough on Natalie and the kids, but I'll do whatever I can to make it easier. Pete, I've never felt this way about anyone else. And I wish I didn't, but I can't help the way I feel.'

Pete feels as if he's been punched in the gut. Shock makes his teeth feel numb, his tongue too big for his mouth as he fumbles for something to say.

'Vanessa …' He swallows. This wasn't the deal, and he thought she knew that. It was supposed to be a bit of fun, thrilling and exciting. Something to lighten the load he had to bear at home. A slip back into the way things used to be, before kids and mortgages and a wife who couldn't stand to even look at him, and he thought Vanessa felt the same way. 'Look, you know things aren't that simple. I have a family, a whole life—'

'I know that, I know.' Vanessa's voice is thick, and Pete prays she isn't going to cry. 'I can't help how I feel! I thought I could just have some fun, but it turns out …' She shrugs, looking defeated. 'I can't. This is more to me than just a fling, Pete.' Vanessa slides from the bed, pulling a silky kimono around her shoulders.

*Fuck.* All Pete can feel is panic, buzzing through his veins. This wasn't meant to happen. 'This is … Look, you know I think you're great, and we have got history together, you're right, but this isn't a long-term thing, I thought you knew that.'

Vanessa's face darkens and Pete feels a mild stirring of panic. *Maybe Vanessa didn't know it was temporary?* But Pete thought they were both on the same page. She said she wanted fun and adventure, not marriage and babies.

'How can you say that, Pete? I thought …' Vanessa's face crumples, and Pete feels like an absolute *shit*. 'Haven't things been amazing between us? I thought you realised you'd made a mistake with Natalie. That we were going to be together.'

'Ness, I never said that.' And he hadn't. But now he thinks about things, maybe he should have been blunt and honest with Vanessa from the get-go and then maybe he wouldn't be in this position now. He thinks back over some of the things Vanessa has said over the past few weeks. The pressure she's put him on to stay longer, even though she knows Natalie and the kids are waiting for him at home. The hints at mini-breaks in the summer; the way she's always free no matter how much they have on at work, and how she has so easily slipped back into affectionate ways with him, as if he'd never left her at all. Things that he has all conveniently ignored, just so he can slide into her bed feeling, if not guilt-free, then at least less guilty.

Pete follows her lead, slipping from the bed and reaching for his clothes. He feels oddly vulnerable, even though he is the one who has just broken Vanessa's heart. 'Vanessa, I love my wife and kids – I know I've said some things I probably shouldn't, but I really do love them, they're my world.' He reaches down and pulls on his jeans, tugs his T-shirt over his head.

'Pete, please. We should talk about this. You can't honestly say you've never thought about what it would be like if we were together properly?' Vanessa pulls her robe tighter around her shoulders – a robe that a couple of hours ago Pete would have been mad to pull off. Now, he feels sick as he looks at her, shame and guilt flooding his veins.

Pete *can* honestly say he's never thought about being with Vanessa properly. He's never once considered giving up Natalie and the kids. He's just been a greedy bastard who wanted to have his cake and eat it. 'I don't ... I don't think there's anything to talk about, Ness.' Pete pushes his hand through his hair, unable to meet her eyes. 'We've gone into this wanting very different things.'

'I didn't,' she says, tears coursing down her cheeks now. 'I didn't go into it thinking anything, Pete. It just *happened*, and when I realised, I thought this was it.'

'What?'

'I realised you were everything I'd ever been chasing. Every man I'd ever dated who didn't quite match up to my expectations, I'd always thought it was because something about them reminded me of my dad, but in reality, it was just that they weren't you.'

'I'm sorry.' Pete doesn't know what else to say. *Christ, I feel sick.* 'I'm not who you think I am, Ness. I'm not the person you want me to be.' He wishes he'd thought this through before just giving in to his animal instincts. He'd been thinking with his dick, never even considering how far things would go. 'This can't... *We* can't happen.' Panic makes his fingers tremble as he tries to tie the laces on his boots. 'I have to go. I'm sorry, I've made a massive mistake. I shouldn't be here, and I can't see you again. Not like this.' Without waiting for a response, and without looking at her, Pete snatches up his phone and wallet and hurries out of the front door. A journey that usually takes him twenty-five minutes, Pete makes it to his own front door in fifteen, pulling on to the drive and checking his phone. He has a missed call and three text messages from Vanessa. Kicking himself for letting things go so far, he deletes the messages unread and blocks her number, before looking up at the dark windows of his own bedroom, where Natalie will be pretending to be asleep. He can see the soft yellow glow of Zadie's night light in the window on the other side of the house, and he rubs his hands over his face. *What the hell have I done?*

# Natalie

Erin is finally sleeping, and Natalie hums an old Taylor Swift song under her breath, feeling oddly serene even as she shoves Zadie's wet sheets into the washing machine for the third morning in a row. Pete seems to be making a bit more of an effort to get home on time the past week or so, and it's improved Natalie's mood drastically, just knowing he will be home in time to help with the bedtime routine. Whatever was so urgent at work – client dinners by the looks of it; the couple of times Natalie checked Find My iPhone his car had been parked near Montpellier Square – seems to have died down, to Natalie's relief, and although he's still not fully present in spirit, at least he's physically available. If she didn't know him so well, she might have been concerned about an affair, but this is Pete. He can barely cope with Natalie, let alone the demands of another woman.

Emily saunters into the kitchen, wearing hot pants and a barely there top, wrinkling her nose at the slight smell of piss from Zadie's sheets. 'I'm going out.'

'Oh?' Natalie starts the washing machine and moves to the tap to wash her hands. 'I thought you were working today.' Emily has worked in the small coffee shop on the edge of town since she was fifteen, and has taken extra hours over the summer.

'I took the week off.' Emily moves to the fridge, opening the door and starting to pick listlessly through its meagre contents.

'You took the week off? Why?'

'To spend it with Jake.' Emily pops a cherry tomato in her mouth and closes the fridge.

'Jesus, Emily. Are you serious? You've taken the entire week off? You're on zero hours, you don't get holiday pay.'

'So what? I am entitled to some time off, you know,' Emily huffs. 'I've revised all year for my A levels, got stressed *to the max* taking my exams seeing as how I got literally *no* sleep thanks to Erin crying all night every night, and now they're finished and you don't even want me to have a day off. Plus, I'm eighteen. I can make my own decisions, I don't need your permission.'

*Why are teenage girls so dramatic?* The thought that she has to go through this phase another two times makes Natalie want to groan aloud. 'I'm not saying you can't take time off. I'm just saying that a week is a lot of money to lose when you're supposed to be saving as much as you can before you go to university. It's OK for Jake.'

'What's that supposed to mean? It's not Jake's fault he can't afford to go to university.' Emily's voice rises and Natalie feels her own temper flare. 'Just because you hate him. I know you do.'

'I don't hate him.' Natalie doesn't *hate* Jake. She just thinks that twenty-one is too old to be interested in an eighteen-year-old girl. And she'd kind of hoped that Emily would find someone with her own level of drive and ambition eventually. Not now. And not a boy from the wrong side of town, whose father is a distant memory, and who doesn't seem to be able to hold down a steady job.

'Yes, you do,' Emily counters. 'You make it perfectly obvious every time you roll your eyes when I mention his name, or when you make comments under your breath about him.'

'Well, I'm hardly going to be his biggest fan when he upsets you all the time, am I?' Natalie says, resisting the urge to roll her eyes right now. 'You came home crying last week over him talking to Lexi Smith after you'd left the pub. And the week before, when you found out he'd liked some random girl's Instagram photo.'

Emily's eyes fill, her mouth turning down at the corners. 'I know the real reason why you don't want me to go out, and it's not even about you hating Jake. You don't want me to have a life, you just want me to stay at home and look after Erin.'

'Emily, that's not fair—'

'No, it's not bloody fair,' Emily shouts, her voice thick with frustration and unshed tears. 'You used to be such a cool mum – I used to actually be able to talk to you – but now all you ever do is mope about and moan and get me to look after Erin. She's your baby, not mine, and I don't want to spend my summer looking after her.'

'Hey, that's out of order. Jake is always tagging along with you when you take Erin out.' Natalie doesn't think she asks Emily to look after Erin that much, but when she stops to consider it now, Emily is the one she turns to for help when Eve is with clients and can't pitch in. 'To be honest, the last time I left her with you while I dropped Zadie at gymnastics, the pair of you didn't do such a great job, did you? I came back to both of you playing *Fortnite*, and Erin with a soaked nappy.'

'I changed her literally an hour before you got back, but you wouldn't know because you weren't here.' Emily swallows, her voice lowering to barely above a whisper. 'Even when you are here, you don't have time for me. Not any more, anyway.'

The words are like a shard of glass piercing Natalie's heart. 'Em, you know I appreciate you, but—'

'Yeah, right.' Emily blinks and a tear slides over her bottom lashes, that she dashes away as if she doesn't want Natalie to notice. 'Erin isn't my responsibility – I shouldn't have to sacrifice time with my boyfriend or my friends to babysit all the time. Annabel invited me to Ibiza with her and Jodie this summer, did you know that? But I said no, because I knew you wouldn't be able to cope with Erin on your own. If things had been different I could have been sunning myself on a beach right now.'

'Oh, Em—'

'No, Mum. I'm not talking about it any more. I'm going out.' There is the honking of a car horn outside. 'That's Jake. I'll be back later, and no, I don't know what time, before you ask.' Snatching up her phone, Emily hurries out of the house, slamming the front door behind her as if desperate to put some distance between them. Natalie sinks back against the kitchen worktop, her good mood punctured, waiting for the inevitable shout to come from Erin.

In some sort of miracle, Erin doesn't wake, and Natalie makes her way upstairs, her hands shaking and her chest aching with unshed tears. In the bathroom she opens the medicine cabinet and pulls out the white box of diazepam the doctor prescribed, that she hasn't quite been able to bring herself to start taking yet. The crushing sense of failure weighing down on her doesn't dissipate as Natalie presses her fingers to the blister pack, popping two pills into her hand. Glancing into the mirror, Natalie catches a glimpse of her reflection, pausing as she raises her hand to her mouth. Dark circles ring her eyes and her blonde hair lies limp against her shoulders. Emily's right – if they hadn't had Erin, then the whole family would probably have gone away in the sun for a week after Emily's exams had finished, and Natalie would have been sporting a bit of a tan, but instead her face is pasty white, and the beginning of a pimple glows on her chin. She blinks once, as if hoping the reflection will change and then, with a sigh, she turns to the toilet, throwing the pills into the bowl and flushing the chain.

Moments later, Natalie's phone rings and she fumbles to answer before the ringtone can wake the baby.

'Hello?'

'Mrs Maxwell? This is Mrs Hendry. Zadie's headteacher.'

'Is Zadie OK?' Natalie's breath catches in her throat and her eyes go back to the white pill box. She shoves it back into the cupboard and closes the door.

'She's fine, but I wondered if you could come into the office.'

'I can come in when I collect her.'

'No.' The word is a sigh. 'We need to see you rather sooner than that, please. As soon as possible. There's been an incident, and we need to talk to you before we can decide on the appropriate action to be taken. I'd rather not discuss it over the phone.'

'Oh. OK. I'll be there as soon as I can.' Natalie ends the call and, with her heart thumping fit to burst, she dials Pete. As usual, there is no answer. 'Pete. Call me. It's urgent, it's about Zadie. I have to go to a meeting at the school.'

Peering into the bedroom, Natalie can just make out the slight rise and fall of Erin's chest. She feels a wave of love, a crashing tsunami that takes her breath away, before dread takes over at the thought of having to wake her to take her into school for the meeting, knowing she'll grizzle and cry all the way through. Stepping out of the room, Natalie hesitates on the landing for just a moment before she lifts her phone and calls Eve.

'Eve? It's me. Are you busy?'

'Always. I've got a client at four o'clock, but today is mostly an admin day sorting things for new clients, so I'm hoping you're calling to save me.' Eve laughs. 'Everything OK?'

'I am so, so sorry to do this.' Natalie feels her throat thicken and she blinks rapidly. 'I have to go to a meeting at Zadie's school and Erin is down for a nap. I don't suppose there's any way...?'

'Of course!' Eve says, and Natalie lets out a long breath of relief. 'I'll be right over.'

By the time Eve arrives, Erin is awake and crying, and Natalie feels terrible for dragging her out.

'Sorry, she was sleeping when I called.' Natalie grapples with a fussy Erin as Eve pushes her way into the hallway. 'Don't feel you have to stay. Hopefully she'll drop off again in the pushchair.'

'Don't be daft, I'm here now.' Barely glancing at Natalie, Eve holds out her arms and Erin bends towards her, her chubby hands reaching for Eve's amber necklace. 'How about I walk up with you and Erin, and then when you go into the meeting, I'll walk Erin back home and meet you here? That way, both of you get a change of scenery.'

Natalie feels a rush of relief. 'That sounds perfect.' She wheels the pushchair onto the driveway and Eve tucks Erin safely in before taking the handles. 'I'll push. Come on, little miss, let's go for a walk.'

They cut through the woods behind the house to get to the park, and as they reach the pond in the centre of the park, Natalie ignores the painful twist in her heart as Erin spies the ducks and begins to squeal.

'See?' Eve says, with a grin. 'I told you she loves them. We'll stop on the way back and feed them, baby girl. Oh, hi!' Eve slows the pushchair to a stop as an older lady approaches and peers at Erin.

'Hello, you little monkey. I hope you're being good for your mummy.' The lady looks up at Eve and smiles, as Eve nods.

'This is the lady we met last time we fed the ducks. We've seen her here a few times now,' Eve says to Natalie, before turning back to the woman. 'This is Erin's mum, actually.'

'Oh. Gosh, I'm sorry, I just assumed...'

'Nice to meet you.' Natalie smiles, but there is an urgent crashing in her chest. 'Eve, sorry, but I really do need to go.' Relief floods her veins when the other woman walks past, but even as Eve chatters away as they make their way towards the school, Natalie can't shake the unsettling feeling that washed over her as she realised the woman had thought Eve was Erin's mother.

Fifteen minutes later, Natalie has waved goodbye to Eve and Erin and is following the school secretary towards Mrs Hendry's office, the thick scent of antiseptic and old school dinners heavy on the air. She smiles as she steps inside, but it soon fades as Mrs Hendry gets to her feet to shake her hand, the smile not reciprocated.

'Mrs Maxwell, as I said on the phone, we've had an incident involving Zadie today, and this time it's fairly serious.'

*This time? What does she mean, 'this time'?* Natalie opens her mouth to speak, but Mrs Hendry rushes on.

'On several occasions Zadie has had to be removed from class for being disruptive, and there have been some reports of bullying.'

'*Bullying?*' Natalie feels sick. Zadie is so sweet and kind, she can't bear the thought of someone bullying her. 'Who was it? Who's been picking on Zadie?'

'Mrs Maxwell.' The headteacher leans in, her voice softening. 'It's not Zadie being bullied. Zadie is the one doing the bullying.'

It's as though Natalie has been slapped in the face – a swift, sharp smack she didn't see coming. 'No. Not Zadie. I know my daughter and she isn't a bully. I want to know who's saying these things.'

'I'm sorry, I know this is very upsetting, but you understand why I need to talk to you? The incident today involved Zadie biting a child, and I will be speaking to their parents, too, so we can get to the bottom of all this.' Mrs Hendry's tone leaves no room for doubt that she is taking this seriously. 'How has Zadie been at home? She's sleeping OK, seems like herself?'

'Yes. She's just … Zadie. She's fine.'

'Sometimes, when something like this happens, it can be down to frustration. And lashing out is a way of expressing this frustration. Sometimes we just need to encourage the child to talk about anything they might be worried about—'

'Zadie doesn't have anything to worry about.' Natalie can hear the heat in her own voice, and she takes a moment to rein it in. 'Everything is fine at home. It sounds to me as though Zadie is unhappy at school, not at home.'

'Mrs Maxwell, I wasn't insinuating anything was wrong at home, but I do think Zadie is a brilliant, bright girl and you should perhaps encourage her to talk to you about how she's feeling, or if there is anything that *might* be worrying her,' Mrs Hendry says, gently. 'In light of what's happened today, I think the best course of action is for Zadie to stay home with you for a few days. We only have a week left until the school holidays start, and I think perhaps she might benefit from some time to reflect on her actions, if you could perhaps have a talk with her.'

Natalie gets to her feet, fury strangling her voice, her words coming out thin and reedy. 'I can tell you now, there is nothing wrong with Zadie. If she's acting up, then it's just a phase, that's all. I'll speak to her, of course I will, but I'm confident things aren't as you say they are.' Without saying goodbye, she sweeps out of the office and back to reception, where she waits for Zadie's teacher to bring her out. *Bullying.* Natalie still can't quite believe it, and it takes every fibre of her being to paste on a smile as Zadie skips towards her, thrilled to be starting her school holidays early. Natalie, on the other hand, feels as though she's failed. Again.

'How was it?' Eve is bouncing a dozy Erin in her arms as Natalie arrives home, packing Zadie upstairs with the threat of talking to her when Pete gets home.

'Oh, God, Eve.' Natalie's voice breaks and the tears she's held back since the row with Emily erupt, like a dam bursting. 'They're saying Zadie's a bully. That she *bit* someone. I mean, what the fuck? That's not Zadie, you know that.'

'Oh, love.' Eve lays Erin down in her bouncy chair, pulling Natalie in for a hug. 'It can all be sorted, don't worry. All kids go through things like this.'

'I just feel so ... *shit*. Like I can't get anything right.' Natalie tells Eve about the argument earlier – about Emily missing out on a girls' holiday because of her. 'And the thing is, she's right,' she says. 'If Em had been home earlier, I would have asked her to sit with Erin instead of calling you. Pete never answered his phone, as usual. He's not working late as much any more, but it's still like he's not really here. Like he can't stand to be around us.'

'Pete's always been selfish, you know that. It seems like he's forgotten he's a husband and a father lately. Acting like he doesn't have responsibilities to come home to. Almost like he's single.'

Eve has never been Pete's biggest fan, but now there is something bitter and spiteful in her tone. She's always thought he could do more for Natalie, to support her with the kids, but Natalie usually brushes her comments aside.

'It feels that way at the moment,' Natalie says, a spark of shame igniting at having slagged Pete off. Erin murmurs, stirring in her bouncy chair, and Natalie sees that Eve has swapped the outfit Natalie dressed her in for a sleepsuit Eve bought. 'Listen, I should let you go, you have a client at four. But thank you for today. Again. I don't know what I'd do without you.'

'No problem. I've fed Erin and burped her, and she played for a bit on the play mat until she got tired again. She's such a little love.' Eve gives Natalie another hug goodbye, and it's only moments after she's left that the doorbell rings again. Thinking it's Eve, Natalie opens the door with a smile.

'What did you forget—? Oh. Hello.'

'Hi.' A woman Natalie doesn't know stands on the doorstep, a big Hermès bag over one arm, a slim paper file in the other. 'Sorry to bother you, but is Pete in?'

'Errrmmm . . . no. Sorry, he's not. He's at work.' Natalie feels her brows draw together in confusion. The woman seems familiar somehow, but Natalie can't place her.

'Oh. Oh, God. That's a bit of a nightmare.' The woman waves the slim file in her hand, the expensive bangles on her wrist jangling. 'I really need to hand these papers over.'

'I can pass them on to him, no problem.' Feeling uneasy, Natalie is horribly aware of her own appearance beside the glamorous woman on her doorstep – aware of her unwashed hair and bare face, next to this woman's sleek dark hair and bright red lipstick.

The woman pulls a face. 'I wish I could just hand them over, but I need to give them to him personally, I'm afraid.'

Natalie pauses to think. 'I could give him a call? See if he can pop home? He's only working on the other side of the village on that new housing development.' *And that way, I can grab his ear for five minutes to talk to him about Zadie.*

'Would you? That would be fantastic.'

'No problem.' Natalie pulls her phone from her cardigan pocket and dials Pete's number. 'Who shall I tell him is here?'

'Just tell him it's Vanessa.'

# *Pete*

Pete's phone vibrates in his back pocket for the third time, and he pulls it out to see Natalie's name on the screen. It rings off before he can answer, and he sees notifications for multiple missed calls, all from Natalie.

'Excuse me,' he says to the water board representative. 'I'm really sorry, I'm going to have to return this call. I'll be five minutes.' The water guy nods and Pete steps away, pressing his phone to his ear.

'Pete?' The phone doesn't even ring before Natalie picks up.

'Everything OK?'

'Pete! Finally, I've been trying to get hold of you all afternoon.' Her voice sounds thick, the way it does when she's been crying, and Pete feels his heart sink. *What is it now?* Every day she seems to call him to rant about something that really could be ranted about when he gets home. Irritation scratches at his insides as he glances over to where the guy from the water board is waiting, his own phone in his hand.

'I'm at work, Nat. I'm in the middle of something really important.'

'Can you come home?' There is a hint of annoyance in her voice and Pete finds himself reciprocating.

'Natalie, I can't just walk off site. I'm in the middle of a meeting with the water company, and I've got another meeting before I leave.' Pete has had this meeting with the water board booked for weeks; he can't just leave. If he leaves now without getting everything approved, not only is he going to hold up the entire project, but he's also going to have to speak to Vanessa and tell her. Pete has somehow managed to avoid Vanessa since that awful evening

91

at her flat two weeks ago, despite the numerous messages from her personal email. The last email just read *please*, and even now his stomach turns over at the thought of it. 'Is it one of the kids?' Pete signals to Dave, his foreman. If it's one of the kids, he's going to have to go. Maybe Dave can get the sign-off in his absence, just so long as he doesn't have to tell Vanessa there's a delay.

'No, it's not the—'

'Then what is it, Nat? Because if I leave site without sorting this out, I'm going to have to go to Vanessa and tell her the entire project is delayed, for God knows how long.'

'Well, if you come home, you can tell her immediately,' Natalie says, 'seeing as how she's here, at our house, right now.'

Pete's mind is going nineteen to the dozen on the way home. *Why the fuck is Vanessa at my house?* He should have responded to her emails, he thinks, even if he just reiterated the fact that there can never be anything between them ever again. *Is she throwing me off the contract?* His heart goes cold at the thought. This contract – it's the making of him and his business. If she throws him off, then… Not only are there financial implications, but there's also his reputation. There'll be speculation as to why he was removed, and that brings his thoughts to his biggest fear. *Has Vanessa told Natalie what's been going on between them?*

As he pulls onto the driveway the front door swings open and Natalie stands there, her arms folded across her body. He can't help but notice she hasn't washed her hair today, and she's wearing the same jogging pants she's worn all week.

'You said Vanessa is here?' Pete asks, as he reaches the threshold. He smiles, an attempt to hide the panic currently firing through his veins, as he tries to read her expression, to see if there's any hint at all that Vanessa has dropped a bomb on his life, but Natalie just looks as she usually does. Tired and pale.

'She's through there,' she says, standing to one side to let him inside. 'In the kitchen.'

His heart in his mouth, Pete slides out of his jacket and heads into the kitchen, frantically trying to figure out how to play things.

'Hello, Pete.' Vanessa smiles at him as if the last time he saw her wasn't in her bedroom, as he told her he didn't want to sleep with her any more. It's been a struggle to avoid her at work, and he does wonder if he was the only one who could feel the tension between them in the design meeting last week. 'I did try to call you, but for some reason I couldn't get it to connect.'

Natalie steps around him, moving towards Vanessa, and as she does Pete notices for the first time that her eyes are pink and swollen. He casts a frantic glance towards Vanessa, half expecting Natalie to slap her round the face. *This is it*, he thinks, as panic claws at his insides, and he tries frantically to come up with a reasonable excuse to counteract whatever Vanessa has told Natalie. *This is the moment when it all comes tumbling down.*

But instead of Natalie slapping Vanessa and then launching herself at Pete, she simply reaches over and switches on the kettle. 'Vanessa, can I make you a cup of tea? Coffee?'

'Not for me.' Vanessa says, not taking her eyes off Pete.

'Why are you here, Vanessa?' Pete asks, as Natalie looks at him sharply. 'I mean, why didn't you see me at the office?'

'You're very elusive,' Vanessa says. 'I did try and catch you a couple of times, and like I said, my call to your phone wouldn't connect. I was passing by and thought I'd drop this file in to you.' She holds out a slim paper wallet. 'Here. There are a few essential documents in there – it's pretty urgent, so you might want to cast your eye over it now, before I leave.'

It's with some trepidation that Pete takes the file, as Natalie stirs the tea and hands him a mug.

'Excuse me one sec,' Natalie says. 'I'm just going to check on Zadie and the baby.' She squeezes past Pete and leaves him alone with Vanessa.

Pete opens the file, his mouth going dry when he sees what it contains. He feels sick as he shuffles through the photographs in the folder, his stomach rolling. Vanessa, in various stages of undress, wearing the underwear he'd been so keen to rip off her just a week ago. Vanessa, naked, her lips jammy with glossy red lipstick as she pouts at the camera. Finally – worst, if at all possible – a photograph of Pete, lying in her bed, clearly naked as he snoozes after a particularly exhausting visit to her flat. He can almost feel the blood drain from his face as Natalie's footsteps move overhead, and then there is the muted cry of the baby.

'Jesus, Vanessa.'

She blinks, watching him as he slides the pictures back into the file. 'I just wanted to talk to you, Pete. You've blocked my number, haven't you? None of my texts are going through, and you could barely look me in the eye at the design meeting last week.'

'So, you came to my *house?*' Pete hisses, always aware of Natalie on the floor above. He runs his hands through his hair. 'I can't believe you thought it was a good idea to just turn up... Natalie and the kids are home, for Christ's sake.'

'How else was I supposed to get hold of you? Maybe you should have answered my emails, Pete. We need to discuss things.'

Natalie's voice filters down the stairs as she speaks to Zadie, and Pete's heart lurches in his chest again. 'We can't talk in here.' He takes her by the arm and gently manoeuvres her towards the front door, before raising his voice. 'Thanks so much, Vanessa, for dropping this off. Let me see you out.'

Pete opens the front door and follows Vanessa out onto the drive, where he tries to give her the file back.

'No, Pete, I don't want it.' Vanessa takes a step back, her eyes going to the first-floor windows above their heads.

Pete follows her gaze. There is no sign of Natalie, but he drops the hand holding the file, not wanting to make a scene. 'Vanessa, I already explained to you this can't happen. Me and you – it's over.'

'How can you say that?' Vanessa's eyes are glassy as she stares at him. 'After everything?'

Pete swallows, the words sticking in his throat. 'Ness, you can't just turn up at my house like this. It's not right.'

'What else was I supposed to do? I love you, Pete. I can't believe you could be this ... this ... *cruel*.' Her voice breaks slightly, and Pete holds his breath. *Please don't cry. There's no way I'll be able to explain that to Natalie if she looks out of the window.*

'I'm sorry, Vanessa. I really am so, so sorry, but there is no us, there can't be, I already told you that. I know I've hurt you, and I hate myself for that, but this really is it. Please don't come here again. Please don't try and contact me unless it's about work.'

Vanessa's mouth drops open in a soundless O, one fist pressed against her chest as if he has physically wounded her. 'You're making a massive mistake,' she says, her voice rising. 'You're just like all the others, aren't you? You're no better than my dad – using me and then casting me aside when you're done.' Tears spill over her cheeks, mascara pooling under her eyes, and Pete feels a flicker of anger.

'You knew my situation,' he says, guiding her towards her car now. He needs to get her off his property before Natalie comes out to see what's taking so long. 'You can't come to my house and threaten me, understand? And as for comparing me to your father? I *want* to stay with my family. I'm nothing like your fucking dad.' He catches her features starting to crumple as he slams the car door in her face and marches back up the driveway into the house, his heart racing, asking himself that same question again. *What the fuck have I done?*

'Did Vanessa leave already?' Natalie begins to descend the staircase, Erin in her arms, and adrenaline spurts through Pete's veins as he realises he's still holding the file. Suddenly afraid she'll ask to see what's inside, Pete lets Natalie reach the hallway before he heads for the stairs.

'Yeah, she just had to drop off some ... confidential stuff.'

'Weird she came here instead of just waiting for you at the office.' Pete tries to figure out if there is an undercurrent to

Natalie's tone – if she is suspicious in any way. 'I can't believe that's the first time I've ever met her,' Natalie goes on. 'She's not what I thought.'

'Oh?'

'Listen, Pete, while you're here, I need to talk to you—'

Aware of the file, hot enough to singe the skin on his palm, Pete cuts her off. 'I need to sort this stuff out. Sorry.' Without waiting for Natalie to reply, Pete hurries upstairs to the spare room that sometimes doubles as an office. Sitting at the desk, he opens the file again, his eyes running over the photo of Vanessa in her underwear. It doesn't attract him in the slightest any more – in fact, it makes him feel ill, sick with shame and guilt. He slams it closed again and pushes his hands through his hair. *What the hell am I going to do with this?* He can't take it to work – he could lose the contract if anyone there finds it. If he throws it away, there's a chance Natalie – or even Emily – could find it in the bin, and that really would be the end of everything. He pauses for a moment, tapping his fingers on the desk as he thinks. *I could keep it.* It could end up being the perfect insurance policy to hold over Vanessa. A smile tugs at the corners of his mouth as he realises he might just have solved his own problem. If he keeps the file and Vanessa carries on harassing him, all he needs to do is turn the tables on her. He could threaten to post them online, or email them out to her clients, effectively blackmailing her into keeping her mouth shut. He can say she's been stalking him: she turned up at his house, threatened to tell his wife they had an affair. He wouldn't be lying, not strictly speaking. Despite the idea of blackmail leaving a filthy taste in his mouth, Pete unlocks the bottom drawer of the desk and slides the file inside, before carefully locking it and heading back downstairs.

In the sitting room, Natalie sits slumped on the sofa as cartoons blare from the television. She doesn't look up as he enters.

'Nat? Why is Zadie home? I thought the holidays didn't start until next week.'

Natalie drags her gaze from the screen, her mouth twisting as she looks up at him. 'Maybe if you could spare five minutes to actually talk to me, you'd know.'

'Nat, I was working. I told you that. What happened? You said you had to go to school for a meeting.'

'I don't want to talk about it now.' She gets to her feet and pushes past him roughly, heading into the kitchen.

Later, Pete lies beside Natalie in bed, as she literally turns a cold shoulder towards him. She hasn't spoken to him all evening, and he had to ask Zadie what happened at school. She gave him some story about the teacher being mean to her, and he's still not any wiser as to why she's been sent home. Exhausted but wide awake, he stares up at the ceiling, picturing Natalie's face as it twisted with disgust when he asked her about Zadie, before it morphs into Vanessa's face, crumpling as he told her he *was nothing like her fucking dad*. Maybe that was a bit harsh of him. There is a pang of regret and he reaches for his phone. He knows how she feels about her dad and that was a step too far, mentioning him.

I'm sorry about today. I shouldn't have said that. Believe me when I say I really didn't want things to end up like this.

Feeling like less of a heel, he rolls away from Natalie's back and closes his eyes.

# *Natalie*

'I'll come with you.' Eve is already reaching for her jacket as Natalie shakes her head.

'It's fine, Eve, honestly. It's just a check-up.' As if she has been primed, Erin lets out a wail, sharp and high-pitched, and Natalie has to resist the urge to shudder.

'I think Erin has just made the decision for you.' Eve laughs as she bends and scoops the baby out of her bouncy chair. 'I'll come with you, then while you're in with the doctor Erin can stay in the waiting room with me. It'll be easier all round – you can talk properly to the doctor without fretting about whether she's going to cry or not.'

'Sure. OK. Whatever.' Natalie feels sluggish and slow, exhaustion making her thoughts cloudy and fragmented as she allows Eve to strap Erin into her pushchair and take the handles. She hadn't slept well after Vanessa's visit, and she can't squash the burning irritation she feels at Pete. She knows he works for Vanessa – theoretically she is his boss – but it still stings that he can walk off site when Vanessa snaps her fingers. Something he apparently can't do when it's Natalie who needs him. As Eve wheels Erin out of the front door, Natalie follows, stumbling over something in the hallway as she does. Eve's handbag. 'Eve, your bag!'

'Can you grab it for me?' Eve calls back over her shoulder, her focus still on Erin. Natalie sighs and stoops to pick up the jumble of detritus that has spilled from the battered leather bag Eve has carried round for almost as long as Natalie has known her. A packet of tissues, a pen with no lid, a piece of rose quartz and – Natalie pauses, with a glance towards the driveway, where Eve is still leaning over Erin – Eve's appointment book. She tries to tuck it into the bag but it gets caught in the strap, slipping to the floor, and Natalie can't help glancing at the pages. Her mouth goes dry as she runs her eyes over the scrawled biro notes, at the names and times scribbled out. Cancellations. Page after page of them. Natalie looks up, towards Eve, who makes a 'hurry up' gesture towards her, and shoves the book into the bag, her mind racing. *Why is Eve cancelling so many appointments?* The way she's been talking, Eve has had more clients than ever, but her appointment book is telling a different story. Natalie turns her back on Eve, her face hot as she pulls the front door closed behind her. *Is Eve cancelling appointments to spend time with Erin and me?* Something about that thought makes Natalie feel oddly stifled and guilty at the same time.

Natalie tries to push the image of the pages of cancelled appointments out of her head as she lets Eve push Erin onto the path through the woods, the full leaves of the trees knitting over their heads and blocking out the sun. She's not sure if Eve has insisted on coming along to help with Erin, or if it's really just so she can make sure Natalie does actually go to this check-up. Natalie hasn't brought a jacket, and she shivers in the chilly gloom of the trees, glad when they step out into the sunshine, although she is sweating lightly as they reach the surgery.

'Natalie Maxwell?' There is only a short wait before Natalie's name is called. She feels sick and anxious as she stands, running her hands over the fabric of her jeans while Eve gives her an encouraging smile.

'Hello, Natalie.' Dr Crawford looks up as Natalie takes a seat. 'How are you?'

'Good.'

The doctor peers at the screen. 'So, you're here for a post-natal check-up, correct? You've had some issues with depression, and I can see you've been prescribed diazepam previously.'

Natalie nods. 'That's right.'

'And how are you feeling?' Dr Crawford gives Natalie a gentle smile, and Natalie wishes this was the doctor she'd seen when she found out she was pregnant.

'OK.' Natalie's eyes fill with unexpected tears, and she blinks rapidly. 'I'm very tired,' she whispers. 'All the time. The baby doesn't sleep much, and my husband works long hours.'

'Do you have support in place?'

'My eldest daughter helps out a bit, when she can.' Natalie blinks again, her mouth dry. She doesn't want to tell the doctor that Emily seems to hate her, that Zadie is in awful trouble at school, that generally, things feel as if they are falling apart, and she is a massive failure.

'How are your energy levels?'

'Low. But it's just because I'm tired. I'll be OK when the baby starts sleeping.' Natalie offers up a watery smile. She doesn't even have the energy to wash her hair most days. 'My friend helps me out a lot. She takes the baby when I don't feel great, she's actually looking after her now.'

'Well, that's good.' The doctor smiles. 'It sounds like you have a good support system in her, and that's what you need right now. And you're taking the pills prescribed to you? How do you feel now you're taking them?'

'Fine. Better.' The lie tastes as bitter on Natalie's tongue as she presumes the pills would if she had actually taken any. As it is, she hasn't yet. She feels as if by taking them she would be admitting that she can't cope, that she really is a complete and utter failure and yet, there's a part of her that needs the security they offer from their little white box in the bathroom cabinet. If she needs them, they are there. She wonders briefly if that's how her mother felt at first. If there's anything Natalie *doesn't* want to be, it's like her mother.

'Great. Well, I'll write you a new prescription and we'll chat again in a few weeks. And keep making use of that friend of yours – she sounds like a godsend.'

*She sounds like a godsend.* The words ring in Natalie's ears as she takes her new prescription and exits the consulting room to see said godsend dandling Erin on her knee as the receptionist leans over, cooing in the baby's face, and Eve presses a kiss to the top of Erin's head.

'...your mummy.' Natalie catches the last fragment of the receptionist's words as the woman straightens, and Eve looks up at Natalie with a smile.

'Here she is!' She turns Erin in her lap towards Natalie, but Erin looks away, more interested in Eve's bracelets.

'I was just saying to your friend here what a good baby she is,' the receptionist says, with a smile.

'And I was just saying she's always good, aren't you, little one?' Eve laughs as Erin's fingers wind around a strand of her hair.

Natalie eyes Eve, watching closely as she patiently untangles her hair, then fusses with Erin's cardigan before placing her back in her pushchair, tucking a blanket over her little legs. *What is Eve implying? That Erin behaves better for her than she does for me?* There is a burning sensation in Natalie's chest, a wave of acid that makes it hard to swallow, and she nudges Eve out of the way and takes the handles of the pushchair, wheeling Erin out into the sunshine.

'What did the doctor say?' Eve asks, her brow furrowed in concern. 'Did she give you another prescription?'

'Yes. I'll fill it later.' Natalie hasn't admitted to Eve that she isn't taking the pills. 'She just asked how I was feeling, and I told her. Tired, stressed and like an old bag lady.' Natalie takes one hand off the pushchair to gesture at her faded leggings.

'I've told you before, Nat, all new mums feel this way to some extent,' Eve says gently. 'You're too hard on yourself. You know I'm always happy to help out if things get too much.'

*Ahh, yes. Eve, the godsend.* Natalie flinches at the memory of the doctor's words. Even the doctor thinks that Eve is more capable than Natalie. *Good old Eve, always ready to step in and stop Erin from crying.*

'Why don't I take Erin for a day soon, and you could go and get your highlights done? Maybe do some shopping?'

Natalie starts to shake her head, but pauses. 'Did I tell you I saw Vanessa?'

'What?'

'Vanessa. Pete's ex, the one he's working with. She came to our house to give him some files. She's not how I thought she would look, to be honest.'

Eve's mouth opens as if she wants to say something, before she closes it abruptly, as Erin lets out a yelp and then a burp. 'Wait, Nat. She's been sick.' Eve is reaching in and rummaging in the changing bag for wipes before Natalie even has a chance to think about it. 'Maybe Pete needs to step up to the plate a bit more. Spend a bit more time at home than at work, if that's even where he is.'

'What?' One minute they were talking about highlights; now Eve has once again decided to go in on Pete, and Natalie doesn't appreciate her tone.

'He's got kids, for God's sake, it's about time he started acting like it. Jesus, Nat.' Eve stands, moving to the bin on the edge of the footpath to throw away the dirty wipes. 'He's never at home – you're left coping with everything, exhausting yourself to the point that you need medication to get through the day while Pete's out there living his best life. It's not on. Sometimes I think you might as well be on your own.'

Natalie can feel her jaw drop. She knows Pete hasn't been around much, but Eve surely has to understand that he's working all the hours God sends to provide for her and the kids. 'He's got a job to do, Eve. If Pete doesn't work, then who pays the bills? He's been coming home on time the last couple of weeks, actually. And he does more than you know – he does a lot when he is around.' Not strictly true, but despite the animosity she's felt towards Pete lately, Natalie still feels the urge to defend him.

'Sure he does,' Eve says.

A wave of resentment bubbles up as Erin laughs at Eve, who is making faces at her, and Natalie looks ahead to the edge of the woods. Something about the way Eve is behaving lately is off: the cancellation of her clients; the way she seems to have ditched her other friends – not that she has many, Pete says Eve changes her friends more than her knickers; her comments about Pete that seem to be getting progressively more and more spiteful. Natalie doesn't know any more if she is too dependent on Eve, or if it's beginning to be the other way round and she feels a sudden longing for space. 'Thanks for today, Eve. I can take things from here.'

Eve looks up, puzzled. 'I thought I was coming back to yours? I was going to help Emily with her packing list for university.'

'Erin needs a nap. I'll catch you later.' Simmering with a mixture of irritation at Eve's comments and an uneasy stirring in her gut, Natalie marches the pushchair towards the woods, her pulse pounding in her ears. As she reaches the path leading through the trees towards the back of the house, she glances back to see Eve standing on the footpath, watching her go, her face clouded with confusion.

Erin begins to cry as Natalie shoves the pushchair over the bumpy dirt track, the wheels catching on a tree root. She is hot, sweaty despite the cool shade, and as she wheels a now screaming Erin through the trees towards the house, the same thought forms over and over in her brain. *Erin is such a good baby. But not for me. Only for Eve. Eve is a godsend.* Sweat prickles on the nape of her neck and Natalie swallows, her mouth dry. *Maybe Eve is a better mother to Erin than I am. Maybe I have made a terrible mistake – maybe I never should have had another baby at all.*

# *Pete*

Pete shuts down his laptop with a sigh and glances at his phone. Five past five. That's it, he's going home. It's Friday, the sun is out, and he'd once again promised Natalie he would be home in time for dinner, and this time he means it. He's got a gift for her, and he wants to do things properly.

It's been a month since his initial showdown with Vanessa at her flat, and ten days since she showed up at his house with that explosive file. Since then, he has been cordially polite to her on site, and the only emails he's received have been from her work email. None of those emails have made any mention of her rescinding the contract, nor did she mention the possibility of it when he happened to bump into her in the site office early one morning. In fact, her face had dropped at the sight of him, and she had made her excuses and left before he'd even really had a chance to think about what he was going to say to her. He's starting to believe that she took on board what he said at the house, and that she's seen sense now she's had a chance to process things.

As he gets into the car, turning the air conditioning up full blast, Pete takes a moment to sit back and just breathe. The last few months have been an absolute horror show, if he's brutally honest with himself. Erin's arrival turned their entire world upside down, far more than he'd expected it to. Between Emily's mood swings, Zadie's school trouble and the *constant* bed-wetting, not to mention Natalie barely functioning … plus the fucking *hole* he dug himself into with Vanessa, Pete is surprised any of them are still standing. But they are. By some complete miracle. And now, today, Pete can see that the way he's behaved is beyond selfish. He put himself before his family, and it just isn't acceptable. It's not who he really is. The realisation that he came within inches of losing them all makes his blood freeze in his veins. Leaning forward, he punches a button on the touch screen of his dashboard, smiling as the car dials Natalie's number.

'Pete?' She sounds frazzled but she doesn't have that sullen tone to her voice, and Pete hopes she's in a good mood. 'What is it?'

'I'm leaving the office now – shall I pick food up on the way? Maybe a Chinese? If Emily is there, keep her home for dinner. I want to talk to you all.' He pauses. 'And if Eve is round... can you get rid of her?'

Natalie has the small kids at the table when Pete walks in with a huge bag of Chinese takeaway and two bottles of wine, as Emily lays down plates at everyone's seat, except for Erin who gets a plastic bowl that she immediately starts to thump on the tray of the high chair.

'Oh, yum, I love Chinese.' Emily takes one of the bags from him, as Natalie gives him a curious look.

'No late meetings tonight?' Her tone is light, but with a slight edge, and Pete thinks she might be being sarcastic.

'The only meeting I have this evening is with four beautiful women,' he says, determined not to let tonight turn out like all the other nights, with Natalie facing away from him in bed as he scrolls mindlessly on his phone, wishing he could go back to before, when things were good. He leans over and kisses Natalie full on the mouth.

'Err... gross,' Zadie says with a grin. She's lost another tooth.

'I know, right,' Natalie says, but she smiles as her cheeks flush and she drops Zadie a wink before moving to the worktop to help Emily with the takeaway containers.

Once everyone is seated and tucking in, Natalie pushes a piece of chicken around on her plate, laying her fork down before she says, 'Aren't you going to tell us what's going on? You said you had something to tell us all.'

Pete feels an odd flutter of nerves in his belly. He hasn't made a grand gesture to Natalie since the tickets to Australia, and look how that debacle turned out. Clearing his throat, he fumbles in his pocket, drawing out a small box. 'Natalie – and you, girls – I know these past few months have been really difficult for all of us. Things have been really up in the air, and I know I haven't been around as much as I should have been.' Pete casts his gaze around the table, guilt turning the few bites of food he's eaten to tar in his stomach. Natalie pauses, her fork halfway to her mouth now. She looks panicked, a rabbit in headlights, and Pete thinks maybe he hasn't gone about this quite as well as he'd hoped. 'What I'm trying to say is, Nat, I know I've let you down recently, and I hate myself for it.' He clears his throat again, hearing the echo of the words he said to Vanessa days ago. 'I've got you something.'

Natalie leans forward, her breath catching as he pops open the lid of the small jewellery box to reveal a diamond eternity ring. 'Pete… Oh my God, I don't know what to say.'

Pete swallows, a lump in his throat building at the emotion on her face. 'You don't have to say anything, just put it on.'

Natalie slides the ring on to her finger above her wedding and engagement rings. 'It's perfect. Thank you.'

'Wow,' Emily breathes. 'That is gorgeous, Dad. You really must have some making up to do.' She laughs, and Pete tries to, but it comes out as an odd wheeze that he covers with a sip of wine.

'So, anyway,' he says, once he's recovered, 'I was thinking… we should throw a party.'

'A party?' Natalie looks doubtful.

'Yes, a party. We can say it's a double celebration – for Emily turning eighteen and for passing her exams. Or a commiseration party if she flunks out.' Pete winks.

'Wow, cheers, Dad.' Emily rolls her eyes, but she's laughing, and Pete realises it's the first time in a long time he's seen his eldest daughter laugh like that.

'I don't know, Pete. A party is a lot of work,' Natalie says. 'Couldn't we just do something a little more … I don't know … low-key? Something for just the five of us?'

'Noooooo,' Zadie cries. 'We want a party!'

Pete reaches out and grasps Natalie's hand. 'Come on, old girl, you used to be the life and soul of the party. It'll be fun. We can invite Stu and Mari, a few of Em's friends—'

'Jake,' Emily interjects.

'Jake,' Pete says, with a glance at Natalie, who presses her lips together. 'Some of the neighbours. We can make a playlist, I'll knock up some cocktails, you can whip up some banging beige food …'

'Oh my God, *Dad*,' Emily groans. 'I don't want a party if it's going to be pure cringe, I'll just go out instead.'

'It won't be cringe, I promise.'

'Pete, I don't know …' Natalie glances at Erin, who wriggles in her seat, her face sticky with rice grains. 'Erin—'

'Will be fine. I'll help, I promise.'

'Pleeease, Mummy? Please?' Zadie steeples her hands under her chin as her words whistle through the gap in her teeth, making Emily laugh.

Natalie sighs before she smiles, although it doesn't quite reach her eyes. 'I don't suppose I have much of a choice, do I? You're all ganging up on me, it's three against one. Looks like we're having a party.'

'Yay!' Zadie jumps off her chair and spins in a circle, her arms wide and her hair flying out behind her. 'Can I get new shoes for the party?'

'I don't see why not.' Pete can't stop the grin that marches across his face, as he takes in the sight before him. Erin is not crying – she's actually smiling and babbling as she reaches out

107

to grab at Zadie, Emily seems to have lost what he thought was becoming a permanent scowl, and as Natalie reaches for her wine glass the light catches the diamond in her new ring. She meets his eyes and raises her glass. *Maybe*, he thinks, *just maybe, everything is going to be OK.*

*The Party*

# Natalie

Natalie shoves another tray of sausage rolls into the oven and wonders again if there is any possible way she could get away with cancelling the party at this late hour. She'd felt ambushed when Pete had suggested throwing a party over dinner last month, mesmerised by the glint of the diamond he had presented to her. In all honesty, Natalie doesn't need a diamond ring. She needs a husband who is present and willing to help out when she feels as though she's drowning. She'd felt unable to say no completely to the party even though she'd tried, not when he'd spent all that money on her, and all three of them – Pete, Emily and Zadie – had been so excited at the thought of having a big celebration, not one of them stopping to consider that perhaps it might be too much for her to cope with. Now, as she grates cheese for sandwiches and Erin grizzles in her bouncy chair, she remembers why they haven't had anyone over for ages. At least the rain that hammered down all night and well into the morning has finally stopped, although that was going to be her saving grace – Pete has invited too many people over for them all to fit comfortably in the house, so rain would have been the perfect excuse to cancel.

'Cheese? Ugh, no one likes cheese sandwiches.' Emily breezes into the chaotic kitchen, snatching the phone charger out of the wall.

'Everyone likes cheese sandwiches,' Natalie says as the oven timer pings and she moves to rescue this round of pastry before it burns. 'Finish those sandwiches off, will you, while I get the next lot of food in the oven.'

'Can't. Sorry.' Emily reaches for her jacket that hangs on the back of the kitchen chair – the jacket that Natalie has been asking her to take upstairs for three days.

'What do you mean, you can't? Emily, this is your party. I could do with some help.' It's only just gone lunchtime and Natalie is already exhausted. Erin is cutting teeth and woke up what felt like a hundred times in the night. At four o'clock this morning Natalie had given up and brought Erin downstairs, feeling a sharp bolt of resentment towards Pete as he slumbered on, oblivious.

'I'm going to get my eyelashes done. And anyway, this whole thing wasn't my idea. I would have just gone out in town with my friends.' Without waiting for Natalie to respond, Emily swings her bag over her shoulder and heads for the front door, leaving Natalie to silently gnash her teeth and pray to God she gets through today without losing her shit.

'Mum. Mum. *Mum.*' Zadie appears in the doorway, an old teddy that she used to sleep with under one arm. It's missing an eye and the faint smell of wee rises from its fur. Natalie can't remember the last time she washed it.

'What is it, Zade?'

'I feel sick.'

Natalie thinks hanging on to that ratty old bear might be part of the problem. 'You haven't even eaten anything yet today, have you?' She'd found Zadie's soggy cereal left in the bowl when Zadie went upstairs to get dressed. 'Do you want some toast? You can have one of these if you don't tell Em.' Natalie holds out a cupcake, knowing she's cementing herself a place in the world's worst parent Olympics, bribing her kid to eat breakfast at lunchtime by offering her cake.

'I don't want toast. Or that. I told you, I feel sick.'

'Jesus Christ,' Natalie mutters under her breath. 'You feel sick, Zadie, because you haven't eaten anything today. You didn't eat your dinner last night either. Your tummy needs food.'

'You gave me pasta for dinner. I don't like pasta.' Zadie's voice takes on a grating whine, and Natalie has to take a deep breath and count to five before she can speak.

'You do like pasta. Everyone likes pasta. You liked pasta when Eve made it for you.' Saying it out loud makes a knot form in Natalie's stomach. If Eve was here, she's sure Zadie would eat whatever she served up for her, just as she's sure Erin would *stop bloody crying* if Eve was here. Natalie shakes away the memory of the animosity she'd felt as she realised on her return home from the meeting with the school that Eve had changed Erin into a sleepsuit she'd bought for her. The same animosity and resentment that had flared when that woman had mistaken Eve for Erin's mother at the duck pond, and again as Natalie left the doctor's consulting room – the idea that Eve was somehow a better mother to Erin than Natalie crowding out any other thoughts.

'Nat? Got any extra chairs in here? And I need a tablecloth for that big table outside.' Pete waltzes into the kitchen, a huge grin on his face as he ruffles Zadie's hair.

'You know where things are, Pete, get them yourself,' Natalie snaps.

'I don't know which tablecloth you want to use. I don't want to get myself in trouble.' Pete waggles his eyebrows at Zadie and she giggles, making Natalie's blood bubble up. Erin continues to cry, but Pete doesn't seem to hear her.

'I don't give a shit which tablecloth you use,' she says, slamming plates onto the worktop. Pete dodges round Zadie, reaching out to pull Natalie towards him.

'Come on, chill out. There's going to be a party.' Pete grasps her hands and moves as though dancing with her. Natalie pulls away, frowning.

'Yeah, there's going to be a party,' Natalie says. 'A party I didn't even want to host, because I'm so bloody tired, and now not a single one of you is helping me, so forgive me if I'm not really in the mood.'

Pete drops his hands and picks up one of the kitchen chairs. 'Outside is mostly set up,' he says, his tone sober now. 'I just need the tablecloth and chairs, and to tie the last of the balloons up. The weather's brightened up now, so we won't need the marquee.'

No, they won't need the marquee. But the ground will still be muddy, and dirt will probably still be tracked all through the house for Natalie to clean up in the morning.

Pete glances at the clock. 'Where's Em?'

'Gone to get her eyelashes done. She'll be back in a little while, and then she's just got to get changed.' Natalie opens another packet of cupcakes, hastily shoving them onto a plate, before rooting through the kitchen drawer to find candles for the main attraction – a three-tier cake with extravagant icing decorations. She looks up as she feels Pete's eyes on her.

'What?'

'Well … it's half two,' he says. 'Shouldn't you be getting ready?'

Erin's muted grizzling dials up a notch, to that unstable place between a soft cry and full-blown yell. Zadie moans under her breath, clutching her belly, and the oven timer pings again, signalling the next batch of beige food is cooked. Natalie leans down and scoops Erin up, shoving her in Pete's direction.

'You're dead right, Pete,' she says. 'I really should be getting ready.'

Upstairs, behind the safety of the closed bedroom door, Natalie stands in front of the wardrobe in her stained grey jogging pants. She has no idea what she's going to wear to this party. Every day for the last eight months (or ten really, if she's honest, ever since she went on maternity leave) she's worn the same three pairs of jogging pants on rotation, switching them out when they get too stained and gross. She pulls out an emerald-green dress, one that is fitted over the bust and then flares at the waist, holding it up to herself before throwing it onto the bed. Her boobs aren't the same since she stopped feeding Erin. A pink sundress, one she wore religiously on their last holiday to Portugal, strains over her hips when she slips it over her head, and she feels sick as she strips it off again and looks at her body in the full-length mirror. She had always felt quite proud of herself, before Erin. She'd been a regular gym-goer, and even though there was a ten-year gap between Emily and Zadie, she had bounced right back to her usual size after Zadie was born. This time, though... She stands there in her greying knickers and grasps at the handfuls of flesh either side of her waist. She doesn't seem to have lost any of her baby weight, despite having no appetite and feeling as exhausted as if she's run a marathon every day. She closes her eyes briefly, blocking out the sight of the thin scar that slices across the skin above her pubic bone, a constant reminder of the traumatic day of Erin's birth.

The image of Vanessa standing on her doorstep rises in Natalie's mind and she swallows, not taking her eyes from the mirror. Vanessa hadn't been what Natalie thought she would be at all. They must be the same age, but where Natalie is soft and rounded, Vanessa is sleek and lean. Where Natalie's face is pale, a cluster of three tiny spots trying to bloom at her hairline, Vanessa's skin had been flawless, her make-up perfect, not a hint of her crimson lipstick bleeding from the confines of her lip liner. Her hair was shiny and thick, not frizzy and dry at the ends like Natalie's, and Natalie feels a sharp pang of envy. When Pete had started work on the contract, Natalie had asked him what Vanessa looked like now, intrigued by this old flame of her husband's, and Pete had just shrugged.

'I dunno,' he'd said. 'Just... like Vanessa. She's got brown hair. She wears those stupid shoes with the red bottoms that you're always going on about, she looks ridiculous on site in them. Not a patch on you, babe.'

Natalie had let him hug her, smiling into his shoulder, but now she thinks Pete must be blind not to have noticed Vanessa's glamorous appearance.

Moving to the bathroom, Natalie hastily showers, wishing she had time to wash her hair before the guests begin to arrive, and then smears her face with moisturiser, her eyes going to the mirror as she does. Not even the most expensive concealer can hide the dark circles and bags that line her eyes, and she looks away, her gaze going to the box of diazepam hidden behind a box of tampons. She still hasn't taken any yet, although the thought has crossed her mind more than once, and she still hasn't told Pete about them. She's not sure why. She doesn't think Pete would judge her, although she knows that he thinks depression can be cured by spending time outside (he's such a dinosaur sometimes), but Natalie also thinks that if she did start taking them, Pete probably wouldn't even notice.

Even though he's coming home on time, and he did try and engage with her in the kitchen this morning, Natalie still can't shake the feeling that ever since Erin was born things haven't been right between them. When they laid Erin on her chest and Pete cried, Natalie thought that any secret resentment he was holding towards her for carrying on with the pregnancy had disappeared, but now she thinks she was wrong about that. He doesn't seem to have connected with Erin at all; he claims he doesn't hear her crying at night, leaving Natalie to get up every time her screams rip through the dark, but Natalie can't understand how he doesn't hear it. He's made more than one bitchy comment about Eve hanging around, and Natalie knows that he probably thinks she's let herself go, but still he doesn't step in to help out. She reaches for her make-up bag, making a sorry attempt with the concealer and brushing mascara on to her lashes as she fights back the thought that comes to the forefront on those long, dark, lonely evenings when she's exhausted and Erin refuses to sleep. *It's almost as if Pete doesn't want Erin here at all.* The terrifying thing about that thought is that somehow, sometimes, Natalie can understand that feeling.

Natalie twists her unwashed hair up into a messy bun, hoping no one will notice the greasy parts, as Pete's voice filters up the stairs.

'Nat! Stu and Mari are here!'

Of course they are. Stu and Mari are always the first ones to arrive. Pulling on the pink sundress and smoothing away the wrinkles that stick to her hips, Natalie draws in a deep breath and takes one last look in the mirror.

'You can do this,' she whispers, blinking back a sudden spurt of hot tears before her mascara can run. 'The party will be over soon. Just hang in there for a few more hours.' And then she hurries down the stairs, a wide smile on her face as she opens her arms to Stu and Mari.

'Guys! So glad you could make it! We've been dying to catch up with you, it's been way too long.'

# *Pete*

Pete feels relaxed for the first time in months as he steps out into the garden, weaving his way between family and friends, a cold beer in his hands. There was a moment this morning when the rain had thundered down, the sky over the woods dark and foreboding as the wind whipped the trees at the back of the house into a frenzy, where he thought they were going to have to cancel the party, but the storm has passed and the sun beats down overhead, and finally it feels as if summer has arrived. Now, the garden is full of all the people the Maxwell family love, and Pete makes sure to enthusiastically greet everyone as they arrive.

'Oh, Peter, she's lovely.' Mrs Noyce from across the street stops him, a glass of Pimm's in one hand, the other holding on to her husband, who must be eighty-five if he's a day. 'You and Natalie must be over the moon.' She nods in the direction of two of Natalie's co-workers cooing over Erin, who has finally stopped grizzling.

'We're very lucky.' He smiles down at her before moving on, clapping Dave the foreman on the back and stooping to kiss Dave's wife on the cheek. Natalie stands on the fringes of the garden, beneath the old apple tree, and Pete is relieved to see she's put on some make-up and she's actually smiling as she talks to the mother of Emily's oldest friend from school.

Heading into the kitchen to grab some more beers for the ice bucket on the table, Pete winks at Emily as she sips from a glass of champagne, almost colliding with Eve, who enters the garden through the side gate carrying an M&S bag for life stuffed with wine, having clearly cut through the woods from her house.

'M&S eh, Eve? You really are spoiling us.' Pete moves aside

so Eve can head into the kitchen, as she gives him a tight smile. Pete rolls his eyes. He doesn't *hate* Eve, doesn't even really dislike her, but he knows that she thinks she's a cut above him and he's not good enough for Natalie. He doesn't really understand why Natalie likes her so much – the woman is always hanging around the house with that judgemental look in her eye, and he knows she's slagged him off to Natalie behind his back.

'Pete!' A hand claps his back as he watches Eve enter the kitchen and he turns to see Stu, wearing a crappy hat with corks hanging from the rim that Pete bought him for a joke about fifteen years ago. 'Brilliant turnout. And lovely to catch up with you guys. It's been ages.'

'Things have been busy, you know?' Pete isn't going to elaborate on exactly what he's been busy doing.

'I know, mate, but even so. We haven't seen you and Nat since before Tenerife. Is everything OK with you guys?' It is unusual for the two couples to go so long without seeing one another. Stu has always been the one whom Pete can talk to about stuff, in the way men don't usually share. Stu has been there since the first year of uni and he's gone through everything with Pete, including his break-up with Vanessa at the end of that first year. Pete can't talk to Stu about what's been going on, though, and maybe that's why he's been unconsciously avoiding him. 'I thought maybe... well, maybe you guys were offended we went away without you?'

'Stu, mate, don't be daft. You know me and Nat aren't like that. Everything is fine. Honestly, pal. We've just been so busy with the baby, but me and Nat are great. We've never been happier.' Pete grins and claps Stu on the back, and if Stu notices that Pete's smile doesn't quite reach his eyes, then he doesn't mention it.

Pete's not sure if it's the buzz from the beer, or the fact that the garden is alive with laughter and the hum of conversation, that's making his heart full, but either way he doesn't want it to change. It's as if the storm earlier today has chased away the dark cloud hanging over his own house, and he can finally breathe. At the end of the garden Zadie pushes Stu's daughter Lola on the swing, both of the two girls bossing around Stu's son, who's two years younger. Emily stands by the table talking to old Mrs Noyce, Jake beside her. Pete watches as Jake slides his hand into Emily's, pressing lightly against her fingers, and Emily turns to him with a smile. Pete isn't too enamoured with the idea of Emily having a serious relationship at her age, but now she's off to university it's something he won't have to worry about too much. No more persistent thud of crappy rap music emanating from Jake's car at all hours as he honks his horn and waits for Emily to scurry out to him. No more tears from Em as they (Pete and Natalie included) try to navigate the ups and downs of young love. No more scraping of Emily's window at night as Jake slides it open and climbs inside her bedroom – Pete and Natalie have argued over whether to confront the two of them over it more than once, but now he's not going to have to lie there with clenched fists, resisting the urge to drag Jake out by the scruff of his neck and throw him down the stairs. Pete gives it until Christmas before Emily fully embraces university life and gives Jake the heave-ho. *Out of sight, out of mind* and all that. A peal of laughter rents the air, familiar and yet not, and Pete turns to see Natalie laughing with a couple of women from her office, as she bounces a gurgling Erin in her arms. It's as though Pete has seen a ghost – a glimpse of the Natalie he knew before Erin was born – and he has to blink for a minute. He can't believe he's behaved like such an idiot. Can't believe that he risked this – risked *everything* – for a woman who belongs buried deep in his past, who means nothing to him and hasn't for a long time.

Smiling to himself, Pete turns down the Spotify playlist Emily made and picks up a fork, banging it against the side of his beer bottle, smiling as his eldest daughter turns and groans when she realises what he's about to do.

'Ladies and gentlemen...' he begins.

'No, Dad. Please don't.' Emily covers her face with her hands, but she's smiling as she does it.

As everyone turns to face Pete, he climbs up onto a rickety garden chair and spreads his arms wide. 'Everybody, thank you so much for coming today, to help us celebrate our Emily's eighteenth birthday.' There are whoops and cheers, and Pete sees Jake's arm slide around Emily, as Natalie glances their way with a smile.

'That isn't the only thing we're celebrating today,' Pete pauses for dramatic effect. 'We're also celebrating the fact that not only did our Em achieve three A stars at A level, but she's also accepted a place this morning to study law at Durham University.' A gasp ripples through the crowd of friends and family, followed by clapping as Stu starts to cheer. 'We've had a year of upheaval in our house,' Pete goes on as, just on cue, Erin lets out a wail, 'and I know you've found it tough studying through it all, Em, especially when you've stepped in so much to help your mum with Erin, but I just wanted to tell you how proud your mum and I are of what you've achieved.' Pete raises his beer, nodding at Stu. 'And just because there's going to be a lawyer in the family doesn't mean you can misbehave, Stu.' Laughter runs through the crowd, but Emily isn't laughing.

'Dad, *stop*.' Emily's face burns a bright, vicious red as she looks up at him, Jake's arm sliding from her shoulder.

'Sorry, Em, I know I'm embarrassing you, but I am honestly so bloody proud of all you've achieved.' His chest feels tight, his throat thick with emotion as Pete scans the small crowd for Natalie, holding out a hand to her as he catches her eye. Rolling her eyes, Natalie puts her half-empty wine glass down and makes her way towards him, allowing Pete to pull her up on to the garden chair next to his. 'This woman here is the backbone of our family, and everything we do, everything we have together, is because of her. Natalie, I want to thank you for giving me these perfect children, for taking care of us all.' Pete stumbles a little over this, knowing that lately all of it has been difficult for Natalie. 'You've given me a pretty much perfect life ever since you *literally* swept me off my feet twenty years ago, and I love you.' Leaning in, he presses his mouth to hers and she resists for just a moment before leaning into him, as their friends and family whoop and catcall, raising their glasses in a toast.

Natalie pulls away, her face flushed, but from the kiss or the wine Pete doesn't know, and doesn't care. 'I love you,' he says again, cheers ringing in his ears, along with the faint grumble of a cry from Erin, and Natalie gives him a small smile but doesn't say it back.

'Now...' Pete turns to the group assembled on the lawn, raising his beer again. 'I say we get drunk!'

It's as he's about to step off the chair that he catches the first glimpse of something that he's not quite sure he's really seeing. A flash of familiar dark hair that makes his heart stop dead in his chest. Pausing, he scans the crowd as people begin to move away, towards the table groaning with Natalie's beige food and ice buckets full of wine and beer bottles. But he isn't mistaken. There, at the fringes of the crowd, raising a glass of wine in his direction as she stares at him, is Vanessa.

# Natalie

Natalie feels herself tense as Pete leans in for a dramatic kiss, forcing herself to relax and return his affection, aware that their entire group of friends and family – and even the old people from across the street; Pete really went to town with the invitations – are watching. As Pete tells her he loves her, all she can hear is the sound of Erin grizzling in the arms of someone else in the crowd, an insistent cry that burrows its way deep under her skin, like the sting of a mosquito. Finally, he lets her go and she pastes on a smile as she stumbles from the garden chair and snatches up her half-drunk wine, Erin's wails growing louder.

'Brilliant speech, eh, Nat?' Stu grabs her arm as she moves towards Erin, pulling her towards him for a hug. 'So bloody proud of Em and I'm just her godfather! You two must be so chuffed.'

'Over the moon,' Natalie says, her eyes running over the crowd as she spots Erin, her cries turning into full-blown wails. She's in the arms of Gina, a woman Natalie has worked with for years, but who doesn't have children and looks wildly uncomfortable as Erin squirms in her arms. 'Sorry, Stu, I have to …' Natalie gives him a brief smile and hurries towards her crying baby, resentment burning in her veins.

Pete is talking to one of his drinking buddies, letting rip a bubbling chain of laughter, seemingly unaware that Erin is crying, and Natalie necks the wine in her glass, a muttered 'for fuck's sake' slipping from between her lips. For a moment – just a brief, tiny moment – Natalie had almost felt content at this party. She's been funny and engaging, making small talk with their guests (even the random old people) with no problem at all as she sips on wine, while Erin is passed around from guest to guest, each of them cooing over her thick, dark hair, and the fact that she's *so good, what a good baby*. She had felt, for a short time, like her old self. Like the Natalie who enjoyed dressing up and putting a bit of make-up on, who enjoyed laughing at other people's not-funny anecdotes while sipping on cold white wine. For just a moment, the burden of responsibility had been lifted from Natalie's shoulders as other people stepped in to look after Erin, but now it's back, like a lead blanket, and she can't stop the bitterness flooding her body as she makes her way towards her crying child while her husband – who just professed his love for her and their perfect children – drinks pretentious IPA and pretends he can't hear the wailing.

'Gina, I'm so sorry, Erin's well overdue her nap.' Natalie has to raise her voice over Erin's ear-splitting cries. 'Let me take her.' She holds out her arms as Gina wrestles with an angry Erin, trying not to feel offended at the relief on the woman's face as she surrenders the baby.

'Nat?' Eve appears at her side, peering at Erin. 'Oh darling, what's the matter?' She pulls a silly face that Erin pauses in her screaming to stare at, and then turns to Natalie. 'Here, let me take her.' She holds out her arms.

'No, it's OK.' Natalie feels her arms tighten instinctively around Erin's hot, frantic body as she lets out another shriek.

'Come on, Nat, don't be silly.' Eve gestures, flicking her fingers in a 'come here' motion. 'Let me take her up for you, the poor thing is exhausted.'

'I *know* she is,' Natalie says through gritted teeth, as Gina and several others look on. 'I'm taking her up for a sleep now.'

'You don't want to miss the party, though,' Eve says, her hands reaching out and seizing Erin around her chubby waist. She gives a tug, as if to wrestle Erin out of Natalie's arms. 'I can take her up for you, and then you can stay down here with your guests, have another drink. It's not like I don't know how to get her off to sleep.'

Natalie's grip tightens and she twists slightly, angling Erin away from Eve, who clings on. Erin's face is red and sweaty, and Natalie's anger is a white-hot wall of rage that washes over her, making her vision dapple with black spots for a moment, as even Erin seems to sense it and take a break from her yelling. 'Excuse me?'

'I just meant—'

'I know what you meant.' Natalie's voice is ice-cold, and her skin still smarts from the sting of Eve returning home with a sleeping Erin in the pram, that day when Natalie came so close to shaking the baby. Her eyes go to Eve's hands, still holding stubbornly on to Erin's waist. 'But I am more than capable of taking my own child up to bed, Eve, even though I know you don't believe that, and I'd appreciate it if you would let go of my daughter.'

'Nat, please, that wasn't what I …' Eve's hands drop to her sides.

'Just back off, Eve, I said I can do it. Erin is my daughter, not yours, and I am more than capable of taking care of her.' Natalie turns to Gina, whose face burns red as she stares down at her glass. 'I'm sure Gina and the others will understand if I have to step away from the party for a short while.'

Eve's face is bleached of colour, her eyes wide. 'Nat, I was just trying to help, that's all.'

'Did it ever occur to you that perhaps I don't always want your help?' Natalie is conveniently forgetting the times she has called Eve to come over when Erin just won't stop crying and Pete is nowhere to be found. All she can see is Eve's smug face as she bumped a sleeping Erin over the threshold, the way she told Natalie to shush so as not to wake her. Eve, preparing a plate of pasta that Zadie wolfed down in minutes after days of not eating for Natalie. Eve, walking around town with Erin in the pushchair, as other people watch and think *she* is Erin's mother. 'I know you've been cancelling your clients to come here instead, and it's too much. You're not helping me, Eve, you're smothering me. When I told you I didn't know what I would do without you, it wasn't an invitation for you to step in and take over my life.'

'Jesus Christ, Natalie.' Eve chokes the words out, shaking her head as her face twists with an expression, something raw and broken, that Natalie has never witnessed on her before.

'I'm Erin's mother, Eve, not you. This is *my* family, not yours.' Aware that she is a little drunk, her anger forcing the acidic white wine straight to her head, Natalie grimaces some semblance of a smile at her other guests. 'If you'll excuse me.' And she sweeps away towards the patio doors just as Erin takes up her screaming again. As she reaches the house, Natalie glances back to see Eve's shocked face, one hand pressed to her mouth. At the other end of the garden Pete stands with Emily and Jake, completely unaware of his crying child and the events that have just taken place, and Natalie feels the swell of nausea in her belly. Making her way upstairs, she's not sure if it's resentment or regret, or just a horrible sense of foreboding, making her chest feel tight and her head feel heavy, but one thing she does know is that she can't wait for this party to be over.

# Pete

*What the fuck is she doing here?* Pete steps down from the garden chair, intent on finding Vanessa and telling her to get the hell out of his house, when he catches sight of Emily and Jake standing together at the end of the garden. Pete pauses, his gut telling him something feels off, when Emily swipes at her cheeks, her head bent low as Jake stands over her, his arms folded across his body. It's clear from the way he's standing that Jake isn't happy about something, and Pete feels a surge of something hot and spiky at the way Emily seems to cower before him.

'Em?' Thoughts of Vanessa forgotten, Pete crosses the garden in what feels like a few steps, coming to stand in front of his teenage daughter. 'Are you all right?' Pete wishes he hadn't made that speech now, regretted it the moment he saw her face fill with colour, but what can he say? He's fucking proud of her. They both are – him and Natalie.

'I'm fine, Dad.' But Emily turns her face away as she sniffs delicately, and Pete knows instinctively that she's not OK. He turns, searching the garden for Natalie, hoping she'll catch his eye and come over and deal with whatever this is, but there's no sign of her. No sign of Erin, either.

'Emily, I can see you're not all right. You're crying, for God's sake.' Pete turns to Jake, who stands there toeing the grass, a mutinous look on his face. 'Do you want to tell me what's going on?'

'Me?' Jake looks up, and there is a flash of anger on his features as his brows draw together and his lip curls. 'Sure, Pete. I'll tell you what's going on.'

'Jake, please...' Emily puts out a hand, and Jake shrugs her off, batting her hand away with more force than is necessary.

'No, Em, I'll tell your dad what the problem is.' He turns to Pete, his eyes narrowing. 'Great speech, Pete. Really brilliant. The only problem is, I thought Em wasn't going to university.'

*Oh*. Pete doesn't know what to say; he's still trying to process the way Jake knocked Emily's hand away. 'Well, Jake, I don't know why you'd think that. You knew she was looking at universities. You offered to take her to the open day at Durham, for goodness' sake! And to be honest, it's not really anything to do with you, it's Emily's decision—'

'Emily told me she wasn't going to university,' Jake says, as Emily covers her face with her hands, a fresh sob erupting. 'She told me she was going to look for a full-time job. Isn't that right, Em?'

Emily looks up, her eyes wet. 'I just said I might, that's all. I never said I was definitely going to stay home and get a job.'

Jake shakes his head, a white-hot rage shimmering around him. 'Don't lie, Em, just because your dad is around. You told me you were going to get a job, and then once we'd saved up we could look at getting a flat.' He looks at Pete. 'She did. That's what she said, all those times we've been looking after Erin together.'

Pete glances at Emily, who looks away, not wanting to meet his eyes. 'Em?'

'We talked about getting a flat, and then maybe once we were settled, getting married and having our own baby, and now...' Jake breaks off and Pete realises that all those times that Jake and Emily took Erin for a walk in the pram around the park, Jake saw it as a glimpse into a life he could have. A chance at the kind of family he'd never had and, deep down, desperately wanted. Pete feels ill at the thought of it – of Emily settling down with a baby, the way he and Natalie did. She's hardly more than a baby herself.

'Ha.' The word slips out of Pete's mouth, a harsh bark of laughter, as Jake's mouth twists. 'Sorry, Jake,' Pete says, 'but are you serious? Emily, are you listening to this?'

'Dad, please don't get involved.'

'Of course I'm going to get involved, Em. He's making you cry at your own party.' All the resentment and anger Pete feels for Vanessa bubbles up, with Jake the new target. 'I'm sorry, Jake, but why on earth would Emily want to settle down and have a baby at her age? She's just achieved three A stars at A level – she's been offered a place at Durham, for Christ's sake. The world is her oyster, so why in the *name of God* would she throw that away?' Pete can hear his own voice rising, knows people will be turning to look at him, but he can't help it, he's just so *furious*.

'Dad, please. Jake, I think you need to go. We can talk about it later.' Emily is sobbing properly now, her chest hitching and the sight of it – of his firstborn crying her heart out over this absolute *loser* – fans the flames of Pete's fury. He reaches out and grasps Jake by the arm, tugging him towards the patio doors.

'Get off me, man.' Jake wrenches his arm away, his rage still smouldering. 'She led me on – she made me think there was a future with her when all along she was just going to leave.'

'No, Jake.' Emily's tears take a breather and she gives him a hard look, one that reminds Pete of Natalie when she's convinced she's right about something. Emily might look like Pete, but she has her mother's grit. 'That's not fair – I never said I would definitely stay. We talked about it, but it was never set in stone. I think maybe you should go.'

Pete takes a tighter grip of Jake's arm, not letting him shrug him off this time. 'You heard her, let's go.'

'Wait. Emily, please, let's just talk about this.' Jake's voice becomes a whine, as several of the party guests turn to stare. There is still no sign of Natalie, but Stu catches Pete's eye and steps forward, ready to help out. Pete shakes his head gently, and marches Jake towards the house, leaving Emily standing in the garden, her face blotchy with tears. 'Emily, just talk to me! Please, tell him to let me stay. I love you, and I don't want things to end like this.'

Emily turns away, her shoulders rounded, and Pete frogmarches Jake into the house, aware of the eyes that follow.

'Time to go, buddy.' Jake is still resistant, and Pete feels his blood boil up again. *Who does this little prick think he is?* 'You need to leave, all right? Emily doesn't want you here – she's made that pretty clear – and after the show you've just put on out there, I don't blame her. You don't belong here, Jake, OK? This party is for Emily and her family and friends.'

Part of Pete knows that telling Jake he doesn't belong will rile the lad even further, but even so, he's not prepared for the way Jake wrenches himself free and pushes his face into Pete's, his hands reaching up to Pete's chest and giving him a small shove. 'You think I don't *belong* here?' Jake's voice is low and full of menace, and Pete can smell the beer on his breath as he presses his face in Pete's. 'Fucking hell, I always knew you were snobs, you Maxwells, but this takes the cake. Do you have any idea how miserable Emily has been lately? Trying to juggle school and exams with looking after Erin, because you and Natalie can't seem to do it yourselves? Neither of you even *see* Emily any more, do you?' Jake shakes his head, his fists clenched. 'I'm the only one who's been able to make her happy, and now she's lied to me because of *you*, but because I don't have a degree, I'm the one who's at fault?'

'Jake, mate.' Pete takes a step back, holding up a hand in a peace gesture, not wanting to admit that his heart is pounding a little harder than it should be. 'Calm down.'

'Calm down? Fuck off, *mate*. You think just because I work in a pub and I was raised by a single mum, I'm not good enough for your daughter?'

A hush has descended now on the party, the air filling with a thick silence as the song on the Spotify playlist draws to a close, and all eyes are on Jake and Pete in the hallway.

Jake turns and looks over the party guests, seeming to deflate in front of Pete's eyes. 'You know what?' he says softly, turning back to Pete. 'Maybe you're right. Maybe I'm not good enough for Emily, and maybe I don't belong here.' He shoves his way past Pete, smacking against his shoulder as he steps out onto the front porch before turning back. 'But I'll tell you something. I might be from the wrong side of the tracks, and I might not be a millionaire, but I'm a thousand times better person than you. None of you, none of your "wonderful" family you claim to adore so much, are perfect.'

Jake faces the partygoers, his eyes skimming over them, pausing briefly on Emily, before coming to rest on Pete's face. 'You're going to regret this, Pete. Trust me.'

# *Natalie*

Natalie wrestles with the baby, trying to pin her down with one hand as she changes her nappy with the other, Erin screaming as though Natalie is murdering her.

'Erin, please.' Natalie's face burns and she feels the prickle of sweat under her arms as the screaming child rolls away, dangerously close to the edge of the changing table. 'Stop!' The word rings out harsh in the still air of the bedroom, and Erin obeys for just a moment before the incessant crying starts up again. Weighty with regret at the way she spoke to Eve, Natalie manages to stuff Erin's legs back into her clothes and grabs the bottle of milk from the dressing table. She could be downstairs, having another glass of wine, if she'd let Eve bring Erin up. But even just the thought of Eve feeding Erin or cooing over the cot makes Natalie's stomach turn over. Pete is right, she thinks. Eve *has* been too involved since Erin was born – it's not normal for someone to want to spend as much time at their house as Eve does.

With the bottle jammed firmly into her mouth, Erin is at last blissfully quiet and Natalie closes her eyes, the wine she drank earlier causing the beginning of a headache at her temples. The peace is interrupted after mere seconds, as the bedroom door is flung wide open, startling Natalie and causing the bottle to slip from Erin's mouth, bouncing as it hits the floor.

'Emily, for God's sake!' Natalie bends from the chair to scoop up the bottle, running her thumb over the end to clear any dust before shoving it back in Erin's mouth before she can cry, with a twinge of guilt. Back when it had been Emily, Natalie would have made herself make up a fresh, sterilised bottle, but who has time for that any more? Germs build immune systems, that's what she's telling herself. 'What's the matter?'

Emily marches into the room, throwing herself on to the bed and glaring at Natalie. 'Dad. That's what's the matter.'

'Oh, not about his speech? It was a bit cringey, but he's proud of you, Em. That's all.'

'Yes, it's about his bloody speech. He's ruined everything.' Emily draws in a breath, and Natalie realises she's been crying. 'Jake didn't know I was planning on going to Durham, and now we've had a massive fight about it.'

'What do you mean he didn't know? He didn't seriously think you were going to hang around here with grades like that?' Natalie pauses, her mind racing. 'Wait. He must have known, he wanted to take you to Durham for the open day. Did you tell him you weren't going to go? Bloody hell, Emily, why on earth would you say that to him?'

'I *didn't* say that – not in so many words. We talked about me maybe staying and getting a job, but I never said I was actually going to.' Emily glowers at her and Natalie looks away, at Erin who sucks greedily at the bottle and yet still manages to kick at Natalie's arm insistently. 'Mum, Dad heard us fighting and he threw Jake out of the house. He's *left* and now it's all over.' Her voice rises to a wail that makes Natalie want to stick her fingers in her ears like a child.

'I'm sure it'll all blow over,' Natalie says. 'You should have told Jake you were definitely going to university. It was probably a bit of a shock to the poor lad if you'd told him there was a chance you might not.'

'Are you even *listening* to me?' Emily's eyes are ringed with puddles of black mascara, tears rolling down her cheeks. 'Dad threw Jake out of the party – he told him he "doesn't belong here". How do you think that made Jake feel? You know he's sensitive about the fact he hasn't got a dad, and his mum doesn't have much money.'

From what Natalie has seen of the young man, he doesn't seem to be sensitive about anything – not for all the times Emily has come home crying about something he said, something he did, some text he'd sent to a girl Emily doesn't know. 'If you and Jake were arguing it's probably best Dad asked him to leave, you don't want to spoil the party for your guests.' Natalie is too exhausted to feel bad for Jake – by the sounds of it, Pete did the right thing, for once.

'Do you actually think that's OK? For Dad to throw Jake out of his own girlfriend's party in front of everyone? How humiliating do you think that was for him?' Emily sniffs, rubbing her wrist under one eye to catch the tears glistening on her cheeks. 'I wouldn't be surprised if that's it now, if Jake never speaks to me again.'

Erin twists her head away from the empty bottle with a high shriek, and Natalie sighs internally, before lifting her and placing her over one shoulder to be winded. 'Emily, I know you think this is the end of the world—'

'I never said that! But it's embarrassing for Jake and for me. And now he'll dump me, and all my friends are going to think I'm some saddo whose dad is an actual psychopath.' Another tear slides down Emily's cheek. 'This was supposed to be a celebration and now everything is ruined.'

'Oh, for God's sake, Emily,' Natalie snaps, the final gossamer threads of her patience worn through. 'It isn't, believe it or not. Jake is not the love of your life, no matter how you think you feel right now. There'll be a time in the future when you won't even remember what he looks like. You probably won't even remember his surname – and if you do, you'll think *thank God my dad threw him out of the party that day, I had a lucky escape.*'

Emily's mouth drops open, but Natalie is on a roll now.

'You might think you're an adult, Emily, but you're still a child. Jake is the first boyfriend you've had, but he certainly won't be the last, mark my words, and if you think your dad and I would let you throw away your future on a kid like that then you're sorely mistaken.' Emily opens her mouth to speak, but Natalie carries on, raising her voice over the music floating up from the garden through the open window. 'I have spent a lot of time preparing this party for you, so I suggest you show some gratitude and get back downstairs to your guests.' Natalie can feel her pulse at the base of her throat, her heart banging hard against her ribcage as Erin belches, and then begins to squirm in her arms again.

Silence fills the room as Emily stares at her mother, her mouth twisted into a petulant pout. 'I can't believe you,' she says, her voice a venomous whisper. 'I can't wait to go to university, can't wait to get away from this house, and from you, you ... *bitch.*'

As Emily storms out of the bedroom, Natalie sinks back into the feeding chair, her face stinging as though Emily's words have slapped her. She's fought with Emily before, of course she has – what mother hasn't with a teenage girl? – but something about this feels different. Emily has never sworn at Natalie before, and there is something distasteful in the flavour of Natalie's remaining anger. The realisation that she could have quite happily slapped Emily's mouth, if she hadn't had her hands full.

Before Natalie can even begin to try and calm down, Erin lets out the familiar grumble signalling a screaming fit, and then the bedroom door creaks open again and Zadie's worried face appears.

'Mummy? Mum?'

'Yes, Zade.' Natalie sighs as she begins to rock a fractious Erin, praying that she can get her off to sleep before the party is over completely. 'Shoes off, please.'

'They're clean.' Zadie looks down at her feet.

'I don't care, Zade. No shoes upstairs, you know the rules.'

'I don't feel well.' Zadie kicks off her shoes and creeps across the carpet, and as she reaches Natalie, she puts a hand on her knee to pull herself into Natalie's lap.

'No, Zadie, get off.' Natalie puts out a hand, pushing gently at Zadie's shoulder. 'You can see I'm trying to get Erin to sleep.'

Zadie's dark eyes fill and Natalie wants to groan aloud. 'But I don't feel well, Mum, I've been telling you all day.'

'Go downstairs and see Dad, he'll give you some Calpol.'

Zadie begins to grizzle, that droning grumble that used to get under Natalie's skin even when she was tiny. Thrusting out her hands, she attempts to push her way into Natalie's lap, knocking against Erin, who lets out a startled squawk. 'I feel sick, Mummy. Like, really, really sick.'

Allowing Zadie to climb into the tiny space that Erin leaves on her lap, Natalie reaches out and presses her hand to Zadie's forehead. 'You don't have a temperature. You probably just need something to eat, Zade, that's all. Go and see Dad, he'll do you a plate.' Natalie half wants to suggest seeing Eve, as she knows Zadie will eat whatever Eve gives her, but everything still feels too raw.

'I don't want to eat,' Zadie pouts. 'I already told you, I feel sick. I don't want any food! You don't even care I feel sick!'

*Oh, for fuck's sake.* Natalie can feel her own temper rising again. Where the hell is Pete? Why does he get to sit downstairs, drinking beer and talking shit with neighbours they barely know, when all Natalie wants to do is pour herself another glass of wine and be allowed to be an actual adult for ten minutes?

'Don't be so silly. If you feel that poorly, you need to miss the rest of the party and go to bed,' Natalie snaps, gently removing Zadie from her lap and getting to her feet. Zadie tumbles dramatically to the floor, and opens her mouth to scream. 'Don't you *dare*,' Natalie hisses, Erin now sleeping peacefully in her arms. She swears if Zadie yells and wakes the baby up she is liable to do murders. 'Don't you dare start that, Zadie. I'm warning you.'

Zadie pouts, an almost comical downturn of her mouth, before she gets to her feet and runs out of the bedroom. Moments later, Natalie winces as she hears the door to Zadie's bedroom slam closed. Moving cautiously to the cot, Natalie gently stoops and places Erin in, holding her breath as she steps away. Erin stirs and Natalie freezes, her heart sinking, before she settles again and Natalie is safe to step away.

Hot, sweaty, and with the thumping headache that only another glass of wine will cure, Natalie lowers herself back into the nursing chair. How is this her life? She blinks, not wanting to allow the tears that ache behind her eyes to escape. Her eldest child thinks she's a bitch. Her middle child accused her of not caring that she feels ill – *always such a drama queen, that girl* – and wildly prefers Natalie's best friend to her. Her youngest child seemingly can't bear to be around her. Her husband can't even be arsed to come home on time from work, and when he does come home all he does is make demands on her, never once thinking that perhaps all she wants is a bit of peace and fucking quiet. Her bones ache with exhaustion; there never seems to be enough time for sleep, for a shower, for five minutes by herself. From the cot comes a sucking sound as Erin places her thumb in her mouth in her sleep, and once again Natalie freezes, afraid she'll wake up. Is this *really* her life? Tiptoeing around on eggshells in case she upsets one of them? Sitting back in the chair, Natalie covers her eyes with her hands and allows herself the tiny luxury of imagining a life without any of them. A life where none of them exist, and she can finally be left alone. A life where she can read a book, lie in the bath uninterrupted for an hour, go for long hikes, drink coffee until ten o'clock at night if that's what she wants, knowing there is no one and nothing to get up for in the morning. Wouldn't it all just be so much easier, if she didn't have them to cater to? Guilt burrows its way under her skin at the thought. It wasn't always this difficult. If she's brutally honest, it's only been the last year or so that everything has felt quite so overwhelming. Peering between her fingers at the cot, at Erin's sleeping form, a tiny mound covered with a thin blanket, Natalie sighs as the truth twists deep in her gut. Wouldn't it all be so much easier if Erin had never been born?

# Pete

Closing the front door on Jake's retreating back, Pete leans his forehead against the cool wood and takes a deep breath. *What a shitshow.* Although he knows Emily will be heartbroken if this is the end of the road for her and Jake, Pete can't help but feel a tiny bit relieved that she might be able to go off to university without Jake as an anchor around her neck. The murmur of voices coming from overhead tells him that Natalie is upstairs with at least one of the older kids, and he lets his breath out in a long stream. He needs to find Vanessa while Natalie is otherwise occupied, and get her out of here.

Pausing as he reaches the open patio doors, Pete looks out onto the garden, his eyes running over the guests in search of Vanessa. For a moment, there is no sign of her and his heart skips, thinking that perhaps she realised what a mistake she was making and left, before a familiar peal of laughter comes from the shade of the apple trees at the rear of the garden and he spots her dark hair.

*Oh hell, no.* Stu stands beside Vanessa, laughing as she reaches out and touches his arm. Mari, Stu's wife, stands to one side, her expression unimpressed, and Pete pushes his way through the other guests until he reaches them, panting slightly. Of course, she would latch on to Stu. She must remember him as Pete's flatmate from first year.

'Pete? You all right, mate?' Stu frowns at him, and Pete nods, his mouth suddenly dry. 'I can't believe Vanessa is here!' Stu gestures in her direction and Vanessa raises her glass to her lips, giving him a coy smile as she does. Mari just raises an eyebrow. 'She was saying you guys are doing a brilliant job on that new housing estate. It must be weird to be working together after all this time.'

'Yeah, it is a bit.' Pete's tone is sharp and Stu frowns for a moment, glancing between Pete and Vanessa. 'I mean ... it was weird to see Vanessa's name in my inbox after so many years. But everything seems to be OK between us – working together, I mean.' Pete's laugh is too bright, too loud, its jagged edges catching in the air. 'Anyway, sorry to interrupt you guys, but could I just borrow Vanessa for a moment?'

'It was so good to see you again, Stu. It's been a long time. What is it? Twenty years?' Vanessa shakes her head. 'And it was great to meet you, Mari. I'm sure we'll run into each other again soon.' Vanessa gives Stu's hand a squeeze, smiling at Mari, and then follows Pete across the grass, her heels sinking into the soft ground. Behind them, Pete hears Mari raise her voice to Stu as they walk away.

Once they reach the patio doors, Pete gives Vanessa a little shove in the small of her back to get her inside, and then he grasps her elbow and drags her into the cloakroom, out of sight of the other party guests.

'Gosh, Pete, there was no need to be so rude. I wasn't going to say anything to Stu about us, if that's what you were worried about.' Vanessa widens her eyes, and Pete tugs at the door handle, making sure it's tightly closed.

'What the fuck are you playing at?' he hisses, pressing his face close to hers. Pete likes to think of himself as pretty easy-going, but this, today, has his blood hitting boiling point. 'Why the fuck are you here? How did you even know we were having a party? I certainly never invited you, and what in God's name do you think you were doing pulling that little stunt with Stu?'

'What do you mean, *that little stunt*?' Vanessa blinks, her face pale. 'I was just chatting to Stu, that's all. It's hardly a crime.'

'I mean, turning up here unannounced. At my house. *Again*. Chatting to Stu like none of this,' he gestures to her, and then to himself, 'has ever happened. Do you think you're being clever?' *How did she know about the party?* All Pete can think is that she's been on his laptop. Looked at his calendar, seen everything that he and Natalie have planned, which isn't much admittedly, but even so. He often leaves his laptop on the desk while he walks around site, and he's not exactly James Bond. His password is NatEm99. Hardly uncrackable. The thought of her poking around his private files makes him feel grubby and unsettled. There's something ... intense about it. Stalker-ish, almost. 'You shouldn't be here.'

'Pete, calm down.' Reaching up, Vanessa winds her arms around his neck and pulls him closer, her perfume invading his senses as her mouth meets his. For a moment – just a brief, tiny moment – there is the flicker of desire in Pete's belly, and then he grabs her hands and pulls them free, pushing her away from him. 'I knew you didn't mean it,' she says, running her tongue over her lips. 'I knew you'd see sense in the end.'

Pete pauses, his eyes narrowing. What the hell is she talking about? Of course he bloody meant it. And then it's as if a light bulb goes on over his head and he sighs, scrubbing his hands over his face.

'Jesus Christ, Vanessa. When I texted you to say I didn't mean things to end like that, I was talking about what I said about your dad. That was wrong of me, I should never have thrown your dad back in your face. But the rest of it ... I stand by what I said.' Pete pushes away the thought of Natalie stiffening in his arms for a second before she returned his kiss after his speech. 'I love my family, Vanessa. I want to be with them, not you.'

Vanessa lets out a sound as though Pete has punched her in the stomach, and when he looks up he sees her face harden, her shoulders pull back. Even so, there is something sloppy about the way she's looking at him, as though she can't quite focus. Too late, Pete realises that in the short time Vanessa has been in his house, at his daughter's party uninvited, she has sunk more than her fair share of wine.

'Vanessa ... Ness ...' Panic chills Pete in a cold wave that drenches him from head to foot. 'Don't ... Don't overreact.' Aware that Natalie is just upstairs – literally *above their heads* – Pete wants to get Vanessa out of the house as soon as possible before she can make a scene. After what's already happened at the party with Emily and Jake, Pete doesn't know if he can handle much more today. In fact, he's wishing he'd never pressed Natalie to hold this bloody party in the first place.

'Are you kidding me?' Vanessa's voice cracks, her mouth tightening into a thin line. 'You are the one who pursued me, Pete. *Oh, Ness, I'm so miserable, my wife doesn't understand me, she's let herself go, she doesn't want to* fuck *me.*' Her voice rises and Pete glances up at the ceiling, praying Natalie can't hear them.

'Ness, please. I think you should go, we can talk about things later.'

'Oh, can we? No, I think we can talk about it now, Pete.' She spits his name in his face. 'You chased me. Taking me out to dinner, kissing me in the office, making it clear you wanted me. Reminiscing about the past ... You knew exactly what you were doing.'

'Vanessa ...'

Her eyes are glassy when she turns her gaze on him now, her mouth trembling as she speaks. 'I waited for you – do you know that? After you ditched me for Natalie. I was so sure you would see sense eventually. We went through so much together – your parents moving to Oz and you staying behind, my mum and her many men – I didn't ever really believe you could just throw it all away, like what we had was nothing.'

'Vanessa, that was over twenty years ago. We were kids.'

'I *waited*,' she says again, a hint of urgency in her voice. 'And then when you came to work on the site, it was like you'd never left. You must have felt it, Pete? We still had that connection. I told you things I had never told anyone before and I thought finally I had someone who would actually *listen* to me, properly. You made me feel special, Pete. You made me think you weren't happy with Natalie. You said she was ill, that she made you miserable. You made me fall in love with you all over again.'

'That's not fair,' Pete says, a sour taste filling his mouth. 'You knew I was married. You knew I had kids – a new baby, for God's sake. You can't honestly have thought I would leave my family, leave a tiny baby?'

Vanessa looks up at him, and Pete realises with a sickening lurch that there is hope in her eyes. Hope, and a steely determination to not let go of whatever she thinks she's found. 'So, if there was no baby then things might have been different? Is that what you're saying?'

*Jesus Christ.* Something hard lodges in Pete's stomach, a sensation so unfamiliar to him – to kind, easy-going Pete who hates to cause a fuss – that it takes him a moment to realise what it is. It's hate. Hate, mixed with a healthy dollop of fear, for this… this *mad woman* who caught him in a moment of weakness and nostalgia and now holds all the cards, who can bring everything tumbling down around him.

'Get out.' Pete feels the ball of hate grow larger, as Vanessa stares at him, until he's sure it's going to burst out of his skin. 'I mean it. Everything that happened between us was a mistake, do you understand? Get the fuck out of my house and stay the fuck away from my family.'

Vanessa lets out a soft huff of laughter, so low it's little more than a breath. 'Oh, Pete, did you really think it would be that simple? Like you said, you're not my dad, so what gives you the right to tell me what to do?' She lifts her chin, giving him a glimpse of the Vanessa he sees at work, and reaches for the door handle. Relief floods Pete's body at the thought that, for all her strong words, she might just leave.

'No man speaks to me like that and gets away with it.' Vanessa pauses at the cloakroom door. 'No man gets to *treat* me the way you've treated me, Pete. Whether you like it or not, this isn't over.' She stares at him, her eyes shimmering with unshed tears before she wrenches the door open, flooding the small cloakroom with music and chatter from the party, the door swinging on its hinges behind her.

Pete's instinct is to hurry after her, out of the cloakroom, to make sure she really does leave, but he knows he has to sit tight for a few more minutes. If someone sees him coming out of the cloakroom seconds after Vanessa, then he won't have to worry about Vanessa spilling the beans to Natalie herself – someone else will do it in a heartbeat. Slumping against the wall, Pete swallows hard against the wave of nausea hitting him, that same old question battering his mind. *What the hell have I done?* Straining to hear the sound of the front door opening, he wonders if he's just made things infinitely worse. Vanessa was intense enough while he was sleeping with her... and she's already shown she's not entirely stable by showing up at his house with that file of incriminating photographs. Who knows how far a woman scorned will go?

# Natalie

Natalie ties her hair back into its messy bun and slicks lip gloss over her mouth before hurrying back downstairs as quickly and quietly as she can. Zadie's bedroom door is shut and Erin is finally asleep, and all Natalie can think about is getting her hands on a fresh glass of that good Sauvignon Eve brought from M&S.

Hurrying through the empty hallway, the baby monitor blinking on the small table there, a red light showing it needs to be charged, Natalie can almost feel the wine hitting her taste buds, but as she reaches the kitchen, she pauses. The refrigerator door is open, someone standing next to it with their head buried deep inside. *Eve*, Natalie thinks. *Eve is the only person here who would feel comfortable enough to root around in my refrigerator.* Even Stu doesn't make his own coffee when he visits, and he's known Natalie as long as she's known Pete. With that pulse fluttering at the base of her throat again, Natalie waits, not sure what to say. Is she still angry with Eve? She thinks so, but it's not a white-hot rage any more, just a simmering bubble. She opens her mouth to speak, but when the refrigerator door swings closed, it isn't Eve standing there holding a bottle of the good champagne Natalie is saving for when they cut the cake. She recognises the woman, who smirks at her, twisting the foil from the neck of the bottle, but it takes a moment to place her.

'Vanessa,' Natalie says as she pastes a smile on her face, although it's a cautious one. 'I didn't realise Pete had invited you to the party.' A ripple of gooseflesh raises the hair on Natalie's bare arms and she isn't sure why. Pete really is taking the cake now. She could kind of understand him inviting the old people from across the street – they would be able to see and hear that the Maxwells were having a party – but to invite his ex-girlfriend, even if she is his boss? Without even mentioning it to Natalie?

'Champagne? Oops.' Vanessa laughs as she pops the cork on the bottle, the bubbles fizzing up and over, splattering the kitchen tiles. She pours a glass and hands it to Natalie, and then pours herself a glass.

'I'm really sorry,' Natalie says, hating herself for apologising – this woman is in her house! Helping herself to her champagne, for God's sake. 'I'm not too sure why you're … Did Pete invite you to this party?'

'Something like that,' Vanessa says, and Natalie realises this isn't the first glass of wine Vanessa has had today.

'I just …' Natalie licks her lips, her mouth dry, not sure why she suddenly feels apprehensive. 'I wasn't expecting to see you here.'

'Life does like to throw a curveball, doesn't it?' Vanessa drains half the glass in one impressive mouthful, reaching towards the worktop for balance. *Definitely half-cut*, Natalie thinks.

'Look,' Natalie says gently, although inside she could throttle Pete. What the hell was he thinking, inviting Vanessa? He must have known it would make Natalie uncomfortable. 'I know you and Pete are working together, and I understand the two of you have history. He told me all about it.'

'Oh, did he?' Vanessa smiles, but it is wavering and doesn't meet her eyes. She reaches for the champagne bottle and tops herself up.

'I think we can both agree that you being here … It's a bit awkward, isn't it? I know it was all a long time ago, and you and Pete are working together now with no issues, but I think it might be best if you leave. This party is for our daughter, and I don't want there to be any … Well, you know. Maybe we could all go out for dinner some time instead?' It's the last thing Natalie wants to do, but she's fully aware that if she offends this woman, Pete could lose his contract.

Vanessa gives Natalie an appraising look, and she is suddenly very, very conscious of her messy hair, the grease lining her scalp, the way her stomach strains at the edges of the tired old sundress she wears. 'Oh darling,' Vanessa says, taking a sip of her champagne, not even trying to disguise the hint of a slur in her words. 'You really have no idea, do you?'

Natalie glances over Vanessa's shoulder, hoping to see Pete, or even Stu. Something about Vanessa doesn't seem right – besides the fact that she's had too much to drink, she seems completely at odds with the poised, articulate woman who came to the house to drop work files off to Pete – but she can't see either of them in the garden. 'No idea about what?' she says.

'I'm rather closer to your family than you think.'

'What?'

'Pete isn't the best husband and father, is he?' Vanessa frowns, giving off an expression that could be concern, though something in her gut tells Natalie this woman isn't concerned for her. 'How *are* you coping, Natalie, with the baby? It must be terribly difficult for you – you're basically a single parent, aren't you?' Vanessa cocks her head to one side, her eyes raking over Natalie. 'Pete at work all the hours God sends ... Coming home long after you've gone to bed ... It must be terribly difficult for you.'

'I'm not sure what it is you're trying to say.'

'Pete's speech was bullshit, wasn't it, Natalie?' Vanessa takes a step towards her, and Natalie feels a frisson of fear run through her. *Where is Pete?* 'All that stuff he was saying about your perfect life, and your perfect family. All lies. I think deep down you know that's true.'

'You need to leave.' Natalie's voice wobbles slightly and she clears her throat. 'Now, please. You weren't invited, were you? Don't make me call Pete to throw you out.'

'Oh, call Pete!' Vanessa throws back her head and laughs, champagne spilling over her fingers. 'I'd just love for Pete to come and hear what I've got to say.' Natalie stares at her, her heart in her mouth, and then Vanessa leans in, close enough for Natalie to smell the alcohol on her breath. 'Pete and I have been sleeping together for months. We're having an affair.'

It's as if someone has taken a sledgehammer to Natalie's knees as she steps back, her legs numb. 'What?'

'Me and Pete. We've been having an affair since Easter.'

'You're lying.' The words are a whisper, slipping out before Natalie can stop them. Her hands shaking, she takes a gulp of the warming champagne, but that only serves to make her mouth even drier. 'Pete would never do that to me, to the girls.' *Pete? An affair?* Natalie wants to laugh; it sounds so preposterous. She's known him for over twenty years. Yes, things have been a little difficult since she found out she was pregnant with Erin, but they're Natalie and Pete. A team. Solid. She's spent twenty years lying beside him – she could map every freckle and scar on his body, could tell you his wildest dreams and his biggest fears. She knows him better than she knows herself. She would know, wouldn't she? If Pete was cheating on her?

'Oh dear. You look a little pale,' Vanessa observes. 'You didn't really think Pete was a good man, did you? That he was actually working all those evenings he came home late. Natalie, don't you know all men are the same? Once a cheat, always a cheat. Isn't that what they say?'

'What do you want?' Natalie is sure she's lying. Revenge, for what Natalie and Pete did to her all those years ago. It has to be.

'Just to tell you the truth!' Vanessa says. 'I can prove to you Pete and I are … close. We've been talking about going to Australia – to see his parents, and to look at a plot of land. He wants to build us a house out there.'

That was their dream – well, Pete's – but Natalie was always going to go along with it, even if it has been slightly delayed. 'That doesn't mean anything,' she says, the words thick, almost strangling her. 'Everyone knows Pete wants to go to Australia some day and build a house. You could have overheard him telling Dave.'

'If I'm lying,' Vanessa says, 'why has Pete been coming home so late every night, Natalie? Do you know where he's been? Because he wasn't at the office, like he told you. He was with me.'

'I don't believe you,' Natalie says, her throat thick.

Vanessa gives Natalie a look full of pity. 'Oh, Natalie. Think about it. You know what I'm saying is true. Why on earth would Pete want to come back to this,' she gestures towards Natalie, to her too-tight sundress and greasy hair, then to the chaos that is their kitchen, 'when everything he really wants is in Montpellier Square.'

*Montpellier Square.* Natalie can see it in her mind's eye now: all the times she checked Find My iPhone and Pete's car was in the car park just down the street from the square. She'd thought he was taking the client out to dinner. Her face burns, and she feels like a fool. What contractor takes their client out to dinner three or four times a week?

'There's more,' Vanessa says, her words coming out in a hiss that makes Natalie think of low-bellied animals, of snakes and worms, of lies and deceit. 'That file I brought over? That wasn't anything to do with work. Ask Pete about it – that'll give you all the proof you need. I mean, I have it right here on my phone, I could show you now. But I think it should come from Pete.' She smiles – a quick, bright flash of white teeth – and then before Natalie can respond, she's gone, leaving Natalie winded and half wondering if she imagined it all.

*The file.* Natalie remembers the way Pete had snapped when he saw Vanessa in the kitchen. She'd thought it was because he didn't want the collision of work and home life, that he'd been annoyed with her for calling him back home, but now ... Swallowing down the nausea that makes her mouth fill with something bitter and unpalatable, Natalie heads for the stairs, wondering where Pete would have put the file, if he hasn't destroyed it already. Her heart sinks at the thought of searching her own bedroom for evidence of her husband's affair, sinks even further at the thought that her searching might disturb Erin, but she has to do it. She has to know for certain. Tiptoeing into the darkened room, she holds her breath as she pulls open the drawer of Pete's bedside table. Rummaging as stealthily as she can, Natalie lays her hands on an old watch strap, a business card for some plant hire rep, earplugs, a tiny screwdriver kit that looks as if it's come out of a Christmas cracker, but no file. She checks the wardrobe, pressing her hands in between neatly stacked T-shirts and inside suit covers. She lifts the mattress, her shoulders straining, but under the bed is clear, too.

As she creeps out of the bedroom, pulling the door gently closed behind her, Natalie glances across to the end of the hallway, to the spare bedroom. She rarely has cause to go in there – only to freshen up the sheets and give it a dust on the odd occasion when they've allowed Jake to stay over, or if Stu and Mari have too much to drink and can't drive home. Pete, though … Pete uses it all the time. He's set up an old Ikea desk and chair, and if he's really under the cosh he'll spend Saturday mornings in there doing his paperwork.

Fire sparking in her veins, Natalie pushes open the door and heads for the desk. There are tidy piles of paperwork on top, supplier invoices, a printed VAT return, drawings that Natalie can't make head nor tail of, but no file. The drawers contain staples, Post-it notes with curled edges and an old packet of gum; all of them are unlocked apart from the bottom drawer.

'Don't be so stupid,' she mutters under her breath, aware that she sounds crazy – that Pete's lies have made her *feel* crazy. 'He wouldn't leave it lying around. He would lock it away.' Running her eyes over the desk, her gaze snags on the plastic pen pot, on the leaky biros and the mound of paper clips, and the glint of a tiny silver key underneath them. She pulls it out, resting it in the palm of her hand as far below, in the garden, someone shouts Pete's name, and then there is raucous laughter and the clink of glasses. Natalie blinks as she stares at the key. It's so light in her hand, but it has the power to change everything.

Stooping, she slides the key in the lock and the bottom drawer glides open. Documents lie in the drawer – Pete's tax return, Erin's birth certificate, a copy of Emily's GCSE results – and there, buried beneath all the other papers, is a slim maroon wallet. Natalie slides it out and sinks down on to the bed. She feels sick and weak, the way she did when Zadie was four and Natalie had gastroenteritis and couldn't even keep water down.

'I don't have to look,' she tells herself, one finger sliding under the flap of the file even as she says it. Her pulse screaming in her ears, Natalie flips the file open, one hand going to her mouth as her stomach rolls over and over, an emotional rollercoaster of fear and pain. Vanessa's face stares up at her, her lipsticked mouth seeming to mock Natalie as her eyes roam further down the photograph, over Vanessa's perfect breasts and flat stomach, no hint of a single stretch mark. Natalie shuffles through, feeling more and more sick as she does, still telling herself that this doesn't mean anything. Vanessa could have just sent the photos to Pete, it doesn't mean he's guilty . . . until she gets to the final photo. Pete, clearly naked, asleep in a bed that is not theirs, in a room Natalie has never seen before but would probably have lusted after if she had seen it in an Instagram post. The ground seems to fall away from beneath her feet, the file and photographs sliding from her lap, and somewhere far away Natalie thinks she hears the sound of breaking glass over the noise of the party. She can't be sure, but she thinks it might be the sound of her heart shattering into a million pieces.

# *Pete*

Finally letting himself out of the cloakroom, Pete heads back towards the garden, a knot of anxiety in his stomach as he searches the grounds for Vanessa. Emily glares as he approaches, moving as if to turn her back on him, but he reaches out and lays a hand on her shoulder.

'What?' she asks belligerently, causing Sam, her best friend from school, to titter nervously.

'Have you seen Mum?' Pete lets her attitude slide, noticing the almost empty glass in her hand, and the way her eyes have the slightly glazed look of someone who has consumed more alcohol than they are used to.

'No,' Emily snaps, 'and I don't want to either. I'm not talking to her.'

Pete sighs. 'What's happened now?'

'I would tell you,' Emily shrugs, casting a sly glance in Sam's direction, 'but I'm not talking to you either.'

Pete doesn't have time for Emily's childish games right now and, resisting the urge to roll his eyes, he makes a mental note to have a word with her in the morning about her attitude. He was so proud of her earlier, of the way she's stepped up to the plate to help with Erin, but it's times like this that remind him that no matter how much of an adult she thinks she is, Emily is still a child. Shaking his head, he moves past her, combing the crowd of guests on the lawn for Natalie's blonde hair. He keeps telling himself he just wants to check in with her, make sure she's OK – especially if she's now had a row with Emily – but he knows it's really that he wants to make sure Vanessa hasn't got to her.

Speaking of Vanessa, there doesn't seem to be any sign of her, either in the house as he marched through from the cloakroom, or outside in the garden. No flash of dark hair, no lilting laugh in the rapidly cooling evening breeze. Pete is just allowing himself the luxury of fully exhaling and going in search of a pint when Eve lurches towards him, stumbling on her wedged heels over the wet, churned-up grass.

'Pete!'

Pete's eyes dart behind Eve, hoping for an escape route, but she's gaining on him and it seems there is no way of avoiding her. He's going to have to make small talk. As Eve trips towards him, Pete groans inwardly. Her eyes are red-rimmed and the tip of her nose is pink and shiny, a dead giveaway that she's been crying. *Great party, Pete*, he thinks to himself. Can it really be considered a celebration when half of the guests are either crying or arguing?

'Eve.' Pete throws on a smile as she reaches him, fumbling in her pocket before drawing out a tissue. 'Is everything OK?' He feels the first flicker of alarm as her mouth draws down. Has she spoken to Vanessa? Does she know what he's done? And then he bats it away, sure that if Eve knew what had gone on between him and Vanessa she wouldn't be crying – she would be screaming blue murder at him.

'Have you seen Natalie?'

'No, not since my speech.'

Eve gives a shuddering sigh. 'So you didn't hear what she said to me.'

'No, Eve, I didn't hear what she said to you.' Impatience makes Pete's tone short, and he glances over Eve's shoulder again, still looking for Natalie's messy bun, for the hot pink of her dress.

'She shouted at me in front of everyone – in front of all your guests,' Eve says, her eyes filling again. 'She *humiliated* me, Pete. All I did was offer to take Erin up for a nap and she just flipped on me, telling me Erin is her baby, not mine, and I'm smothering and interfering . . .' She gasps out a sob. 'And that I should just *back off*.'

'Well, she does have a point,' Pete says, distracted by movement at the edge of the patio doors. The light is beginning to fade, and for one heart-stopping moment he thinks it's Vanessa stepping out into the garden, but then he blinks, and he sees it's just Mari, making her way across the garden towards Emily.

'What the *fuck*, Pete?' Eve's voice is sharp, her brows knitting together as she turns her face to him. Her fists clench and her mouth tightens in fury.

'No, I didn't mean … Look, all I'm saying is, you do spend a lot of time at our house, Eve. I have to agree with Nat on that score. I know you think you're helping, but in all honesty, you're kind of making things worse.'

Eve stares at him, saying nothing, leaving him to fill the silence.

'It's great, you know, that you've been such a good friend to Natalie, but she needs to be able to bond with Erin on her own. You coming in and taking the baby out and getting her off to sleep, or cooking for Zadie and then throwing it in Nat's face that Zadie will eat for you and not for her—'

'I beg your pardon? That's not what's been happening at all!'

'All I'm saying is, just chill out a bit. Give Natalie some space. You *are* smothering her, and by doing that you're damaging her ability to bond with Erin properly. At the end of the day, Eve, you're not a Maxwell, and you never will be.' It feels good to tell Eve what he really thinks. He has had to listen to Natalie defending Eve's presence in their house for so many years – *She's lonely, Pete. She just wants company, Pete* – but recently Natalie has taken to spouting off about how Eve is always trying to take over with Erin, how smug she is when Zadie eats every scrap off her plate – and he's had to listen to Eve slag his husband-and-parent skills off for sixteen years. He's pretty sure that Eve was over the moon when Erin put a spanner in the works for their plans for Australia – and if Erin hadn't come along, he's no doubt that Eve would have tried to persuade Natalie it was a bad idea. There's no way Eve would give up Natalie and the kids without a fight;

it's almost as though she thinks they belong to her – as though they're her family, not his. There is a warm wave of relief that finally Natalie seems to have seen the light as well, and he wishes she was there so he could high-five her.

'Pete, none of what you've just said is true.' Eve's voice takes on a steely tone. 'Throwing it back in Natalie's face that Zadie ate my pasta? That's just fucking ridiculous. I don't just turn up at your house, Pete, day and night – not that you would know because you're never there. Nine times out of ten, I come over to your house because Natalie has called me and *begged* me to come and help her.' Eve's face takes on a triumphant expression as she realises that Natalie has never told Pete she calls Eve for help when Pete isn't around. 'That's right – she calls and begs me to take the baby. I've found her sobbing her heart out while Erin screams in another room more than once.'

Pete blinks, not sure he's hearing right. Natalie has been complaining about Eve coming over to the house so much – why would she do that if she was the one calling Eve? 'Maybe she has asked you to come over and help once or twice, but, Eve, you're cancelling your clients just so you can come over here. Natalie told me she saw your appointment book. You let yourself into our house, for Christ's sake. Where the fuck did you even get a key?'

'You bastard,' Eve hisses, her nostrils flaring as a vein begins to pulse at her temple. 'You really are a piece of shit, aren't you? Answer me this, Pete – if Natalie thinks I'm so mental, and such a stalker, why am I the one she told first about her pregnancy? Why am I the one who went to the dating scan with her?'

Pete wants to laugh, can feel the corners of his mouth tugging up into a smile. The woman really is bonkers. 'No, Eve, I think you'll find I was the one who went to the scan with Natalie.'

Eve crows with laughter, loud enough to make people turn and look in their direction. 'Come on, Pete, you've had two kids before. Didn't you wonder why there was only one scan at twenty weeks? Natalie had a dating scan at twelve weeks – three weeks *after* she told me she was pregnant.'

Pete feels all the air go out of him, the way he did when Stu took him down in a particularly fierce rugby tackle back when they played for the university first team. 'She didn't even know she was pregnant until she was twelve weeks gone,' he says.

Eve laughs again, shrill and rusty, the sound making Pete think of screws tightening into brickwork, the screech of metal on stone. 'No, Pete, that's just what she told you. Natalie found out she was pregnant when she was seven weeks. She told me two weeks later… it must have been around the end of May last year? She told me when we had lunch together, and when I asked, she said she hadn't told you because she didn't know how you'd react.'

Pete can't find the words to express how he feels right now. He thinks back to the beginning of that summer – of looking at university brochures and discussing degree courses with Emily, and how he had come home to find Natalie asleep, a pair of Emily's baby bootees clutched in one hand. He'd thought she was feeling sentimental about Emily flying the nest, when in reality… He swallows, feeling sick. Eve isn't lying.

'Maybe,' Eve leans in, hissing the words so he has to fight to hear her over the strains of Post Malone coming from the speakers, 'you should pay more attention to what's going on with your wife, instead of spending your evenings in that fancy gastropub in town with someone who isn't your wife.' Pete's gut clenches, as Eve looks him up and down with disgust. 'I guess I should leave the party now, Pete. Go back to my sad little lonely life, and leave you to your perfect family. It's clear you Maxwells don't want me around, and clearly I made a mistake thinking I meant more to you all than I actually do. But before I go, I do have one more thing to say.'

'What?' Pete is barely listening; he feels numb, as if he doesn't belong in this body.

*Natalie lied to me.* The thought flashes across his mind.

'I used to feel sorry for the two of you, you know? I thought it was such a shame neither of you could appreciate what you had. I couldn't understand how you were both so miserable, how neither of you seemed to be able to find happiness in this gift you've been given in Erin.' Eve shakes her head before she raises her eyes to his, her face solemn. 'After what I've seen lately, I don't think either of you deserve that happiness.'

# Natalie

Natalie blinks, her face blotchy and stiff with dried tears as she catches a glimpse of herself in the mirror over the vanity table. Glancing down, a wave of nausea hits her as Vanessa's face pouts up at her from the photographs where they lie scattered on the carpet. Sliding off the bed, Natalie scoops them up, shoving them back inside the file and locking it back in the drawer, before sliding her fingers over her dress. She feels dirty, tainted, as if there isn't enough soap in the world to make her feel clean again.

'Where's Natalie?' The words drift up through the open window from the garden below, and Natalie realises she's been gone for too long. Regardless of the fact that she's just found out her husband has been sleeping with his ex-girlfriend (*who is slimmer than you, prettier than you, and probably more enthusiastic in the sack than you,* a spiteful voice whispers in her ear), it doesn't change the fact that she still has a house full of guests and at least another two or three hours to get through before she is alone. *I can't do it,* she thinks. *I can't go out there and pretend like nothing's happened.* All Natalie wants to do is curl up into a ball and sob her heart out, right after she's punched Pete hard in the face. Her limbs feel watery, her head spacy and disconnected, and she realises she's felt this way before, as a child. After a full day of crying and accusing Natalie and her father of all kinds of things, her mother had self-medicated a little too hard, and it was at two o'clock in the morning that Natalie had watched the paramedics load her unconscious mother into an ambulance. A few hours later, her father had knocked on her door and told her to get ready for school. Natalie had felt this way then – weirdly disconnected, her arms and legs wobbly, sure she would fall as she tried to stand. But she hadn't. She'd been twelve years old, and it had taken everything she had to put on her uniform and pack her school bag, all the while knowing the neighbours had seen her mother being taken to hospital in the middle of night, knowing the other children would surround her, wanting to know what had happened. Now she thinks about it, there have been so many times that she's felt this way – none of them as bad as the hospital incident – after endless rows with her mother, a hard ball of hurt and anger in her chest as she forced herself out of the door, forced herself to carry on.

*I* can *do this*, she thinks, as she smooths her hair in the mirror and fans at her hot cheeks. *Just treat it like all the other times, one foot in front of the other. All I need to do is avoid Pete until the party is over.*

Stepping out onto the landing, she peeps in on Zadie, relieved to see a huddled mass in her bed, the covers pulled up high and the curtains drawn. Maybe she did feel sick after all, Natalie thinks, a pinch of guilt nipping at her. Hurrying down the stairs, hoping that not too many guests comment on her absence, Natalie halts abruptly on the bottom stair as Pete turns away from the front door, his face drawn.

He looks up, an expression she can't read crossing his face. 'Natalie.'

At the sound of her name, all plans to avoid him evaporate as Natalie is buffeted by a tsunami of rage, so burning and fierce that for a moment her vision blurs. 'Pete. Have you got something you want to tell me?' She watches as a range of emotions flit over his features – annoyance, anger, and something that looks a little bit like fear.

'I could ask you the same thing.'

Natalie steps down so she is face to face with him, although her face is more in line with his chest. 'How could you, Pete?'

'How—'

'Not only did you sleep with that ... that *whore*, but to invite her to our party? To the party we're throwing to celebrate *our daughter's success*? What kind of monster are you?' She watches as the colour runs from his cheeks, leaving him looking bleached out and pale. 'Yes, Pete, I know all about your girlfriend. I know it's been going on since Easter. I know you've told her I'm a shit wife and you're *so* unhappy. Perhaps you could have given me a bit of a heads-up on how you were feeling.'

Pete runs a hand through his hair and blows out a long breath. He looks oddly fragile, a cracked hourglass with the sand running out of it. 'Nat, it wasn't like that. I don't know what she's told you—'

'Enough, Pete. She's told me enough—' Natalie breaks off as one of the guests – she thinks it's Dave the foreman's wife – heads towards the cloakroom, giving them a quick smile. 'Hi. Yes, the loo is just there.' Natalie smiles, afraid her face might crack as the woman knocks on the door, only to find it occupied, and then stands waiting outside. Natalie grabs Pete's arm and drags him halfway up the stairs, out of sight. 'Vanessa couldn't wait to divulge all the juicy details, but let's be honest, Pete, she didn't really have to tell me much, did she? The proof was all there, right in front of my nose.'

Pete says nothing as Natalie hisses the words at him, aware that anyone in the hallway could potentially overhear their conversation.

'The file, Pete.' Natalie sighs, suddenly weary to her bones. What has she done to deserve this? Is she really that much of an awful person that she deserves to have her whole life ripped away from her? 'It was all in the file. Remember that day? When your mistress came to our house to deliver disgusting photos of herself to you, right in front of me? Did it give you some sort of kick, to see me there making a *fucking cup of tea* while she handed you naked photos of herself?' Natalie shudders, the images burnt on to her retinas.

'Of course not—'

'Did you have a good laugh at my expense when you were alone together? At poor, sad Natalie who has no idea what's going on in front of her eyes?'

'Natalie, please just listen—'

'And then the speech! Oh God, Pete, that cringey, maudlin speech.' Natalie lets out a laugh, looking up at the ceiling to disguise the fact that her eyes are smarting again. 'All a bunch of lies. Everything you said, about how much you loved us, how proud you were – it was all just a load of rubbish. All the time you've been shagging that woman behind my back.'

Pete swallows and reaches out a hand as if to pull Natalie towards him, but she raises her hands and takes a step back. 'Natalie, please, I swear it wasn't the way you think it was. I do love you, and I am so—'

'You love me?' Natalie shakes her head, the words bitter on her tongue. She can barely look at him, at the face she's loved for over twenty years. She'd seen him first, long before she'd knocked him flying with her books. He'd been at the bar with his arm around a girl with long, dark hair trailing halfway down her back, but Natalie knew what she was doing, that day when she crossed the quad and knocked him over. Natalie hadn't thought about the dark-haired girl again after that day, and neither, it seemed, had Pete. (*Had that girl been Vanessa? Had she come to visit Pete on campus?* Natalie doesn't know; she hadn't even looked at the girl's face.) Now it looks as though it's come back to bite her. *Once a cheater, always a cheater.* 'If you loved me,' she says, her voice rancid with spite, a toxic anger lacing every word like belladonna, 'you wouldn't have been spending all those evenings having sex with your *ex-girlfriend*, while I was here alone, taking care of your children. Up half the night with your baby, exhausted and lonely, wondering why my husband would rather be at work than with me. If you loved me, you would have been here. You would never have lied to me.'

Pete stares at Natalie, his face thunderous.

'Let's talk about that, shall we?' he says, as a chill runs down Natalie's spine at his icy tone. 'You're not exactly innocent in all this.'

'What are you talking about?'

'When did you find out you were pregnant with Erin?' His eyes never leave her face, and she feels as if she's just stepped into a lift, her stomach dropping away.

'I told you when.'

Pete laughs, a sneering snicker of a laugh. 'When, though, Natalie? How many weeks were you?'

*He can't know.* She licks her lips, worrying at the tingly dry patch on the corner of her mouth that she just knows is going to turn into a cold sore. 'I told you. Twelve weeks.'

'Fuck's sake, Nat. I might not have been honest with you about Vanessa, but you're standing here lying to my face.' Pete shakes his head and for a moment she thinks he's going to walk away. 'Eve told me. She told me you found out you were pregnant weeks before you said anything to me – you told her before you told me! You took her to a scan, for fuck's sake.'

Natalie's chest feels tight, and for a moment her breathing falters as she takes in the betrayal. *Eve told him.* Pete is still talking, but she can't hear him over the roar of her pulse, the crashing of blood in her ears. 'What?'

'You left it so long to tell me because you had already made the decision,' Pete says. 'You knew if you left it long enough, it would be too late for us to have any other option.'

'No,' Natalie says, her head still spinning from the fact that Eve – Eve! – has betrayed her confidence to Pete. The two people she loves best in the world have shattered her trust in a matter of minutes. 'That wasn't the reason, Pete.' She faces him, stares at him long and hard. 'I didn't tell you before because I didn't know if you would have my back.'

'That's ridiculous. I've always had your back.'

'Except for when you had Vanessa on hers,' Natalie says tartly.

'I didn't tell you because I knew you would want to get rid of the baby, and I knew that wasn't what I wanted. I might not have told you straight away, but that's small fry compared to what you've done. You've destroyed our family, Pete. Everything you said out there was lies. I should just throw you out now, tell all our guests what you've done.'

'Natalie, this wasn't all me.' Pete's voice is low, and she has to strain to hear him. 'You have to take some responsibility for what's happened.'

'Are you kidding me?' Natalie's hackles rise, but as Pete reaches out and grips her hand, she falls silent.

'You knew I wouldn't want another child, and you kept the pregnancy from me for weeks. Even though I told you I wasn't happy about having another baby, you went ahead and did it anyway, without any regard for how I might feel or how it might affect our other kids.' She tries to pull away but he won't let her, his fingers digging into the back of her hand. 'I was lonely, too, Nat. You pulled away from me – I could go for days without you exchanging even a word with me – and you don't seem to see what's going on around you at all. Look at Zadie. She's not eating, she's wetting the bed, playing up at school. And Emily can't wait to get away to university.'

'You keep giving Zadie juice—'

'No, Nat.' Pete's voice is firm – the voice he uses when the kids are playing up, or when a client is refusing to pay an invoice. 'You have to stop burying your hand in the sand.'

'You don't know what's going on, Pete, you're never here! Instead of coming to school with me when they said Zadie had been bullying people, you were off having a roll in the hay with that … that …'

'Zadie's behaviour has got nothing to do with juice at dinner – she's playing up because our whole family dynamic has changed, and you have to take some responsibility for that.'

Natalie sags against the wall, feeling sick with the realisation.

She had never seen it that way, had never thought of it at all. All she's been able to focus on since the day Erin was born – since before, really; since the day she first felt that crippling exhaustion and nausea – was just making it through to the end of the day without killing anyone or wanting to throw herself under a bus.

'None of that excuses what you've done,' she says, but she can hear in her own voice that the fight has gone out of her – for now, at least. 'But maybe you're right. I was so focused on this baby, on the idea of a new life, that maybe I didn't properly think about the effects it would have on our family. Maybe this is all my fault. Maybe I was the one who made a horrible mistake.' As she raises her eyes to look at him, tears spill over her cheeks, dripping onto her dress and darkening the hot pink to a deep rose. 'Maybe if I hadn't gone ahead with the pregnancy then none of this would have ever happened. Maybe it would have all stayed the same, and we would still be happy, Emily and Zadie would be happy. Maybe it would have been better all round if Erin wasn't here at all.'

# Pete

Natalie stares at him for a moment, her eyes wide and red-rimmed, as Pete tries to piece together a response – something that won't place all the blame on her, that will acknowledge what he's done without firing up her temper again – but before he can speak, she presses a hand to her mouth and hurries back up the stairs.

Pete turns and walks down the stairs, freezing in horror as he rounds the corner into the hallway. Vanessa is standing by the cloakroom door, her jacket over one shoulder. Her face is pale and there are the faintest smudges of black mascara beneath her eyes. She stops dead for a fraction of a second, before she puts her head down and moves to push past him, towards the front door, leaving the scent of alcohol on the air.

'Vanessa!' Pete hisses after her. *How much of that exchange with Natalie did she hear?* That's his first thought before a surge of anger makes his blood warm, his pulse beating loudly in his ears. 'Vanessa! Do you know what you've done? What the hell did you say to her?'

Vanessa pauses at the front door, her hand on the latch. 'Just the truth, Pete.' Before he can respond she is out of the door, leaving him alone in the hall, shaking with rage. Everything is falling apart, just as he'd feared. Scrubbing a hand over his face, Pete takes a deep breath. There is still a house full of guests, his daughter – even though she's not exactly a ray of sunshine today – is supposed to be celebrating her eighteenth birthday, and his wife is in no fit state to host, thanks to his actions. *Two more hours*, he tells himself. *Just a couple of hours more and then I can kick people out without it looking weird, and then I can try and piece my life back together.*

Wearily, Pete moves to the kitchen, forcing a smile at the guests who linger in the doorway, pushed inside by the dimming light outside and the unseasonable chill in the air as the sun drops ever lower in the sky.

'Beer bucket is dry.' Stu appears beside him, and Pete realises that could be another reason why people are hovering near the kitchen. 'You OK, bud? Em seemed a bit upset earlier, but Mari had a word with her, and I think she's OK now.'

'Oh, great. Yeah. Yeah, all good.' He hands Stu a box of Budweiser, and as people begin to drift away Pete turns to the top cupboard – the one that is a jumble of old medicines and sun creams – and fumbles at the back. A sigh of relief escapes him as his fingers snag the square corner of the box, and as he pulls it towards him he can almost taste it, can almost feel the nicotine rush as the fresh scent of tobacco rises from the Benson & Hedges packet. Checking to make sure he is unobserved, he tucks the cigarettes into his shirt pocket and moves quickly through the garden, towards the apple trees at the back. Beyond the trees there is a fence with a worn gate, the timber split in places and the paint flaking away in crumbly layers as he jiggles the rusting bolt. On the other side is peace. The woods stretch out before Pete, the ancient oaks, ash and hazel trees clustered as far as the eye can see, keeping the house blanketed from the world outside.

It would be easy to get lost – the trees are so densely clustered together in some parts and the stream can be treacherous, especially after heavy rain – but Pete knows these woods like the back of his hand. He spent his childhood playing in them, making dens when he was a little kid, hearing the haunting legends attached to them and then sitting round a campfire with his mates when they were teenagers, telling ghost stories, trying to scare his little brother. Now he cuts through them several times a week – they all do. The route through the village to the shops and the school takes in a treacherous main road, but to cut through the woods, following the carpet of old leaves making up the woodland trail, twisting its way along the stream, is safe and quiet, the kids able to run ahead. He used to make dens with Emily in these woods, and again with Zadie when she was younger. Never quite taking his eyes off them, knowing how it easy it is to get lost, whether you know the woods well or not.

The thought of a tiny Zadie brings forth thoughts of Natalie, and he slides his hand into his pocket and pulls out the cigarettes, almost dropping the lighter in his haste to get one lit. As he inhales, the sharp acrid smoke hitting his lungs in a rush that makes his head spin, he's aware that once again he's lying to Natalie. He'd promised to quit smoking after they'd been to the scan at twenty weeks, and he'd seen Erin dancing on the screen, her tiny hands and feet waving and kicking.

After he'd pulled out his cigarettes on the way back to the car, Natalie had frowned. 'Seriously, Pete? When are you going to quit? You're going to have three kids that depend on you. You can't be there for them when your lungs are all black and wizened.'

He'd stubbed the cigarette out immediately, snapping the rest of them in half and shoving them deep into the bin before pulling her in and kissing her on the head. 'You're right. Filthy habit. Time to quit.' He'd meant it when he said it – of course he had – but he'd still found himself asking the cashier for twenty B&H the next time he'd stopped at the garage for petrol. *Just for emergencies*, he'd told himself. Well, if this doesn't count as an emergency, he doesn't know what does.

As Pete lets out a stream of smoke, he finds himself hoping it doesn't cling to his clothes before he shakes the thought away. He's done far worse lately than hide the occasional illicit cigarette from Natalie, and goose pimples rise on his arms as he thinks of her face, the way she had looked at him when she confronted him about Vanessa. He's never seen her look at him that way before. She'd looked at her mother that way, the day her parents told Natalie and Pete to abort their accidental pregnancy or Natalie would no longer be welcome in their home. Natalie had stared at her mother, and then simply got to her feet and walked out of the room, with a quiet, 'Come on, Pete.' Natalie had never spoken to either her mother or father again after that day.

Is this really it for them? Is Natalie really going to call time on their marriage without giving him a chance to properly explain? Pete knows that deep down he can forgive Natalie for lying to him about when she found out she was pregnant; if he's honest, he thinks he could probably forgive her anything. He knew the moment she sent him crashing to the concrete with those bloody books in her hands that she was meant to be his, and by the time he'd dropped her back at her halls after their first date, he knew he was going to marry her. He remembers coming back to the flat he shared with Stu and telling him that very thing, while Stu scoffed and laughed and offered him a hit on his bong.

*It can't be over. There has to be a way for me to salvage this, to make her realise that we're meant to be together.* Pete stubs out his first cigarette, scratching it hard against the concrete fence post to make sure all the embers are out, before pulling another from the pack. The day Natalie told him she was pregnant with Emily was the best day of his life. He'd already been thinking that he wanted to propose to her, but was unsure of how she would respond. They were in their final year, working on their dissertations, and Natalie had expressed an interest in travelling with a group of girlfriends afterwards. Pete couldn't stomach the thought of her not being there, of her travelling around Europe without him, even though he would never have stopped her if that's what she wanted. He would have waited for her. But as it turned out, he didn't need to wait for her. She told him she was pregnant, and it seemed the most natural thing in the world to propose after that. If he remembers rightly, he thinks he cried a little bit when she said yes. Has he really thrown all of that away for a woman he doesn't even care about? Pete doesn't know what he was thinking, starting an affair with Vanessa. It almost felt like an accident, even though he knows it wasn't – that part of him enjoyed the attention, that there was a layer of nostalgia there, as if Vanessa represented a life before kids and marriage – but if he confesses that to Natalie, she's liable to kill him.

At the thought of Vanessa, he feels a fresh surge of anger run through him, and he snaps the lighter, bringing the flame to the end of a fresh cigarette. *What the fuck was she thinking, telling Natalie like that?* If she thinks this will drive him into her arms, she's got another think coming. He doesn't want to see her ever again – but he will, just to tell her what he thinks of her. Pete will take great pleasure in telling her he never wants to lay eyes on her again, in telling her that if she contacts his family, he will kill her. He only hopes that none of the other guests were privy to her big reveal; that none of them witnessed her rip Natalie's world apart. Especially Eve. She'll be thrilled with this news.

*Eve.* Pete takes a deep drag on the cigarette and holds the smoke in his lungs, imagining it seeping into his bloodstream. She's another problem. What was it Princess Diana said? *There are three of us in this marriage.* Something like that, anyway, and that's exactly how Pete feels, even more so after his confrontation with her earlier. How could Natalie confide in her before Pete, knowing as she does how Eve feels about him? Pete knows Eve has spent years whispering in Natalie's ear about how Pete isn't good enough for her. He thinks of what she said to him earlier, before she flounced out of the party. *You should pay more attention to what's going on with your wife, instead of spending your evenings in that fancy gastropub in town with someone who* isn't *your wife.* Does she know about Vanessa? Or did she just see them that night of the leaving drinks? His mouth is dry as he breathes out a long ribbon of smoke. If Eve knows about the affair with Vanessa, it will be all the ammunition she needs to have Natalie packing his bags and throwing him out on the street.

Pete blinks, squinting as smoke curls around his head, suddenly seeing himself in a dingy one-bedroomed flat on the outskirts of Maidstone, pacing as he waits for Natalie to drop the girls off to spend the weekend with him. He sees himself at the McDonald's near the Lockmeadow cinema complex, Happy Meals on the table as Zadie picks listlessly at her food and Erin screams, the other parents – whole, happy families – casting him sympathetic glances, as they wonder what he must have done to become the weekend dad, the dad who doesn't even know his kids any more. And where would Natalie be? Suddenly feeling sick, he stubs out this cigarette, too, even though it's barely half-smoked.

Pete might be upset with Natalie for lying to him, but what he's done is far, far worse, especially as he knew deep down that she wasn't coping very well with things. Instead of facing things head-on, he has to admit he has buried his head in the sand, too. It's been easier to slope off with Vanessa than to sit down with Natalie and ask what's wrong, what can he do to help fix it. He thinks of her face as she told him that maybe all of this was her fault. Her eyes had been curiously blank, her voice thin and list-less, croaky with tears. Pete might have lied about a lot of things, but one thing he said to Vanessa is true. Natalie isn't well – hasn't been well since Erin was born – and Pete was too afraid to do anything about it, choosing instead to hide away at work, or in Vanessa's bed. Now, his stomach churns and his hands shake, and his tongue feels fuzzy and thick with the taste of cigarettes. He thinks of the way Natalie spends so much time slumped on the sofa, or lying blank-faced on the bed, of the disconnect she seems to feel between herself and Erin. *She hates me, Pete.* His mother had suffered awful post-natal depression after the birth of his younger brother, although he didn't realise it at the time – he'd only been five, after all – but she'd since described it to him as having a fierce black dog snapping at her heels. She'd once confessed that the thought had crossed her mind that perhaps Pete and his brother would be better off without her. *Is that how Natalie feels?* He knows Natalie has been struggling – thinks now that maybe she is depressed – but surely, *surely*, she wouldn't do anything to harm herself or the baby? Would she?

# *Natalie*

As she heads back upstairs to the sanctuary of her bedroom, Natalie feels woozy and drained. She feels the way she did last time she went for lunch with Eve and it turned into a night out, months before she found out she was expecting Erin. Her head spins, her vision blurring the outline of the bed into an indistinct blob, as she stumbles inside and closes the door, leaning against it and shutting her eyes, before hurrying into the en suite bathroom.

*Vanessa wasn't lying. Pete cheated on me.* Suddenly nauseous, Natalie's mouth fills with saliva and she retches over the toilet, giving herself an eerie case of déjà vu. She spent a lot of time in this position in the early days of her pregnancy. Finally, her stomach muscles aching and her mouth sour, there is nothing left to come up, and Natalie stands on shaking legs, moving to the sink. *Pete really did cheat on me.* As she leans down and slurps cold water directly from the tap, swishing it around her mouth, Natalie feels sick again. Even though she had seen the file, had looked at the photos Vanessa had hidden in there, part of her was still hoping all of this was some terrible mistake. That Vanessa had somehow faked the photo of Pete asleep in her bed. If there had only been the pictures of Vanessa, naked and hungry, Natalie could well have believed it was all a set-up – there was something in the other woman's eyes as she said Pete's name that made Natalie think perhaps she was a bit unstable, desperate, even – but there is no explanation for the photograph of Pete. *He must have seen it. Why didn't he get rid of the file?* A horrible thought strikes her as she raises her eyes to the mirror, dabbing at her mouth. What if Pete kept the file in the hopes that Natalie would find it? What if he wanted her to know about the affair – he might even have told Vanessa to spill the beans. Pete's never been the bravest, and that would have made things easier for him – he didn't exactly deny it when she challenged him. Something clenches deep inside her gut, and Natalie presses her hand to her stomach. Somehow, the thought of that is even worse. The thought that it wasn't just a quick shag, a roll in the hay to boost Pete's ego. The thought that Pete might actually be in love with this woman – this woman who shared a part of Pete's life that Natalie wasn't around for – that he might leave Natalie and the kids for her, makes her feel physically ill.

Her reflection in the mirror is puffy and pasty, her skin dry in some patches, oily in others, her make-up sweated off in the stress of trying to hold herself together throughout the party. Her hair, escaping from the messy bun she tied it in, is greasy at the scalp, in desperate need of a wash, while the ends are dry and brittle, split ends making it frizzy and unmanageable. Natalie hasn't had a haircut since just before Erin was born eight months ago, hasn't had her highlights done for even longer. No wonder Pete looked elsewhere, she thinks. She's a different woman from the one who sat across from him and told him they were going to have another baby. At the thought of that night, fresh tears spring to her eyes. While Natalie knew Pete would be resistant to the idea of another baby initially, she honestly thought it would be different from how the past few months have turned out.

Natalie had thought when she made the decision to go ahead with the pregnancy that Erin would be like Emily and Zadie – both easy, happy babies. There had been teething problems with Emily, of course. Natalie was barely more than a child herself when she was born, and she often felt as though she was winging her way through bringing her up, but Emily was placid and slept well, and Natalie had often wondered why some mothers complained all the time. Zadie had been the same, and as Emily was almost ten when Zadie was born it had all felt rather easy.

Natalie had been back at work six months after Zadie's birth, and Zadie was at a brilliant nursery she'd found, so Natalie never really felt as though she'd had to sacrifice anything for her. Erin, though … Natalie sighs. Erin was difficult before she was even born, keeping Natalie up all night with heartburn and needing to wee every hour, it felt like. And then the birth … Remembering the fear and panic of that day, and the trauma of the days that followed, is enough to make Natalie's pulse triple.

Maybe that was when she should have realised nothing was ever going to be the same. Pete wasn't around a lot in the early days with Emily, as he worked day and night at a construction consultancy firm, and then when Zadie was born Pete had already gone freelance and was in the process of setting up his own company. Natalie hadn't felt any resentment towards him because she knew he was doing it all for them. This time, though, she should have known when Pete took that phone call in the hospital room, leaving her alone and in pain, that things were already different.

'You stupid, stupid woman,' Natalie whispers at her own washed-out reflection. 'Client dinners? And how many times can a drainage run get blocked?' She should have known. Although now she's being truly honest with herself about things, didn't a part of her enjoy the fact that Pete wasn't around? Yes, she struggled with Erin – the child never sleeps, and God knows if there's one thing Natalie needs, it's sleep – and she could have done with Pete's help, but she's not convinced he would have even been that much help. Look at how he is with Zadie – he never wants to discipline her; instead he just tuts at her and tips her upside down on the sofa until she laughs. No, the truth is that a tiny part of Natalie enjoyed not having Pete at home. She liked the brief hour or two when Erin did settle for the night, when she could watch reality TV without Pete's judgement, without having to make conversation when all she wanted to do was stare blankly at the flickering screen in front of her. She often felt a wave of relief at getting into bed before he came home, making sure her breathing was deep and even when she heard the front door open, so he wouldn't slide his hands under the baggy T-shirts she's taken to sleeping in, pressing himself against her back in that insistent way he has.

*Maybe it's my fault.* Can she blame Pete for looking elsewhere when she did turn her back on him? They haven't slept together since before Erin was born, Natalie afraid of hurting her hysterectomy scar at first, and then just full of bottled-up resentment towards him, so much so that every time she thought about sleeping with him, it felt like some sort of reward, one Pete didn't deserve. God, what a mess. A horrible, heartbreaking mess.

Natalie opens the door of the bathroom cabinet, intent on pulling out make-up wipes to fix her face before going back to the party for the final hour or so, telling herself she's faked it all day, she can fake it for a tiny bit longer, when the white box of diazepam catches her eye. It's still hidden behind the tampons, still unopened, but now she gently eases it out and tugs out a blister packet. *Maybe Eve is right. Maybe I do need a little bit of help.*

Natalie has always been resistant to the idea of medication, an idea that seems a little outdated now that mental health isn't something to be hidden or kept secret, but growing up in a household where her mother popped a pill for every ailment (even those that didn't exist) pressed Natalie into avoiding even paracetamol if she could. Now, though, she understands. The thought of having to go back to the party, knowing Pete lied to her, knowing Eve betrayed her, knowing Emily hates her, is almost too much to bear. She can't do it without a little bit of help, something to blur the edges a little so it doesn't feel so painful. Pressing against the foil, she pops two pills into her hand. The box says take one, and she falters for a moment before filling the small water glass on the side of the sink and throwing back both of the pills with a slug of lukewarm tap water. Almost immediately she feels better.

She can do this. Moving silently across the carpet, Natalie perches on the end of the bed, on Pete's side, listening out for any noise from the adjoining bedroom where Erin sleeps. There is only silence, and Natalie lets out a long breath. *Just ten minutes, that's all I need.* Just ten minutes to let the pills kick in and then she'll go back down the stairs, back to the party. Natalie shuffles round, so her head rests on Pete's pillow, smelling the faint scent of Tom Ford Ombre Leather emanating from the pillowcase. She loves that aftershave; she buys it for him every Christmas. She doesn't know if she'll ever be able to smell it again without thinking of today, of this party. Flipping over the pillow, Natalie closes her eyes, feeling as though her limbs are melting into the mattress. She thinks about Pete and Vanessa, wonders if Pete really will leave her and go and shack up in that fancy flat in Montpellier Square. She finds the idea isn't as devastating or as terrifying as it was a short while ago, her emotions dulled and pleasantly numb. If she'd known the pills were going to make her feel like this, she would have taken them a lot sooner. The last thought she has before oblivion creeps in, darkening the corners of her mind, is about Pete. If they could turn back the clock, would Pete want to get rid of the baby? If she'd told him when she first saw those two pink lines on the test, her heart turning over in her chest, does she think Pete would have tried his hardest to make her change her mind? *Maybe.* Maybe if she had the time again, she would change her mind herself. All she can think right now is that she would do anything to fix things, to have things go back to the way they were before.

# *Pete*

As Pete inhales and lights his third cigarette, he feels nauseous, remembering why he thought he should give it up in the first place. He stinks now; he can smell the cigarette smoke on his own clothes and hands, and he feels a wave of self-loathing. He knows he should return to the party – between the confrontation with Vanessa, his hissed argument with Eve, and now the bomb that has been dropped on Natalie, he knows he's been too absent, and that people will begin to notice he's not around. That could be a metaphor for his entire life at the moment, Pete thinks, but still he doesn't move from the shelter of the treeline at the edge of the woods, not quite ready to return and put on a fake smile and exude false joviality.

He's not sure how long he stands there, cigarette smoke hanging in the air as raindrops from the earlier storm drip from the summer leaves onto the mulchy floor below, long enough for his back to begin to ache and his hands to get cold.

'Dad?' Pete's ears prick up at the faint call of his name. It's Emily's voice, and the impatient tone tells him this isn't the first time she's called out to him. 'Dad!'

Stifling a sigh, Pete swipes the cigarette over the fence post and collects his butts, before reaching over to unlatch the bolt and slipping back into the garden. As he stuffs the cigarette butts deep into the compost bin (*hiding the evidence*, he thinks) Emily is still calling him, but he can't see her as he emerges from between the apple trees.

'There you are!' Stu appears beside him, clapping him on the back so hard he almost winds Pete. Stu is clearly a little worse for wear, his eyes slightly bloodshot and sleepy in a way that weirdly reminds Pete of Bagpuss, that old cat that used to be on the telly. 'Where the hell have you been, bro? I've hardly seen you all night.'

'Oh, you know what it's like,' Pete says, his stomach clenching. 'It's like a wedding – when it's your own, you never get to see half the people you want to.'

'I still can't believe Vanessa was here,' Stu says. 'Even more than that, I can't believe Natalie was OK with you inviting her – Mari would have had my guts for garters.' Stu lets out a roar of laughter as Pete tries on a smile that wobbles across his face.

'I thought I heard Emily calling me?' Pete changes the subject, not wanting to talk about Vanessa. Not now. Not ever.

'Oh, yeah.' Stu looks surprised, and Pete realises he's had even more to drink than he'd first thought. Stu has always been a bit crap at holding his drink, and Pete wouldn't be surprised if Mari carts him off home soon. 'Mari was talking to Emily, she said something about the cake.'

'Is Natalie not about?' Pete scans the guests, but there is no sign of his wife.

'Not seen her. Emily was calling for her, too.' Stu nudges him with a sly wink. 'Nipped off for a quickie, did you? I wish Mari was still that adventurous.'

Pete feels suddenly nauseous again, and it's got nothing to do with the dose of nicotine he's just inflicted on his body. 'I had better go and see what Em needs.' Clapping Stu on the shoulder, he heads for the kitchen, letting out a sigh of relief when he sees Emily at the kitchen worktop, rummaging in one of the drawers.

'Did you call me?'

Emily whips her head around, her eyes narrowing. 'Where have you been? I've been calling you for ages.' Before he can come up with a valid excuse which is not 'fighting with your mum' or 'smoking so many cigarettes I want to puke', Emily carries on. 'Mari said people are starting to make noises about leaving, and we should probably cut the cake. I can't find a lighter for the candles and I don't know where Mum is.'

Pete hadn't realised how late it was. The sun is below the treeline now and the garden has taken on a distinctly gloomy air, the first prickle of stars beginning to stud the sky. 'This is the perfect time to do the cake,' he says. 'How is anyone going to see the candles in broad daylight?' Overwhelmed by a surge of affection, he pulls Emily towards him, kissing the top of her head. 'Sorry about earlier. For my crappy speech and for arguing with Jake.'

Emily scowls up at him, but she doesn't pull away. 'Go and find Mum, will you? We can't do the cake without her. And you stink of fags.'

Pete gives Emily one last squeeze and reaches into his pocket to toss her the lighter. 'Don't tell Mum.' He is about to step away into the hallway to go in search of Natalie when a shadow falls across the doorway.

'Mum.' Emily looks up. 'We need to do the cake before people start to leave.'

Natalie nods and moves slowly to the kitchen drawer, pulling it open and rifling through the old takeaway menus and bunches of keys; no one knows what they unlock any more. 'We need a lighter.' Her voice is thick and oddly blurry.

'We've got one,' Pete says, a flutter of nerves rippling in his belly. He's almost afraid to look at Natalie in case she says something about Vanessa and what he's done in front of Emily.

'Oh.' Natalie blinks, and Pete moves across the kitchen and lifts the heavy cake. The three of them step across the garden, Emily's voice ringing out above the music as she tells everyone it's time to cut the cake. Stu reaches out and lowers the volume on the speaker, and as Pete places the cake on the table, he can't help but notice that Natalie seems a little unsteady on her feet. Where did she go after she hurried away from him? He knows it's a party, but has she been drinking? Pete saw her with a glass of wine earlier, but unless she's been knocking it back secretly, he doesn't think she's had enough to get plastered.

There are exclamations as people drift over to the table and spy the cake. It's an extravagant three-tier affair with stars exploding out of the top, Emily's name written in intricate swirly icing across the cake board. Natalie would usually make the kids' birthday cakes, but for obvious reasons this year it was never going to happen. Emily had asked Pete for his bank card and ordered her own cake, and now Pete thinks perhaps he should double-check his bank statement to see how much it actually cost. However much it is, it's worth it to see the smile on Emily's face now, after what happened earlier. Ignoring the ripple of unease spreading through his body at the memory of Jake's last words to him – *You're going to regret this, Pete. Trust me* – Pete leans over and takes the lighter from Emily, cupping his hands around the candles until all eighteen of them are lit. A pitchy rendition of 'Happy Birthday' fills the air, and as Emily leans down and blows out the candles, Stu pulls out his phone and takes a short video.

'Let's have a photo of all of you together,' Stu calls out. 'Em's last birthday at home.' Pete wants to shake his head at that, wanting to say that he always wants Emily to celebrate at home, that he doesn't want anything to ever change, but instead he just reaches out to put an arm around Natalie's shoulder. She frowns, looking down at where his hand rests on her shoulder, and then steps away, placing Emily beside him, then Zadie, then herself, coming to stand on the edges.

'Pete, if you just want to do a little TikTok dance for us, we know how you love a knees-up when you've had a drink,' Stu says, waving the phone in his direction. 'I reckon I can get you to go viral.' Emily groans as the rest of the guests laugh, but Natalie stays poker-faced.

'Say big birthday bollocks!' Stu shouts as Mari nudges his arm and old Mrs Noyce sucks in a shocked breath. Zadie laughs, and Stu presses the button on his phone, immortalising the moment forever. As Emily claps and reaches for the kitchen knife to start cutting up the cake, Pete watches Natalie as she steps to one side, visibly distancing herself from them all, and his heart turns over.

Emily hands out slices of cake, rich buttercream oozing between the layers of vanilla sponge, and as Stu reaches the table, he holds out the phone.

'Lovely pic, don't you reckon? I could probably be a professional photographer.'

'In your dreams, Uncle Stu,' Emily laughs.

Pete leans in and takes in the photo. Emily looks radiant, despite her earlier tears, and Pete is half glad he threw Jake out when he did. Zadie grins up at the camera, a smudge of dirt on her cheek and that bright gap in her teeth all you can see as she smiles widely. Pete is also smiling, and he thinks as he looks at the photo that you could almost think they were a happy family. Almost think there is nothing wrong, until he looks at Natalie in the picture. Her face is oddly blank, her dark eyes curiously vacant.

'Send me that photo, Uncle Stu,' Emily says, 'I want to put it on my story.' Stu AirDrops it to her phone, but as soon as Emily sees it, she wrinkles her nose.

'What's wrong with it?' Pete asks, expecting her to say that her hair looks shit, or the lighting isn't right.

'It's Erin,' Emily says. 'She's not in the photograph. It's not really a family photo without her, is it?'

Pete hadn't even thought about Erin as Stu snapped the picture, and he feels a greasy slick of shame wash over him. 'Well, no, I suppose not.'

'Is she still sleeping?' Emily asks. 'I know Mum won't want to get her up because it is late, but she's been asleep for a while, so she's bound to be getting up for a bottle soon.' The unspoken words hang in the air – *Erin never sleeps.*

Pete realises Erin has been asleep for a while – the baby monitor hasn't flickered to life for at least an hour or so, and she will be due a bottle shortly. He glances in Natalie's direction, as she accepts a glass of white wine from Mari with that same blank expression on her face. No, she definitely isn't herself, and Pete doesn't think it's just the shock of finding out what he's done.

'Zade?' Pete calls out to his youngest daughter, who – despite allegedly feeling sick – is hovering at the edge of the table in the hopes of snagging a second slice of cake. 'Do me and your mum a favour, would you? Will you go upstairs and check on Erin, see if she's still asleep? Emily wants to have a photo taken of all of us together.'

'I'm just having cake,' Zadie grumbles. 'I don't want to. She'll be asleep anyway.' There is that familiar ominous whine to her voice, and Emily rolls her eyes good-naturedly, handing her another plate of cake.

'Don't blame me if you puke,' Emily says, turning to pass the cake knife to Pete. 'Here you go, Dad, you finish slicing the cake and I'll go and get Erin. If she is awake Zadie can't carry her downstairs anyway.'

'Thanks, love.' Pete watches Emily hurry across the grass towards the house, an ache in his heart as he berates himself again for throwing everything away for nothing.

Natalie stands at the other end of the table, and Pete picks up a paper plate with a slice of cake and makes his way towards her. As he reaches her, she looks up at him in a way that makes his heart stutter in his chest. Her face is expressionless, and Pete has the horrifying sensation that what he's done might have just pushed her over the edge – might be the thing that breaks his beautiful, funny, fearless wife. Without thinking he reaches for her, pressing a kiss to her forehead and breathing in the scent of her face lotion, along with the faint tang of old wine, and she stiffens before pulling away.

'Mum? Mum!' At the sound of her name, Natalie turns her head, shaking it slightly as if she can't quite focus. 'Dad!'

Emily's voice is laced with panic and something snakes down Pete's spine – a primal fear that raises gooseflesh on his arms. 'Dad, it's Erin. She's not in her cot. She's not there. She's not anywhere.'

*The Mistake*

# Pete

Pete stumbles over the gnarled roots of the old oak trees making up over half the woodland, his breath coming loud and ragged in his ears. When Emily had first come down and told him Erin wasn't in her cot, his initial instinct had been to laugh in disbelief, then annoyance had taken over. Had Emily checked properly? How could Erin not be there? But when he'd stood over the empty cot in the darkened bedroom, confusion had muddled his thoughts, causing something unpleasant to flutter in his stomach as he gripped the edge of the cot, his knuckles white.

'Dad? I swear I checked, she's not there.' Emily had followed him up the stairs, her face white as she peered over his shoulder.

'Go downstairs,' he'd barked. 'Stay with your mother. No, ask Stu. Ask Stu, Mari, anyone downstairs if they've seen Erin.' He'd pushed past Emily and hurried towards his and Natalie's bedroom. *Had Natalie taken Erin to their bed to lie down with her? She'd done that before.* But when he'd pushed open the bedroom door the room was empty, the imprint of Natalie's body still etched on the duvet, the press of her head ingrained on his pillow, and something cold and icy had enveloped him.

Now, he runs through the woods, half-blind in the darkness that seems to have fallen like a curtain, and half-drunk on fear as his feet sink into the damp mulchy leaves, sweat prickling at the nape of his neck. 'Erin!'

'Pete, wait a minute.' Stu appears beside him, frantic and sweaty – no sign of the tipsy Stu who had laughed and taken photographs just a short while earlier. 'Come back to the house, we'll call the police.' He reaches out and grabs Pete's arm.

'Go back inside, Stu,' Pete says, shrugging free and not slowing his pace, his eyes frantically scanning the trees for something – anything – that will point to where his baby is. 'Wait with Nat, please, someone needs to be with her. I can't . . . I have to look for Erin.' He doesn't look at Stu, only aware that he's not beside him any more when he slows, his chest straining.

Pete bends, sucking in a breath and cursing the fact that he hasn't been to the gym once this year, regretting the cigarettes he smoked earlier. He is aware now of others in the woods, of the crack and rustle of twigs and leaves underfoot as guests from the party join in the search. Stu's voice carries on the fresh night air, his best friend directing the other searchers, trying to take control of a situation that has already spiralled. Pete feels helpless, a desperation to find Erin clawing at his insides. Resting his hands on his thighs, he pulls in sharp, ragged breaths that make his chest ache. 'Erin!' He calls for her, even though he knows she can't respond. From the garden comes the sound of his daughter's name being shouted by multiple voices, followed by the keening tones of someone crying. Emily, he thinks; it sounds like Emily. For a moment his blood runs cold; he thinks maybe Erin's been found and it isn't good news, but then Emily takes up the mantle, her voice raw as she calls her little sister's name. After a moment he can breathe despite the rawness in his chest, and he takes off again, his feet sliding on the wet forest floor. The air is damp and chilly now the sun has disappeared, and he can't help but wonder what Erin was wearing. Did Natalie put her down in the little T-shirt and leggings she wore to the party? Or did she change her into something warmer, something cosy to sleep in, thinking that was her down for the night? The sky overhead is mostly clear, prickled with stars, and all he can think is that if she's out here in that tiny little T-shirt, she'll freeze.

Ploughing on through the trees, peering at the clusters of bushes lining the wooded trail, Pete knows his thoughts aren't rational, but panic floods his mouth with a sharp metallic taste, and he can't think straight. When he'd first seen the empty cot he'd thought maybe Natalie had already been in to pick her up, even though something in the back of his mind was telling him it wasn't possible – that Natalie had been with him; then he thought perhaps one of the guests had heard her crying and gone in to bring her downstairs. When a sweep of the rest of the house and garden had shown no sign of Erin, Pete had glanced out of the window at the woods, an almost tangible sense of foreboding clutching at his gut. With every haunted legend he'd heard about the woods ringing in his ears, he'd sprinted for the rusty bolt on the back gate, shoving his way through the rickety fence out into the woods, the thought that someone had taken her, *must* have taken her, beating like a pulse in his mind.

*The bolt on the gate.* Pete's feet slow momentarily as the clouds overhead part and bright puddles of moonlight stretch through the gaps in the leaves of the trees. *It was open.* As he had reached for it, his fingers fumbling in panic, the gate had swung open easily, adding fire to his panicked thoughts. He remembers hearing Emily call his name before they cut the cake, and stubbing out his fag before heading back into the garden, but he doesn't remember whether he pulled the bolt safely home or not. *Erin could be out here. Someone could have taken her.*

To his right is the stream, usually barely more than a trickle at this time of year. Now, though, Pete becomes aware of the sound of rushing water, the stream swollen to the size of a small river with the heavy rain earlier in the day. *What if she's in the water?* The thought makes his limbs liquefy and he calls again, his voice breaking as he scans the dark horizon. 'Erin? Erin!'

As he reaches the edge of the woodland path, only patchy blackberry bushes and mounds of damp leaves separating him from the stream, Pete pauses, straining to hear any sound at all that might be Erin. The stream really is more of a river as he looks out over it, moonlight rippling over the swirling water, not sure if he's hoping to see something or not. It's swollen to the very banks, water beginning to lap at the edges of the blackberry bushes. Another burst of heavy rain and the harmless stream will erupt over the forest floor. Panting, his pulse crashing in his ears, Pete looks out over the stream, but there is no sign of Erin. No familiar ear-splitting wail. No cries or shouts at all, and Pete realises he can no longer hear the calls of Erin's name from his own back garden. Following the trail alongside the stream, Pete slips and slides in the mud, the movement of the leaves releasing the papery stink of rot. That, combined with the silty tang of the river on the air, makes his stomach turn. There is something about that smell, sulphurous and thick, that makes him think of caves and drains, dark places from which there is no escape.

Pete makes his way along the woodland path, his shoes picking up mud and leaves. There is a glimpse of white from the corner of his eye and he whips his head in that direction, only to see a barn owl taking flight from the branches of an oak tree, its wings wide and majestic as it swoops across the sky. Owls mean mice and rats, and Pete's stomach turns again. He knows these woods are full of vermin – they'd had a rat problem at the house not long before Natalie had fallen pregnant. When the pest control guy turned up and informed Pete they had rats, not sweet little field mice, Pete had made the conscious decision to tell Natalie it was just mice. Nothing to worry about. *Another lie*, he thinks, his brain feeling scrambled. *Is Erin's disappearance payback for all of the awful lies I've told?* There is a pain in his chest as he struggles on, branches and thorns clawing at his arms as he battles his way through an overgrown patch, his ears ringing with the effort of drawing in enough oxygen to keep going.

'Erin!' Pete's voice rings out in the heavy silence, broken only by the rush of the stream. His feet are cold, damp seeping in through the tops of his trainers, the suede ruined, and all he can think is that if Erin is out here, hidden somewhere among the bushes, moss and fallen trees, there isn't much time left to find her. Reaching the turn in the path leading out towards the village, where Eve's house sits on the other side of the trees, Pete slows to a jog. This is the path everyone uses to cut through the woods towards the main road, and his heart double-beats in his chest painfully. If someone took Erin, it would only be a matter of minutes from this point before they could be out on to the main road and into a car, speeding her away, never to be seen again. Pete pushes the thought away, not wanting to entertain what that could mean for himself and Natalie, for their family. He's far enough away from the house now that he can no longer hear the calls for Erin, the sound of Emily crying for her little sister. Behind him, something cracks – a twig or a branch. Pulse racing, Pete turns, only to see the bushy tail of a fox disappearing into the undergrowth. *Owls, rats, foxes, badgers.* There is no end of animals and pests in this wood that could harm Erin, but still Pete finds the idea of Erin being here, in the dark, damp woods, preferable to her being stolen away in a stranger's car.

Cold, sick, and with a throat raw from screaming Erin's name, Pete pushes on, following the rough track littered with the remnants of the season's bluebells towards the village, the same thought beating inside him like a drum as the distant wail of a siren fills the air. *How could this have happened? How could Erin have disappeared from her own bed, in a house full of people? And more importantly, who could have taken her?*

# *Natalie*

The sitting room is full of people, and Natalie feels an odd tickle of irritation. She'd told Pete he had invited too many people for them all to fit comfortably in the house, and for a moment she can't quite understand why they are all inside. Then she remembers. *Erin. Erin is not in her cot, is nowhere to be found.* Someone has called the police, she heard them – Mari? – talking about it, but there is no sign of any police officers yet. Mari is sitting on the armchair across from where Natalie sits on the sofa, Zadie pulled tightly into her lap. Zadie's eyes are wide, and she sucks determinedly at her thumb. Natalie wants to tell Zadie to take her thumb out of her mouth, that her teeth will be crooked, but she can't find the words. She has no idea where Pete is, and part of her is glad about that. Natalie doesn't want to see Pete, doesn't want to talk to him. The other part of her is desperate for him to come back from wherever he's gone, to be able to lean against his shoulder, for his arms to come around her and prop her up the way he has so many times before.

'Holding her …' a voice is saying behind her. 'Natalie … sleep.' Natalie thinks it's Gina, her colleague from the office, telling someone how she was holding Erin before Natalie took her upstairs for a sleep. Either that, or they are all talking about Natalie herself, and how she never gets any sleep any more. All around her, voices are calling out for Erin, or talking about where they all were the last time they saw her. There is a hushed air about the room now, following the initial buzz of panic, with many of the guests starting to move out into the garden, Erin's name on their lips. Wearily, Natalie blinks. She knows she should be grateful that people are concerned, that they are looking for her missing child, but it's pointless calling out for her. Erin is only eight months old; it's not as if she's going to reply to them.

As people mill around her, Natalie tries her hardest to connect the dots. There is an undeniable frisson of fear in the air, so tangible you can almost taste it, but it doesn't seem to have the same panicking effect on Natalie that it's having on her guests. She knows it's awful – she knows this is the worst thing that could ever happen to a mother – but the combination of too much diazepam and two glasses of Sauvignon on an empty stomach means she feels oddly disconnected from what is going on. It almost feels as though she is watching events through a mirror, a layer of glass separating her from real life, protecting her from the pain that surely she is about to experience. Or through a TV screen. Yes, that's it. Natalie feels as though she is watching this all happen to someone else – some TV drama starring Jill Halfpenny or Nicola Walker; it's always those two women the awful stuff happens to – and any minute now Erin will start up her incessant wailing and Natalie will feel that familiar sense of exasperation at once again having to pause her show for the millionth time.

Leaning forward, Natalie rests her elbows on her knees and covers her face with her hands. Her cheeks burn hot, her palms cool against her skin, and she is grateful to be able to feel *something* at least. Everything else is numb. A hand lands on her shoulder and begins to rub her back soothingly. It makes Natalie think of when she was little, and she would curl up in her mother's lap and she would rub her back until she fell asleep. For a sharp, painful moment Natalie misses her mother, the need for her like a splinter under her skin that brings tears to her eyes. It's been a long time since Natalie felt like that about her mum, probably not since Zadie was born. The hand persists in its gentle stroking of Natalie's back, and she keeps her eyes closed, hidden behind her palms. A familiar floral fragrance fills her nostrils, and she thinks it might be Eve's perfume. *Didn't Eve leave?* Natalie had thought that Eve left after she had snapped at her so fiercely before taking Erin up to bed. She didn't remember seeing her when they cut the cake, but maybe she came back? Part of Natalie hopes so. She hates fighting with Eve – they've only ever argued a couple of times before, and both times it was over Natalie's defence of Pete. She leans back, pressing against the warm palm, hoping it's Eve and that this means they're going to be OK. Natalie is going to need her to get through this, and the affair Pete's been having with Vanessa. Natalie half expects tears to spring to her eyes when she thinks about Erin, about Pete, but there is nothing, and it is with flushed cheeks and dry eyes that she looks up, when someone taps her gently on her knee.

'Natalie?' A dark-haired woman in a neat trench coat and ugly black shoes is crouched beside her, and Natalie frowns in confusion. *Who invited her to the party?* 'Natalie, my name is DI Travis. I'm a police officer, I'm here to help you look for Erin.'

'Erin ...' Natalie's tongue feels thick, too big for her mouth, and she licks at her dry lips.

'I need to ask you a few questions, OK?' The woman leans in, rocking forward on the balls of her feet, and Natalie wonders how long before she gets pins and needles. 'How old is Erin?'

'She's ... uh ...' Natalie has to think for a moment, her brain fuzzy. 'Eight months? I think she's eight months.'

The police officer exchanges a glance with someone above Natalie's head and then smiles gently. 'Excellent. Natalie, I know this is difficult for you, but I need to ask you a few things to help us focus our search for Erin, OK?'

Natalie nods, but everything still has the weird, shimmery feel about it, as though she's in a dream. Any moment now Erin is going to shriek that strident, piercing yell meaning she needs her nappy changed, and Natalie will wake up with her pulse pounding in her ears and her hands shaking, rudely ripped from sleep once again as Pete slumbers on, oblivious, beside her.

'When was the last time you saw Erin tonight? Did you put her to bed yourself?'

*Did I?* The combination of wine and prescription drugs has made time seem to melt together like an ice cream on a hot day, dripping and oozing. 'I ... She was ...' Natalie stumbles, her mouth feeling drier and drier. 'Could I have ... some water please?'

The police officer nods at someone behind Natalie, and then the palm disappears from her back. Emily's figure appears in Natalie's peripheral vision, and then she feels the sag of the sofa cushion beside her as Emily takes a seat. She reaches out and Emily twines her fingers through hers, holding her tightly, like she used to on the walk to playschool.

'Mum put Erin to bed at about eight o'clock,' Emily says, her voice strong and clear.

'So ... around two hours ago?' DI Travis asks, her pencil scratching away in a little notebook as she jots down Emily's words.

'About then,' Emily says, with a quick glance at Natalie. Natalie wants to agree but her head feels so heavy, too heavy for her neck to support, and she just blinks. 'Erin was crying after my dad made a speech, so my mum took her upstairs to feed her and get her settled for the night.'

'Natalie, is that right?'

Natalie looks up. 'Yes ... I fed her and put her to bed in her cot.'

'I was there,' Emily says, a blush rising on her cheeks, presumably at the memory of their argument. 'I came up to see Mum and she was sitting in the nursing chair giving Erin a bottle. She was about to put Erin down when I left and came back downstairs.'

'And that was the last time either of you saw Erin?'

Emily nods, casting a quick glance in Natalie's direction. Natalie also nods, before gratefully taking the glass of water that is handed to her. She takes long sips of the cold water, almost immediately feeling better, if not that much clearer. 'I put Erin in her cot and—' She breaks off, thinking, trying to piece together the events of the evening in her cotton-filled brain. 'I came downstairs, and we cut the cake. Pete asked Emily to ... to check on Erin.' Her throat thickens and she hastily gulps at the water again, coughing as it goes down the wrong way.

'OK. Take your time,' the detective says soothingly.

'Erin was asleep,' Emily says, her voice rising. 'There was no need for anyone to go upstairs after Mum put her in the cot. She was sleeping. We all know not to disturb her when she's gone down because Mum—' She breaks off, looking down at her bitten fingernails.

'Thank you, Emily,' DI Travis says, 'you've been really helpful. Can I just have a quick word with your mum, though? Perhaps you could go out in the garden and see if your dad's back yet? Someone said he's gone out to look for Erin.'

Emily nods and, with one last anxious look at Natalie, slides off the sofa and heads for the patio doors, where Stu holds out an arm and wraps it around her shoulders. Mari comes to stand on the other side of her, forming a protective barrier. Zadie hovers at Mari's side, staring at Natalie, still with her thumb in her mouth.

'Natalie?' DI Travis pulls Natalie's attention back to her. Her mouth is pursed, and Natalie can see tiny fine lines etched around her lips, and at her eyes. She must be the same age as Natalie, or thereabouts. 'Did you know the battery on the baby monitor has run out?'

Natalie looks up, her brow creasing. She didn't know that, did she? *If I had known I would have plugged it in at the wall*, she thinks. She was always nagging Pete to do it. 'No,' she whispers, 'I didn't know that.'

'OK,' The detective says. 'It's OK, Natalie. It just means that if someone did go into Erin's room, nothing would have been picked up on the monitor down here, that's all.'

Natalie swallows, a sick feeling cutting through the drugged numbness. *Is this detective implying it's my fault for not charging the baby monitor? Is it my fault?* 'I didn't ... No one would need to go up there. She was asleep.' Even as she says it, Natalie is aware she probably isn't making any sense.

'I have to ask you,' DI Travis says, 'is there anyone you can think of – anyone at all – who might have wanted to harm Erin?'

'Erin?' Natalie sits up, pressing one cold hand to her mouth. 'She's … She's just a baby. Why would anyone want to hurt a baby?' A fuzzy half-formed thought tries to break its way through the cloud of diazepam. No one would want to hurt Erin, would they? She's only been on this planet for eight months, has never done anything to warrant anything bad happening to her.

The detective gets to her feet, wincing as she does so. 'No one at all?'

Natalie shakes her head, but the half-formed thought persists, becoming clearer the longer she holds on to it. There is no one who would ever want to harm baby Erin, but after the events of the past few hours, there are plenty of people who might want to hurt Natalie directly, including her own husband.

*Pete. Vanessa. Eve. Maybe even Jake.* The list of names pours through Natalie's mind like quicksand, none of them certain enough to stick. Her head spins, and her stomach pitches; she thinks she might be sick.

'Sorry. Excuse me.' Without waiting for the detective to stop her, Natalie gets to her feet and rushes from the room, one hand clasped tightly over her mouth.

# Pete

At the edge of the woods, looking out on to the main road, Pete presses his hands over his face, fighting back the sobs threatening to choke him. The idea that someone could have come through the woods to a waiting car makes his blood run cold, makes him want to scream and rage until his throat is raw. Dropping his hands, he looks up and down the road, almost hoping for any sign of disappearing tail lights, but there is nothing.

*She has to still be here. She has to be in the woods.* Pete knows he could be fooling himself, but he refuses to give up hope, refuses to give up on Erin. Turning back towards the pitchy darkness of the trees, he steps into the shadows, his pulse thudding hard and insistent in his ears. He had raced along the forest path earlier, scrambled through bushes, skimmed past the stream in his haste to find her, but now he pauses for a moment. He needs to think logically, to comb every inch of the woods, searching for any kind of clue that someone had brought Erin through here. Pete's seen enough true crime shows to know how it works – how the police do fingertip searches, collecting any tiny thing that might help the investigation. Pete has also seen enough true crime shows to know there isn't always a happy ending.

Swallowing down his fear that Erin may not be OK – or worse, that she may never be found – Pete turns his attention to the forest floor in front of him, his eyes raking over the carpet of dead leaves for any sign of a disturbance not caused by his own harried dash. *How has this happened?* This is the thought that keeps springing into his mind as he searches, on high alert for any sound, wishing for the faintest whimper or cry to reach his ears. There were only supposed to be people he and Natalie love and trust in their home today, and the idea that one of them – someone he *knows*, for God's sake – could be responsible for Erin's abduction makes him feel physically ill. The idea that someone could be vicious enough to walk into his home and take his child … He shivers, his skin breaking out in goose pimples rippling along his arms. He might have been a twat, might even be a terrible human being, but he and Natalie aren't bad parents – they've never left the kids alone, they've never hit them, they've only ever wanted the best for them … Pete wants to cry as image after image of Erin, alone, crying, possibly hurt, some masked captor looming over her, flash in front of his eyes.

Passing the thicket of blackberry bushes that he and Natalie take Zadie to in the summer – the one with the juiciest berries that stain Zadie's mouth and clothes until Nat is despairing of ever getting the stains out – a flash of white catches his eye, and Pete comes to an abrupt halt, his heart stuttering in his chest. *What was Erin wearing?* He's sure Natalie had dressed her in pink leggings and a white T-shirt for the party. Dread cloaking his shoulders, Pete feels dizzy for a moment as he steps forward, the faint cries of Erin's name floating on the air every now and again as the rest of the searchers work their way through the woods.

'Erin.' Her name is a whisper as Pete pushes the brambles aside, the thorns clawing at the sleeves of his T-shirt. His mouth is dry, and he struggles to swallow as he fights his way in. 'Erin … Oh, God—' The noise that erupts from Pete's throat is half sob, half laughter as he gets close enough to see what the brambles are hiding. *A napkin.* The square of white that Pete convinced himself was a scrap of Erin's T-shirt is a paper napkin, blown in from the road. Backing out, Pete doesn't know whether to be relieved or disappointed. He finds his way back to the path, his eyes straining in the dark for anything, any sign at all that Erin has been here. He calls out her name, hoping she'll hear him and cry, but there's nothing, just the rustle of the wind in the trees, and the faint calls of her name from the other side of the woods.

The path forks at the midpoint between the road and the house, the right-hand fork looping round towards the stream before rejoining the main path a little further on. After following the main path out, now Pete follows the right-hand fork back towards the house, and as he reaches the old oak – that sturdy, dependable old tree, the site of so many memories for Pete, from smoking his first illicit cigarette when he was fifteen, to picnics with Zadie and Emily from almost as soon as they could walk – Pete stops, overwhelmed by a crushing sense of failure. Erin isn't here, in the woods. Surely, he would have found her by now. He rests one hand against the trunk, feeling the rough bark scratch at the pads of his fingertips, as a choking sob erupts from deep in his chest. On top of everything that has happened today, he's going to have to go back to the house and tell Natalie he couldn't find her. That he searched and searched but Erin is gone, and he doesn't know what that's going to do to her – to them. Pulling in a deep breath, Pete steps around the far side of the tree, mentally running through how he's going to tell Natalie that Erin really is gone, when his eyes go to the hollow at the bottom of the trunk, to the faint smudge of white almost glowing in the moonlight.

'Oh my God.' Pete slides in the wet mud as he bends down, almost too afraid to blink in case he's hallucinating. 'Oh my God, Erin.' He reaches out for the bundle tucked inside the damp hollow – something that could have been so easily mistaken for litter, casually tossed aside – and scoops it up, holding it close. The tiny body feels solid, weighty in his arms, and tears leak from his eyes, dripping from his chin onto her pale face, her lips tinged with blue as she lies there, so still and silent. Pete feels dizzy as he takes in the gnawed edges of the plastic bag that Erin was laid in, torn and shredded by razor-sharp rodent teeth, and his arms tighten around her. *Cry,* he pleads silently. *Please, Erin, cry. Please don't let me be too late.*

# *Natalie*

Natalie pushes open the door to Erin's bedroom, her eyes adjusting to the gloom to see the outline of the empty cot. She still feels spacy, as though she's not really here, and she moves to Erin's bed, to the empty space where her baby should be sleeping.

*She needs feeding*, Natalie thinks, her eyes going to the tiny alarm clock that used to sit in Zadie's bedroom. It's one of those ones that sends gradual rays of light into the room, so you can teach your child to only get up when it's light. It never worked for Zadie, and now she's old enough to get up and put the telly on herself, Natalie moved it into Erin's room for when she's ready. Now, a knife twists in Natalie's chest as she realises Erin might never be ready. She might never crouch beside a toddler bed, telling Erin to only get up when the light comes on.

*She'll need feeding*, Natalie thinks again, still nauseous, even though she leant over the toilet and retched but nothing came up. *She'll be screaming, crying in that fierce, furious way she has, where her face is bright red, screwed up in anger, her little fists pumping.* The thought of it, something that only hours ago would have caused her blood pressure to rise, makes Natalie feel oddly nostalgic. She would give anything to hear Erin cry right now.

Downstairs she can hear people talking, the solemn tones of DI Travis wafting up the stairs, and Natalie presumes she's asking where the guests were when Erin disappeared. Footsteps creak on the landing outside the bedroom and Natalie wonders which one of the police officers has been sent up here to keep an eye on her. Probably that young one, the one whose eyes were too wide as he took in the scene in the sitting room, giving away his lack of experience. There is a grizzly cry from below, one

Natalie recognises as belonging to Zadie, an overtired whine that she wheels out whenever she's been up too late, and then she hears Mari shushing Zadie, and imagines her wrapping her arms around her middle daughter to comfort her. Natalie knows she should go back downstairs and check on Zadie, make sure she's not upset, but she can't. She feels rooted to the spot; her feet welded to the floor.

Natalie's eyes go to the window above the cot, and she reaches forward and pulls up the blind. Below, in the garden, someone has turned on the outside lights and the patio heater, and she can see some guests milling around outside. All of them wear looks of concern, Gina pressing her hand to her mouth and shaking her head, as if she can't believe what has happened. Natalie can imagine the horror they are feeling at being caught up in something so terrible, the underlying feeling a sense of relief, that sense of *thank God this isn't happening to me.* Emily stands at the bottom of the garden, looking out onto the woods, her arms crossed over her body as if cold. She is stood by the gate, alone despite the groups of guests who still linger, and Natalie can recognise tiny Emily in her, in the way she shifts from foot to foot, a little ball of anxious energy. Beyond the garden, the trees shake in the wind and there are glimpses of light, flashes from phone torches as people – torchlight rests on a figure and Natalie can see Stu and that awful orange shirt he wore to the party – comb through the woods, searching for her missing child.

*How has this happened?* Natalie blinks, a single tear sliding unnoticed over one cheek. *Yesterday I was miserable – I thought I hated my life, but if I had known what was to come… I would have been more grateful*, she thinks. There is a shout from the woods – a hoarse cry – and her heart turns over in her chest. Flashes of torchlight whip through the trees, and then she sees Pete, emerging from the thick darkness where the woods meet the end of the garden. His trainers, new brown Adidas Munchen trainers that he spent a small fortune on, are splattered with river mud, and it coats the bottom of his jeans in wild splashes, and in his arms, he holds a tiny bundle. His face is stricken as he races through the back gate, shrugging Stu off as he reaches for whatever Pete is holding.

Natalie presses her hands against the cold glass of the window, her heart crawling up her chest and into her throat as time slows down. *This is all a dream*, she thinks. *This can't really be happening, because if it was real and Pete was carrying Erin, then Erin would be crying, and whatever Pete is carrying now is still and silent.*

'Mum?' The word is thick and heavy, pressed between lips numb with fear and dread. 'Mum.' Emily steps into the room and comes to stand beside Natalie, her arm wrapping around her mother's shoulders. 'You have to come downstairs.'

Natalie knows that. But she can't. Because if she leaves this room, this spot beside Erin's cot, then her world as she knows it is about to change irreparably, and she doesn't know if she's strong enough to cope with that.

'Dad found her,' Emily chokes out, her voice scratchy and raw in a way that makes her sound years older than she really is. 'Mum, Dad found Erin.'

Somewhere outside, there is the wail of sirens, drawing closer and closer, until all Natalie can hear is the scream ringing out in the empty bedroom, but she's not sure if it's the sirens or if the terrible wail is coming from somewhere deep inside her.

# Pete

Pete feels light-headed at the thought of how close he came to almost missing her altogether. A couple more steps and he would never have seen her, tucked away like that. He presses his hands over his eyes for a moment. He doesn't know what it was – instinct or something else, something more … spiritual – that made him pause as he approached the old oak tree beside the stream, just before the path rounds the last corner back into the forest, but he prays his thanks to a god he doesn't believe in that he did.

It was the lettering on the M&S bag that caught his eye, a ghostly white against the dark plastic, tucked away in the hollow of the oldest tree in the woods. The tree is a favourite of everyone in the village, old and young alike – the older people love it because it's been there since they were kids, and the kids love it because it's the best tree in the whole wood for climbing and hiding. As he had crept forward, his heart hammering in his chest, and he had seen her tiny face, so still and white, her lashes resting on her cheeks, it was as if the forest floor had fallen away beneath his feet. Any good memories he had of that tree – of showing Emily the best way to climb up into its thick branches (to Natalie's horror), of collecting acorns with Zadie from the foot of the tree so she can 'feed the squirrels' – all of that has been erased by the sight of Erin wedged into the hollow, ghostly and silent.

Now, Pete sits in the back of the ambulance, a shiny silver sheet around his shoulders as he watches the paramedics work on Erin's tiny body, desperately praying that any minute now he'll hear that familiar wail, the one that usually makes his toes curl up and his whole body sigh. Despite the warmth of the foil sheet he can't stop shivering, his muscles contracting over and over until his entire body begins to ache. He feels sick, his stomach rolling, as every time he closes his eyes he sees Erin's little face, the way she had laid so still, wrapped in her blanket and the Marks and Spencer carrier bag. He keeps hearing the way her name had slipped involuntarily from his lips as he made his way over the wet, boggy ground to get to her, his heart stilling in his chest as she made no response. No cry, no gasp, no whimper, just a thick, unsettling silence. He can still smell the cloying sulphurous scent of the river on the air, clinging to the mud and leaves that stick to the soles of his trainers. His hands stink, too, even though the paramedics gave him wipes to clean them, after he'd slipped and fallen in the mud in his haste to get to Erin. The carrier bag lies on the ambulance floor by Pete's feet now, the slick of mud from his hands obscuring the lettering, and he closes his eyes, feeling off-kilter.

'Excuse me.' The paramedic brushes past him as she reaches for something on the trolley, jolting Pete back to the present, and he reaches out and grabs at her arm.

'She's … Erin's going to be OK, isn't she?' Pete realises as he asks the question that he's not sure he wants to know the answer.

The paramedic pauses for a second, an expression he can't read flitting over her face before she gives him a tight smile and rummages wordlessly through the trolley.

*Suspicion.* Is that what Pete can see written all over her face? He wants to carry on talking to her, to tell her this isn't his fault, but she turns back to Erin, who is still silent and motionless on the stretcher.

She's so quiet. Pete realises he doesn't think he's ever heard Erin be this silent for so long. Even when she is asleep she mumbles and tuts to herself, rolling and fidgeting in her cot and rustling the blankets all night long. He knows that Natalie thinks he doesn't wake up, that he doesn't hear a thing once his head hits the pillow, but, he confesses to himself with a sickening twist to his stomach, he does. He does wake up and he does hear Erin, but he actively chooses to not get up and see to her. Natalie is at home with Erin on her own all day long – Emily is at sixth form or her summer job and Zadie is at school – and still Pete comes home to no dinner and an untidy house. At the risk of sounding like a massive bastard, Pete doesn't see how Natalie can expect him to get up all night long with Erin and then get up at five o'clock in the morning to do a full day on site. Now, trying to catch a glimpse of his baby daughter between the paramedics as they move swiftly and quietly around her, he wishes he could take it all back. The stark realisation that everything could be ripped away from him, even if Erin does make it through what has happened to her tonight, makes his eyes smart. If only he could have it all back, could have things the way they were before this night, then he'd do it all so differently. He'd get up with Erin, he'd deal with Zadie's tantrums, he'd be supportive of Emily and Jake's relationship, if only things could go back to the way they were twenty-four hours ago.

*Twenty-four hours.* Is that all it's been since everything was normal? The ambulance driver slams the back doors of the ambulance closed and the paramedic turns to Pete.

'We're going to head to the hospital now, Mr Maxwell. I know you're worried, but please, when we arrive, let us do our job. The sooner we get Erin inside and with the doctor, the better.'

Pete nods blankly, pulling the silver foil sheet more tightly around his shoulders. Still Erin is silent, her face so white she looks like a porcelain doll. Her fingernails are tinged with blue, and the oxygen mask covering the lower half of her face is so tiny it looks like a toy. There is a rumble as the engine starts, and then the ambulance is away, the siren shattering the air as they career through the village and out onto the main road to the hospital.

As they speed through the dark streets, Pete thinks over the day, unable to tear his eyes away from Erin's silent body. Just yesterday – hell, just this morning – Pete's life was OK. Yes, he'd fucked things up with Vanessa, but she was dealt with. He had a wife who loved him, even if she wasn't always present, and three beautiful kids. Someone today has conspired to take all of this away from him. But who?

As the ambulance takes a corner at a swift pace, Pete has to hang on tight to save himself from falling off the narrow seat he's perched on, the stink of the river mud rising from his trainers as he moves. The rest of the journey to the hospital passes in a blur, Pete unable to think about anything except Erin and the scream of the siren in his ears. As soon as the ambulance screeches to a halt outside the accident and emergency department, the doors are yanked open and Pete finds himself shoved to one side as the waiting doctors and paramedics wheel Erin out of the ambulance, rain splattering the foil around his shoulders. He feels clueless, a useless spare part as the doctors and paramedics shout phrases that make no sense, until he hears the word 'unresponsive' and his heart seems to stop dead in his chest.

Erin is wheeled into A&E as Pete runs alongside, trying desperately to keep up. There is a moment where the lights overhead seem too bright, and he is unable to hear anything over the wheels of the stretcher as they scuff over the hospital linoleum, and he thinks for a heart-stopping moment that he might faint. He can't take his eyes from the slight mound her body makes under the blanket; she seems smaller than ever, if that's at all possible. Her face is hidden by the oxygen mask, and as the doctors rush her into a private room Pete feels as if he has lost all control for the first time in his life.

'Mr Maxwell, please.' A nurse firmly stops him at the door to the room where they have Erin, one hand up to prevent him from entering. 'You can't come in here. I have to ask you to move to the waiting area.'

'You don't understand.' Pete's voice is croaky, his throat dry and sore from shouting for Erin. 'That's my baby... Erin, she's my daughter.'

'I'm sorry.'

Behind the nurse, Pete sees a doctor tilting Erin's head back, a thin tube being pushed down her tiny throat. His own throat closes over and once again he feels the threat of tears. The nurse firmly closes the door behind her, and Pete moves to the small window to the side of the room. There is no way he's going to sit on some plastic chair in the middle of a waiting room full of sick people. He needs to be here, needs to keep his eyes on Erin at all times. He's let her down enough tonight; there's no way he's letting her down again.

Pete watches helplessly as the nurses attach sensors to Erin's hands, wires trailing to a machine beside the bed. More pads are pressed onto her tiny chest, and Pete is struck by how white and waxy her skin looks as the doctor attaches the pads to another machine and a high-pitched beeping fills the air, constant and repetitive. A nurse taps the end of an empty syringe and then inserts it into Erin's arm, and Pete's eyes follow the line Erin's blood makes along the attached tube into a small vial. Pete feels almost woozy as he watches the nurse draw Erin's blood, a thick, dark maroon, a shocking contrast to the paleness of her skin. He feels it again: that overwhelming sensation that he has lost control of things for the first time in his life. Even with Vanessa telling Natalie about their affair, he still thought he could fix things – could take control of the spiralling situation – but not now. Not over this. Pete presses his forehead to the window, the cold glass welcome against the heat of his skin, as a metallic taste fills his mouth. The taste of fear.

All he can do is wait.

# Natalie

Natalie sits in the back of the police car, desperately trying to draw in enough oxygen. Her cheeks burn and it's hot and stuffy in the car, the windows tightly closed and the heater blowing hot, dusty air despite the fact that it's the middle of August. She wonders if Pete is at the hospital yet, the ambulance screeching away before she had even fastened her seatbelt. Pete's face had been pale as he'd climbed into the back of the ambulance, Erin's tiny body disappearing inside ahead of him, cradled in the paramedic's arms. Her feet had automatically started to follow them, but then the police officer was at her side, gently taking her elbow and guiding her towards the waiting police car.

The familiar streets fly past in a blur, as rain begins to splatter the windows. Natalie sighs, still feeling oddly numb as she watches the world through the passenger window, the glass beginning to steam up as Natalie's breath hits it. She'd thought the storm was over, that the weather was meant to turn tonight and they would wake up to blue skies in the morning, but apparently not. Somewhere, deep and buried, she thinks she should feel relieved that Pete found Erin before the rain started, but she still feels as if this is all a terrible dream that she'll wake up from at any moment. She blinks and a single tear runs down one cheek, slipping into the corner of her mouth, leaving the salty taste of heartbreak on her tongue.

'Natalie? Nat?' DI Travis taps gently on her knee to get her attention and Natalie drags her gaze away from the rain-washed streets outside. She can still faintly hear the sound of a siren in the distance. 'I was asking why you had people over to the house tonight. Were you celebrating something special?'

Something about the way she asks the question tells Natalie that the police officer already knows the answer, but she draws in a breath of that fuggy, stuffy air and replies. 'Yes, Emily – she's our eldest daughter – it was her birthday. It *is* her birthday, her eighteenth.' The words feel jumbled, as though she can't put them in the right order. 'We were having a party to celebrate, because she got her A level results this week and she's going to university.' For a moment Natalie can't remember where Emily is going, before the name presents itself on the tip of her tongue. 'Durham,' she says with a cold wave of relief. 'Emily's going to go to Durham.' She thinks of the way Emily's lip curled as she spat her anger at Natalie in the bedroom, wonders if she'll ever be forgiven for not dishing out sympathy at Emily's distress over Jake leaving.

'Wait a minute.' Panic clenches at Natalie's insides, turning her hot, then cold. 'Zadie. Where is Zadie? Who's looking after her?' She twists in her seat, looking out of the rear window as if she'll be able to see the house, see Zadie.

DI Travis puts out a hand, as if to calm Natalie. 'She's OK, she's back at the house. Emily is there with her, and also a lady called Eve? She said she's a close friend of yours.'

Natalie sits back, her pulse slowing. *Eve is there*. Natalie knows she should be glad, should feel grateful, but she doesn't know how she feels about the thought of Eve taking care of Zadie.

'I've also left one of our officers at the house,' Travis says, 'so you don't have to worry – your girls are safe.'

Natalie nods, aware that she is biting the skin around her fingers, the way she always does when she gets anxious. She pulls her hand away, tucking it under her thigh. 'Thank you.'

'So, Natalie, can you tell me who else was at the party? It seems like you had quite a crowd.'

'Just friends and family,' Natalie says. 'Eve, Stu and Mari – that's Pete's best friend and his wife. Emily's best friend from school and her mother. The neighbours across the street – Noyce, that's their name.' Natalie pauses. 'Emily's boyfriend, Jake, for a short while.' Adrenaline floods her veins at the thought of the other guest – the uninvited guest – and she almost feels a shiver of pleasure at the thought of the police turning up on her doorstep, followed by rage at the thought of Pete bringing all this to their door. 'And Vanessa. I don't remember her surname, I'm afraid, she works with Pete. She's an *old friend* of his. I would suggest you ask Pete about her.' There is no disguising the venom that leaches into her voice as Natalie says the other woman's name, and she realises for the first time that she doesn't feel quite as foggy as she did. DI Travis says nothing for a moment, but there is the tiniest raising of an eyebrow as she reaches for her pocketbook.

'OK, we'll speak with Pete about her. We can get her details from him.' Travis scribbles the names down in a spidery, scratchy scrawl, before she flips the pocketbook closed and smiles at Natalie. 'We're nearly there now,' she says, patting Natalie's hand. Natalie recognises the road they are speeding along, and remembers with a pang that the last time she travelled this way, it was Pete speeding along and patting her hand as she puffed and panted in the seat beside him, Erin on her way.

'What time did the party start?'

'About three o'clock. It wasn't meant to go on this late.' Natalie swallows and glances out of the window again. Rain still pours, and it looks more like November than August outside.

'I have a daughter, too,' The police officer says, and Natalie looks at her in surprise. She doesn't look like a mum. She's too put together, too neat and tidy to be a mum, Natalie thinks. Maybe her daughter is Emily's age and she's over the worst of it all. 'She's five,' Travis goes on, and Natalie has to rethink things. 'She just started school this year – that was an eye-opener, let me tell you.' The detective smiles wryly.

'It can be difficult,' Natalie says quietly, thinking about Zadie and how the school accused her of bullying. 'Some of them struggle a little bit.'

'Some of us mums do, too,' Travis says, a smile tugging at her lips as she runs her eyes over Natalie's face. 'I'm one of the oldest mums in the playground. I feel like every time I walk in to pick her up, I'm half expecting someone to think I'm her granny.'

Natalie doesn't respond.

'They're a bit cliquey, the other parents in the playground,' Travis says, brushing her fringe out of her eyes and picking invisible lint from her trousers. 'I'm not sure if they don't want to speak to me because they know I'm a copper, or if it's just the age difference. I'm afraid I'm not at all up to speed with *Below Deck* and TikTok.'

'Me neither,' Natalie says, avoiding her gaze, although that is a lie. She loves watching *Below Deck* when Pete's working late. At that thought she gets that sharp pain in her stomach again and shifts, pressing a hand to her belly, a gesture not missed by the police officer.

'All of my friends' kids are much older than my daughter, so I really do feel like a fish out of water sometimes,' Travis says. 'Do you find that, too, Natalie?'

'Not really. Stu and Mari's kids are still quite small. We had Emily very young.' What does this woman want? Why is she telling Natalie about her trials as a mother? Natalie isn't interested in this woman's experiences of having a child later in life. Shouldn't she be out looking for whoever took Erin from her cot? Natalie sighs, resisting the urge to face the window again. It all feels too much. Too heavy.

'Of course … Emily.' The police officer nods. 'Her eighteenth, you said? You must have been barely more than a child yourself when you had her.'

'Twenty-two,' Natalie says. 'I got pregnant in our last year at university.'

'Wow. That must have been a shock.'

'It was. But we were both pleased. Really happy.' Natalie's eyes fill with tears and she blinks, her vision softening.

DI Travis fumbles in the pocket of her trench coat and hands Natalie a tissue. 'I'm sorry. I didn't mean to upset you.' Silence fills the car for a long moment as Natalie gets her emotions back under control. She doesn't like this police officer; there's something false about the tone of her voice, the things she says. As if she wants to come across as kind and understanding, but something about it doesn't sit right for Natalie. Maybe it's just that she feels guarded – today has shown her she can't trust anyone around her.

'Quite an age gap you guys have, isn't it,' Travis says, 'Between Zadie and Erin? Was she a little surprise?'

Natalie feels the ghost of a smile on her face. 'You could say that.'

'I remember when I told my husband we were having a baby.' Travis gives a small huff of laughter. 'You could have knocked us both down with a feather. Both of us had given up, if I'm honest, we thought we were just destined to not have kids, but then along she came. Our little gift.'

'Oh.' Natalie doesn't care. She doesn't care that this woman had a miracle baby. She doesn't care that the husband was shocked. All she cares about is getting to the hospital and finding out if her own baby has survived being left outside in a cold, dark wood.

'It must have been a shock for you guys, too?' The detective is still talking. 'When you found out you were having Erin? Someone told me at the house she wasn't a planned baby.' Natalie feels the words needle under her skin. *Who told her that? Was it Eve?*

'It was a surprise, yes.' Natalie leans forward in her seat, as they approach the final roundabout that takes them to the hospital. They'll be there any moment, and she feels a spurt of adrenaline run through her veins. Will Erin be OK? She swallows, her mouth dry at the thought of what awaits her at the emergency department.

'What about Pete?' The question hangs in the air as Natalie

takes a moment to absorb it. 'How did he take the news you were pregnant? Was he pleased? Once he got over the initial shock, I mean.'

Natalie pauses, mulling over her response. Her initial reaction is to say whatever she usually says when people remark on the fact that they've had Erin so late after their other children. To say of course they were thrilled, of course Pete was happy to become a father again. But to say that now would be to lie, and Natalie doesn't want to lie to the police. She doesn't think Pete would lie either, and she squashes down the spark of fear that ignites at the thought of telling the truth.

'Natalie?' Travis prods gently, her intense gaze focused directly on Natalie's face like a searchlight. 'How did Pete react when you told him you were pregnant with Erin?'

Natalie drags her eyes up to meet DI Travis's face, her heart frantically crashing against her ribcage. 'He was ... overwhelmed,' she says eventually. 'We both were. Neither of us were expecting another child, and discovering I was pregnant ... Well, it meant we had to change our plans.' Natalie has been as honest as she feels she can, but doesn't say what she wants to say, what she believes to be the truth. That Pete was horrified to learn that Natalie was pregnant. That Pete never wanted Erin at all.

# *Pete*

Pete thinks he's probably walked miles in the minutes since they arrived at the hospital. After pressing his face to the window of the hospital room, his heart in his mouth as Erin was poked and prodded and strapped to various machines, the same nurse had come out and told him in no uncertain terms that he was to leave. Now, he paces in a shabby waiting room, the walls scuffed and the hospital blue lino cracked in places. If there was anywhere that reeked of despair and desperation more, Pete isn't sure he could find it, but still he can't stop pacing, his filthy trainers squeaking on the lino as nervous energy floods his veins.

The nurse has promised the doctor will come and find Pete the minute there is any news, the moment he is allowed to see Erin, even if it is through glass, and while he realistically knows it's only been a short while since he was escorted to the waiting room, time is elastic and it feels like days – weeks – since they left him in here.

The door handle turns and Pete pauses in his pacing, suddenly not sure he wants to know what the doctor has to say, but when the door opens it isn't the doctor standing there.

'Nat. Oh God, Nat.' Pete stumbles towards her, tripping over his own feet, his arms outstretched.

Natalie's face is washed of colour, her hair slipping out of the messy bun she stuffed it into for the party. She still wears the hot pink sundress, but now there is an old chunky cardigan around her shoulders, one that she usually wears only at home, when the weather is really cold. It makes Pete think of Christmas, of Natalie standing in a steaming hot kitchen pulling a roast out of the oven. It looks oddly out of place in this cold, sterile room, with posters advertising counselling on the walls.

'Where is Erin? Is she OK?' Natalie's voice is thick, the words coming out in a strangled choke. As she draws the old cardigan tighter around her body her hands shake, and Pete feels a surge of guilt as his gaze reaches her eyes. Salt stains her cheeks, her face drawn, and she looks fragile, as if one tiny push could break her like glass. *This is your fault*, a voice hisses in Pete's ear – the sound of his own conscience. *You've done this to her.*

Swallowing down the guilt choking him, Pete moves towards her. 'I'm still waiting for the doctor. They said in the ambulance she's going to be OK… She's in the best place, Nat. She's going to be fine.' The lie sits heavy on his tongue, bitter and tangy, and he swallows hard as he reaches out and pulls Natalie towards him. She freezes, her body going rigid, and before he can speak, she pulls away, crossing her arms over her body and stepping towards one of the plastic chairs against the wall.

'Nat…' He wants to tell her he loves her, that he's sorry – so, so sorry – but movement in the doorway alerts him to the fact that they are not alone. In fact, their entire exchange has just been very closely observed.

'Pete?' A dark-haired woman who looks vaguely familiar steps into the room. 'My name is DI Travis. I brought Natalie here in the police car.' She smiles, and Pete feels himself relax a tiny fraction. 'Would you mind just stepping outside with me for a moment?' She looks at Natalie. 'Natalie, I'll send my colleague in to sit with you, all right?'

Natalie nods, and Pete sees that her expression isn't quite as blank as it was back at the house. Still, though, it doesn't seem as though the full force of what has happened has hit her yet.

Once out in the corridor, Pete pulls the door to the waiting room closed behind him, feeling as if this will protect Natalie from anything the police officer has to say, but instead of speaking to him here, Travis gestures for him to follow her into an empty office further along the hall.

'Take a seat.'

Pete feels a flicker of alarm. The office is tidy, the desk clear, and on one side of the table is a single chair. On the other side are two more chairs, one of which is already occupied by another police officer. DI Travis squeezes around the edge of the desk and sits beside him.

'This is my colleague, DS Haynes,' she says. 'We just have a few questions for you, Pete, that's all. I've already had a good chat with Natalie on our way over here.'

Pete doesn't know if that's allowed. All he knows about police procedures is what he's seen on the telly, and they always say you have to have a lawyer present before they can formally question you. At the thought that this is just an informal chat to find out exactly what happened earlier tonight, he feels able to breathe again.

'I want to ask you about this evening, Pete,' Travis says, her voice clear in the quiet room. Her tone seems friendly and Pete shifts in his seat, trying to appear relaxed, even though his pulse is still clattering. 'There was a party at your house, is that right?'

'Yes, that's right. For Emily – our daughter's – eighteenth birthday.'

'Lovely.' She gives him a brisk smile. 'Did anything happen at the party that perhaps wasn't ... expected? Someone showed up you didn't invite, or any kind of altercation? We're just trying to find out exactly why someone would want to take Erin.'

Pete's mouth goes dry. Where does he even start? 'There was ...' He clears his throat. 'There was a little bit of friction earlier on in the evening. My daughter hadn't told her boyfriend she was planning on going to university, and he became quite upset about it. They had a ... Well, they had words about it, and Emily was quite upset. I asked Jake to leave.'

'How did Jake react to that?'

'Well, he wasn't too pleased,' Pete says. A nugget of something that might be fear worms in his belly. *Could Jake have done this?* 'He told me I would regret throwing him out of the party.'

DI Travis raises her eyebrows at this. 'Sounds like he was pretty angry.' She glances down at her open notebook, the pages filled with scratchy writing as though a drunk spider had fallen in a pot of black ink. 'No other arguments? Altercations?'

Pete shakes his head slowly, before pressing a finger to his lips. 'Oh, I think my wife had words with a friend of hers.'

'Would that be …' She consults the notebook again. 'Eve?'

'That's right. Natalie was growing concerned that Eve has developed an unhealthy interest in our family.' Pete doesn't mention the fact that he was the one who initially said this to Natalie. That he's the one who thinks Eve is slightly crazy. 'She's always at our house. Always telling Natalie how to deal with Erin's sleep problems, even though she doesn't have any experience raising kids. She doesn't have any children of her own,' he clarifies. 'Eve left the party,' he goes on as the detective leaves a pregnant pause. 'Someone should probably see where Eve was when Erin disappeared. She left the party, but she could easily have sneaked back in. She's quite familiar with our house – she knows which bedroom Erin sleeps in.' As he says it, Pete feels a flicker of something that could be vindication, mixed with horror. Vindication because if Eve did do this, then Pete was right about her all along – horror because that would mean Natalie will feel responsible, and Pete is already afraid of her fragile state of mind. He knows this statement will lead the police to Eve's door, will presumably lead to her being questioned, but what he's saying is true.

'OK.' Travis nods as her colleague scribbles notes in his own notebook. 'What about the other guests. Was there anyone there who perhaps shouldn't have been at the party? Someone who heard about it and turned up anyway? You know what it's like.

There's always someone who thinks they're entitled to an invite, isn't there?'

Pete licks his lips, his tongue like sandpaper. *She knows about Vanessa. Someone has told the police that Vanessa was there – who, though? Natalie? Stu?* Pete presses his foot to the floor, trying to stop his knee from jiggling under the table. 'Could I possibly get a drink of water?' He tugs at his collar. The room is stiflingly hot, the way hospitals always are. DI Travis nods, and there is a brief pause in her questioning as she waits for her colleague to return with two plastic cups of water.

'So Pete, back to the party – any uninvited guests?'

Pete sips at the water, the taste flat and metallic. 'No,' he says eventually. 'Oh, wait... a woman from my office. She turned up, I guess she must have heard us talking about it in the office – I invited Dave, my foreman, you see – and assumed it was an open invitation. She left once she realised.' Pete lets out a nervous caw of laughter. 'We're not teenagers, it's not like someone plastered it all over Facebook and all the local hoodlums turned up.'

DI Travis allows herself a small smile, as if the thought of teenagers using Facebook is amusing to her. 'You understand we have to ask?'

'Of course.' Pete can feel sweat prickling under his arms, and he wonders if he should have been more forthcoming about Vanessa.

'So, Pete, I have to ask you this – I've asked everyone I've spoken to so far. When was the last time you saw Erin?'

'I don't know...' Pete's brow creases and he tries to think back, past the row with Natalie, past the confrontation with Vanessa. 'After my speech, maybe? I made a speech at about seven-thirty? Sometime around then. That's the last time I remember seeing Erin. Someone from Nat's work was holding her so Nat could come up and stand next to me.'

DI Travis nods. 'And where were you at the time Erin disappeared? We believe the time frame was between approximately

8.30, when Natalie fed her and put her in her cot to sleep, and ten o'clock, when your daughter went to check on her.'

'I was...' Pete feels a flutter of panic. He doesn't know for certain; after his speech everything became a bit of a blur.

'According to other guests at the party you cut the cake with Emily at around ten o'clock. So really, we're looking at a period of roughly ninety minutes before this. We have a photograph of you, with Natalie and your other girls with the cake, time-stamped at 9.54. Natalie put Erin to bed at around 8.30.'

'I was outside,' Pete says, his heart knocking out a triple beat in his chest. 'Smoking.'

'In the garden?'

'At the end of the garden, on the other side of the gate. Just on the edge of the woods.' A spurt of horror heats Pete's veins as the two police officers exchange a glance. 'Natalie doesn't know I still smoke,' he says quickly. 'I didn't want her to see me.'

'Did anyone else see you out there?'

'No.' Pete doesn't know why this makes him anxious, his knee still jiggling under the table.

'But we'll find the cigarette butts behind the gate if we look?'

Pete runs a hand through his hair, feeling as nauseous as he was after smoking those cigarettes. 'No. Natalie uses that gate all the time to cut through the woods with the girls. I didn't want her to know.' He pauses for a moment, replaying the moment that he dug the cigarette butts deep down inside the compost bin. Would they still be there? Would they have disintegrated in the damp, mulchy clippings? 'I hid them in the compost bin.'

'Right.' Travis writes something in her notepad, and Pete feels the prickle of sweat in his armpits. 'We can check that.'

Pete feels a shimmer of alarm, enough to make his bladder feel full. 'You'll find the cigarette butts there. I stubbed them out on the fence post.' He trails off. He still hid his tracks, even though he was caught up in his own head about Natalie, praying his marriage isn't over, and Vanessa, wishing he'd never even spoken to her in the first place. A sign of a seasoned liar, for sure. 'I'm not lying.' As soon as the words escape he wishes he could take them back.

DI Travis gives him another of those gentle smiles. 'I didn't think you were lying about that, Pete.' She flips the pages on her notes, pausing at something she's scrawled. 'How are things at home? Before the party, I mean. How are things between you and Natalie?'

Pete shifts in his seat, his bladder uncomfortably full now, but still he sips at the water. 'Fine. Everything at home has been fine.'

'Really? It's quite an upheaval, surely, having a new baby, even when you do have other children.'

'Well, yes,' Pete says, that shimmer of alarm growing stronger. There's something about the way the police officer is looking at him that makes him feel on edge. 'Obviously Natalie and I are both tired – you forget how much time and energy a small baby takes up.' He flicks his gaze to the younger DS beside her, wondering if he has children, too. 'I've been working really long hours, and I know Natalie has been exhausted. Things have been a bit of a struggle for her. The birth wasn't straightforward, and I know she's finding things tough at the moment. Erin doesn't sleep much.' DI Travis doesn't respond, a thick silence filling the room as Pete fumbles for something to say to erode it.

'But that doesn't mean … It's been hard, but I love them so much,' he says in a rush, the words falling over one another. 'All of them – my family is my world.'

'I don't doubt that at all,' Travis says, but she doesn't smile this time. 'Pete, tell me how it felt when Natalie first told you she was pregnant. I should imagine that was the last thing on your minds.' *At this stage in your life.* The words hang in there unspoken.

'I was thrilled,' Pete says. 'I was excited we were going to have another baby.'

'OK.' The word is a statement, not a question, as Travis shifts in her seat. 'The reason I ask, Pete, is because when I spoke to Natalie she suggested perhaps you weren't that thrilled.'

*Oh.* Pete feels his stomach drop away, and places the plastic cup of water on the table before his hands can begin to shake. 'I ...'

'She said you had to change plans you two had made, and I got the impression this wasn't something you were happy about.' There is an undertone to her statement, one that insinuates Pete is a liar, and he's not. *He's not.* She just doesn't understand.

'It's not that I wasn't thrilled,' he says – although, let's be honest, he wasn't exactly over the moon. 'It was more ... I was shocked, that's all. It was a complete surprise. Natalie and I had never even discussed having another baby after Zadie was born. Two was enough. That's what I thought, anyway.'

'But Natalie didn't agree.'

'No. Well, she didn't do it on purpose.' *Did she?* Pete has never thought about things that way before, and he frowns as he tries to recall the conversation they'd had that night in the Italian restaurant. Natalie didn't get pregnant on purpose; he's sure of it. Almost sure. 'We had plans, me and Nat. Plans we'd made years before when the girls were small, and Natalie getting pregnant threw the whole thing off-kilter.' He still feels raw about that perfect plot of land they'd allowed to slip through their fingers. 'We were going to build a house in Australia – that was always the plan, but then ... Well, the plot got sold, and we couldn't do anything about it because Natalie was pregnant.'

'So Erin being born really put a spanner in the works for you.' As the police officer fixes her dark gaze on him, Pete feels his stomach drop away to the floor. *This isn't an informal chat*, he thinks, as hot spurts of panic race through his veins. *They think I was the one who left Erin in the woods.*

# *Natalie*

Natalie pulls her cardigan tighter around her body, as she sits on the hard plastic chair in the waiting room. Despite the hot stuffiness of the hospital, she just can't seem to get warm, and she wishes Pete was here before she remembers what he has done, and then she thinks she doesn't want Pete to come near her ever again.

No one has been in yet to tell her how Erin is doing, and she glances at the clock on the wall for the hundredth time. The remains of the diazepam have worn off and now Natalie feels as if every nerve ending is exposed, the thought of Erin not making it home unbearable. Pete still isn't back from wherever DI Travis took him to, and the police officer who was supposed to wait with her has gone off in search of a hot chocolate in the hopes it will warm Natalie up. Alone, Natalie runs through the evening over and over in her head, frustrated by the patchiness in her memory. She remembers hissing at Pete, the stabbing pain in her gut as Vanessa gleefully told her she was sleeping with him, the way Eve's face had crumpled as she told her she was interfering and overbearing. Then everything falls away, fuzzy and indistinct, as if someone has drawn a veil over the evening until the moment Emily appeared to tell them that Erin wasn't in her cot.

*I can't sit here. I can't just sit and wait, I need to see Erin.* A desperate urge claws at Natalie's insides, the primal instinct to be with her baby overriding every instruction given to her by the nurse, the police and Pete to wait here. She gets to her feet and hurries out of the waiting room, following the ICU signs until she reaches the room Erin is in. Pressing down on the handle, Natalie exhales as the door slides open, and she tiptoes across the room to the tiny plastic cot where Erin lies.

Her baby is unrecognisable. That's the first thought she has, her heart filling her chest to the point that she feels she can't breathe. She wants to reach out a hand, to feel Erin's tight grip around her finger, but she's too afraid, scared she'll shatter into a million pieces if Erin doesn't respond. Tubes snake out of Erin's throat, pushing her tiny chest up and down as she struggles to breathe, a rhythmic beeping telling Natalie that this machine is the one keeping her daughter alive. Her skin is waxy and white, not the pink flush she usually carries on her cheeks, or the furious red of her angry wailing. Natalie has a pain in her sternum that surely must be her heart breaking. How could she have thought for one minute that Erin was a mistake? How could she ever have thought that life would have been better without her in it? Now, the idea of Erin not coming home makes Natalie want to scream and cry, to bargain with the devil, do *anything* for her baby to be all right.

*I need answers.* As the door swings open, Natalie turns to see a nurse entering Erin's room.

'Please. I need to know what's happening with Erin. Is she going to wake up? Why isn't she awake?' Her hands knot together as the nurse stops and shakes her head.

'Mrs Maxwell, I'm sorry, you can't be in here. Please, you need to go back to the waiting room. Someone will be along to see you just as soon as they can.'

'I want to be with my daughter.' The words are almost a shriek, tinged with pain and anguish as Natalie stands firm, her hand reaching out to grip the edge of the plastic cot.

'I understand that, but Erin is about to be taken down for some tests. Doctors are going to give her a quick ultrasound, and then we'll come and find you, I promise.' The nurse tries to reassure her, but Natalie can hear the clipped, tense edge to her voice, and she notices the nurse already has her hands on Erin's cot, ready to wheel the plastic bed down to the right department.

Natalie nods, feeling deflated, her hand dropping back to her side. Of course, she has to let them do whatever they need to do for Erin, to make sure she's OK. Watching as the nurse wheels Erin into the lift, Natalie waits until the doors close before she heads back to the waiting room, feeling empty without Erin beside her. If you'd asked her a few days ago what was the best thing anyone could have given her, Natalie would have said an hour away from the baby. Now, all she wants is Erin in her arms.

Another half an hour passes and, just as she is about to get to her feet and go looking for a doctor, a nurse – for anyone who can tell her anything about what is happening with Erin – the waiting room door creaks open. Natalie stands so quickly that for a moment she is light-headed, and she has to blink to refocus, as the chair behind her hits the wall. 'Oh. It's you.' She sags back down into the chair as Eve enters the room, her hands filled with an overstuffed carrier bag, Erin's changing bag hanging from her shoulder.

'Have you heard anything?' Eve's voice is hushed as the heavy door swings closed, shutting out the beeps of machines and hurried footsteps as hospital staff move between wards.

'No. Not yet.' Natalie looks up at her friend, trying to read the look on her face. She knows the words she said to Eve at the party were vicious, but Eve doesn't seem to have let them affect her at all. 'Why are you here? I thought you were staying at the house with Zadie. That's what the police told me. You haven't left her alone, have you?' Even as she says it, she knows Eve would never do that. She was horrified when Natalie told her she'd left Zadie in bed asleep once to pop to the shop.

'There's a family liaison officer there,' Eve says. 'She said I should go, and Emily agreed with her.' Natalie's not sure, but she thinks there might be a bit of bitterness to Eve's tone. Maybe the things Natalie said to her didn't just slide off like water from a duck's back. 'Emily wanted to try and get Zadie to bed for a little while. The poor thing is exhausted, and it's long past her bedtime.'

Natalie glances again at the clock, actually taking it in this time. It's almost one o'clock in the morning.

'How are you, Nat?' Eve's face is full of concern, and Natalie can't help it; the spark of irritation she's felt towards Eve over the past few weeks has ignited into a full-blown flame that she can't seem to extinguish.

'How do you think I am, Eve?' Natalie stands, not wanting Eve looming over her. 'My baby was taken from her cot in the middle of the night, dumped in the woods and right now I don't even know if she's going to make it, so how the bloody hell do you think I feel?'

Eve's mouth drops open, and for a moment nothing comes out, and then she says, 'I'm sorry, Natalie. Of course you're all over the place. I don't know what I was thinking.' She slides the changing bag off her shoulder and tucks it on the empty chair beside Natalie, and then holds out the carrier bag in her hands. 'I brought a few things for Erin.'

Natalie takes the carrier bag and peers inside.

'I brought her dummy, I know she struggles to get off to sleep without it,' Eve says. 'And a fresh change of clothes and a clean blanket. I took one out of the airing cupboard, because Erin's usual blanket...' She trails off. Erin's usual blanket was tucked around her tiny body in the woods. 'And the changing bag...' She gestures vaguely towards the chair. 'I filled it with wipes and nappies, and I made up a few bottles, just in case. I know they probably have milk here, but—'

'Thanks.' Natalie knows she's being short with Eve, knows she should at least try and show some gratitude, even if it is fake, but she can't. She should have been the one to put Erin's things in a bag, to make up fresh bottles so she doesn't get hungry, but she hadn't even thought about it. She'd just blindly followed the police officer out to the car.

Eve moves awkwardly to the chair beside Natalie and lowers herself into it. 'Do the police have any idea who could have done this?'

Suddenly exhausted, Natalie pulls Erin's spare blanket from the bag and sits in the chair next to Eve, pressing the soft fabric to her face. If she breathes in and closes her eyes she can still smell Erin on it, under the floral scent of fabric softener. 'I don't know.'

'Well', Eve persists, 'do they know who the last person was to see Erin before she disappeared?' She pauses, frowning. 'I mean, it's difficult, isn't it? It was a party, after all. Did any of the guests see anyone else go upstairs after … you put Erin to bed?' The memory of their brief argument seems to bring a hint of colour to Eve's cheeks as she stumbles over the words.

'Me. I was the last one to see her,' Natalie says. 'At least I'm assuming it was me, I was the one who fed her and put her down, after all.' She shakes away the gap in the evening, the missing stretch of time where she's not too sure where she was or what she was doing.

'Gosh.' Eve's eyes widen. 'The FLO said the baby monitor was out of charge.'

'Yep.' The word is like a chip of ice. 'It seems no one – *I* – didn't realise, given everything else going on at the time.'

Eve looks as if she wants to respond, but clamps her mouth closed, the two women sitting in silence until the police officer returns with a cup of lukewarm hot chocolate for Natalie.

'Did you see the doctor out there?' Natalie asks, aware of the desperation in her voice. The police officer shakes his head and perches on the chair in the far corner of the room, as if to be as unobtrusive as possible.

'It's unbelievable, isn't it?' Eve shakes her head, tears spilling over and beginning to run down her cheeks. 'That someone could do something so awful to a little baby like this.'

'Yes, it is.' Natalie wonders if she should comfort Eve, but shouldn't it be the other way round?

'I just honestly can't believe it. Erin is so precious. Such a tiny, precious little thing. She's such a good baby. The very idea someone could sneak into her room without being noticed and just *steal* her away like that...'

Natalie feels that familiar prickle, the needles that dig under her skin when Eve says things like this, *hints* at things like this. 'What are you saying, Eve?'

'Nothing. Nothing.' Eve shakes her head again. 'I just find it so shocking this has even happened. When the house was full of people, someone just... Who could do something like this, something this evil, knowing they risked her life? She's a *baby*, for goodness' sakes. How did nobody see what was happening?'

'Someone did do it, though, didn't they?' Natalie says. *What is Eve saying? That I am a terrible mother? That I should have seen what happened? That Pete is somehow responsible, seeing as he never wanted Erin in the first place?* 'And maybe that's my fault for not charging the monitor, maybe it's Pete's fault for wanting to host this fucking party in the first place. Maybe...' Her voice breaks. 'I don't know, Eve. I don't know how someone could have gone upstairs and taken my baby without anyone noticing.'

'What about Pete?' Eve asks, her voice barely above a whisper.

'What about him?' Natalie snaps. She hopes Eve doesn't know about Vanessa – not yet. Natalie isn't ready to talk about that, and certainly not with a police officer in the room.

'Do you know...? Do you actually know where Pete was when they found out Erin was missing?'

'He was with me and Zadie, we had just cut Emily's birthday cake.'

'I mean... before. Not when they found her missing. Where was he when she actually disappeared? People were saying no one saw him for a while before they realised Erin was gone.' Eve looks down at the bag at her feet, unwilling to meet Natalie's eyes.

The air seems to go out of the room, and Natalie pauses, trying to draw a breath as she glances in the direction of the police officer. He is looking down at his hands, picking something out from under his nail, and doesn't appear to be listening.

'What the fuck is that supposed to mean?' Natalie hisses, two angry red dots burning their way on to her cheeks. All of a sudden she feels incredibly warm, and she throws off the cardigan.

'Nothing,' Eve says, her voice low. 'I didn't mean anything by it, but they're going to ask you that question, Nat. Whether you want to admit it or not, things have been tough at home, and having Erin has affected yours and Pete's relationship.' She pauses, fixing her sharp blue eyes on Natalie. 'Natalie, you have to be honest with yourself. Pete never wanted Erin in the first place.'

The anger that washes over Natalie is almost cleansing, as it strips away any last vestiges of fuzziness from the diazepam, leaving her clear-headed and absolutely furious.

'Are you kidding me?' Her voice rises to a screech and the police officer looks up from his nails. 'Are you actually going to accuse Pete? I know you hate him, but for fuck's sake, Eve.'

'Natalie, I'm just asking the question the police are going to want answered, that's all.' Eve is on her feet too, now, and for a brief dizzying moment, Natalie can picture herself wrapping her hands around Eve's throat, choking her into silence.

'I can't believe you. The nerve … The *audacity* of you.'

'Nat, I'm worried—'

'You don't need to be worried about me,' Natalie snorts. 'Thanks for bringing Erin's things, but you didn't need to, I could have got Stu and Mari to do that.' She knows those words will sting Eve, wound her like tiny darts. Eve has always been jealous of Stu and Mari, of the years of shared history they all have together without Eve. 'I think it's time you left.'

'Natalie, please, I want to make sure Erin is OK.'

As Natalie turns on Eve, the police officer gets to his feet, reaching out to gently tug her away from the woman she thought was her friend. 'Erin is not your concern,' Natalie says, her voice dangerously quiet now. 'None of us are your concern.'

'OK. OK, I'll leave.' As if sensing that Natalie is teetering on the edge, Eve gets to her feet, tucking her phone into her pocket.

Natalie watches her move to the door, her heart in her mouth, half expecting Eve to refuse to leave at the last moment, half expecting her to demand to see Erin. As she reaches the door, Natalie can't stop herself from calling out to Eve.

'Erin doesn't need you around, Eve. All she needs is her *family*. No one else.' Eve's face is blank, but as she blinks Natalie thinks she can see fresh tears in her eyes. 'So thanks for bringing her things in, but please don't come back to the hospital. Please respect our privacy.'

'Of course.' Eve bows her head in a nod, reaching for the door handle before she turns back to Natalie. 'But I just want you to think about things, Nat, that's all. You must know you can't trust a word Pete says.'

Natalie feels the room spin for a moment as the force of Eve's words hit her full on. 'Like I can trust you? I know you've been cancelling your clients so you can come over to our house. Why? So I can feel in debt to you, feel guilty for pulling you away from your busy practice?' She shakes her head. 'Don't you dare put this on me, or Pete. It's like you're obsessed with us.'

Eve pulls back as if she's been slapped. 'Natalie, I just wanted to help ... but Pete—'

'I don't want any explanations from you, Eve. And as for Pete ... If you've got something to tell me, then just say it.'

'I'm sorry, Nat, this was a mistake. I shouldn't have come here.'

'Just *say it*, Eve. Whatever it is, just say it and then get out.'

Eve lifts her chin, and meets Natalie's gaze head-on. 'OK. Pete's a liar, Nat, and you know it. If he's so innocent in all of this, then where has he been lately, while you've been at home alone, struggling to keep going? Maybe he should have been spending more time at home with you and the children, and less time at Montpellier Square.'

# *Pete*

Pete has been in the office with the two police officers for well over half an hour and they don't seem to be showing any sign of wrapping up the conversation. He shifts in his seat; the temptation to just get up and tell them he'll speak to them later is overwhelming, but he's pretty sure it won't go down too well.

'I'm sorry,' Pete says eventually, 'but is this going to take much longer? I'm sure you can understand I'm waiting to hear if my daughter is going to be OK...' He breaks off, his throat thickening. 'Sorry, it's just that the doctor will go to the waiting room if there is any news and I won't be there. They won't know where I am to tell me.'

'The doctors already know where you are, and they'll update us as soon as there are any developments.'

Pete's eyes go to the clock on the wall, registering it's just gone one o'clock in the morning. How much longer before they're able to tell them how Erin is? He doesn't know what time they arrived at the hospital, but it feels like hours ago.

'We're trying to build up a picture of what happened tonight,' DI Travis says. 'It's important we collect as much information as we can.' She glances down at her notepad, at the indecipherable writing there. 'Tell us about Vanessa, Pete. The woman from your office. What's her surname?'

Pete feels his heart stutter in his chest. He thought they were done discussing Vanessa. 'Taylor. Vanessa Taylor.'

'Do you have a contact number for Vanessa? We'll need to speak to her, seeing as she was at the house this evening.'

'No, I don't,' Pete says, running his thumb over the locked screen of his phone. He doesn't. He blocked her number. 'She lives at Montpellier Square, though.' He gives them her address. Will they think it's odd that he knows her address, but doesn't have her number in his phone? His palms are sweaty, and he can feel a muscle begin to twitch in his upper eyelid. He wonders if this is what guilty people feel like.

'Vanessa isn't just a woman from your office, is she, Pete?' Travis asks. 'The two of you have history together.' DS Haynes looks up now, his face drawn. He has pockmarked skin, as if he suffered badly with acne as a teenager, and his hair sticks up in little tufts all over his head. He's young, barely more than Emily's age, and Pete can't seem to take him seriously, not when he sits beside the immaculate DI Travis. 'Eve Sanders told us she believes you and Vanessa Taylor are having an affair. Is that why the affair started? Because you were unhappy with the fact your wife was pregnant?'

Pete feels as though someone has punched him in the stomach. He leans forward, gasping a little as he reaches for the plastic cup of water and takes a sip. He was a fool to think that the police wouldn't find out he'd had an affair with Vanessa. *Eve knew about Vanessa all along – even if she didn't have proof, just raising the idea of it with the police is the ultimate revenge on me for everything I said to her.* He wonders if she enjoyed telling the police about her suspicions, if she relished the thought of making him look like a terrible husband and father.

'I didn't ... No.' Pete falters. 'That's ... That's not why I had an affair with Vanessa.'

'No one could blame you,' Travis says, with what appears to be a sympathetic smile. 'I mean, a baby you didn't want, your entire family life disrupted, a wife who didn't want to know you. Men have done far worse for less.'

'No,' Pete says, his voice rising. 'It wasn't like that. That's not how it was.' He pauses, trying to gather his thoughts into some sort of order so he can explain to Travis exactly what it was like. 'I didn't actively choose to have an affair with Vanessa, I didn't want to at all. It just kind of... happened. She invited me – us – to the pub at Easter and Natalie didn't want to come.'

'Is that when it started?'

Pete shakes his head. 'No, not that night. It was a couple of weeks later. We went for drinks at a leaving do, and I walked her back to her flat after – it was late. She invited me in for a coffee. We kissed that night, nothing more. I thought that was it, just a silly, drunken mistake, but then...' He trails off. He'd thought that was all it would be, but now that he thinks about it, maybe Vanessa wasn't thinking the same way.

'It all felt... organic, I suppose, at the time, but now I think of it, I think Vanessa... I don't know, set her cap at me? Like she was determined for something to happen between us again. She would turn up in my office when I was working late, talking about the past, the things we used to do, the people we used to hang out with, and she would listen to me when I... well, when I complained about Natalie, I suppose.' Pete swallows, his throat jagged and sore as if he's swallowed glass. It was bad enough Natalie finding out about the affair, but to have it aired to strangers – to *police officers* – makes him feel like the lowest of the low. He looks away, unable to make eye contact as a slick wave of shame washes over him, leaving him feeling greasy and tainted somehow. 'It felt like it was inevitable something more would happen between us, and now I think about it, I feel as though Vanessa engineered it all.' He feels like a mug, Pete thinks. That's how he feels. Manipulated by his dick, like thousands of other men before him.

'Are you still seeing Vanessa?' DI Travis asks, an eyebrow raised.

'No,' Pete shakes his head vehemently. 'Definitely not.'

'And how did she take it? I'm assuming you broke things off with her?'

'Not well.' An icy draught blows over Pete, even though there is no air conditioning in this room. 'Really badly, actually. She turned up at my house with a file containing... ahh, naked photographs of herself.' A violent heat creeps up Pete's neck, staining his skin a bright pink. 'I told her to get out, that I didn't want anything to do with her any more. She started on at me about Natalie, telling me she was a terrible wife and a shit mother, and that was the last straw for me.' Pete remembers the gleeful look on her face as Vanessa spat the words at him, almost as if she relished the idea of Natalie struggling, drowning in her attempts to keep them all above water.

'And then she turned up uninvited at your daughter's birthday party.' DI Travis jots a note in her book, chewing her bottom lip as she does. 'What about access to the party – did you have to physically let people into the house? Or were people coming and going as they pleased?'

Pete pauses for a moment, trying to remember. Stu and Mari had knocked, but once the party was in full swing neither he nor Natalie had the time to keep answering the door. 'We let the first guests in, but once the party got underway most of the guests were using the side gate to let themselves into the garden.' Pete remembers seeing Dave and his wife coming in that way. 'The patio doors were open from the kitchen out into the garden, so if people needed to use the loo or get drinks that's the way they would have gone in and out.'

'So no one would have had any access through the front door?'

Pete shakes his head. He had let Jake out that way after the argument with Emily, but everyone else had gone through the side gate – he's sure of it. 'The front door is the kind that slams closed and locks itself, unless you put it on the latch. Natalie is forever worried Zadie will lock her out one of these days.'

'Any other exits from the house besides the front door and the side gate?'

Pete nods. 'The back gate. The gate at the back of the garden leads directly out into the woods. That gate was locked, though, up until I went out to have a cigarette. I unlocked it to go out, but I don't remember if I locked it again. The gate was open when I went out to look for Erin.'

'Do you have a Ring doorbell, any cameras up around the house?'

'No.' Pete had wanted to get a Ring doorbell, but Natalie refused, saying she couldn't bear the chime of it. She was even more resistant after Erin was born, convinced that the chime would wake the baby.

'So,' Travis shifts in her seat, as if she is also slowly going numb from sitting for so long on the uncomfortable plastic chairs, 'if Vanessa came to the party uninvited, she would have had to let herself in through the side gate, but no one saw her?'

'Not that I know of,' Pete says. 'Most people at the party already knew each other – it was close friends and family, mainly – but even if she had let herself in the side gate, I don't know that anyone would have challenged her. I didn't see her come in. The first time I saw her was when I noticed her standing on the grass when I finished making my speech.'

DI Travis and DS Haynes exchange a glance, and Pete feels it again – that little flicker of fear that tells him they are thinking something he's too frightened to voice. That he knows something about Erin's disappearance.

'Did you see Vanessa leave the party?'

'Yes.' Pete doesn't elaborate, doesn't want to think about that awful argument with Natalie on the stairs.

'Could she have returned at some point without being noticed?'

'Of course she could. By that point – it was well after my speech and Natalie had already put Erin down to sleep – most people were pretty well oiled, and she'd already been seen at the party. No one would have thought it strange she was around.'

'OK.' DI Travis taps her pen against her chin. 'What about the other guests? Did anyone leave the party unexpectedly? Could they have left and then returned?'

Pete pauses, thinking of Jake storming out, of Eve telling him she was leaving, of Vanessa standing by the front door, her hand on the latch after she must have heard what was said between him and Natalie. 'It's possible, yes. Do you think Vanessa has something to do with Erin's disappearance?' She could have flicked the latch up as she left, stopping the door from locking. Pete goes cold at the thought that this might be all his fault. He knows Vanessa had sworn to get her revenge on him, but he thought that was just her telling Natalie about the affair, in order to cause the implosion of his marriage. Could she really have it in her to steal a child?

'We have to consider all the options,' Travis says. 'Moving on, do you remember if Natalie was wearing make-up for the party?'

'What?' Pete's head spins at the change in direction, not sure what relevance this has to anything.

'Make-up. Was Natalie wearing make-up for the party?' Travis repeats, patiently.

'Yes, I think so.' Pete can't honestly remember. All he remembers is thinking she looked pretty when she came downstairs when Stu and Mari arrived. Everything else has been wiped out by the events of the rest of the evening. 'Why? What does this have to do with Erin?'

Travis leans forward, her gaze solemn. 'The blanket Erin was wrapped in ... There was a red stain on it when the paramedics removed her from the bag. At first they thought it was blood.' She watches him, gauging his reaction as Pete raises a hand to his mouth. *Blood?* 'It wasn't,' she says, and Pete visibly relaxes. 'It was red lipstick – we're pretty certain it's MAC Ruby Woo. I'm asking because if Natalie was wearing that lipstick when she put Erin down to sleep, then there is a reasonable explanation for the lipstick being there. If Natalie *wasn't* wearing red lipstick, then we need to know who was, and how it came to be on the blanket.' DI Travis opens up her phone and slides it over to Pete. It shows a photograph of Erin's blanket, the faint smudge of bright red lipstick standing out like a gash against the white wool.

Pete sees Natalie in his mind's eye, stepping down the stairs in her pink sundress. She wasn't wearing red lipstick, he's sure of it. In fact, he's pretty sure that Natalie has never worn red lipstick, not even before Erin was born. Another image rises in his mind, amid a crashing wave of raw, unbridled anger. There is one woman in his life who religiously wears red lipstick. One woman who will do anything, it seems, to destroy his life. *Vanessa.*

# Natalie

Natalie stands there speechless, adrenaline leaving her breathless as she debates what to do. Eve knows about Montpellier Square, knows what Pete has been doing, but how? Did she follow him? A horrifying thought floats into Natalie's mind. *Did Eve take Erin in an attempt to frame Pete? Is that why she asked if I knew where he was when Erin disappeared?* Decision made, Natalie hands her still full cup of hot chocolate to the police officer and heads for the lifts down to the ground floor. Jabbing impatiently at the buttons, she hopes she can make it downstairs before Eve leaves the hospital. She is about to push open the swing doors to the stairs when the bell pings and the lift doors open. Natalie steps in beside a doctor with a stern face and a clipboard, and an older lady clutching a mangled tissue in her hands, pressing it to her nose in tiny dabs. Her eyes are red-rimmed and Natalie looks away, towards the mirrored walls. Immediately she wishes she hadn't. Her reflection in the glass is set, her lips a thin white gash, and the tiny lines that she's recently noticed around her eyes and mouth have deepened into gorges. Her skin has a waxy sheen to it, as if she's in the middle of a bout of flu.

After stopping at every floor, the lift finally reaches the ground floor and Natalie is alone. Hurrying through the doors, she rushes through the accident and emergency department and follows the signs for the car park, her breath coming in short pants as her sandals slip on the wet pavement. The rain has finally stopped, but the air has an unseasonable chill and Natalie shivers as she casts her eye around the car park, searching for Eve's car. She has almost given up hope when she sees movement at the parking pay station, and then Eve crosses the tarmac in front of her, the street lamp illuminating her slight figure.

'Eve!' Natalie runs across the car park, ignoring the puddles splashing over her feet and up her bare calves, as the lights on Eve's car flash. 'Eve! Wait a minute.'

Eve pauses, about to step into her car. Her eyes are wide and alarm flits across her features before she realises it's just Natalie. 'God,' she breathes, pressing a hand to her chest, 'I thought I was about to get mugged. What is it?' Her hand goes to her mouth. 'Oh no. It's not Erin, is it?'

'No,' Natalie frowns. 'I wouldn't chase you down out here if it was about Erin – I would be *with Erin*.' Natalie thinks this is a prime example of how important Eve believes she is to their family – important enough that Natalie would leave her daughter to tell Eve any news. 'What did you mean upstairs? You said Pete should have been at home instead of spending time in Montpellier Square. What did you mean?' Natalie's hand shoots out and grips the car door, so Eve can't close it if she gets into the car.

Eve's gaze drifts to Natalie's hand on the door, and then back to her face. 'I didn't mean anything by it. I'm sorry, I'm tired and I wasn't thinking. I shouldn't have said it.'

'You knew.' Natalie feels winded, as if all the air has been knocked out of her. 'You knew Pete was having an affair and you didn't tell me.'

'It wasn't my place to tell you, Natalie.'

Natalie isn't buying that, not one little bit. 'Bullshit, Eve. There's nothing you love more than running Pete down, so why not tell me something you know is going to blow my marriage apart? Isn't that what you've been waiting for? Something to prove you right about Pete?' Natalie pauses, drawing in a breath.

'That's not true, Nat. I might not like Pete – in fact, I think he's a right shit – but I wasn't going to come between the two of you. He can do that all by himself.'

Natalie's voice rises, echoing in the empty car park. 'You think Pete had something to do with this. With Erin's disappearance.'

Eve scoffs. 'I never said anything of the sort—'

'You don't need to!' Natalie half screeches as Eve takes a step back, raising her hands as if to ward her off. 'You've made it perfectly clear what you think about him. What has he ever done to you, Eve? Even before you knew about the affair, you hated him. You're so... so *down* on him all the time, and he doesn't deserve it.' If someone had told Natalie a couple of hours ago that she would be defending Pete – Pete the *cheat* – she would have laughed in their face, but now standing in front of Eve, Natalie has never felt so passionately about him as she does now.

'You're deluded,' Eve says, fury making her voice tremble in the still night air. 'I can't believe that after all this time you can't see what he's really like. Even after you know he cheated on you.' She takes a step towards Natalie, her eyes never leaving her face. 'He was with that other woman when you were crying at the bottom of the stairs. He was with her when Zadie was playing up at school and you had to meet the headteacher alone.' She eyes Natalie with disdain. 'Pete was with *her* when you called me, afraid of what you might do to your own baby.'

Natalie can't speak, winded by Eve's mention of that awful, desperate phone call. 'No one asked you to be there.'

'Yes, you fucking did!' Eve shouts, drawing attention from a man who hurries past them into the emergency department, his head lowered as if to drown them out. 'It was me you called, not Pete, because you knew he would never respond to you. It was *me* who took care of Erin when you couldn't, *me* who spent time with Zadie, when all she wanted was a little bit of attention and you couldn't give it to her. It was me, every time, when it should have been Pete. So forgive me if you think I'm unreasonable for thinking he's a complete piece of shit.' Eve takes a breath, her chest hitching, but Natalie can tell she isn't done yet, not by a long shot.

'Pete should have been the one doing all of this. Pete should have been the one supporting you, not me,' Eve says, quietly. 'Pete should be grateful he even has a family like yours to come home to. He doesn't deserve you.'

Natalie's veins spark with something deeper than plain old rage. It's the innate instinct to lash out and knock down whatever is threatening her family. 'What is it that you want, Eve?'

'I want you to see what *you* have,' Eve says, her voice breaking now. 'If Erin was mine, I would take such good care of her, I would worship the ground she walked on, but you – neither of you seem to appreciate what you have. You need to wake up, Natalie, to the fact that you are lucky to have a healthy baby at your age – to have three beautiful kids, which is all I ever wanted – and to the fact that Pete will never give you what you deserve.'

'None of this is my fault,' Natalie says, the words tumbling out before she has a chance to process what she's even going to say. All she knows is that she wants to make Eve hurt the way she is hurting right now. 'It's not my fault you don't have a family, Eve. It's not my fault none of your many, *many* boyfriends want to marry you, and it's not my fault you can't have children.' Eve opens her mouth, her face a bleached, sickly white in the glow of the street lamp overhead, but Natalie holds up a hand. 'I've tried so hard to include you in our family, to make you feel welcome, and in return all you've done is try to turn me against Pete.'

'I was trying to show you that you deserve better than him.'

Natalie laughs, a bitter brisk bark that hangs in the air. 'Why can't you just admit it? You were jealous, Eve, you always have been, even when I tried to make you a part of it, even when Pete told me you were obsessive and annoying, and that something wasn't right about the way you were so fixated on our family. The way you were constantly looking for a way in.' She pauses before she leans in close, so close she can feel Eve's breath hitting her cheek. 'I know what you did.'

What little colour is left in Eve's face drains away and she swallows hard. 'Natalie, I—'

'You told Pete I knew I was pregnant. You told him I told you first!' Natalie shakes her head, as Eve lets out a long exhale. She looks almost relieved, but Natalie is too furious to question why. 'I trusted you, Eve, and you couldn't even tell me my husband was lying to me. Does it make you happy? Knowing you've had a hand in destroying my marriage?'

Eve's eyes narrow, and she yanks open the car door again. 'I don't think telling Pete you lied about your pregnancy is the nail in that particular coffin.'

Natalie pulls her hand from the door as Eve slides into the driver's seat and shoves her key towards the ignition, fumbling it and dropping it into the footwell. 'I will never, ever let you take Erin from me, do you understand?' That look of relief on Eve's face when Natalie brought up the pregnancy flashes in front of Natalie's eyes, and she steps back, something dark and ugly stirring in her gut. 'Where did you go, Eve? When you left the party after Pete's speech? Where were you?'

Eve finally manages to get her key in the ignition and she guns the car into life with a roar. 'I am not to blame for your family's problems, Natalie. Instead of looking at me, perhaps you should be looking a bit closer to home. I think everything else that needs to be said has been said. Go back to your baby.' Without another glance at Natalie, Eve speeds out of the car park, her brake lights flashing only briefly as she reaches the junction back out on to the main road.

Drained, Natalie leans against the street lamp, willing her heart rate to return to normal. She's not going mad, she's sure of it. The look of relief on Eve's face just now – it was almost as if Eve had expected to be accused of something else, far worse than telling Pete a secret. *Where did Eve go when she left the party?* Natalie thought she went home, but then Eve was there when the police turned up, after Erin was reported missing. Did she hear the sirens and come back? Or had she returned prior to that? Natalie closes her eyes, thinking about Pete running back into the house, shouting that he'd found her. Erin, a tiny bundle in his arms, wrapped in a carrier bag. *Oh, God.* Natalie wraps a hand around the cold metal of the street lamp, keeping herself upright, the pavement suddenly tilting beneath her feet. Erin had been found inside a plastic Marks and Spencer's bag. The same bag that Eve had brought to the party, filled with expensive wine.

*Erin was found in the hollow tree, beside the woodland path.* The woodland path leading from the back of Natalie's house, all the way out to the village, to the street that Eve lives on. Eve uses that cut through all the time. And she would know about the tree – of course she would. Natalie's hand goes to her mouth, and she's surprised to taste salt on her lips. She's crying again. Eve has been with Natalie on numerous occasions during the summer holidays when they've taken Emily and Zadie – and even Erin, this year – to the hollow tree for a picnic and to try and catch sticklebacks in the stream.

Natalie's eyes go to the illuminated windows of the hospital, to the third floor where Erin is being looked after by the doctors in the ICU. She still doesn't even know if Erin is going to survive the ordeal she's been through tonight, and at this thought Natalie's feet turn towards the building and she begins to run, back inside, back to her daughter. With every footstep, Eve's words rebound in her mind. *If Erin were mine I would take such good care of her.* Eve has made it clear to Natalie that she thinks she is a terrible mother. *Did Eve take Erin to prove that to the rest of the world?*

# *Pete*

Pete hurries back to the waiting room, his guts a roiling turmoil of fear, anger and frustration, but when he pushes the door open, there is no sign of Natalie.

'I think she stepped outside for some fresh air,' The police officer sitting in the corner says before Pete can ask the question, the smell of hot chocolate and antiseptic on the air making Pete's stomach turn.

'Is there ... ?'

The police officer shakes his head. 'No news, not yet.'

Pete steps back out into the corridor, pulling out his phone and scrolling to Vanessa's contact details. Unblocking her number, he dials, frustration flooding his veins when it goes straight to voicemail. He dials again, with the same result, but doesn't leave a message. He thinks for a minute, scrolling across the apps on his screen when he pauses, his finger hovering over Snapchat. He never uses the app, only has it because Vanessa encouraged him to download it because the messages disappear once read. Now, he opens up the map in the app, to see Vanessa's icon hovering over her flat in Montpellier Square. *I could go there, demand to know if she was responsible for Erin's abduction.* He thinks of Erin, hooked up to all kinds of machines. He needs to be here, for her, for Natalie. *But if Vanessa is responsible, I need to know.*

Pete's phone buzzes, his heart leaping as Emily's name flashes across the screen. 'Em? Everything OK there?'

'Dad.' Her voice sounds tired and thick, the way it does when she's been crying. 'Is Erin OK?'

'Still waiting for news, sweetheart. Are you girls all right?'

240

'Can we come to the hospital? Jake said he could drive us.' Emily's voice breaks and Pete feels his heart crack. 'Eve left, but the police officer is still here and Zadie is frightened. I tried to get her to go to bed, but she just keeps crying about Erin, saying she's scared she's going to die.'

'Stay there, Em. I'll come home, get Zadie settled and then I'll come back. Mum will stay here with Erin.' Pete hangs up, promising Emily he won't be long, and then pulls up the Uber app, thanking God that there's a car just three minutes away.

As the Uber driver speeds towards town, Pete can hear his pulse pounding in his ears. He hasn't felt rage like this for years – maybe ever. Erin in hospital, Zadie terrified, Emily crying. His family, hurting. He knows he should go straight home, wrap his girls in his arms and reassure them that everything is going to be fine – even though right now he doesn't know for sure – but the image of DI Travis leaning in to tell him about the red lipstick on Erin's blanket preys on his mind, and he clenches his fists, anger burning in his gut. *Vanessa*. He has to know, has to confront her, to watch her face as he tells her he knows what she did.

'Excuse me, mate.' Pete leans forward and taps the Uber driver on the shoulder. 'Could we make a quick stop on the way?'

Fifteen minutes later, the car pulls up outside Vanessa's building, and Pete glances up at the top floor. A single lamp burns in her sitting room window, and he hurries up the front steps, jabbing at the buzzer repeatedly until she opens the door.

'Pete? Oh my God, are you OK?' Vanessa answers the door in a silk kimono, her expression concerned but not unwelcoming, as she stands to one side to let him in to her immaculate flat. 'Come in.'

'I'm sorry about Erin,' she says as he walks down the hall into the sitting room. The Tiffany lamp emits a soft glow, aided by the help of several large Diptyque candles burning brightly in the fireplace, and the television mouths silently to itself in the corner. 'I've been so worried about you. I was going to call, but then I didn't know if...' She lets out a long breath. 'My God, I can't believe this has happened. Can't imagine what you must be going through. Is she going to be OK?'

'We don't know yet.' Pete's voice is gruff, and he starts as Vanessa's hands slide onto his shoulders and ease his jacket off. 'That's part of the reason I'm here.'

'Well, I'm glad you came.' Her voice is soft, her breath tickling the nape of his neck. She drops his jacket, and then slides her arms around him from behind, hugging him to her. She feels warm and familiar, and for one dizzying second it's as if none of this has ever happened. It's as if Pete has just slipped back here after work, and Natalie doesn't know anything about the affair, and Erin is safely tucked up in her cot.

'Don't, Vanessa.' Pete pulls her arms away and turns to face her. She blinks at him, her hair falling over one shoulder, the kimono sliding from the other one, leaving it bare.

'I'm sorry.' She steps back, and Pete can almost believe for a moment that she is.

'Things are touch-and-go with Erin,' Pete says, his eyes never leaving her face. 'Someone knew when they took her out to the woods that she could potentially die out there. What kind of person does something like that?'

Vanessa's eyes narrow. 'Why are you here, Pete? Shouldn't you be at the hospital?'

'What the fuck are you playing at, Vanessa?'

Vanessa stares at him for a long moment, before she shakes her head and pulls the kimono back up over her shoulders. 'Pete, I—'

'Your lipstick was all over her blanket! What the hell were you trying to achieve? Did you just want to hurt me? Hurt Nat? Is it revenge for me dumping you? Because you're sick in the head if it is.' Pete feels breathless, as if it is painful to get the words out, a crushing weight sitting on his chest. 'Erin is just a *baby*.'

'Jesus Christ, Pete, you really are losing it.' Vanessa picks up the crystal tumbler sitting on the coffee table and sips from the amber liquid inside.

'Did you think if Erin wasn't around I'd leave Natalie? That I'd come and set up a nice, cosy home over here with you?' Pete steps towards her, his hands itching to slap the glass away from her mouth, to smash it to tiny shards all over her expensive oak flooring.

'Pete, I never went anywhere near Erin, not even when she was being handed around the garden like a little dolly.' The words ring hollow, and as she sips at the whisky in her glass to cover the flush rising on her collarbone, Pete knows she's lying. 'Don't you think there was more than one woman at the party wearing red lipstick?'

Pete does know that – he's thought about it in the Uber on the way over here – but it can only be Vanessa. No one else would want to hurt him like this. 'You wear it every day, the same shade as the one in the photo the police showed me.' Pete moves to the small clutch bag on the sofa, the same one Vanessa brought to the party. He tips it out, letting out a yelp of triumph as a lipstick rolls out, MAC written in silver where the lid meets the rest of the case. He stoops, scooping it up and twisting it out to show what he's now certain is the exact shade on the blanket. It is worn down, the end slightly mangled. 'See? I knew I was right. You asked me if things would be different for us if there was no baby to keep me with Natalie.'

'You're crazy, you know that?' Vanessa snatches the lipstick out of his hands.

'My child could have *died*. She still might! Can't you see what you've done?'

'The only thing I've done is follow your lead, Pete. I never took Erin from her bed,' Vanessa says. 'You might think I'm mad, and do you know what? Right now, I'm inclined to agree with you.' Vanessa steps towards him, and he can smell her perfume, fused with the peaty scent of the whisky. 'I must have been *stark, raving mad* to have ever got involved with you. I loved you, Pete, but not enough to kidnap your child. It's crazy you could ever even think that.' She blinks, and a tear falls onto the silk of her kimono. 'I wanted you to be with me because you wanted to, not because I forced you.'

Pete snorts, not buying it for a second. 'So that's why you told Natalie about us? That's why you turned up uninvited to Emily's party? Because that wouldn't be forcing my hand, would it?'

'You really can't see it, can you?' Vanessa says, her mouth twisting, the tears drying up. 'When I turned up at your house that day, Natalie answered the door with a glass of wine in her hand. It was four o'clock in the afternoon, Pete, and she was already drinking.'

Pete doesn't want to believe that. The party was the first time he's seen Natalie with a drink since before Erin was born – but even as he thinks that, he remembers the way she seems so sluggish in the mornings, the way she complains of a headache most days. Has she been drinking? Would he really have missed it if she were?

'Erin was crying,' Vanessa goes on. 'Screaming her head off, but it was like Natalie couldn't hear it. I asked her if she wanted me to go and pick Erin up, but she just waved me away and said she was leaving Erin to "cry it out".' She makes quote marks in the air. 'Natalie was more concerned with whether I wanted to join her in a glass of wine than whether her crying child was OK. To be honest, Pete, it really made me feel quite uncomfortable.'

'And you thought the solution to all of this was to offer me naked photos of yourself in front of my wife.'

'For fuck's sake, Pete, aren't you listening to me?' Vanessa moves to the sofa and Pete realises she's a little unsteady on her feet. It's hardly surprising, given the amount of wine she sank at the party, and it seems that she has carried on the party here alone, if she really didn't take Erin to the woods. Just Vanessa and her decanter of Johnnie Walker Blue. 'The house was a fucking tip, clothes and toys scattered everywhere, although I suspect you're already aware of that. Your baby daughter was screaming her head off, and all your wife cared about was getting another glass of Sauvignon into her.'

Pete says nothing, just waits for her to continue. If he's honest, he doesn't know what to say. He came over here so fired up, convinced after his conversation with DI Travis that it must have been Vanessa who came back to the party to steal Erin away from them in an attempt to force Pete back into her arms, leaving her lipstick smudge on the blanket, incriminating herself. But now... Standing in front of Vanessa, he doesn't know what to think. Vanessa is still talking, her voice muted, threaded with strains of exhaustion.

'Natalie did eventually pick Erin up,' she is saying, 'but she was still odd... disconnected, and I just put it down to the fact she'd been drinking. Erin was sweet when she finally stopped crying.' Vanessa lets a smile tug at the corners of her mouth. 'I almost felt broody for a moment.' She glances up at Pete, the smile falling away when she sees the stern look on his face. 'Anyway,' she goes on, 'I complimented her – I told Natalie I thought Erin was cute and she told me, "Looks can be deceiving." She said Erin was by far the most difficult child she'd ever had, and she honestly didn't know how to cope with her.'

Pete's mouth is dry and he desperately wants to sip at the whisky, the very scent of it making his mouth water, but he doesn't want to return to the hospital with the smell of fresh alcohol on his breath. He doesn't doubt that DI Travis would pick up on it within seconds, and he already thinks she is suspicious of him. 'That doesn't mean anything,' he says. 'Vanessa, with all due respect, you have no idea what it's like to have a new baby. You have no idea how difficult it is, how demanding. Just because Natalie said that doesn't mean anything at all – she was probably just exhausted.'

Vanessa stands, scooping up his jacket and handing it to him. 'I know enough to know it isn't normal to be half-cut at four o'clock in the afternoon when you have two small children to take care of. I know enough to know it isn't right to leave a baby screaming and in distress.' She pushes him out into the hallway, his jacket half on, and reaches for the handle of the front door, staring into his eyes. 'I know that all I ever wanted to offer you was a sanctuary, Pete. Away from a life you told me made you so miserable. Away from the woman you told me pushed you away, never wanted to talk to you, never had time for you. A sanctuary from the bedlam you called home.'

With a gentle shove to the small of his back, Pete finds himself in the corridor, Vanessa filling the doorway with her body. 'Natalie isn't well, Pete, anyone with half a brain can see that.' She gives him one last long look. 'If I were you, I'd be looking much closer to home for whoever it was that did this to Erin.'

# Natalie

Eve's tail lights long gone in the distance, Natalie hurries back inside the hospital on unsteady feet, the smell of old dinners and disinfectant making her feel queasy. *Eve was definitely being shady about Pete*, she thinks as the lift ascends slowly back to the third floor. *Why else would she ask where Pete was when Erin went missing?* Something about it feels off to Natalie, but she can't put her finger on it and she presses her hands over her eyes. It feels as if Eve wants Natalie to think that Pete did this. *Is Eve trying to cover her own tracks by placing the blame on Pete? Or does Eve think that if Pete is out of the picture, I'll draw her into our family as a substitute for him?* Natalie doesn't know where Pete was when Erin disappeared, but she doesn't know where Eve was either. She isn't even sure where she herself was when Erin was taken from her cot, and the drugs mixed with the wine have left her cotton-mouthed and vague. That, and the fear that in that short space of time where her memory is fragmented and patchy, she did something so awful she's blocked it out completely.

Natalie has to focus on Erin now – on being the mother that Erin deserves. She steps out of the lift, heading towards the room where Erin was before, but it's empty. Erin is still down for her ultrasound, so Natalie heads for the waiting room and pushes the door open, expecting to see Pete sitting on a chair in front of her.

'Where is Pete? Has he not come back yet?' Worry gnaws at Natalie's insides as she opens the door to see only the police officer, the cold cup of hot chocolate on the table. *Are the police still questioning him?* The butterflies become a swarm, the anxiety almost painful. Why would they still be questioning Pete if he hadn't done anything wrong?

'Mrs Maxwell?' The police officer is watching her with concern. 'I said Mr Maxwell did come back here, and I told him you'd stepped out for some fresh air. I assumed he went outside to find you. Did you not catch up with him outside?'

'No.' Natalie frowns. She had expected Pete to be here waiting for her, waiting for news of Erin. She supposes it's possible that they could have missed each other in the lifts, but even so she would have thought he'd be back by now.

'Maybe he's gone for a cigarette,' she says, pulling her phone out of the pocket of her sundress. Pete thinks she doesn't know that he still sneaks the odd fag, but of course, she does. She only wishes she'd been a bit more alert to all the other things he's been hiding from her. She jabs at the phone screen, dialling his number, but when the call connects it's to voicemail.

'Shit.' Fury at Pete and panic over Erin combine to leave Natalie jittery and on edge. *How fucking difficult is it for Pete to answer his phone?* A seed of doubt begins to grow in her mind, fertilised by Eve's comments. Pete wouldn't, would he? His daughter is lying in hospital; surely he wouldn't ... That now-familiar rage bubbles up at the thought of where Pete could be, and Natalie opens Find My iPhone, hoping to prove herself wrong.

*Montpellier Square.* The blue dot representing Pete pulses over an old apartment building in Montpellier Square. *Vanessa's flat.* Natalie throws her phone onto the table with a crash, startling the police officer. How could Pete do this, now of all times? Natalie feels drained, hollow, as if Pete has ripped all the stuffing out of her, and she covers her face with her hands. She never knew it was possible to feel this hurt, this broken.

'Natalie?' DI Travis's voice is soft as she peers into the waiting room. 'Could you come with me, please?'

Natalie looks up, dropping her hands into her lap. 'Really? Right now? I'm waiting for Erin to come back from her ultrasound and Pete ...' She swallows, trying to dislodge the lump in her throat.

'This really won't take very long.'

'You've never been in this situation, have you?' Natalie feels a surge of inner strength. This is her *child*. She needs to be near her. 'Wouldn't you want to be near your child at a time like this? Would you want to be answering questions?'

DI Travis's face is blank. 'Like I said, it won't take long, and I'm sure you'd rather do it here, than down at the station.'

Natalie nods and swipes her hands over her face, slicking away tears before she follows Travis to an office further down the corridor. Another police officer sits on the other side of the desk, and he stands as Natalie enters, introducing himself as DS Haynes.

'I want to go back to the beginning,' Travis says, 'to when Erin was first born. I understand you struggled a bit with adjusting to having a third baby.'

*Is that what Pete told them?* Natalie sits forward, arranging her hands neatly in her lap under the table. 'It was difficult, yes,' she says. 'I suppose I didn't realise how much of an impact it would have on the family, going from two children to three.' Natalie finds herself picking at her nails under the table. 'Erin doesn't sleep very much. I struggled with that – with the exhaustion.'

Travis nods as if she understands, and Natalie remembers her saying in the car that she had a young daughter. 'Natalie, let's talk about post-natal depression. I understand that was a big part of this for you. Did you suffer from it before, when you had Emily and Zadie?'

'What? I don't—'

'How long have you been taking diazepam for?'

Natalie feels a horrifying sensation creeping over her, bringing a chill to her very core. The chat in the car with DI Travis wasn't just one older mother to another, sharing their experiences. It wasn't Travis being friendly. It was her feeling Natalie out, trying to judge whether she could have been responsible for this.

'I don't know where you've got your information,' Natalie says coldly, 'but I am not suffering from post-natal depression. I've been a bit low, yes, but that's exhaustion, not depression. Anyone would struggle to cope on two or three hours' sleep a night.'

'And the diazepam?' Travis gives nothing away as she glances at her colleague and then back to Natalie. 'Forgive my ignorance, Natalie, but I'm sure the doctor wouldn't usually prescribe that just for exhaustion.'

'I didn't take them,' Natalie says.

'Four tablets are missing from the blister pack we found in the bathroom.' Travis's tone has lost any hint of warmth, and Natalie can feel the glacial chill radiating from her. 'If you didn't take them, who did?'

'No, I did take them.' Natalie feels tongue-tied, as if the detective is trying to trip her up. 'I flushed two of the tablets away ages ago. I did take those other two tablets, but I never took any before today, that's what I meant. You can check the prescription – it hasn't been refilled.' She pauses, her throat thickening. 'I only took them tonight because ... because I found out Pete had been sleeping with Vanessa. I'd also had an argument this evening with Eve, over the way she was with Erin.' Had it really only been a few hours ago that Pete was standing on a rickety garden chair, making his ridiculous speech? Had it really only been a few hours since everything had come tumbling down? 'Everything felt overwhelming, and seeing as everyone – Eve, the doctor – had been on at me to take them, telling me I would feel better if I did, I thought I might as well.'

DI Travis nods, steepling her hands under her chin. 'Of course, Natalie, I understand. Having a young baby can be very overwhelming on its own, and with everything else that happened at the party ...' She pauses for a moment. 'Tell me, Natalie. Have you ever felt at any point as though you might want to harm Erin?'

Natalie's mouth falls open, but no words come out. What can she say? There was that terrible phone call to Eve – one she wishes she'd never made. She'd been terrified that day, afraid of herself and her own actions. Has Eve told them about the phone

250

call? About the way Natalie had cried down the phone, begging Eve to come over before she did something she would regret?

'Natalie?'

'No.' She shakes her head violently, shaking away the thoughts of the phone call, of the hours she can't seem to recall tonight. 'I wouldn't ... I could never.'

DI Travis doesn't respond; instead she jots a note in her sprawling, spidery writing in the notebook as Natalie watches, gooseflesh rising on her arms at the horrifying realisation that there is every possibility the detective thinks Natalie is the one to have abducted Erin.

'I can't believe you could even ask me that.' Natalie forces the words out, her throat dry. 'I don't understand how any parent could hurt their child, and I could never hurt Erin. She's ... She's just a baby.' She can feel a pulse at her temple, an insistent beat thudding in time with the headache tightening across the back of her skull. She wouldn't hurt Erin; she couldn't. But even as she says it, Natalie thinks about the phone call she made to Eve that awful day, about the way just for a moment she could have easily picked Erin up and shaken her.

'It's more common than people realise,' Haynes says, his tone sombre.

Natalie feels the sting of his words like tiny needles under her skin. 'I'm not like those people,' she says. 'I'm not a bad person.' She looks at DI Travis, holding her gaze in what she hopes is a clear and open (*innocent*) way. 'You must understand, you have a young child. It's exhausting, and sometimes it can be very, very difficult, but that doesn't mean—'

'Isolating, too,' Travis says. 'Did you feel isolated, Natalie? After all, Pete was at work – or so he said – such long hours, and you were left with the baby all day and most evenings.'

'I didn't ... I mean, I was lonely. Sometimes.' The words taste bitter on her tongue. She *had* been lonely, and there were times when she had thought that perhaps if she hadn't continued with her pregnancy then she wouldn't feel this way. 'I didn't feel isolated, though. Not really. I had Eve, and Emily was home a lot during her study leave, and then after her exams.'

'Let's talk about Emily.'

'What about her?' Natalie's chin lifts, a rush of maternal energy running through her at the thought of her eldest child. 'She has nothing to do with this.'

'What's your relationship like with Emily? How do you get along?' DI Travis watches Natalie curiously, as if expecting her to crumble. 'Lord knows I'm not looking forward to my daughter reaching her teenage years – she's headstrong enough already.'

'Our relationship is fine,' Natalie says, hesitantly. 'We've always been close.' And they were. Before, anyway.

'She doesn't resent you for having another baby? I should imagine it was a big upheaval for her, what with her A levels and applying for university.'

'No, of course she doesn't.' Natalie can feel her blood pressure rise, anger flushing her cheeks. 'Emily isn't like that.'

'Really?' Travis sits back in her chair, an unimpressed look on her face. 'Only, the two of you were overheard arguing upstairs, when you went to put Erin to bed. She told you she wasn't here to look after the baby only you wanted, or words to that effect. Isn't that right?'

'Well—'

'What was it that pushed Emily over the edge tonight, Natalie?'

'The edge? She wasn't pushed over *the edge*.' The fury washing over Natalie creates a red mist, blinding her for a moment. Who does this woman think she is? 'How dare you.' Her voice is icy despite the heat raging in her veins. 'Yes, Emily and I have had words before over her looking after Erin, but she's got nothing to do with this. She loves Erin, and she's been nothing but helpful in the months since she's been born. Of course she's going to feel resentful sometimes – what child doesn't when they have a new sibling? But Emily and I are closer than we've ever been and nothing is going to change that.' Natalie's throat is thick with unshed tears, an aching in her chest signalling the start of a tremendous crying jag if she can't keep herself together for just a little bit longer.

'It just seems an odd time, that's all. For a row like that. At a party. For Emily.' Travis gives nothing away, her face a blank canvas. 'She called you a bitch, Natalie. That tells me she was pretty upset, and it was all over Erin. What was it that triggered her? Was Erin crying again? Was Erin taking up all of your attention, when it should have been Emily's day?'

'Yes ... no. *No*. It wasn't just about Erin, Emily was just ... being a teenager. Of course she didn't want to look after her baby sister all the time – what teenager does? But the argument at the party, it wasn't only about Erin.'

'She told you she couldn't wait to get away, isn't that right? Emily told you she couldn't wait to leave your house for good,' Travis presses on, as Natalie feels a crushing sensation in her chest. 'Maybe Emily just couldn't take it any more, the constant pressure on her to pick up your slack. Emily was happier before Erin was born, wasn't she, Natalie?'

'No. No, that's not true.' Natalie shakes her head, her heart in her mouth because even as she speaks, she knows what DI Travis is saying *is* true. Emily *was* happier before Erin came along, but they can't honestly think Emily would do this? 'You can't ... You can't think ...' Natalie tries to draw in a breath but she can't, as a thick, gulping sob erupts from her chest, hollowing her out.

*Emily would never hurt Erin.* Natalie knows that as sure as she knows her own name. *Someone heard Emily and me arguing in the bedroom.* Natalie can't think who would have been upstairs in order to hear them, and then she remembers the baby monitor. The police said it had run out of battery, but if it was still working when she and Emily were arguing, any of the guests at the party could have overheard them. Anyone could have overheard her daughter telling her how much she hates her. Folding her arms on the table in front of her, Natalie lays her head on them and finally lets the dam of tears break. Natalie sobs in a way she hasn't for years – not since her mother and father told her and Pete that if they weren't going to terminate their pregnancy with Emily, then they didn't want to see her again. She had come home that day, back to the poky flat she and Pete had fallen in love with on the outskirts of Maidstone, and cried her heart out in the bathroom, without Pete's knowledge. Now she cries until there is nothing left, the ache in her chest is gone and her face is sore and itchy with salt.

*Everything is falling apart.* The thought comes like a neon sign, blinking on and off in her head as she reaches for a tissue and blows her nose, patting her face dry, aware of DI Travis scrutinising her every move. A little over a year ago, everything had been perfect. Natalie had loved her job, working in HR at a charity. It didn't pay a lot, but it meant she could chip in for holidays, and take the kids on days out in half-term. She and Pete were rock-solid back then. They were a golden couple, an example to the rest of their friends. Even Stu and Mari had had hiccups before, but Natalie and Pete had had a smooth run; it was rare for them to even argue. Emily and Zadie had been happy. Emily hadn't hated Natalie – yes, she'd lied to the police officers, she does feel as if Emily hates her right now, but they'll get over it, they always do – and Zadie wasn't in trouble at school. Wasn't wetting the bed and refusing to eat. All of it has changed since Erin came along, and if Natalie is brutally honest with herself, she hates her life right now.

'Do you envy Emily, Natalie?' Travis speaks, her tone low and serious. 'Do you wish you could walk away from it all?'

'No,' Natalie whispers, her voice hoarse. But that is another lie. There have been so many times in the last year when Natalie has wanted to pack her bag and walk out of the door, without even saying goodbye to the rest of them. How many times has she wondered how long it would take for them to notice she wasn't there? Those days when Erin would have her up four or five times during the night, while Pete snored on completely oblivious, and then she would cry all day, no matter what Natalie did to try and soothe her. Those days, they were the days when Natalie could have walked out and never looked back. There have been a number of times when Natalie has stood over the cot, willing a restless Erin to *please, just go to sleep*, wondering why her youngest child hates her so much, a feeling that is only exacerbated by Eve waltzing in the door and getting Erin off to sleep within minutes. Natalie knows she should feel grateful for the brief respite that Eve's magic touch brings, but in all honesty, it just makes Natalie feel even more inadequate. Even more surplus to Erin's requirements.

And now, Pete. Pete and Vanessa. Natalie's mouth fills with saliva and she presses her hand to her lips, suddenly sure she's going to vomit. Maybe this is all Natalie's fault, too. Maybe she should have given him more attention, not turned her back on him and pretended to be asleep as soon as she heard the front door open. As soon as the thought rises in her mind, Natalie is disgusted with herself. The affair is Pete's doing, nobody else's. How are they ever going to get over this, even if Erin is OK? Natalie can't imagine going back to the house, to the home they've shared, raised a family in, acting as if nothing has happened. She wouldn't be surprised if Emily found a way to leave for university as soon as possible – she said she couldn't wait to get away from Natalie, and if there is no Pete to keep her there … Natalie's eyes fill with tears again and she feels a bone-crushing weariness. It feels as if she is at the root of all the problems in her family. It's her fault Pete had an affair, her fault Emily wants to leave, her fault Zadie is playing up, all because she insisted on carrying on with the pregnancy.

A cold wave of fear washes over Natalie, leaving her shivering in her sundress. She tucks her feet up onto the chair, pulling the dress low over her ankles, and wraps her arms around her knees.

If she thinks she is the most likely suspect to have done this – to have taken Erin out to die in the woods – then it stands to reason that DI Travis and her colleague will be thinking along the same lines. Natalie is sure, *positive*, she could never have done this, but what if the police have already made their minds up that she is responsible? You hear of it all the time, people being convicted of things they haven't done. She can't go to prison. She'll die if that happens. The thought takes her breath away, and she knows she is on the verge of a panic attack, her pulse crashing in her ears. *What if they find me guilty? I can't leave them, can't leave my family. Who will take care of them all?* The thought of the press hammering at the door, taking photos of Zadie and Emily as they try to go to school, of Pete having to cope without her, makes her want to die. *How will any of them cope if I'm convicted of trying to murder my own child?*

# *Pete*

Pete jumps into the waiting Uber and tells the driver to get him home *now*. He feels sick, disgusted with himself at ever taking a second look in Vanessa's direction, but underneath that there is a swirl of confusion, a foggy cloud where he can't make head nor tail of anything any more. He had been so sure that Vanessa was responsible for Erin's abduction, that the lipstick on the blanket must have belonged to her. For Vanessa to flat out deny it, and then throw Natalie's name in his face, should really make him want to defend his wife to the ends of the earth, but deep down, if he's honest, there's a tiny part of him that thinks it's not impossible. Natalie has been so erratic, so completely unlike herself, that he can't honestly say it's an impossibility. It's a thought that makes sour bile rise in the back of his throat, and he wishes he'd drunk that whisky after all.

The Uber pulls up outside the Maxwell house a short while later, and Pete is relieved to see lights blazing in the downstairs windows, his heart lifting at the thought of seeing his girls, of laying eyes on them and knowing two of his children, at least, are OK. He checks his phone as he slips out of the Uber and makes his way up the front path, his heart skipping a beat as he sees there is a missed call from Natalie. His breath catching in his throat, his fingers shake as he calls her back, suddenly sure that she was calling about Erin. That something dreadful, the worst possible thing, has happened. He turns to see the tail lights of the Uber wink as the driver reaches the end of the cul-de-sac and gets the urge to raise a hand, to tell the driver to wait. Natalie's phone rings three times before her voicemail cuts in, and Pete hangs up without leaving a message, intent on checking on the girls and getting back to the hospital as quickly as he can.

Letting himself into the hallway, he is aware of the muted conversation coming from the kitchen. The detritus of the party is still littered around the house, empty glasses and paper plates left stagnating on the coffee table in the sitting room, although it does look as though someone has made a cursory effort to tidy up a little. He wonders if whoever it was, was told to stop cleaning in case of removing evidence, and the thought of his home being a crime scene makes that sour bile rise up again.

'Dad?' Emily turns as he enters the kitchen. The family liaison officer is at the kitchen worktop, making a round of tea, and Jake hovers by the sink, an uncertain look on his face. Emily flies across the kitchen, burying her face in his chest and wrapping her arms around him so hard he feels winded.

'Hello, love,' he manages to choke out.

'How is Erin?' Emily lifts a tear-stained face up to look at him. 'Is she OK? Where's Mum? Are they coming home?' She looks to the kitchen door as if expecting Natalie to walk in carrying Erin at any moment.

'They're … ahh … They're still at the hospital, love,' Pete says gently. 'The doctors are taking care of Erin as we speak.' His gaze flickers towards Jake, who looks away and begins to wipe over the draining board with a damp cloth, just for something to do. 'Where's Zadie?'

'I managed to get her into bed, but I don't know how long she'll stay asleep. She fell asleep on the sofa and Jake carried her up.'

'What's he doing here?' Pete asks Emily in a low voice. 'I thought—'

'I called him and asked him to come back,' Emily says at full volume. 'Sorry, Dad, I just didn't want to be here on my own. Sorry,' she says to the FLO, who just smiles.

'Well, that was good of you, Jake,' Pete says graciously. Jake nods and takes a cup of tea from the worktop, handing it to Pete without meeting his eyes. 'Thanks.' Pete takes the tea, a flicker of suspicion sparking to life in his veins. *Why won't Jake meet my eye? Is it purely because he is embarrassed over the way he behaved in front of me earlier?* Pete feels a wave of shame when he thinks about the way things played out. Or is it something more sinister? He thinks again of the scrape of Emily's window at night, when both she and Jake think he and Natalie are asleep. Jake couldn't have done that this evening, as Emily's window backs on to the garden and everyone would have seen him, but... Pete takes a sip of the tea, his eyes never leaving Jake's face, as Jake looks at Emily, at the floor, anywhere except Pete's face. Could he have sneaked in through the front door? Pete has no doubt that Emily will have given Jake the code to the key safe at some point before now, so what would stop him from letting himself back into the house after Pete threw him out? The thought raises conflicting emotions for Pete – relief that perhaps Vanessa didn't do this, thereby relieving Pete of some of the burden of guilt, mixed with disgust that this boy could be responsible for hurting two of his daughters this evening. Pete's chaotic thoughts are derailed by a muffled cry, and he turns to see Zadie in the doorway.

'Daddy?' Her eyes are full, her thumb wedged into her mouth, and as Pete turns towards her he catches the acrid scent of urine rising from her direction. Her pale pink pyjama bottoms are darkened with it, and Pete wants to cry.

'Come on, Zade, let's get you upstairs for a bath, and I'll sort your bed out,' Emily says, moving towards an exhausted but upset Zadie.

With a glance towards Jake – Pete still thinks he could be responsible; after all, didn't he say he'd make Pete regret things? – Pete steps forward, reaching out and wrapping his hand around Zadie's wrist. 'I'll do it, Em.'

'You're sure?' She looks at him uncertainly and it's as if she's stuck a knife in his chest. How absent, how disconnected, must he have been that Emily feels it automatically falls to her to sort Zadie out after an accident? It's his job, Zadie is his responsibility.

'Of course, Em. I'm her dad. I'll get her all cleaned up and then I'll head back to the hospital to see Mum and Erin.' He gives her a quick kiss on the cheek. 'Drink that tea and then try and get some sleep, OK?'

Upstairs, Pete runs Zadie a quick bubble bath and strips the wet bedding from her bed, replacing it with fresh sheets from the airing cupboard. The door to Erin's bedroom stands open, and as he pulls the sheets from the cupboard he finds he is unable to look in that direction. He is unable to look at the empty cot, the cushions on the nursing chair still crumpled and squashed from where Natalie leant against them for Erin's last feed, and as he moves to the bathroom he reaches out and pulls the door closed.

In the bath, Zadie is subdued. Usually – or at least, the times that Pete can remember; it's been a while since he did bathtime – Zadie is exuberant, at her happiest in the water. She clowns around, making beards and Mohicans out of the bubbles, telling stories about dolphins and mermaids. Not now, though. Maybe it's just that she's tired, but Pete's heart hurts at the thought that Zadie is upset over Erin.

'All clean, pickle,' he says, reaching in to pull out the plug. He wraps her in a towel, scruffing her hair in the way that usually makes her shriek with laughter, and then helps her with her pyjamas. As Pete lifts her into bed, she smells of strawberry shampoo, the way she always has since she was a tiny baby. 'You go back to sleep, OK? I'll be home in the morning when you wake up.' He hopes so, anyway.

'Daddy?' Zadie's voice is muffled, the duvet pulled right up past her chin.

'What is it, Zade?'

'Is Erin going to die?'

Pete's ears ring at the words, his stomach turning over. 'No, darling, of course she's not. She's going to be just fine.'

Pete feels the sharp sting of tears behind his eyes and blinks rapidly before he leans over and kisses her, praying that it's true, and as he pulls the door gently closed, his phone begins to ring.

# Natalie

'Enough.' Natalie swipes her hands over her face, her fingers sticky with tears, and shoves her chair back. 'I've done what you asked. I've answered your questions, and now I'm going to find out what's happening to my daughter.' Ignoring DI Travis as she calls her name, Natalie almost tips her chair over as she rushes from the stifling, cramped office and out into the corridor.

She can't sit there and listen to them insinuate that she is responsible for Erin's abduction – or worse, that *Emily* could have something to do with it. She's going to find a doctor and demand answers – they've been here for hours with no word of Erin, and she can't bear to wait any longer. She's her mother; she has a right to know what is going on. As Natalie approaches the ICU reception desk, somewhere behind the door an alarm shrieks into life, and all of a sudden people are running everywhere. Nurses drop pens, clipboards, mugs of tea and sprint through the wide double doors into the ICU corridor. Unobserved in the chaos, Natalie slips through the doors, hoping to get close to Erin, when her heart seems to stop in her chest. The alarm is still screaming from a room off the corridor, a team of doctors and nurses surrounding the bed as they frantically try to help their patient. As one moves away, Natalie's stomach drops. *The patient is Erin. The alarm is screaming for Erin.*

A nurse exits the room and Natalie pushes her way in, watching in horror as a doctor leans over Erin's fragile body, his fingers pressing down on her chest. Natalie is frozen, a still tableau in a flurried blur of movement as the hospital staff work on Erin, that incessant alarm scraping down to Natalie's bones.

'Please … That's my baby,' Natalie chokes the words out, grabbing at a nurse's sleeve. 'What's happening? Is she going to be OK?'

'You can't be in here.' The doctor barely raises his head, his eyes on Erin. 'Get her out of here!'

'That's my daughter.' Natalie can hear the wail in her voice, the words suffocating her as she struggles to breathe. 'Erin … What's happening? Please, tell me.'

The nurse – Natalie realises she's young, a student, maybe – takes Natalie's arm firmly. 'You really can't be here. Let the doctor help Erin, I'll come myself to the waiting room when they—'

'No,' Natalie half shrieks. 'I know all about your waiting room, I've been in there half the night waiting to hear if my daughter is going to be OK. Please, please can someone just tell me what's going on?' She peers over the nurse's shoulder as she is dragged towards the door, trying desperately to see into the room, to catch a glimpse of Erin. All she can see is doctors, bent over Erin's tiny frame as they work frantically, the alarm blissfully quiet at last.

'Please, Mrs Maxwell.' The nurse grips her arm and skilfully manages to manoeuvre her out of sight of Erin's room before Natalie has even realised. 'You have to trust us.'

'The alarm …' In the corridor now, Natalie's legs feel as though they might give way and she sags against the wall.

'There have been some complications with Erin. Her breathing. It's been irregular, and there was a brief moment as we brought her back to her room where she stopped breathing completely.' Natalie feels the blood drain from her face, the room beginning to spin. 'Here.' The nurse sits Natalie down in a chair in the corridor, perching beside her as she grasps her hand in hers and rubs briskly, bringing warmth to Natalie's ice-cold skin. 'That's why we have the alarms – we had the team go straight in there the minute she stopped breathing. They're doing everything they can to get her stable again.'

'She's going to be OK, isn't she?' Natalie's eyes burn with tears and she thinks to herself that she'll do anything – *anything* – if Erin will just be all right. *I'll get help. I won't yell at Emily any more. I'll even forgive Pete.*

'She's in the best possible hands,' The nurse repeats. 'How about I walk you up to the waiting room? You can wait there, in privacy, and I'll bring you a cup of tea.'

The thought of tea, after the rancid hot chocolate and the wine swirling in her belly, makes Natalie feel even more sick. 'No, thank you,' she manages. 'I need to find my husband and tell him what's happening. He'll be waiting.'

The nurse pats her hand and leaves Natalie in the corridor. Her legs feel oddly shaky, as if she's just been on a long run, and she finds her stomach is swollen with butterflies as she fumbles for her phone. *Pete. I need to tell Pete.* Her finger hovers over his name in her contacts. She doesn't know what she'll do if he doesn't answer. The thought of him at Montpellier Square while Natalie is here, watching Erin battle to stay alive, makes her blood bubble like lava. She holds her breath as the call connects. It rings once, twice, three times and then, 'Nat?'

The relief Natalie feels at the sound of his voice almost finishes her off. Her throat closes over and, even though she thought she was all cried out, sobs make her words almost indecipherable. 'Pete. Oh my God, Pete. You have to get here now, it's Erin.'

# Pete

Pete screeches into the hospital car park, punching the steering wheel in frustration as the ticket barrier takes an age to lift and let him in. He throws the car into a parking space, feeling sick as he moves towards the bright lights of the emergency room. He keeps replaying Natalie's terrified words as she told him he had to come back *now*, the way Emily had looked up at him, her mouth twisting in horror.

'Dad? What is it?' Fear had given Emily's voice a biting tone that shredded Pete's last remaining nerves.

'I have to go,' he'd said as he'd hung up on Natalie, shoving his phone into his pocket and ripping open the kitchen drawer to find his car keys. 'I have to get back to the hospital. I should never have left in the first place.' Pete shoved old takeaway leaflets, birthday candles and more – an insurmountable amount of crap – out of the way, desperately trying to find his car keys, to no avail.

'Here.' Jake held out a hand, Pete's car key dangling from his index finger. 'You left them in the fruit bowl.'

'Right. Cheers.'

Jake had followed Pete out into the hallway, right out on to the driveway to where Pete's car is parked. 'Pete?'

'What, Jake?'

'Erin … Is she going to be OK?'

Pete had looked up at the boy – *man* – who is probably going to break his eldest daughter's heart. The boy who quite possibly was the one to take Erin from her bed. The sky was beginning to lighten as Pete started the engine, the sun rising on what looks to be a clear, summer's day, and in the dawn light Jake had looked like a child, concern crossing his features.

Pete had punched the car into first gear, suddenly afraid that this would be the last time he left this house with their family still intact, giving Jake one last look before he tore out of the driveway.

*I should never have left the hospital.* The thought comes back to him as he reaches the doors to the staircase, afraid that if he waits for the lifts he'll be too late. His vision swims with images of Erin, of wires coming out of her, of the oxygen mask swamping her face in the back of the ambulance. He pictures her tiny chest struggling to rise, her little rosebud mouth struggling to draw in air. He should have been here, with Natalie. But he'd been so convinced Vanessa was involved, so sure he would find out the truth when he confronted her, that it had blinded him to what was really important.

As he reaches the doors leading to the ICU, he spots Natalie's blonde hair as she paces, her fist pressed to her mouth. His heart turns over at the look on her face. She looks broken, a burnt-out shell.

'Nat. Natalie, I'm here.' Pete runs towards her and pulls her into his arms, the relief as she tightens her arms around him overwhelming.

'I think we're losing her, Pete.' Natalie's voice is muffled as she sobs against his chest. 'The alarms ... They were screaming, and they wouldn't let me stay with her. I'm so scared.'

Pete presses a kiss to the top of her head, inhaling the familiar scent of her. His hands are shaking and he presses his fingers into her back, trying to hide it from her. 'We won't lose her, Nat. I promise.' He knows he shouldn't say it, but he wants to believe it so badly. 'Erin's a fighter.'

Natalie nods, her cheek rubbing against his shirt, and then she pulls away. 'She's in there.' She points to a room further down the corridor, and Pete grabs her hand and pulls her towards the door.

*Please, God.* Pete presses his hands to the window as the nurses cluster around the bed, carrying out their checks and blocking his view of Erin. *Please let her be OK.* 'This is...' Pete can't finish the sentence.

'She looks so tiny. So helpless,' Natalie says, pulling her arms across her body. Dark circles ring her eyes, and her mouth is pinched and drawn. 'I can't lose her, Pete.' The thought that last night might have been their last night together as a family of five makes Pete's heart turn over in his chest. Even if Erin *is* OK, will Natalie ever forgive him for what he's done? The thought of not being with her, of not sleeping beside her every night, the idea of someone else sharing her life instead of him, is enough to make him go mad. How could he have been so stupid? How could he have risked it all for Vanessa – for some romantic nostalgia that never even really existed?

Natalie's shoulders heave beside him, tears streaking down her cheeks. 'Come and sit down. You look exhausted, and Erin is going to need you when she's feeling better.' *If she gets better.* The words hang in the air, unspoken. Pete gently leads Natalie to the chairs on the other side of the corridor, close enough that they are right there when the doctor has something to tell them. He sinks into a chair beside her, unable to bear the sight of Erin hooked up to those machines.

As they wait, Pete feels winded with regret. They've worked so hard, him and Natalie, building a home, a life together, and now all of it could be thrown away because of his actions, because of what he did.

Pete reaches out and links his fingers through Natalie's silently, wondering desperately how he can fix this. *We could move away.* The thought isn't entirely unwelcome, although he's long since given up on the idea of moving to Australia. But they could move away, to a different area. *Maybe if we move somewhere new with no memories attached, we could make things work.* Somewhere further down south, closer to the coast. Cornwall, maybe, or even Wales. There's loads of construction work all over; he could move the business relatively easily. Dave could complete the new build contract, while Pete builds things up in another city. Far from all of this. Far away from Vanessa. Far enough away that maybe he can repair the damage he's done.

Hope flares, and Pete begins to pace the short distance between the chairs and the door to Erin's room, his feet aching despite the comfy trainers he pulled on hours ago for the party. Natalie has leant her head back against the wall, her eyes closed, her cheeks carrying a consumptive flush against the rest of her pale face. They could go on holiday first, he thinks, to Australia. He'll tell Natalie they don't have to build a house over there, but they could go and spend a few weeks with his parents. It would be good for the girls to spend some time with their grandparents, and he knows his mum would love to help take care of Erin. It could be a proper holiday for Natalie; they could go to the beach, and out for dinner or drinks. She could relax for the first time in a long time. He'll give up his dream of moving there, if it means Natalie can give him another chance to put their family back together and Erin will be OK. He'll do whatever it takes, whatever Natalie wants, if things will just work out.

'Mr and Mrs Maxwell?' The doctor is peering out of Erin's room, the rim of his glasses glinting in the bright light of the corridor. Pete freezes.

'Here,' he says, his voice a croak. 'We're here.' Natalie's eyes spring open, and they exchange a glance saturated with fear as the doctor steps out, pulling the door to Erin's room closed behind him. His face is grave, and Pete swears his heart stutters in his chest, a missing beat that makes him feel faint. He doesn't think he's ready to hear what he has to say.

# Natalie

Time seems to stop for Natalie as the doctor steps out of the room, his face strained and sober. There is no longer the screaming of the alarm coming from Erin's room, and surely, *surely* that can only be a good thing?

Pete steps forward, but Natalie knows he is as terrified as she is, not just by the way his hand snakes out and grips hers tightly – so tightly she can feel her wedding ring cutting into her fingers. She wants her pills, she thinks, suddenly longing for their chalky, bitter taste, her free hand going to her pocket as if she might magically find them there. Two of those little white pills would make her strong enough to hear whatever Erin's doctor has to say.

Forcing her feet to cross the short distance between the chair and the door of Erin's room, Natalie feels as if she's walking the green mile, knowing that whatever the doctor tells them in the next few minutes will change their lives forever. *She can't be gone.* The thought flickers through her mind. *I would know. I would know if Erin wasn't here any more.*

Pete looks at the doctor, his hand still gripping Natalie tightly. 'Is she ...?' He trails off, as if he can't bear to say it out loud.

'Erin's going to be OK,' The doctor says, glancing from Natalie to Pete. 'She's had some breathing issues, and we are concerned about pneumonia. We've started her on an IV of antibiotics, and fluids as she's dehydrated, but Erin is going to make a full recovery.'

'Thank God.' Natalie closes her eyes, tears rolling down her cheeks. It's as though something drops away, a load that Natalie wasn't sure she could carry any longer. *She's OK. She's going to be OK.* Pete stumbles back, landing on the plastic seat of the hospital chair, and he leans forwards. His elbows are on his knees as his hands cover his face and he cries in a way she's never heard him cry before. His shoulders heave and the sobs ripping from his throat are raw and guttural, a wave of pent-up emotion. For a moment, Natalie can't move, and then she kneels beside him, pulling him into her arms and murmuring in his ear until finally the sobs subside.

Pete pulls back, his eyes red, his cheeks flushed, and she has the weirdest sense of déjà vu – a flashback to the day Erin was born, and how they'd waited for her scream that didn't come for the longest time. That was the last time she saw Pete cry, she thinks. When Erin's yell had finally filled the room and they had ridden a wave of relief together, both of them giddy with happiness.

'She's going to be OK, Pete,' Natalie whispers, tears darkening the denim of Pete's jeans as sweet relief floods her veins. 'She's going to be OK.'

# Pete

It's not just the news that Erin is going to be OK that makes Pete weep into Natalie's hair as her arms automatically go around him; it's the familiar feel of her in his arms, something that he took for granted for so long and is now determined he never will again.

'She's really going to be all right?' Natalie's hands cover her face as the news sinks in and she lets out a long moan, her shoulders juddering. Pete gets to his feet, pulling Natalie up with him and holding her tightly against his chest as she cries. The relief is almost overwhelming.

'She is,' The doctor says, with a tired smile. 'We're still in with her at the moment, but we're hoping later on today we'll be able to move her to a paediatric ward. We'll want to keep her in for a few days, just for observation, but Erin is going to be fine. I'll let you know when you can come in and see her.'

'Oh, thank God. I thought . . .' Natalie breaks off and Pete squeezes her tightly again. He knows exactly what she thought. He had thought the same thing. Natalie's head rests against his chest, and while he wishes he could just brush everything else under the carpet and behave as if nothing has happened, he has to make things right with her.

'Nat?'

She looks up, pulling away slightly as if she just remembered what he's done. 'What?' She fumbles in her pocket, pulling out a used tissue and pressing it to her eyes.

'I'm sorry. I'm so, so sorry, for everything.' His throat thickens again and he has to blink rapidly. 'I did everything wrong, right from the very beginning. I should never have reacted that way when you told me you were pregnant. I mean, what kind of bloke does that?' He hates himself, can taste the disgust on his tongue. 'I should have been over the moon – I love you, we're a family, Erin was meant to be the icing on the cake. The only thing I regret more than my reaction that night is ...' The words are clunky, sticking in his throat, and he wants to cough. 'What happened with Vanessa.'

'Pete—'

'There's no excuse for what I did, for how I behaved.' Pete looks at Natalie now, at the woman he's loved for over twenty years, and he doesn't understand how he ever thought that she wasn't enough. 'I was looking for something that was never even missing in the first place, I just thought it was. Everything I've ever needed, ever wanted ... it was all there right in front of me the whole time.'

Natalie sighs, pressing the tissue to her eyes again before shoving it up the sleeve of that ratty old cardigan she loves so much. Pete loves the sight of her in that cardigan right now; he'll never complain about it again. 'Pete ...' she says, her voice hoarse. 'This isn't all on you. It isn't all your fault. I'm to blame as well, and I'm sorry.'

She looks up at him and for a moment time slides away, and she is that quirky nineteen-year-old student, with the self-cut fringe and smudgy eyeliner, who knocked him to the floor. 'I was struggling with Erin,' she says quietly, 'and instead of doing the decent thing, instead of coming to you and saying you were right, another child *has* upset the balance of our family and I'm not coping very well, I pushed you away.' She draws in a shuddering breath. 'I punished you for being right, Pete. Instead of coming to you for help, instead of going to the doctor sooner and being honest about things, it was easier for me to be mad at you. It was easier for me to pretend to be asleep when you came home and to blame you for Zadie wetting the bed than it was to tell you maybe I'd made a mistake having another baby.' Tears roll silently down Natalie's cheeks, but she doesn't seem to be aware that she's crying. 'I don't blame you, Pete, for…' She swallows, as if the words she's about to speak are painfully sharp. 'For having an affair with Vanessa. I pushed you into it, with my own behaviour.'

'Jesus, Nat.' Just when Pete thinks his heart couldn't feel any more broken. He pulls her back into his arms, resting his chin on her hair. 'No, that's not how it was at all. Vanessa… I don't ever want you to blame yourself for what happened with Vanessa. That's all on me. I was weak and stupid and… I wish I'd been as strong as you are.' He pulls away, gripping her by her upper arms and looking into her eyes. 'I am so sorry, Nat. I've never been sorrier for anything in my life, and I…' He breaks off, suddenly nervous, afraid of what her response will be, but he has to ask her. 'More than anything, I want us to be able to get over this. Do you think you could ever forgive me for hurting you so badly? Do you think…? Do you think we could fix this?'

For a long, heart-stopping moment, Natalie doesn't respond. She looks down at his hands gripping her tightly and Pete feels his stomach drop away. *She's going to say no*, he thinks, and he doesn't know how he'll cope with that.

'Yes.' The word is barely a whisper. Natalie finally looks at him, her blue eyes filling with yet more tears. 'At least… I hope so. When I checked to see where you were earlier and you were at Vanessa's flat, I thought…' A sob escapes, ringing out in the quiet waiting room.

'Oh, God, Nat. No. It was nothing like that, I swear. I went home to check on the kids, and the police had said there was lipstick on the blanket Erin was found in. I was so angry with her, I thought… I had to ask her, that's all.' For a moment Pete thinks he might have just undone everything as Natalie freezes, before she relaxes into him again. Pete feels as if all the air has gone out of him, he's so relieved. Leaning down, he presses his mouth to Natalie's, tasting salt on her lips. 'I swear to you, Nat, I'll never fuck up like this again.'

Natalie takes a step back, holding up one hand. 'There's just one question I have to ask you, Pete, before we can even begin to start again.'

'What is it?' Pete will answer any question she has. He'd fly her to the moon if that's what she wanted, if it meant they could fix things.

'Do you...? Do you think I could have done this to Erin?'

'What? My God, Natalie, no.' Pete shakes his head. He hadn't thought it, not really. Even when the police were questioning him and he'd had that brief flicker of doubt, he knew deep down in his bones that Natalie could never be responsible for something like this. 'What about you?' he asks, with a flutter of nerves. 'Did you ever think maybe I was responsible for taking Erin?'

Natalie shakes her head, her eyes never leaving his face. 'Never, Pete. You might be a lot of things, but you love your kids. It never crossed my mind that you could have been responsible.'

Pete feels a chill at the thought running through his mind. *If neither I nor Natalie is responsible for Erin's abduction... then who is?*

# Natalie

Pete offers to be the one to go back to the house to pick up Emily and Zadie, to bring them to the hospital to see Erin, but Natalie finds herself desperate to see them, to hold them in her arms, so she says she'll go, even though she feels a war waging inside her. Guilt at leaving Emily and Zadie at home all night with no idea at what's going on, and fear that if she leaves Erin's bedside, she'll take a turn for the worse. It's only when Pete swears he won't take his eyes off Erin that she makes her decision, eager to race home and kiss her girls.

Natalie presses her foot hard on the accelerator through the quiet streets towards the house, glad the Sunday drivers are all still in bed as the sun rises over the horizon, spreading warm lilac and peach rays across the sky. She is exhausted but wired, buoyed by Erin's survival and the fact that she can tell Emily and Zadie their baby sister is going to be fine. As she hurriedly parks on the drive, she almost runs the few steps to the front door.

'Oh.' Jake is the last person Natalie is expecting to see as she reaches the house, but there he is, standing at the open front door with a cautious smile on his face. He looks pale, dark, purple circles sprouting under his eyes, and Natalie realises he hasn't slept at all. 'Jake. I wasn't expecting you.'

'Sorry. Emily called me and told me what happened. She asked me to come back.' Jake closes the door behind Natalie and follows her through to the kitchen, where a squat blonde woman in a police uniform sits at the kitchen table. 'I sent Emily up to bed once Zadie was asleep, but I thought perhaps I should wait up, just in case Zadie woke again in the night. I know she's had a few night-time accidents lately and I didn't want her to come downstairs and there only be a stranger in the house.' He glances at the family liaison officer. 'Sorry, Sally, no offence.'

'None taken. I'll get a pot of tea on, shall I?' The FLO fills the kettle, moving around Natalie's kitchen in a way that tells her this isn't the first cuppa Sally's had to make this evening.

Natalie gives Jake an appraising look. 'Thanks,' she says, 'I really appreciate that.' Maybe she's got Jake wrong after all. Maybe he isn't a hooligan in training, a loser destined for a council flat and a stint behind bars. What he's done this evening is more thoughtful than Natalie would have expected from any adult male.

'Erin ... Is she ...?' Jake swallows, one hand reaching up to rub at his neck.

'She's going to be OK.' Natalie still wants to cry as she thinks about Erin's tiny body with all those tubes coming out of her. 'I should wake Emily.'

Leaving Jake downstairs in the kitchen with the family liaison officer – and probably his fiftieth cup of tea of the night – Natalie creeps into Emily's bedroom, perching on the end of her bed for a moment. Emily still sleeps the way she did as a little girl – with one arm flung over her head and one knee raised. Natalie has never understood how she can be comfortable like that all night long, but Pete sleeps the same way. Watching her now, Natalie feels her heart squeeze. How stupid she was to think that any of this was too much for her.

'Em?' She leans in, tickling Emily's face with the ends of her hair. 'Em, wake up.'

Emily's eyelashes flutter and she pouts, before one eye creeps open and then the other. 'Mum?' There is a blissful moment where Natalie can see Emily has forgotten all about what happened the previous evening, the way you do when you wake up from a deep sleep, and then her eyes widen and the memory crashes in. 'Mum, you're back.' Emily pushes into a sitting position, and wraps her arms around Natalie's neck like she did when she was small and she'd had a nightmare. 'Is Erin going to be OK?' Her voice is muffled, her breath hot against Natalie's neck.

'She's going to be fine, love.'

'Oh, thank God.' A hot wetness seeps into the shoulder of Natalie's cardigan as Emily beings to cry. 'I've been so worried, I never meant to fall asleep, I wanted to wait for you...'

'Shhhh. It's all right, Em. Jake stayed awake downstairs. He's a good egg.' Emily pulls away, a frown on her face. 'Yes, I said it. But I'm not saying it again.' Natalie feels a smile tug at her lips.

'Let me get up.' Emily pushes the duvet back. 'I want to come and see Erin. Can I give her a bottle? She is downstairs, isn't she?'

Natalie puts her hand on Emily's knee, stilling her. 'She's at the hospital, love. She had some breathing issues and they're concerned about pneumonia, so they're keeping her in for a few days for observation. It's going to take a while for her to fully recover, but she's in the best place, and Dad is with her right now.'

'You should be with her, too,' Emily says. 'I can take care of Zadie, don't worry.'

'No, love, you've done enough for us,' Natalie says. 'I'm going to grab a few bits and then I'll take you girls to see her, if you want? If she's awake I know she'll want to see you.'

'Really?' Emily smiles. Her hair is tangled, and there are dark smudges of mascara under her eyes, her lips stained with the remains of Natalie's favourite MAC lipstick. She looks like a child who'd got into her mother's make-up bag. 'Let me shower quickly and I'll be ready.' She throws back the duvet and jumps out of bed, as Natalie watches her hurry towards the bathroom, all messy hair and long legs.

Moving along the hallway, she enters Zadie's room, smiling as she sees the little bundle huddled under the duvet. There is the slight scent of urine in the room and her heart sinks.

'Zadie? Zade? I need you to get up, my girlie.' Natalie pulls back the covers but the bed is empty, the bundle Zadie's ratty old bear instead of her sleepy little body. 'Zadie?' There is a sharp spike of fear, a horrifying sense of déjà vu as Natalie turns, taking in the bedroom. Zadie isn't here.

Natalie runs along the hallway to the bathroom the two girls share, peering in on her own empty bedroom as she does, and hammers on the door.

'Em? Emily? Is Zadie in there with you?'

Emily opens the door, steam filling the room as the shower runs behind her, her toothbrush stuck in her mouth. 'Wha—?'

'Zadie,' Natalie repeats impatiently. 'Is she in the bathroom with you?'

Emily spits and wipes her mouth. 'No? She's in bed, isn't she? Dad tucked her in when he left earlier and we haven't heard a peep since.'

'She's not there.' Natalie feels as if someone has punched her in the chest. How can she have one daughter back, only to lose another? Emily is already out of the bathroom and heading for the stairs, calling out to Jake to look for Zadie in case she's sneaked downstairs.

On legs that feel like jelly, her knees wobbling, Natalie calls out for her middle child and runs into her own bedroom. It's still empty – of course it is – but even so, Natalie pushes open the door to the en suite, checks the wardrobe, under the bed, and then she heads back to Zadie's room.

It smells of Zadie when Natalie enters. There is still that faint scent of urine that she doesn't think will go away, the smell of strawberry shampoo layered on top. She peers under Zadie's bed, in her wardrobe, too. Nothing.

'I'll call DI Travis.' Sally, the FLO, appears in the doorway, eerily calm. Natalie supposes she sees this kind of thing all the time.

'Yes,' Natalie chokes out. 'And Pete. I need to call Pete. What if…?' She breaks off, unable to vocalise what she's thinking. *What if the same person who took Erin has taken Zadie?*

# *Pete*

'Nat?' Pete can't take his eyes off a sleeping Erin even as he answers the phone to his wife. 'Erin's OK, you don't need to—'

'Pete, oh God…' Natalie's voice is a broken croak, and Pete's arms break out in gooseflesh as she gasps. 'She's… Zadie—'

'Nat? Natalie, what is it? Calm down.' Pete doesn't mean to be so abrupt, but he can't make sense of what Natalie is trying to tell him. He hears her draw in a deep breath and then finally, he can understand her.

'It's Zadie,' she says. 'She's gone. She's not in her room, she's not here, I can't find her.'

Immediately something sharp and spiky floods Pete's veins, his hands beginning to shake. 'I'm on my way.' He hangs up and, with one last look at Erin, whispers, 'I'll be back, baby girl.'

Pete hurries past the ICU reception, calling out DI Travis's name to the nurse there as he does. She points towards the waiting room where Pete and Natalie have spent so much of their evening, and he breaks into a sprint, his breath coming hard and fast in his ears as he shoves the door open, his mouth dry. Travis and Haynes are sitting closely together, Haynes talking quietly in his phone, both of them with dirty brown cups of coffee in their hands.

'Pete?' Travis frowns as she gets to her feet. 'What is it? Did something happen?'

'Zadie's gone,' he puffs, winded and slightly sick. 'I need to go home, Natalie called.'

Travis immediately throws her coffee cup into the bin and pulls on her jacket. 'I'll take you. Tell me exactly what Natalie said.'

'She just said Zadie isn't in the house – she can't find her anywhere. Erin…' Pete feels his eyes fill with tears. 'What about Erin? She's going to be on her own.' He feels torn – the idea of leaving Erin here alone, even though she's going to be OK, is unbearable, but *Zadie*… He needs to find his little girl.

'Haynes will stay with Erin.' Travis is already bustling Pete out of the door and down the corridor towards the lift. 'We have the number for your friend – Stuart, is it? DS Haynes will call him and ask him to come in and sit with Erin, too, if you'd like? This way, come on.'

Pete lets Travis guide him on leaden feet towards her car, feeling oddly numb as his mind races. *How has this happened?* He'd left Zadie tucked up in bed, Emily, Jake and the FLO downstairs. Could someone have sneaked into the house and taken her? Pete doesn't understand how, but he supposes it could be possible. He presses his pounding head against the window as Travis reaches over and switches on her siren, the scream of it cutting into his thoughts.

'I've spoken to the team,' Travis is saying. 'Another unit is being dispatched to the house. Pete, we will find her, OK? We will find Zadie.'

*And what if you don't?* Pete wants to ask. What will he do then? What will any of them do? Just when he'd thought that things were going to be OK, he's staring down the barrel of a fresh nightmare. He can't imagine a life without Zadie. Without her wit – so sharp for an eight-year-old; Pete was always so sure she'd be a stand-up comic one day – without her relentless questions about the most random things, without her whingeing that she's bored the moment there's a single minute of downtime. Pete draws his hands across his face, feeling the prickle of stubble under his fingers. That was one of the things he usually found infuriating about Zadie, especially after a long day on site, but now he'd give anything to listen to her whine about there being nothing to do, if it just means that they'll find her.

The police car zips through the familiar streets, the speed adding to Pete's sense of urgency. Fear burns like bile in the back of his throat as they hit the outskirts of West Marsham and Pete realises he's utterly terrified at the thought of going home. *How will we carry on*, he thinks desperately, as DI Travis slows a fraction for the speed humps through the village. *How will we ever go on if Zadie is gone for good?*

# Natalie

'Who's been here?' Natalie demands as Sally, the FLO, hangs up after calling her team. 'Was it Eve? Did Eve come back here?'

'No, Mum,' Emily says, her face a sickly white. 'No one came back here. It's just been me, Jake and Sally.'

Natalie shakes her head, pushing past Emily and Sally down the stairs and out towards the patio doors into the garden, biting her tongue. Emily was asleep; how would she know if anyone came to the house or not?

'Zadie!' Natalie's voice rings out in the early morning air as a breeze picks up, cooling her hot cheeks and lifting her hair from the nape of her neck. *The gate.* At the bottom of the garden the gate swings open and, before she can think about what she's doing, Natalie is running over the wet grass, dew seeping into her sandals as she heads for the woods.

'Natalie?' Jake appears beside her, his breathing even as he easily keeps pace with her. 'Where are you going?'

'The tree,' she puffs. 'The tree where Erin was found. What if she's there? What if whoever took her left her there, too?' Her feet slow as she approaches the fork in the path leading to the old oak.

'Zadie?' Reaching the tree, Natalie steadies herself on the trunk as her feet slide in the mud, her muscles aching as she stoops to peer into the hollow.

'Nat.' Jake places a hand gently on her arm. 'I've already checked. She's not here.'

Natalie feels as though her heart might crack in two. 'Then where is she? I can't ...' she gasps, unable to say it out loud. *I can't lose her. I can't go through this twice in one night.*

'Let me take you back to the house, come on.' Silently Natalie lets Jake lead her by the hand towards the open patio doors at the back of the house.

'She's not out there,' she says numbly, as Sally meets her at the door, Emily letting Jake pull her into a hug.

'She's definitely not in the house? You've checked everywhere?' The FLO watches as Natalie paces, her hands going to her scalp, tugging at her hair.

'*Yes*,' Natalie almost shouts, before she stops, her hand going to her mouth. 'Wait.' There is one place she hasn't checked, hadn't even thought about. Pushing past the FLO, Natalie hurries to Erin's bedroom. The room is dark, the blackout blind lowered now, blocking any hint of the early morning sun. Even so, despite the gloom, Natalie can see the cot is empty, and no Zadie sits on the nursing chair.

'Oh God, Zadie, where are you?' The words come out in a low moan, and Natalie sinks onto the nursing chair, wishing she could turn back the clock to the previous evening, before all of this happened. She wouldn't let any of her children out of her sight.

At first, she thinks she's imagined it as she stands, ready to head downstairs and back out into the garden where she can already hear Jake calling Zadie's name again, but then it comes again. The faintest sniff. The sniff of a child who has been crying uncontrollably, and her heart stops.

'Zadie? Zade?'

The sniff comes again, and Natalie goes to the wardrobe behind the door, half-filled with Erin's tiny outfits. As she yanks the door open she almost collapses with relief, hot tears stinging her eyes as she sees a huddled Zadie, tear-stained and exhausted, tucked into the bottom of the wardrobe. She clutches Erin's teddy to her chest.

'Oh. Oh, thank God. Emily! Emily, I've found her!' Natalie feels faint, her ears ringing. 'Blimey, Zade, you gave me such a fright.' Natalie gets to her knees and holds out her arms, waiting for Zadie to shuffle into them. 'What are you doing in here, silly thing? Didn't you hear me calling you?'

Zadie crawls forward and climbs onto Natalie's lap, her little body hot and sticky through the thin fabric of Natalie's sundress. 'I was scared,' she says.

'Oh, darling, you don't need to be afraid.' Natalie presses a kiss into Zadie's hair, her arms wrapping tightly around Zadie's little body as she waits for her own frantic pulse to subside. As Zadie settles against her, Natalie pulls her phone out and calls Pete.

'I've found her. Pete, she's here. She's safe.'

Pete's voice on the other end of the line is warm with relief, as he tells her he's on his way with DI Travis, and Natalie turns her attention back to Zadie. 'Everything is going to be OK, Zade, I swear. Erin's going to be all right. Do you want to go and see her when Dad gets here?'

Zadie hesitates for a moment before she nods.

'Right, well, we need to wash your face, don't we?' Natalie stands, her legs still shaking as she scoops Zadie up on to her hip and carries her into the bathroom. She sits her on the side of the bath and runs a flannel under warm water and begins to swipe at Zadie's tear-stained face.

'Zadie, you gave us a heart attack!' Emily swoops into the bathroom and clutches Zadie in a fierce hug. 'What were you doing, hiding like that?' Emily gives her little sister an extra squeeze before letting her go and glancing at Natalie. 'Are we still going to the hospital?'

'Of course.' Natalie rinses the cloth and returns to Zadie, pausing for a moment as she swipes the flannel over Zadie's hands, over the smudges of lipstick on her fingers. Shaking her head, she gives Zadie a wobbly smile, and then lifts her off the bath and swats her on the bum. 'Go downstairs with Emily for something quick to eat. I'll bring you down some clean clothes and your shoes.'

As Zadie heads for the stairs, Natalie gives herself a minute to compose herself before she moves to the bedroom, anxious now to get the girls in the car and get back to the hospital – back to Erin – as soon as Pete arrives. She pulls out shorts and a T-shirt for Zadie to change into, and then turns to the wardrobe to hunt out the new Crocs that Zadie demanded for the party, taking some small comfort in performing mundane, everyday chores after the ordeal of the last twelve hours. *I'll never complain again*, Natalie thinks, a sense of peace washing over her as she rummages in the depths of Zadie's wardrobe. She'll never wish time away, never wish they would all leave her alone, she'll be *grateful* for what she has. This life, this old life that she thought was so overwhelming, is all she wants now – just Pete and her girls, that's all Natalie needs.

*That's odd.* Natalie knows she put Zadie's new Crocs in the bottom of the wardrobe when she brought them home. She'd pulled the label off and set them neatly in the bottom, beside Zadie's PE plimsolls, and now they're gone. Sitting back on her haunches, she surveys the room.

*They have to be here somewhere.* She saw Zadie wearing them when she was pushing Lola on the swing, right around the time Pete was about to make his speech. She remembers, because the stark, crisp whiteness of them stood out against the grass. Turning back to the wardrobe, Natalie pulls out the other pairs of shoes, stacking them neatly beside her, until the floor of the wardrobe is clear. Thrusting her hand in, she gropes around in the dark recesses at the back, letting out a hiss of triumph as her hand brushes something plastic. *The Crocs.*

'Bingo.' Natalie tugs the shoes towards her, the smile fading from her face as she turns them over in her hands. She bought these shoes brand new two days ago, and Zadie has only worn them to the party. So why are they shoved to the back of the wardrobe, the soles rimmed with dark mud? Natalie peers at the soles, her heart galloping in her chest. A slimy strand of river weed wraps its way around the strap at the back of the shoe. Zadie wore them to the party, but she hadn't left the garden yesterday, so the most Natalie would have expected would be grass stains on the white plastic. *They were clean*, she thinks, *when Pete made his speech. When Zadie came into Erin's bedroom when I was feeding her.* Panic scratches at Natalie's insides. *Zadie had lipstick on her hands. Red lipstick.* Natalie thinks she might vomit. She can't process why the shoes have strands of river weed on them, why the soles are covered in the same thick mud marking the path through the woods alongside the stream. The path that becomes swampy and thick with viscous mud every time there is heavy rain. The path that Zadie walks every day when she goes to school, or to the shops, or to visit Eve's house – that Zadie knows like the back of her hand. The path leading to the hollow in the old oak tree where Erin was found.

# Pete and Natalie

*Oh, God.* Natalie drops the Croc as if it burns her hand, that familiar nausea rising as she looks at the shoes.

'Mum?' Emily appears in the doorway. 'Zadie's just having some toast and then we'll be ready to leave.'

'Great, love. Listen, can you get Jake to drive you straight to the hospital? I don't want Erin left on her own. Leave Zadie here, I'll bring her in a little bit.' Natalie doesn't wait for Emily to respond, just picks up the shoes and makes her way downstairs.

DI Travis's car screeches to a halt outside the house sooner than Natalie expected, but even so she is pacing the driveway, a sick, nervous energy flooding her veins as Pete tumbles from the passenger side.

'Pete ... I ...' Natalie launches herself into the familiar safety of Pete's arms. 'Zadie's here. She's safe, but ...' She swallows, waiting until DI Travis steps out of the car and approaches them before lowering her voice. 'I think I know who took Erin.'

'What?' Pete pulls back, his face draining of colour. 'How ...?'

Travis looks grim as she takes in Natalie's solemn face and the way her fingers tremble as she reaches out and grasps Pete's hand tightly. 'Let's talk inside.'

Her heart sinking, Natalie leads them both into the kitchen, where the family liaison officer is once again filling the kettle. Emily and Jake have already left for the hospital, and Zadie is upstairs. Natalie points to the shoes on the table wordlessly, her throat tightening.

'These are Zadie's?' Travis moves to the table, pulling a pen from her breast pocket. She pokes at the shoes, flipping one of them over so the muddy sole is exposed, the river weed clinging stubbornly to the strap as it dries.

'Yes.' The word is barely a whisper, and Pete comes to stand beside Natalie, his arm around her shoulder as if to prop her up.

'Could she have worn these before the day of the party?' Travis asks, her brows knitting together.

'No.' Natalie shakes her head, wrapping her arms across her body as if to ward off what's coming next. 'I bought these for her on Thursday afternoon, after Emily picked up her A level results, when I was picking up party supplies. She wore them for the first time at the party. When I was feeding Erin, right before I put her down to sleep, Zadie came in wearing them. They were clean then.' Natalie pauses, her throat closing over. 'She... She had smudges of lipstick on her hands when I came home. Red lipstick. Pete said there was red lipstick on Erin's blanket.'

Travis puts her pen back in her pocket and turns to Pete and Natalie. 'I think we should probably have a chat with Zadie.'

Pete feels something lodge in his gut as Natalie heads upstairs to fetch Zadie – something heavy and obstructive. Guilt, he thinks; guilt that he hasn't been able to protect any of the girls in his family. 'Please...' he says to the police officer, his voice choked. 'Please don't... She's just a baby.'

'We just need to talk to her, Pete.' Travis has dropped the iron persona and almost seems human. 'We need to get to the bottom of what happened here last night. Oh, hey! Hi, Zadie!' She slaps on a big grin, but Zadie eyes her warily before her eyes go to the Crocs on the table. 'Can we have a little chat together? Me and you and your mum and dad? My name's Lucy, by the way.'

Zadie's thumb goes to her mouth, but she nods.

'Let's go and sit on the sofa, shall we?' Travis holds out a hand and Zadie lets her lead her towards the sofa in the sitting room. Pete and Natalie follow, Pete squeezing Natalie's icy cold hand as they do.

'So, Zadie, I just wanted to have a little chat with you about your new shoes. They're pretty smart, hey? They're kind of dirty, though. Do you know how they got all this mud and stuff on them?'

Zadie stays silent, her thumb still wedged in her mouth, but her eyes fill with tears and a fierce blush crawls over her cheeks, staining them a deep crimson. Natalie feels her own eyes smart and she steps forward, crouching on the floor beside where Zadie sits on the sofa.

'Zade?' Natalie reaches out and lifts Zadie's chin so she has to look at her. 'Did you take Erin out to the woods last night?'

There is a long silence, one in which Pete can hear his own ragged breathing and the crash of his pulse in his ears and then, slowly, Zadie nods. A tear slides down one cheek as she looks up at him and nods. 'Am I in lots of trouble?'

Natalie slides onto the sofa beside Zadie, feeling as if her heart will break as she wraps her arms around her, and Zadie sniffles, her face hot and wet with tears. Pete comes to sit on the other side and does the same, wrapping his arm around Zadie from the other side, both of them forming a protective barrier around her.

DI Travis comes to sit on the floor in front of the sofa, so she is at eye level with Zadie. 'Can you tell us what happened?' she asks in a gentle voice. 'What happened at the party that made you think you should take Erin out to the woods?'

'I didn't mean to hurt her,' Zadie says quietly as Natalie gently eases her thumb away from her mouth. 'Erin cries a lot and that makes my mum cry a lot, too. Ever since the baby came home my mum cries every day.'

Her words are like a punch to Natalie's gut. She'd thought she'd hidden the way she was feeling from Zadie quite well, but clearly not well enough.

'So what happened last night, Zadie? Something did happen, didn't it, to make you think you should take Erin outside?' Travis leans forward, her eyes never leaving Zadie's face.

Zadie swipes a hand over her cheek and then over her shorts, smearing tears into the fabric. 'I didn't feel very well, and I told my mum I felt sick but she just told me to go to bed. I did go to bed for a bit, but I didn't want to miss the party either.' She sneaks a look at Pete and Natalie from under her lashes. 'So I went and sat at the top of the stairs so I could hear the music.'

'And then what happened?' Travis puts a reassuring hand on Zadie's knee. 'You're not in trouble, Zadie, but I do need you to tell me what happened.'

'Mummy and Daddy were fighting.' Another fat tear slips its way down Zadie's cheek as Natalie closes her eyes, feeling sick with shame and regret. 'I heard Mummy say it was a mistake having Erin and everything would have been OK if we didn't have her. She said none of this would have happened if she didn't have the baby.'

'Oh, Zadie.' Natalie presses a kiss to the top of her head, trying not to let her tears fall.

Pete closes his eyes, each word like a tiny jabbing knife stripping away the top layer of his skin. Like Natalie, he had thought that he'd hidden the way he was feeling, and he'd been so wrapped up in Vanessa that it hadn't even occurred to him that Zadie would notice he wasn't there every evening. He's a terrible father, a terrible husband. He has to make things right.

'I thought maybe if Erin wasn't here, then Mummy and Daddy would be happy again and everything would go back to how it was before. I wouldn't wee the bed any more. I wanted to ask Eve to look after her because I know Eve loves her, but I thought she would say no. I thought if I left her in the tree, someone would see her on the way home from the party and maybe take care of her.'

'Oh, Zadie, my love.' Natalie feels as if her heart has been ripped out and handed to her on a plate. Poor, poor Zadie, thinking she could be the only one who knew how to fix this horrible mess.

'I didn't want to do it,' Zadie cries, gulping back a huge sob.

'I love Erin, she's the best baby in the world, but I just wanted Mummy and Daddy to stop fighting and for Daddy to come home.'

Pete reaches out behind Zadie's back and links his fingers through Natalie's as tears stream down Natalie's face. 'Am I going to prison?' Zadie asks him, turning her stricken face to him. 'Please don't be mad at me, I'm sorry, Daddy.'

'No, Zadie, you're not going to prison. I'm not mad at you, sweetie.' Pete's mad at himself, at the whole sorry situation.

'Zadie, no one is cross with you,' DI Travis says, 'but things like this ... You can't fix them, OK? The only people who can fix big things like this are the adults. In future, if you're worried about something you must always, always speak to an adult. Erin is going to be all right, but things could have been very different.'

'Zadie, everything is going to be all right.' Natalie grasps her hand tightly, and glances at Pete.

'We promise you,' Pete says. 'All grown-ups fight sometimes and sometimes we say things we don't mean, but it never ever means Mummy and I don't love all of you girls.' He pauses, holding Natalie's gaze. 'Or each other. We are a family, and we're going to stay that way.'

'It's all going to go back to the way things were,' Natalie says.

Later, DI Travis has left, Jake and Emily are holed up in her room, with Zadie as a chaperone on the bed between them as they watch cartoons on Netflix, and Natalie and Pete are back at the hospital with Erin.

'I meant it,' Pete says as they stand over a sleeping Erin, laid peacefully in her hospital cot. 'What I said to Zadie. I love all of you, so much. I can't believe we nearly lost it all.'

Natalie pauses, then comes round to his side of the cot, wrapping her arms around his waist. 'I meant it, too,' she says. 'Everything is going back to the way it used to be.'

They stand there for a moment, motionless, not caring about the people who seemed so eager to watch them crash and burn, or whether they are the subject of village gossip, an unspoken vow rising on the air between them. *Nothing like this can ever happen again.*

# *Epilogue*

## Four months later

Natalie gasps with laughter as the wind whips her hair across her face.

'Mum, your hat!' Emily snatches it out of the air as the wind carries towards the ocean, her own joy written all over her face. If you had told Natalie on that dreadful night four months ago that she would be celebrating Erin's birthday a few days after Christmas on the beach, with her family all around her, she would never have believed you. She would never have believed it would be possible to come back from what happened that night, but here they all are.

'No, don't eat that!' Zadie laughs as Erin digs her hand into the sand, raising a fistful towards her mouth.

'Pete, put the camera down and sort your baby out, will you?' Natalie hurls a packet of baby wipes at him and Pete grins, snapping one more picture of her before he moves to wipe Erin's hands clean. 'Zadie, you need more sunscreen. Come here.'

Zadie squirms as Natalie slathers sunscreen over her nose and cheeks. *Some things haven't changed*, Natalie thinks with a grin as she finishes rubbing it in and pecks Zadie's greasy cheek with a kiss. Zadie is still a pest for having enough sunscreen on her and Pete still can't do a good job at wiping Erin clean. She leans over and takes the wipes from him, gently brushing at Erin's chubby cheeks.

Erin has made an almost full recovery after her ordeal, the suspicion of pneumonia coming to nothing. She has been left with a weak chest and Natalie and Pete have been warned that she may need to use an inhaler in the future, hence their idea to come away for Christmas and to celebrate Erin's first birthday. Natalie wasn't sure she could have stood the thought of hosting another party at home – not after the way things went at Emily's party that night – and at least here there's no chance of them running into Eve.

At the thought of Eve, Natalie's heart twists in her chest. She hasn't seen or spoken to Eve since a few days after Zadie's confession. While Eve had nothing to do with Erin's abduction, what transpired between them in the months leading up to it had been too big for either of them to come back from. Natalie thinks she might have been able to forgive Eve's insistence on being so involved in their lives, but she couldn't forgive Eve for not telling her about Pete and Vanessa.

'Penny for them?' Pete appears, standing over and blocking the sun.

'Just thinking,' she says, 'about how everything turned out OK in the end.'

'I wish we could have figured things out in a less traumatic way.' He stoops down and brushes her lips with a kiss.

'Peter! Put that girl down for one minute!' His mother's voice filters across the sand, and Pete groans. 'I've got a special birthday cake for a special girl.' Pete's mother makes her way across the beach, his father not far behind her, carrying a huge elaborate cake with a single sparkler in the top. Erin will never remember this birthday, and Pete told his mum so when she confessed to spending a hundred and fifty dollars on the cake, but she said that as this is the first birthday in years the entire family have been together, she's entitled to go all out.

Natalie helps Erin blow the candle out, and then Pete taps on the side of his beer bottle. 'Guys, I just want to make a quick speech.'

Emily groans, and Pete hears Jake's laughter coming from her phone speaker, where she is facetiming him into the celebrations.

'It's a quick one!' Pete protests, as his brother punches him on the arm. 'I know my speeches are shit, but I just want to say … it's been a roller coaster of a year. Past couple of years, actually, but I want to tell you all how grateful I am to have you. If there's one thing I've learnt, it's that family is everything, so with that in mind …' Pete reaches down and pulls Natalie to her feet, as she stumbles, spilling her sparkling water into the sand. 'Nat and I have got something we want to tell you.'

Natalie looks up at him, her heart bursting. Everything feels so different, in a good way. What happened might have almost broken them, but Natalie has grown, and she thinks Pete has too. Now, she waits up for him on the rare occasion he's late home, so they can share a glass of wine and talk about their day. Pete makes sure to take the younger girls out on a Saturday morning, so Natalie can lie in and get some time to herself. If he pisses her off, she tells him. The bond that existed between them is slowly repairing itself, the filaments twisting back together, stronger than ever. It doesn't matter how tough things get for them going forward – because they will, that's the way life is; neither of them will ever again think this precious family they've created is a mistake.

Pete squeezes Natalie's hand before dipping into his pocket and pulling out a sheet of paper. 'We wanted to tell you all that that parcel of land just behind Mum and Dad's house? Well, the original offer fell through and … we've had our offer on it accepted. We're going to build a house.'

Pete's mum lets out a squeak of joy, her hand going to her mouth as her eyes fill with tears. Pete's dad wraps Natalie in a hug, as Emily lifts Erin and she and Zadie come and join them. In the midst of the joy, both of them surrounded by the family they love, Natalie and Pete catch each other's eyes and share a private smile. *Everything really is going to be all right.*

# Credits

Orion Fiction and the authors M.J. Arlidge and Lisa Hall would like to thank everyone at Orion who worked on the publication of *The Mistake*.

**Editor**
Sam Eades

**Copy-editor**
Steve O'Gorman

**Proofreader**
Alex Davis

**Editorial Management**
Anshuman Yadav
Jane Hughes
Charlie Panayiotou
Lucy Bilton
Patrice Nelson

**Audio**
Paul Stark
Louise Richardson
Georgina Cutler

**Inventory**
Jo Jacobs
Dan Stevens

**Contracts**
Dan Herron
Ellie Bowker
Oliver Chacón

**Design**
Nick Shah
Deborah Francois
Helen Ewing

**Photo Shoots & Image Research**
Natalie Dawkins

**Finance**
Nick Gibson
Jasdip Nandra
Sue Baker
Tom Costello

**Production**
Ruth Sharvell
Katie Horrocks

**Marketing**
Helena Fouracre
Lindsay Terrell

**Publicity**
Ellen Turner

**Rights**
Rebecca Folland
Tara Hiatt
Ben Fowler
Alice Cottrell
Ruth Blakemore
Marie Henckel

**Sales**
Catherine Worsley
Dave Murphy
Victoria Laws
Esther Waters
Group Sales teams across
Digital, Field, International
and Non-Trade

**Operations**
Group Sales Operations team